New York Times bestselling auth[...] in rural Oregon with her three [...] husband, whose chiseled jaw a[...] continue to make her swoon. S[...] she takes several times a day from her office to her coffee maker is a true example of her pioneer spirit.

USA TODAY bestselling and RITA® Award–nominated author **Caitlin Crews** loves writing romance. She teaches her favorite romance novels in creative-writing classes at places like UCLA Extension's prestigious Writers' Program, where she finally gets to utilize the MA and PhD in English literature she received from the University of York in England. She currently lives in the Pacific Northwest with her very own hero and too many pets. Visit her at caitlincrews.com.

Jackie Ashenden writes dark, emotional stories with alpha heroes who've just gotten the world to their liking only to have it blown apart by their kick-ass heroines. She lives in Auckland, New Zealand, with her husband, the inimitable Dr. Jax, two kids and two rats. When she's not torturing alpha males and their gutsy heroines, she can be found drinking chocolate martinis, reading anything she can lay her hands on, wasting time on social media or being forced to go mountain biking with her husband. To keep up-to-date with Jackie's new releases and other news, sign up to her newsletter at jackieashenden.com.

Nicole Helm grew up with her nose in a book and the dream of one day becoming a writer. Luckily, after a few failed career choices, she gets to follow that dream—writing down-to-earth contemporary romance and romantic suspense. From farmers to cowboys, Midwest to *the* West, Nicole writes stories about people finding themselves and finding love in the process. She lives in Missouri with her husband and two sons and dreams of someday owning a barn.

Also by Maisey Yates

Secrets from a Happy Marriage
The Bad Boy of Redemption Ranch
The Hero of Hope Springs
The Last Christmas Cowboy

Also by Caitlin Crews

Christmas in the King's Bed
His Scandalous Christmas Princess
Chosen for His Desert Throne

Also by Jackie Ashenden

Promoted to His Princess
The Most Powerful of Kings
The Italian's Final Redemption

Also by Nicole Helm

Badlands Beware
Close Range Christmas
Hunting a Killer

A GOOD OLD-FASHIONED
Cowboy

MAISEY YATES
CAITLIN CREWS
JACKIE ASHENDEN · NICOLE HELM

HQN

ISBN-13: 978-1-335-91131-5
A Good Old-Fashioned Cowboy
Copyright © 2021 by Harlequin Books S.A.

Recycling programs
for this product may
not exist in your area.

How to Find Him
Copyright © 2021 by Maisey Yates

How to Win Him
Copyright © 2021 by Caitlin Crews

How to Hold Him
Copyright © 2021 by Jackie Ashenden

How to Love Him
Copyright © 2021 by Nicole Helm

Copyright © 2021 by Jeff Johnson, interior illustrations

This edition published by arrangement with Harlequin Books S.A.

For questions and comments about the quality of this book, please contact us at CustomerService@Harlequin.com.

HQN
22 Adelaide St. West, 40th Floor
Toronto, Ontario M5H 4E3, Canada
www.Harlequin.com

Printed in Spain

Contents

HOW TO FIND HIM

Maisey Yates

This book is dedicated, yet again,
to my dearest friends. Jackie, Nicole and Caitlin.
My day would be boring without your texts.
I'd get a lot more done. But it would be boring.

PROLOGUE

"Old friends are the bricks and mortar of your life."
— Nora Roberts

ON A SLOWLY cooling summer night, the crickets chirping their low hum of incessant noise, stars spread out like a wave of celestial glow, four girls sat around a small campfire and planned their future.

"After Princeton, I'll probably stay on the East Coast," Kit said. Though college was a far-off proposition, it was what her father wanted for her, and so it seemed a foregone conclusion that was what she would do.

"I'm not sure what I'll do after med school, but I'll want to work at a hospital bigger than this area. Dad always says the important work is done in underserved communities." Charity didn't know what that meant quite yet, but that was what was expected of her. What else was there to do?

"I don't know what I'll do, but I want to live in a city. A *real* city with fancy stores and important people." Hope smiled dreamily. She didn't need a concrete plan yet. She just knew she wanted *more*.

Pru frowned at all of them. "But if you do all that, we won't be together." Her marshmallows were burning and no one noticed. "I'm staying right here, with my own piece of the ranch." There was no doubt for her that the Riley ranch, where they were prepared to camp tonight just a ways from the main house, would be her future. Always.

"Maybe we'll figure out a way to be together," Kit said. "When you're important, you can do whatever you want. We'll visit."

"Yes," Charity agreed. "We'll just have to go on vacations together." She fiddled with the compass necklace that hung from her neck. Pru's mom had taken the four of them to the mall just this afternoon. They'd saved up their chore and birthday money so they could go buy matching necklaces. No BFF broken hearts. Something grown-up. Special.

They had searched the store, high and low, for something they could all agree on. Something the store had four of. When they'd been about to leave, Kit had gone over to the cashier and asked her if she had anything that fit the bill.

They'd walked out with four delicate necklaces with tiny compasses at the end and promised to wear them. Always.

"We can always take summers off," Hope said. "Go somewhere fun and exciting together."

"I can't just take summers off from the ranch," Pru said, pouting.

"Sure you could. You could take turns with your brothers. Maybe not a whole summer, but we'll find time to be together," Hope said firmly.

"I don't understand why anyone would want to leave Jasper Creek."

"Maybe you will," Kit said philosophically. "And maybe we'll change our minds and want to stay." She knew she wouldn't, but she had more faith in Pru eventually wanting to leave. There was so much out there. Why would anyone want to stay?

Pru held on to them changing their minds. After all, Jasper Creek had everything anyone could ever want. Why would anyone want to leave? "If you guys leave and don't like it, you have to promise to come back home."

"I promise," Hope said, though she couldn't imagine *wanting* to be in boring old Jasper Creek. She knew Kit agreed, but they kept it between themselves because Pru was so fiercely defensive of *home*.

"Sure. We'll all promise," Kit agreed with an easy shrug.

"We should come home and open our stores," Charity said, fingering the compass, the gold seeming to come alive in the firelight. Just this afternoon, they'd pretended to run stores on Main Street, a game that even as they approached the ripe old age of thirteen they hadn't left behind.

"Yeah, when we're old—like, really old. Like when we're thirty, if we're all unhappy, anyone that doesn't live here has to come home."

"And open the stores. You can't forget that part," Charity said. She liked the idea of a place that was all hers. Every time they played make-believe store owners, she felt in charge of her own life. Like she could do whatever she wanted.

"It's a pact," Pru said firmly.

Kit nodded thoughtfully. "A pact needs words. Symbols. A talisman." Like in all the books she read. She looked down at her necklace, then wrapped her hand around the compass. "Okay, everyone hold on to their compass and repeat after me." Kit considered. "Best friends we are, and always will be. If life doesn't give us what we want, home is where we'll return."

"It doesn't rhyme," Pru said with a frown.

Kit rolled her eyes. "It doesn't have to *rhyme*, it just has to mean something. We need to look at the fire, hold our necklaces, and say it all together."

Pru grumbled a little bit, but after a few practice tries,

they said the words and looked deep into the fire. Immediately, there was the lone howl of a coyote, and then a few answering calls as the wind gave a little gust sending the flames just a little higher.

"Woah," Hope breathed.

"It's a coincidence," Pru insisted, though she looked around nervously.

"It's a sign," Kit said firmly. "We made a pact. The universe heard us and responded."

"You need to lay off the poetry books, Kit," Pru said disdainfully, but her heart jittered all the same. Like they really *had* made a pact with the universe.

But the feeling faded with sticky marshmallow roasting and plenty of chocolate. They ate, they chattered, determined to stay up *all* night lying there on the grass looking up at the stars.

Charity had gone to a science camp last summer and learned the constellations, informing them the arrow-looking one was Aquila. They'd searched it out every night they were together ever since.

"It'll always bring us back," Charity said softly. "Whether we're thirty or not. Pacts with the universe or not. We'll always come back."

She reached across to find Kit's hand, then Kit gripped Hope's, and Hope Pru's, until they were a connected chain, looking up at the stars, thinking about what their futures might hold.

And knowing, no matter what, the thing that would always bring them back together was each other.

CHAPTER ONE

Hope's Story

"I HOPE YOU like salmon." Hope Marshall shut the front door of the quaint farmhouse behind her and shouted across the porch at her friends. They were sitting around a campfire, roasting hot dogs and marshmallows in a scene reminiscent of their childhoods.

Except Hope couldn't remember feeling stressed, exhausted, and like a royally flattened pigeon during her childhood.

"I do not, Hope," Kit, formally known as Katherine, said from her position by the fire. "And I think you know that."

One of Hope's dearest friends in all the world, Kit believed in bracing honesty, fierce loyalty, and scarves that could also pass as blankets.

Her friend was currently swathed in one of those very scarves, her dark hair a blunt frame for a pale face that resembled an antique doll, with large eyes and a perfectly drawn mouth. She somehow managed to effect a posture of lounging in the old yellow canvas-and-aluminum lawn chair she occupied.

Hope made her way down the wooden steps and paused for a moment, looking back at the big white farmhouse they'd rented for the summer.

It had the right kind of front porch for drinking lemonade, with wild, erratic flowers growing up to touch the top of the staircase railing.

It had been owned by June Gable, a sweet older woman that Hope could scarcely remember from town picnics and church services. June had passed a while ago and the ownership of the home had fallen to her granddaughters, who now rented it out to guests.

Two of them, Keira and Bella, lived on ranches near this property spread, with their respective husbands, and had told them they would be on hand for anything they needed.

The house and its contents—antique furniture, old board games, bakeware, and stacks of books and magazines—were all there for them to use.

Hope had already made use of the kitchen by throwing some fudge together. Anything to get her mind off her incessantly buzzing phone.

Her parents. They were so upset. So, so upset and sending messages every few minutes to that effect. The weight of their disappointment was beginning to grind Hope into fine powder.

So she ignored her phone.

For now.

She sat down in a chair next to Kit and looked around at the three of them, all lit up in the glow of the fire.

The whole air was that deep twilight color that settled on everything it touched and painted it blue. There was no competition from streetlights, not here. She'd gotten used to her bright, noisy corner of Chicago.

But the distant memories of the life she'd had before seemed a lot less distant here. Especially surrounded by the women she'd grown up sharing it with.

"Handily," Hope said, "there is also beef, and a limited number of vegetarian options."

She bent down and fished a marshmallow out of the bag sitting on the ground, then took one of the stretched-out wire hangers from where it was propped against a rock and speared the sugary treat.

"No one wants secondhand squash," Pru said in her extremely straightforward manner. "Also, I question the kind of friends you had in Chicago that so many of them chose salmon when there was steak."

"James's family," she muttered.

"I could eat the salmon…" Charity, a bright, brilliant doctor who was also—in the grand tradition of those working in the medical profession—a champion martyr, made the offer with a gravely sacrificial tone.

"What was I thinking?" Hope asked, shoving her marshmallow into a glowing pocket in the fire. She hadn't roasted a marshmallow since…well, since she and the girls had gone camping after high school graduation, but apparently roasting marshmallows was like riding a bike. "It was like… I couldn't get away with his heirloom family ring without being hunted down by the cops so I thought… I know, I'll take the food."

Wedding food that she had packed in dry ice for her drive from Chicago to Jasper Creek, Oregon, her heartbreak and humiliation echoing in her like a drumbeat as she left that life behind.

As she headed toward home.

Humiliation had blossomed into rebellion as she'd driven. She'd given James Field Warner IV nine years of her life. And he'd given her a cooler full of salmon.

She refused to give him credit for anything else. The

positive move that had resulted from this had nothing at all to do with him. It was Charity, Pru, and Kit.

Like always.

Even though they'd gone their separate ways after high school, they always found their way back to each other.

There was a constellation at the Riley Ranch—Pru's family ranch where they'd spent all their summer days—clearly visible on warm nights.

It'll always bring us back.

Charity had said that, like a prayer. Hope hadn't believed her, not then. Not when her dreams had been so much bigger than an Oregon sky and a small town.

But here she was.

They'd made a promise under that sky. And again, after her wedding-that-wasn't, they'd sat under the stars, surrounded by the most beautiful white gossamer canopy that they had rented for the whole night, along with the venue, and had passed around the bottles of champagne meant for a toast that would never happen.

HOPE GRABBED HOLD of her compass necklace—the necklace her now-not-going-to-be-her-mother-in-law had disparaged while they were dressing for the wedding.

"That's very down-market."

"It's symbolic."

Now that James had called off the wedding and she was sitting in an empty venue, with only her friends, she had to wonder what it was symbolic of.

She'd been worried it had been symbolic of her own... she wouldn't have called them doubts until just now. But as the wedding had drawn closer she'd started dreaming. First, of home, of pine trees swaying overhead as she lay in the back of a pickup truck.

Of clear, diamond-dust skies with no streetlights.

And then—much more concerning—of strong, masculine arms that did not belong to her fiancé.

Nope.

The man who was making her wake up sweaty, hot, bothered, and very aroused was not the man she was supposed to marry, but the man she'd left behind.

Brooks.

And as loudly as the sound of Jasper Creek whispered through the trees, whispered to her soul, in the weeks leading up to the wedding-that-wasn't, Brooks's name had been even louder.

Brooks, she rationalized, lying there with her friends, was not the real issue. It was what he represented. A time when there had been endless possibilities.

A time when getting to third base in the bed of a pickup truck had been the height of excitement and what had come next hadn't mattered at all.

"I'm thirty and I was supposed to be married. Instead I'm dumped. In front of...everyone. Every friend I ever made in this town."

Brooks.

"We made a deal," Charity said, softly. "We made a deal that if we were thirty and miserable we'd go back home and open the shops, remember?"

"There's no way the shops are still for sale," Pru said.

"They are. I drive down to Jasper Creek sometimes. From Seattle," Charity said, the words like she was admitting to an illicit tryst. "And I always see the buildings. The old yarn shop...and last time I was there, there was a sign offering penny rent to the person who can rehab the businesses by the centennial in August."

"That would be an insane amount of work," Pru said,

ever the pragmatist. "No one could do it." But there was also a keen edge to her voice, because if anyone liked taking on the impossible and then making it look easy, it was Pru. Even if she'd never admit it.

"I guess no more work than rebuilding my life," Hope said, an echo of home still reverberating in her chest.

An echo of Brooks.

"You have a career," Kit said.

"Yes," Charity said, "but there's a reason I drive back to Jasper Creek and...and Hope, you need a change."

Charity neatly turned the topic back to Hope, and Hope was just miserable enough to allow it, rather than press her friend for more details on her own situation.

"I need more than a change," Hope said. "I need a new everything."

"Why dream?" Kit asked, standing abruptly. "Seriously? Why dream? Why not do it?"

"You're going to...leave New York?" Pru asked, skeptical.

"My apartment is the size of a closet, and I work so much I can barely enjoy any of the perks of being there."

"You realize this is insane," Pru said, and yet again, Pru's love of accomplishing the insane was apparent, even in her scathing tone.

"Well, so are we," Kit said. "Historically."

"I might have already found a place to rent," Charity said. "It's the cutest farmhouse you've ever seen."

"YOU DIDN'T *ONLY* get fish," Pru said, bringing her back to the moment. "You got your wedding dress."

Hope groaned. "Well, who cares? It doesn't fit me now because the minute he jilted me I started eating carbs again and haven't stopped. That gown was for a woman who was going to be in the society pages, stared at and judged by a braying mob of old-money elites." Just saying that made her feel a profound sense of relief. That she was here, and they were there. And it was all…behind her now.

She'd followed her dreams. Not her broader life dreams but the dreams she'd been having before the wedding. Which was…maybe stupid. But it had brought a sense of relief, a sense of peace that nothing else had.

Her phone chimed from her pocket, the sound like nails on the chalkboard of said peace.

"Is your mom still texting you?" Kit asked.

"Um. Well, yes." Her mom and dad had retired to Maui a few years ago—how nice for them—and her mom hadn't gotten on a plane to check on her well-being but she had been sending a lot of messages.

So had everyone, though most had been less judgmental than the ones that had come from her mother.

The steady stream of messages she'd gotten since she had been *jilted* and also *lost her mind* and moved away from her friends and her life in Chicago was…intense.

She pulled her phone partway out of her pocket and saw that the banner said *Mom*.

No. Not right now. She couldn't deal.

"We got to keep our bridesmaid dresses too," Charity said, as if that was an added bonus.

"Do you have a lot of occasions to wear lilac gowns?" Hope asked. "That look like a tangle of netting you might find on a beach?"

Lilac. She didn't even like lilac. Her nearly-mother-in-law liked it and said it looked great on Henrietta, her nearly-sister-in-law and thus the railroading had begun.

"I could cut it way above the knee and go stand on the

corner of Main Street in town and try to attract customers to our shops," Pru said.

"Prudence," Hope said, because she knew Pru hated her full name. "That is shocking."

"What will be shocking," Pru said, lifting her marshmallow near her face and squeezing it gently to test it, "is if we don't get these shops open by the Jasper Creek centennial and our rent ends up going so high I wouldn't be able to pay for it even if I did stand on the street corner, and our dreams will end before they've even started."

"Ah!" Hope said with mock brightness. "A metaphor for my almost-wedding."

"While you know I find grimness to be the little black dress of emotions," Kit said, "I hate to see you wearing it all the time."

"I'm fine, *Katherine*." Hope stared into the flames and ignored the stinging in her eyes. "I just need sugar. And to not think about it. Let's talk about the shops, please."

The shops at least were a good thing. One very good thing happening in her life.

"Then let's move to the living room," Charity said. "I need a couch."

"Does anyone want a salmon snack?" Hope asked, pulling her marshmallow from the flame and blowing on it before tearing into it with savage relish.

"No," they all answered, getting up from the fire and assuming long-held roles.

Pru made sure it was dead out with water and a shovel. Charity collected chairs. Kit grabbed the food. It made Hope's heart feel too big for her chest.

These girls had been a constant in her life since childhood, and they'd been distant these last few years because of life and geography but they were here.

They weren't the ones messaging her, or offering fake sympathy.

They'd rallied.

They'd gathered.

And they were showing her how to dream again.

They'd given up their lives—and while they had their own reasons, her misery had been the trigger point for them. And here they were, sitting around a fire with her, no judgment, just lots of sugar and warm memories.

"I made fudge," Hope said, as they headed toward the house.

"That we will take," Kit said.

As her friends went into the house and to the living room, Hope detoured into the kitchen to grab her pan of fudge and pour herself a cup of hot water from the kettle, dunking a tea bag into it before joining everyone.

It was a warm, well-lived-in room that had a sense of history from the walls down to the floorboards.

From her pocket, her phone dinged again.

"Silence your cell phone," Pru said.

"Fine," she said, digging in her pocket and taking it out as she set the fudge on the coffee table.

"All right," Pru said, standing. Which surprised Hope not at all. Pru was a big one for taking charge and making pronouncements. "The first meeting of our Main Street Renovation Coalition has come to order."

"I am philosophically opposed to meetings that could've been emails," Kit said.

"I'm tired of meetings in general," Charity said.

"Too bad," Pru said. "We have to make sure we're on the same page. Or I'm liable to just start painting the shops lemon yellow. I like yellow right now. If you leave the walls unpainted I may have to paint."

"They're brick," Kit said, deeply shocked.

"I'm just saying. It would benefit us to be on the same page."

"Yes," said Charity. "My official medical opinion is that lemon yellow walls are a health hazard."

Hope's phone buzzed and she saw her mom had texted again and she looked down at the phone, typing a response as quick as she could. She knew Pru was still talking.

"House rules," Pru said. "I think we need some house rules. Boundaries."

Hope looked up. "What?"

"House rules," Pru repeated, looking at her with grave concern.

"We'll get to house rules in a bit," Kit said. "I think the first order of business is making a pact that whatever happens, we don't kill each other. Friendship is more important than anything. Even stores."

"The pact is why we're here," Hope said, glancing back at her phone. And then she sighed. "A pact is what got me out of my past life, and I am deeply grateful for it. So actually, yes. Let's make a pact. That we remember why we started this. Because we want to do something we love. I want to sell candy. Because as much as young Hope wanted to escape Jasper Creek and see the bright lights of the big city, she also really loved sweets. And she really loved this town, even if she couldn't admit it."

"Are you going to talk about yourself in the third person the whole time?" Kit asked. "Because I left publishing, and I'm no longer working with authors. So my patience for that is done."

"You know what I mean," Hope said. "I want to get back to where my life was not a disaster. And that was somewhere here. I thought I knew what I wanted but I didn't.

And nothing made that clearer than when my relationship blew up and there was nothing to stay for. I lived in Chicago for twelve years and I didn't feel like I wanted to stay when the wedding collapsed. That says everything there is to say about that life. It was just everything moved so fast I was sucked into it. I was sucked into…hustling. And being involved with people who mattered and fancy lunches and…"

And suddenly her mind was back to evenings spent in the bed of a pickup truck, with ill-gotten beer and a cowboy…

"What?" Kit asked, eyeing her too keenly.

"What?" Hope repeated.

"You got dreamy."

"Oh, I…it's just… I don't know. I think it's nostalgia. It's being here. It's making me miss things. Want things."

"You have to be careful with nostalgia," Pru said. "It's how you end up with bangs, even though you already know you hate them."

Kit glared at Pru from beneath her own bangs.

"*I* don't want bangs," Hope said. "I want to feel…happy again. Everything I was in Chicago I want to be…not that. I want… I want to walk barefoot through the grass and go to small-town parades and…" *Brooks.* No. She would not mention her ex-boyfriend's name. It wasn't about Brooks anyway. "I might want to make out with a country boy."

Kit looked suddenly wistful. "I do miss men whose hands aren't more manicured than my own. Which you can't see from an online dating app."

Charity frowned. "Oh, those are the worst."

"They sound the worst," Hope said. "I've been in a relationship for years, and I've never had to do it and…and I don't want to. I don't want to meet a man in my phone." She brandished the device. "I'm sick of fake connections

and technology. I want something real. Cold beer and rough hands and…"

Why was it Brooks that she saw?

Her first love.

"We lost you again," Pru said.

"My point is," she said, trying to root herself to the moment and not to memories of Sullivan Brooks and his magic hands. "Modern life has failed me. My pursuits have failed me. I was about to make the worst decision of my life. I was about to get married to a man who organized his sweaters by color and got me less hot than an average sexy dream."

Kit frowned deeply, looking her up and down as if she were ill. "That's a cry for help, Hope. The fact that you never mentioned that is telling."

"Well, I wasn't…letting myself realize it. And up until the wedding I was having these dreams—these fantasies—about home—Jasper Creek–home, not Chicago—and other men—" *just one man*, but she wasn't admitting that "—and it was a sign, and I nearly missed it! Well, no more. Now, when the universe speaks, I will listen. Because Lord knows I should not be making my own decisions. The universe should make my decisions for me."

Hope stood up, and as she did, a large, fat magazine fell off a nearby shelf with a thunk. She must have disturbed the shelf, she rationalized, even though she was pretty sure she hadn't touched anything. But there it was. An old-fashioned magazine with a date stamp on it that read 1945. A women's magazine with a pair of smiling girls with their hair in victory rolls and dresses that went down past their knees.

The cover proudly proclaimed that this particular issue held secrets.

50 Ways to Catch—and Keep—a Man!

Well, ten points to the universe.

"*This* is how people used to do it," Hope said, bending down and picking it up. And as she did, an odd sensation passed over her skin. Goose bumps rising up on her arms. She brushed it off. "Maybe this magazine holds the secrets to all our problems."

She opened the page up and howled with laughter.

"Oh my gosh, look at this. 'Foolproof Tips to Land Yourself a Husband.' And there are sections: How to Find Him, How to Land Him, How to Keep Him, How to Love Him."

"Is that last one sexy?" Pru asked.

"It's 1945," Hope said. "I think sexy was showing the seam of your silk stocking." She looked back down at the magazine. "Wear a Band-Aid on your face. People always ask what happened! Join an outdoors club; men like a woman who isn't afraid of nature." She looked up at her friends. "Get a dog."

"Are those real?" Kit asked.

"Yes," Hope said. "Deeply real. Wear a wedding dress! What better way to show you're ready and willing!"

"Well, there you go, Hope," Pru said. "Maybe that's how far back you need to go to fix your life. Modern dating hasn't worked. Anyway, you have the dress already."

"It hasn't worked for any of you either." They all grumbled. "It's *true*."

"But you're...sad," Charity said.

Hope frowned. "Thank you."

"I didn't mean it like that! I meant that you're all unhappy. And I don't want you to be unhappy. We don't want you to be unhappy."

Suddenly she was very aware of the pity aspect of it all. Yes, they were all here for their own reasons, whether they were sharing them or not. But it was all for her benefit, and while that was deeply supportive it also suggested…well, a high level of feeling very sorry for her.

But she felt…somewhat sorry for herself and as much as it was a low moment it was also…they were here with her.

One for all, all for one, as they always were. Always had been.

"Have you all been talking about me?"

Pru nodded. "Yes. Out of grave concern for you because that two-timing blue-bellied skink wasted enough years of your life and you deserve to be happy."

"I'm happy. I'm here. I'm with you guys." Her phone buzzed. "It's fine."

"What if," Kit said. "You draw a tip every day. It will be your way of consulting the universe, and perhaps getting some country-boy action."

Pru laughed and Charity bit her bottom lip. "Well," Charity said, "that's one way of shaking things up."

"Hey, if I do it, we all have to do it," Hope said.

"Why?" Pru asked. "I'm not looking for a man."

"It's not about looking for a man," Hope said. "It's about spontaneity. If we're going big, if we're making changes, let's make changes." She could sense growing skepticism around her, but these tips had amused her more than anything had for days and it felt like something—an opportunity, a sign, she didn't know what. She didn't really think she'd find a man—and honestly, for anything other than pleasure, she didn't want one. But it reminded her of simple games they'd played as kids. Of slumber parties when they'd laughed till their sides ached. Nostalgia. And okay, maybe it would be bad bangs. But maybe it would be just what she needed. What *they* needed.

"I propose," Hope said, "that if *any* of us break a house rule, we have to draw a tip."

"There are no house rules yet," Kit pointed out.

"There *will* be," Pru said, giving her a determined look.

"I volunteer to write them down," Kit said, producing a notebook out of the folds of her scarf. It was clear that Kit had accepted the turning tide and figured she'd position herself to be at the forefront.

"Just because you write them down doesn't mean you'll be exempt from them," Pru said, clearly sensing the same.

Kit shot her a penetrating glare. "I would never think such a thing, Prudence."

"You would," Pru said. "And since I can feel you trying to do so, I say that the first house rule is that anyone who says 'the city,' meaning New York City, as though it is the only city in the entire world, must draw a penalty dating tip."

Hope took her phone out again and started surfing through her messages while her friends continued to talk. The conversation became fuzzy around the edges.

"It *is* the only city in the world," Kit said. "The one true city."

"The ruling stands," Charity announced.

"No cell-phone dating," Pru said.

"Easy," Kit said.

"No cell phones *at all*," Charity said.

"What?" Hope's head popped up.

"No cell phones. If you use one, before the Grand Opening of the Main Street shops, then you earn a penalty."

Pru nodded slowly. "We have a lot of work to do. Cell phones are a distraction."

"But also can be helpful," Kit said. "What if I need to look up a video of a parakeet playing the piano?"

"You're actually reinforcing my point."

Hope's phone kept vibrating and suddenly, she wanted

this. All of it. Her parents were texting and texting and if she wanted change—real change—she needed to disconnect. Detach. And suddenly it was all clear. Maybe it was another message. Just like the magazine. "They'll go in the safe," she said. "I saw one down in the basement below the shops. Phones in the safe."

"Why?" Kit asked.

"Because," Charity stood up, looking at Hope, then back at Pru and Kit. "We are here together. We are trying to recapture something. Find the joy of...life. And back when we used to have...joy. And life. We didn't have smartphones. Hope can't focus because she's so busy handling the drama."

Hope looked down at her phone, her throat getting dry. "Yes. I need to be done with it. I need a break. A clean break. This is...we were happy here. We were happy back then."

Everyone looked at her.

"We're in this together," Charity said.

"I don't really care," Kit said.

She clearly did care a little, but wouldn't go against a group mandate, not in the end.

"I can do it," Pru said, looking down at her phone. "It's just a phone."

She clearly didn't feel like it was just a phone, but would never admit it, because Pru would never act like something was hard.

"Then it's settled," Hope said. "Tomorrow we disconnect. No phones."

"Just...messages from the universe," Kit said, her tone gently mocking.

"Are you telling me you don't believe in fate?"

Kit looked wounded. "You know I do. Fate, destiny, and true love."

"We're surrendering to fate," Charity said.

"But we still need rules, because we're not surrendering to anarchy. No unauthorized cooking of seafood," Pru declared.

"I have *all that salmon*," Hope said, now feeling unfairly targeted.

"You must gain permission to fill the house with the smell of fish. It is good and right that you do so."

"But it's…"

"We are helping you. *We care*," Kit said seriously. "You don't want all that salmon, do you?"

"I hate salmon," Hope said.

"Then no one needs to eat it!" Kit declared.

"If we were in high school we would have just filled James's car with it and called it a day," Pru said.

Hope couldn't help it. She laughed. "We would have," she said. "Oh, we would have. We'd have filled it up with fish and taped it shut!"

"We were badasses," Charity said wistfully.

"Small-town badasses," Kit said. "But sure."

Hope sighed. What had happened to that girl? She'd gotten lost. In Chicago. In James's family. In James. In wanting nicer clothes and a better house and a shinier car so she could keep up with her shiny friends.

But really, what had she gotten out of the last nine years?

A nine-year relationship that had been worse than boring by the end, with a man who fit like an old pair of jeans: faded, worn, and too tight.

And she wanted…something more.

Her Brooks dreams were emblematic, not of wanting the

man who'd once broken her heart, but of wanting something new. She was sure.

Something simmered in her belly and the image of a cowboy filtered through her mind. She knew exactly who he was, even if she tried to keep herself from thinking his name again.

She was awash in regret, just like that.

She had always been…cautious when it came to physical relationships.

She hadn't even lost her virginity until college. It was one of her regrets. That she hadn't given it up to Sullivan Brooks when she'd had the chance.

Maybe that was why he haunted her sweaty, erotic dreams.

He represented unfinished business.

"We have to make an effort to talk to people," Hope said. "In town."

"*Male* people?" Pru asked, lifting an eyebrow.

"Not necessarily. But…could be. Maybe."

"But we're here for friendship," Charity said, touching the compass around her neck. They all reflexively did the same. "So regardless of the magic universe, we can't let men steal friendship."

"All right," Hope said. "Friends first. This house is a sacred space. No men *here*. No hookups here. No ditching for dudes."

"And," Pru continued, "you will all attend the weekly meeting for the Main Street Renovation Coalition in our living room. Failure to do so…"

"Will result in a penalty," Kit said. "And, calling an excess of meetings, in addition to the weekly meeting, will also be met with a penalty."

"Great. No cell phones. Being social. Meetings. And…"

Hope looked around the room, then down at her phone which was still lighting up. And suddenly everything felt simple. Suddenly it really did feel like going back in time. "You guys, I think this is actually going to be pretty great."

"Me too," said Kit.

"I knew it would be," said Charity.

"Don't be smug," said Pru. "But, you're right. It's going to be great."

Charity grinned. "I guess we aren't too old to play store after all."

CHAPTER TWO

THE NEXT DAY, they assembled in the basement of the Main Street Shops, a large space that was open and continuous beneath the four buildings that they were occupying for their stores.

The town of Jasper Creek had been revitalized in recent years, certainly coming a long way from the blocks of empty shops that had sat vacant for years when the girls were in school, but the end of Main Street, where their grouping of shops sat, was still in disrepair.

It was a priority for the town to change that. But economies in small towns were tricky, dependent on tourism, good weather, and a lack of wildfires. Smoke from fires could handily halve business during the typical high season, or so Charity had told them during the last meeting, as though she were reciting from a brochure.

Charity had done most of the legwork when it came to securing the leases, liaising with the city council, and presenting their plans for the stores. Charity planned on reopening the yarn store that had shuttered after the elderly owner's health had declined, and still had all of the stock in place, arranged as if the Closed sign had been turned yesterday instead of several years earlier.

Pru was reviving the old feed store on the corner that had shuttered sometime around their high school graduation. It was full of old boxes of dusty junk including a large wooden Victrola and the bumper of what Pru estimated to be a 1930s-era Ford truck.

The Victrola had gone back to the farmhouse, and they'd put it in the living room, along with the small collection of 1940s records they'd found.

The candy store and the bookstore—to be manned by Hope and Kit—were blessedly empty. They were small spaces that had to be offered up for a pittance since no one was chomping at the bit to take them on.

Except for them.

And they were…maybe a little bit nuts.

But it felt good. It all felt good.

Pru stood proudly behind an old navy-blue-and-gold safe. "I have the combination," she said. "Now I just have to figure out how to get it open."

"I believe in you," Charity said, crunching a chip from a small bag she'd just fished from her purse.

Kit was clutching two very large coffees she'd gotten from Keira's Coffee Cart, squinting against the light. Hope had a hot chocolate and a bag of Swedish Fish and was Not At Home to looks of judgment.

Pru wrinkled her nose and started working the gold wheel. It took her fifteen minutes to get it open.

"Put them in," Pru said, firmly conducting the rules now that they were set because it was just who she was as a person.

Pru stuck hers in first, followed by Kit, then by Charity. Hope stared down at the phone.

The phone that had become a source of extreme anxiety over the last month.

Constant messages about the wedding, then the misdirected text from her fiancé just hours before the actual wedding telling the wrong woman he was going to meet up with her rather than get married. And then afterward the steady stream of condolences, which she was sure were actually judgments carefully wrapped in sweetness. The messages from her parents which were pure judgment.

She'd been glued to it. Unable to look away even as it stole pieces of her sanity. And letting go of it felt hard.

She blinked, feeling rocked by the realization that she was literally clinging to her past.

"In it goes," she said, quickly stuffing it inside.

Pru shut the door with a loud click. "And it's done."

It was Kit who held up the jar containing strips of paper, each one with a tip for landing a husband.

They had not been cut out of the actual magazine. Kit had looked at everyone in extreme horror, proclaiming the periodical to be a piece of literary history, and had demanded that Pru write them down on a piece of paper, which she had.

They had then gone into a jar which had been decorated with hearts by Charity.

She shook it. "Hope, you must choose one."

Hope blanched. "Have I made it very clear that I find this to be silly?"

"You have," Charity said, nodding gravely. "But there's nothing to be done. This is for your happiness. Your future."

Hope made a scathing face. "I look forward to all of you failing and breaking rules, and getting one of your own."

"Anyway," Kit said. "The odds of you actually running into an eligible bachelor on the Main Street of Jasper Creek are very low."

"Very, very low," Charity agreed.

"Maybe I can find myself an octogenarian to hit on." She reached into the jar and snagged a piece of paper. "Oh Lord…"

"What?" her friends chorused.

"You have to read it," Kit said.

"'Pretend to trip. A gallant man will lift you up off the ground and offer assistance.'"

"Well, that's the best thing I've ever heard," Kit said.

"Good thing I'm not going to find a man worth tripping over."

"Okay," Pru said. "Enough jawing. We have stores to open."

"Yeah, well," Charity said, looking sulky. "It's going to take ages. My store might already be an existing thing, but it's a nana shop, and you know yarn is much more hipster these days."

"In Jasper Creek?" Kit questioned.

"Farm-to-table restaurants have cropped up all over," Charity pointed out.

"Because the farms are right over there," Pru said, gesturing. "Anyway, this was *your* idea. And my feed store is currently stacked full of junk, which I was not adequately prepared for."

"I have a lot of unsalable itchy wool," Charity said. "Wool can be treacherous."

"And you would know that how? You don't knit, Charity," Hope pointed out.

Charity looked suddenly wistful. "I used to love going into that store. It was quiet." Her dreamy expression suddenly went tight. "Somehow there was always less pressure there."

It was the closest Charity had come to really talking about…much of anything. She'd been gung ho about the endeavor but hadn't said anything about her break from medicine apart from vague comments about stress.

Charity was the mom friend. The one who had snacks

and Band-Aids in her purse and who always seemed to have it together.

Hope couldn't help but wonder if that was actually true right now.

"Well, this feed store is the closest I'll get to ranching since my dad portioned the ranch out to my brothers and not me." Pru's voice went hard.

Kit patted Pru's arm. "It wasn't right. You would have done a great job with it. But you'll do an amazing job with this."

"Of course I will! Agriculture is my thing."

"I'm going to spend my days surrounded by romance novels," Kit said. "I can't imagine anything better. It's what I always wanted. I could just never... You know how my dad is. Romance isn't exactly considered literature in his eyes."

"Is anything?" Hope asked. "Or does it all fall short of his dangerously imperious gaze?"

"He would call your verbal prose purple and embarrassing, Hope."

Hope shrugged and took a handful of Skittles out of her purse. "I could live with that." She sighed. "Oh, I missed sugar. And the candy store was always my favorite. So many samples... I can't wait."

"Well then," Pru said. "We better get moving. The centennial is in August and we need to be open for it or...well, it's all a loss."

"It won't be a loss!" Charity said, raising her hands in triumph.

"Conquer that yarn," Kit said.

"I'm a doctor," she said. "I can handle anything."

They all went up their individual staircases, into their stores, and Hope found herself surrounded by silence.

Silence and…bins. Because she had wanted to put together a candy shop comprised almost entirely of bins, rather than shelves.

This was…hers.

Well, okay, they were leasing, and if they didn't get the businesses running by the deadline they wouldn't be able to afford them. But it was still more hers than anything she'd had for the last…nine years.

A rebellion and a revolution.

Candy, her own business.

Not to please her parents, not to please James. Not to please his parents.

Just her.

The silence suddenly felt like a symphony. Because it was *her* silence.

Just like this place was hers.

Suddenly she caught some movement out of the corner of her eye. A tan cowboy hat. A white T-shirt. Blue jeans.

Brooks.

And this wasn't a dream.

She turned and then pitched forward suddenly, going ankles over shoulders down onto the ground and creating a massive crash.

She lay there on her back on the wooden floor, staring at the ceiling. It was a nice ceiling. Old stamped plaster. This was not how she thought she might examine the ceiling. But thankfully, her pride seemed to be wounded more than anything else. Luckily, she was in the building and no one had—

She heard the sound of the door open and froze.

She hadn't locked the front door after she'd come in.

"Hey, sorry to barge in but I saw someone fall. Everything okay?"

Oh *Lord*.

His voice. It was still so good. Like gravel and honey and he was just so damn hot. And why was this happening to her? Why was any of this happening to her?

He was the first naked man she'd ever seen and right now those fantasies—which had been building on each other for months now—were clear and present and oh my...

Also the fact *he'd* seen *her* naked...

Agh.

"I'm fine," she shouted from on the ground. She was behind the bins. Maybe he wouldn't come over. Maybe, he wouldn't know it was her. Maybe.

"I don't normally barge in where I'm not invited but I saw you fall and..."

Suddenly, it wasn't the ceiling she was staring at. It was his face. His beautiful face that had only improved with age. The strong, firm line of his jaw had been etched in her memory long ago, and she was slightly distressed to discover that she had not embellished any of it. His dark brows were locked together, a deep groove between them. Concern was evident in his blue eyes which then, turned to...something else: a strange, slow smile that did not seem all that...friendly.

"Hope. Hope Marshall."

"Yes. It is me. And this is just about right for life right now."

She sat up. He reached down that large, masculine hand which occupied a very particular place in her dreams.

She swallowed hard, and took hold of it.

It was so rough. Years of hard work, she suspected. It was tempting to imagine what it might feel like to have Brooks's hands on her skin. She knew what it was like to be touched by a man who hadn't done a day's work away from a desk in his life.

But she'd been touched *all over* by Brooks's hands.

And then she realized two things.

That she was *staring*.

And that the man-catching tip had *worked*.

She found herself being hauled to her feet, and once she was back on solid ground she winced. Apparently, she had done a little bit of damage to her poor body.

"I didn't know you were back in town," he said.

"Yeah. It was…not planned."

Silence ricocheted off the redbrick walls around them.

He crossed his arms over his broad chest and rocked back on his heels. "I heard about your wedding."

So much for putting that in the safe with her phone. She cleared her throat. "Oh, in that you heard there wasn't one?"

"Yeah," he said, a muscle in his jaw ticking.

"Is it…?"

"All over town? Yes. Your mom called Lettie Beamish, who then called my mother, who told my grandmother, who told everybody at church on Sunday."

"Good. Good."

"They're all praying for you."

"I would expect nothing less."

"But, I didn't hear that you were coming back to town."

"So the Jasper Creek grapevine had a breakdown in the system? Shocking. Yeah. I… I'm leasing this place. The whole street. With Charity, Pru and Kit."

That shocked him. "Really?"

"The city council was desperate. They said anyone who could renovate it by the town centennial could lease them for basically nothing. And we have this dream and… Anyway."

He looked around the ramshackle shop, full of upturned bins. "And this is going to be...?"

"It's a candy shop," she said. "You know, there used to be one in town. When we were kids. It had all kinds of old-fashioned candy and homemade fudge. I got the recipe before I left to go to school. I make it all the time. It's that thing that I give away as gifts and... Everyone loves it. But it doesn't exist anymore and I've always thought that it should."

"I thought you had big dreams," he said, his voice going hard. "Dreams that were way bigger than here."

She swallowed. She deserved that. Because when she'd broken up with him it had been all about how what she wanted was bigger than Jasper Creek and bigger than him.

"Yeah, well that didn't work out, did it?"

"Did you have a job over there?"

"I kind of fell into interior design, which wasn't really my plan." It was funny that she didn't feel like taking on the responsibility of the decor for the stores, but interior design wasn't her passion or anything. It just was. And it had been for places that were nothing like this. "But I did hospitality and worked in a hotel for a while and then one of the people who came and stayed there ran this business, and she got me involved. I don't know. I enjoyed it, but it wasn't my passion. Still, I was pretty successful at it, and I think everyone thought I was nuts walking away. Or rather, driving away. With a cooler full of salmon."

"It might've been the salmon that made people think you're nuts."

"Sure," she said.

"I'm sorry," he said. "For what it's worth."

"Thank you." They just stared at each other for a long moment and her heart started to beat faster. She took a breath, trying to dispel the tension in the air. Trying to get rid of last night's revelation. That she would really like to have some sex. With a man who was not James.

And that she had specifically thought of this man.

This one that got away from her when she was too young to know well enough what she wanted. When she was too young to know what a man could make her feel.

Like you know now?

Maybe she didn't.

Her sex dreams about Brooks had been more moving than actual sex with James ever had been.

You were going to marry him.

She shoved that disturbing thought aside.

That was very much the wrong thing to be thinking while she was standing there staring him down. "So what kind of candy are you selling?"

"The…the sweet kind."

"Sure."

"I'll be making some of it. The kind that will be on the counter. Bonbons and things like that. Truffles, peanut butter patties, fudge. And I will try to get a hold of some local things…"

"Well, that was what I was going to mention. I make candy."

"You do?"

Of all the coincidences. She had gone back home, run into her ex-boyfriend, only to discover that he…made candy.

"I mean, that's not my business. But, I have a maple syrup farm."

"Do they have maple syrup outside of Vermont?"

"If not, then I'm living a very strange and dangerous hallucination."

"Right. So you tap trees and things like that?"

"Broadleaf maple. But I make maple syrup, extract, and classic maple candy."

"I can make maple fudge," she said.

"Well, that would work for me. But if you're interested in carrying the products in your store…"

"I would be. Very much."

"So what was your plan for the day?"

"I'm…sorting out bins."

"How would you like to come out and see where the maple syrup is made?"

CHAPTER THREE

BROOKS HAD NO idea what the hell hallucination he was having. He was staring down the only ex that had ever hurt him, inviting her to come to his maple syrup farm.

When he'd heard about Hope's canceled wedding he'd been overtaken by the strangest set of emotions. He used her name as a curse, generally speaking, and when her engagement announcement had made the rounds in town— marrying that hoity-toity rich asshole she'd been with for years—his heart had turned to stone.

Hearing that her wedding had been canceled—that he'd left her at the altar—Brooks had been...well he'd been pissed off and he wasn't sure why.

Pity for Hope wasn't generally in his emotional wheelhouse.

He couldn't quite say why the fury at Hope Marshall lingered within him the way it did, but he really, really bore a grudge against the woman.

He supposed it wasn't all that fair. It was a bit like inviting a bear to a picnic and then getting mad when the bear wanted to eat *you* instead of a peanut butter sandwich.

A bear was going to do what a bear was going to do.

And a snotty little rich girl was going to marry an equally snotty rich douchebag, and definitely wasn't going to stay with the boy from the wrong side of the tracks.

And you *broke up with* her, *remember?*

No. He didn't really think of it that way, actually. Because Hope had already been out the door at that point. He'd just shut it behind her. And he didn't see much point in being broken up about that.

And now she's coming to the ranch.

Hell.

Now she was coming to the ranch to get a gander at his maple syrup supply, which was not exactly how he'd imagined this little reunion going.

He couldn't deny there was a bit of poetic justice in walking into her store just in time to see her flat on her ass from a fall on the heels of hearing about her broken-up wedding. Yeah, he'd been a little bit happy about that too.

More than a little.

And he may or may not have gotten a couple of beers in him last night and had a rant at Garrett Roy down at the bar about it. But then, having one or two too many and having a rant about Hope was essentially his hobby. And had been for the past twelve years.

He could see the dust trail before he saw her car, coming up the long driveway that led to his house.

Hope had never been to his house back when they'd been dating. He'd never have asked her to that shack his dad passed off as a dwelling. Ever. She knew where he was from but she'd never seen it. He'd never wanted her to.

She pulled up and parked the shiny little black car which now had a fine film of dust on it, and he tried not to think of it as a metaphor for *them*.

She opened the car door and the first thing he saw was one fine bare leg, her skirt riding up as she pushed herself out of the seat and then adjusted her ponytail.

Yeah. She was so damn pretty. As pretty as she'd been

back in high school, and too good for him—too soft, too everything.

She said nothing. She was looking around the spread, wide-eyed.

"What?" He turned and looked at the big ranch house behind him. "Did you think I lived in a hole in the ground?"

She shook her head. "No."

"Must have me confused with my old man."

He did his best to moderate his tone. Not for Hope in particular. Really not.

"No, I just…well, I'll be honest. I didn't expect that you were going to make a fortune farming maple, or however you say that. And how exactly did you end up doing that?"

"Oh, I think there's a few conversations we might need to have before we have that one."

"Like?"

"How the hell did you end up out here running a candy store?"

"Well, that would be related to the canceled wedding."

"I figured as much."

He stared at her, her blue eyes, her pretty blond hair. Her cheekbones were sharper than the last time he'd seen her, but she still had that full, lush figure that he'd always liked.

He'd seen a picture of her a couple of years ago. She'd been looking downright thin, and he hadn't liked it. Then he'd been mad that he'd thought about it at all. But it hadn't stopped him from having a thought.

Many thoughts.

He had remembered the way she used to look at him. Full cheeks, sweet and sunny, like he might be something special. And he had always known that eventually the look in her eyes would dim. Sooner or later.

Then, she'd gone and gotten accepted into a college across the country.

And hell, he'd always known that she was headed that way. And he wasn't going to hold her back. His life was going to look different, and he knew that. Things just weren't the same for them. Maybe if he were some kind of brain trust he could've gotten that scholarship or something, but he wasn't. What he knew was hard work. What he valued was hard work. Not sitting and reading and studying and remembering facts. Hope was the one who was good at that. But then she hadn't even gone off and done anything with it. She just got engaged.

To the kind of rich prick he'd always known she was secretly waiting for.

Back then, she had been too young and naive to even make the most of their ill-fated relationship.

If you were going to date beneath you, you ought to at least enjoy getting dirty.

But no. Hope had held on to her virginity through their entire relationship, and then gone off to college, where he imagined the man with the biggest bank account had been given that honor.

"Can you not look at me like you want to roll me in maple syrup and put me on an anthill?"

"Well damn, Hope, still descriptive as ever."

"Hopefully more so. I like to think I've improved with age."

She had. Dammit. "I'm not looking at you any kind of way."

"You are. Let's get one thing straight, Sullivan Brooks, I did not come back to town to go toe-to-toe with you, or... for any reason to do with you. You happened to walk into my candy store right as I—"

"Fell."

"Yes, I fell. I *did* fall. It's basically been that kind of month."

She sighed and reached into her car, and produced an insulated bag. "But I would like to see your facility. And… I brought you some salmon."

"You brought me salmon?"

"I did. Preportioned salmon. As a peace offering of sorts."

"Babe, I fish. I have a freezer full of salmon. And venison. And elk. I'm pretty self-sufficient in the meat department."

"Please take my salmon, Brooks. *Please.*" She looked wide-eyed then. "I will trade it for this delightful tour of your maple farm."

"And if I don't take the salmon?"

"We don't have to be cordial to each other. We can just be exes. And you know what, we're not even significant exes. We dated *in high school.*"

Not significant. Hell and damn.

"You *loved* me in high school," he said.

Her mouth dropped open and her cheeks went pink. "You are…the worst. You really are."

"Hey, I'm just reminding you of how it was."

He remembered her tear-streaked face as she asked him to just say whether or not he loved her. Like it would change anything. She could say whatever she wanted, but that didn't make it true. The girl could tell herself that she loved him, but that didn't mean she did.

"It's not my favorite memory," she said, her jaw tight. "Show me the syrup. Please take the fish."

"I'll take the fish. If you explain the fish."

She let out an exasperated breath. "Fine. The fish is from the wedding." She cleared her throat. "I stole it."

"You *stole* the fish."

"I did. Because my in-laws paid for the wedding. And it just seemed like a petty way to get back at them for everything."

"His parents didn't leave you at the altar. He did."

"Fine. He did. But they were...not a fun part of the whole thing." She stood there for a moment, and there was a hardness to her features that he didn't remember ever seeing there before. "You know when it's over and you realize you should have known a lot sooner?"

That got him. Right where he pretended he wasn't still tender for her. "Yeah, Hope. I do."

"I'm not talking about us."

"No. You're right. Let's take the salmon into the house, then I'll take you out back to see the trees."

He let her into the house, and it wasn't at all because he wanted her to see how nice of a place it was.

No.

He wasn't *that* petty.

It wasn't because he wanted her to see all the top-of-the-line appliances, half of which he didn't know how to use. He'd had them installed just because he could. It wasn't because he wanted her to see how nice the kitchen cabinets were, or the fact that he had made something of himself.

"This is a nice place," she said, walking over to the refrigerator and opening it, taking the salmon out of the insulated container and putting it inside.

"Thanks," he said.

"I'm glad to hear that you've...done well for yourself."

"You never asked about me?"

"My parents aren't exactly invested in the Jasper Creek

gossip chain. You know they think they're better than everyone else. And now they live in Hawaii, where they can be better than everyone else in nicer weather."

"Oh right. Your *parents* always felt that way."

"Don't start. Twelve years, twelve minutes. It doesn't matter, it's the same conversation. You think I think I'm better than you."

She remembered how it had started, being paired off in science. It was a cliché, honestly. Study buddies.

Her very first experience with sexual chemistry had been the result of science class, but it hadn't helped either of them get a passing grade.

He'd been standoffish when they were first paired up, grumbling about snobs.

Sorry, the only snob here seems to be you, she'd said.

That had made him laugh. From there they'd formed a truce and she'd felt sweaty whenever he'd gotten too close or touched her hand passing her a pen.

Then in the lead-up to their presentation they'd been studying in her room, while her parents were out at a community theater production and she'd gone from never having kissed a guy to second base in about fifteen minutes. All it had taken was for him to get close. To look at her with those eyes and sparks had just gone off.

It had been exhilarating.

They'd connected *there*. They'd struggled when it had come to getting to know each other. Her house bothered him. It was big and fancy and he never wanted her to see his.

You still think I'm a snob!

Look how you were born, Hope. It's not your fault. Your parents won't even let me in the door now that they know I'm more than a study buddy. You just don't see it.

Oh, thanks, Brooks. That makes me sound like not just a snob, but a dumb, pitiable snob with no control over her thoughts.

And when you graduate, where are you going? You staying here?

I...no.

Because you're too good for Jasper Creek. Too good for me.

And because they were seventeen they'd quit fighting and kissed instead.

"You *are* better than me, Hope Marshall. That's just a fact."

"I'm not better than you."

His stomach went tight, and he ignored it. The two of them left the house, and he made his way down the front steps to the trail that went straight off into the maple grove. "I bought this place from a man who'd started it and didn't have the patience to see it through. The trees were already mature, ready to tap. And now, well, as shopping local has become a bigger thing, getting your syrup from where you live has become a little bit of a bigger issue. I'm able to off-load the stuff at farmers markets, in CSA boxes. Honestly, I do more business than I can keep up with. It's been a lot more successful than I anticipated. We do the candy and things to go in the online store, but it would be nice to have it in a storefront."

"I love the idea. I love the idea of using the syrup to make candy. And fudge."

"You always did have a sweet tooth."

She laughed. "Not for the last couple of years. And now I can't seem to stop." She bit her lip, and everything in him went on red alert. Damn that girl, she always could get his body to sit up and beg like a sad puppy dog.

"I have a bag of Skittles in my purse. I ate most of it on the way here."

"Not Skittles," he said, feigning horror.

"James's family doesn't eat sugar," she said. "They think it's bad for you. And that your body becomes addicted to it, and that we are all slaves to overly manufactured poison. Something about your adrenals? Do you know how long it's been since I've had Skittles?"

"How long?"

"Well…twenty minutes," she said, sticking her hand into the bag and pulling out a couple pieces of candy, then popping them in her mouth. "But before that, quite some time."

He frowned. "So, what was going to be in your wedding cake?"

"We weren't going to have a wedding cake. We were going to have cheese. A four-tier cheese platter. At *my* wedding."

"That doesn't seem right." The girl he'd known, she would have wanted buckets of candy. And a big cake in bright colors.

"I don't even know who that was. And coming back here, setting up the candy store… I don't know, I feel more like me than I have for a long time."

He stared at her, and the question rose up inside of him. Who was she? Because yeah, he remembered that she'd been a little hummingbird who existed on sugar. And he remembered that she was blonde, and that she was pretty.

And he remembered that he had been the recipient of the first blow job she'd ever given, and that his was the first male member she'd ever seen.

Yeah, he remembered *those* things.

He also remembered that he was the first man to ever go down on her, and that he was responsible for her very first orgasm in the front seat of his pickup truck. It was an inconvenient thing to remember while standing there staring at her out in the middle of the trees.

But he couldn't say if he really knew who she was. Not for certain.

But then, what did that even mean? She was fancy. She'd gone off to live a fancy life and it had bitten her in the ass. And maybe the real reason she was back here was that being around people who were a little bit smaller than she was had always made her feel good. At least, that was what he'd always wondered—if what she'd really liked was feeling as though she had the advantage in whatever relationship she was in.

"Well, come out and see the trees."

They walked on back to the maple grove and stopped at the first tap and bucket.

"So, this is it." He wasn't really sure what he'd intended to accomplish with this. What had seemed clear before seemed a lot less so now that she was here.

"How did you...? I mean, seriously, why this? Why did this interest you?"

"Beef is pretty saturated around here. Dairy...just not that interested. But I always did like working the land. This place came up for sale about the time I was looking to buy. I did a little research and saw that since most of the start-up was done for me, I could make it profitable pretty quickly."

"How did you get the money to buy the place?"

"Work." She stared at him. "That's something that you do, and you get a paycheck for it. It's not when your dad gets out his wallet."

"Wow. How many years have you been waiting to say that?"

"'Bout as long as you've been waiting to eat a Skittle."

"Right. Okay. So, I don't exactly want to do business with someone who's going to be mean to me every time he opens his mouth."

"Why is that?"

"Because I'm done. I was with someone for nine years who was pretty mean to me, actually."

And just like that, his blood nearly boiled over. "He what?"

"It wasn't good, Brooks. That's all. And I don't… I don't want to talk about it. I never have. Not even with the girls. I just… It's not like he hit me or anything. But he liked so much about me, and then there was so much he didn't like. And I didn't really know that until… You know, it was like he had buyer's remorse sometimes."

"I'm sorry. That's not okay."

"I know. I agree. I just got so caught up in it. In all of it and I… You don't want to hear this," she said.

"Maybe I do."

She sighed heavily and looked around. "There was a type. A type that most of his friends were with. And you know, for all that my family was fancy around here, they were not fancy to his family. And I wasn't particularly… the right fit."

"What does that mean?"

"I was…me. You know? I have…" She poked her stomach. "This."

"A body?"

"Fat. And hips. And boobs."

"You are listing literally all of my favorite things about you."

"I am not."

"You are."

"Well, they weren't his favorite."

The feeling that rushed through Brooks wasn't one he could easily articulate. Rage that another man had touched her. And that he hadn't appreciated what had been there to touch. And a hefty dose of desire that he'd hoped he'd left somewhere in his rearview mirror twelve years ago, about the time he told Hope that he didn't love her and never would.

He'd destroyed things then. Ended them completely. And that was supposed to be it. She wasn't supposed to be coming back to town, opening candy shops, and being every bit as sexy to him as she'd always been.

"So, do you want me to bring candy and syrup by later?"

"Yes please. Can I take some syrup now?"

"Sure."

"I just want to test out some fudge recipes at home."

They went down the path that led to the big old repurposed barn. "Here it is," he said. "The sugar shack."

She walked inside, and her jaw went slack.

"First of all, it smells like heaven in here. Second of all, *sugar shack*?"

"That's what they're called."

"Well, I want to call my candy store that."

It gave his chest a strange hitch to hear her say that. It reminded him of a different time. A different life. Where they'd ignored everything that was different and found common ground that felt sacred.

He preferred to ignore that.

He walked over to one of the spigots that came off the final filtering station and grabbed a plastic container. "Use the name if you want," he said. "I don't own it. And consider us square for the salmon."

He really didn't want that salmon.

He poured a hefty amount of syrup into the container and handed it to Hope.

"Thanks. I'll… I can share the recipe for the fudge. Once I get it right."

"Can't you just find a recipe online?"

"Brooks. It's not going to be as good as what I can figure out."

He believed her.

He walked her out toward the car, and he was left with the strangest sensation that the air wasn't quite as sweet after she got in and began to drive away.

Hope Marshall was back.

And somehow, he'd gone and gotten himself tangled up with her just like he had before.

Just like he'd promised himself he'd never do.

CHAPTER FOUR

"IT'S MEETING TIME, HOPE," Pru shouted from the living room.

"Meeting!" The shout from all the girls was accompanied by a banging sound that seemed like a substitute for a chant.

"I'm not breaking any rules! I'm just a second late because I'm making fudge. And you should all be grateful!"

The sound of the Andrews Sisters was filtering into the kitchen from their new Victrola, like they were playing the soundtrack of her demise even as she finished her candy-making.

She poured the fudge in its liquid state into a glass dish, and then ran toward the living room, where she was met by a mock-sorrowful-looking Charity, who was holding out the glass jar filled with slips. "I don't make the rules."

"You were a hundred percent part of making the rules," Hope grumbled, giving her friend the evil eye while she reached into the jar and grabbed the slip.

"I take no joy in it," Charity said.

"You're a liar!"

"I had to cry," Kit said, deadpan. "A lone, solitary tear. In front of Browning West, he of the very large hands who was not—as we had hoped—dissipated from years of hard living, but even more beautiful than he was in high school."

Browning West was the sort of man you didn't forget. And he was helping Kit out with the shelving in her store, a development Hope was very much intrigued by. The bad boy of Jasper Creek High School who made most girls spin fantasies they didn't quite understand. Not Hope, though. She'd been hung up on Brooks.

Brooks.

"And I feel bad for your pride," Hope said. "I do. But do you smell what is coming from the kitchen?"

"It'd better not be salmon," Pru groused.

"No. It's not salmon, because I have no desire to incur a fish-based demerit. It's maple fudge, because you'll never guess who I ran into a few days ago…"

"Who?" the girls asked in unison.

"Sullivan Brooks."

"Sullivan Brooks?" Pru asked. "As in, Sullivan Brooks, the only penis you ever saw when we were in high school?"

Her face went hot. She did not need to be thinking about Brooks's…*that.*

And it was really hard to do because he still looked so hot, and he was bigger all over, really. Broader shoulders, broader chest. Bigger muscles. Bigger thighs. It made her wonder about other things too. Of course, they'd been pretty damn big back then, and had maybe contributed to some of her skittishness in regard to actually—

"Yes. *That* Sullivan Brooks."

This was why she hadn't told them yet.

"That's not even fair," Pru said. "Kit got to see Browning West, you saw Sullivan Brooks…what do Charity and I get?"

"Knitting," Charity said, her tone sullen. "And Thingz. *With a Z.*"

Hope didn't envy Charity's position. Taking on a legacy was harder in some ways than starting from scratch. And the name was as outdated as the stock in the store and

Hope had a feeling that there would be resistance to a name change from the citizens of Jasper Creek.

"And no hot men. The best I'm liable to get is a glimpse of Grant Mathewson at Sunday dinner and no thank you," Pru said.

Grant was Pru's older brother's best friend, and she knew that the whole situation with him was contributing to her crossness. Which, honestly, made Hope think that the Pru-ricane protested a bit too much.

"Well, this whole meeting had nothing to do with his… with *that*." Her face was hot. Lord. She was a grown woman and not a virgin and there was no reason for her to be getting overheated talking about naked men. "And everything to do with one," she held her finger up, "the fact that I fulfilled my last slip. And two," she held up a second finger, "that I am working with Brooks on a deal with his maple syrup. So, the slip did work, just not for what it was intended for."

"I'm sorry, you have to back up," Kit said, swaying in time with the music. "Because we need full details on how you saw Brooks *and fell down*."

"I did not see Brooks and then fall down," she said, gesturing with the unread slip of paper still clutched in her hand. "I fell down, and Brooks saw me through the window and came to make sure I wasn't dead."

"Which you obviously weren't," Charity said.

"I wasn't. But I could have been, and I didn't have a cell phone to call for help. I couldn't even reach the wall to knock and signal Charity for her medical expertise."

"I'm not currently practicing medicine," Charity said, her expression bland. "So I couldn't have helped either way."

"You took an oath, Charity."

"I did. It's true. And I always keep my oaths."

"Anyway. He has a maple farm. And I make candy. And now I'm making maple fudge. And all of you could try some except that you're mean and you made me draw a slip while I was only doing good things for you."

"And we feel awful," Kit said, "but read it."

"Bitches," Hope said, with absolutely no venom. She unfolded the slip and recoiled with great drama. "No. No, I cannot!"

"You can't what?" Charity asked.

"I can't...have him *smell me*."

"Him?" Kit asked, amusement toying with the edge of her lips.

"Oh, you know what I mean. It's just that I have an appointment with Brooks and it's actually likely to be him."

"Smelling you?" Pru asked. "Smelling. That's a hard pass."

"Can I pick again?"

"No, you can't pick again," Charity said. "I am sorry, but those are the rules."

"You're not sorry," Hope said. "And you can sit there looking sweet as pie all you like, Charity, but it's a ruse now like it was a ruse back when we were kids. You didn't make it through medical school because you're *sweet*."

"Smelling," Pru repeated. "Explain."

Hope made an exasperated sound. "'Ask his opinion on which perfume you should wear. Offer him a sniff.'"

"Offer him a sniff!" Pru hooted now. "Oh...oh no."

And the worst part was that when Hope thought of Brooks leaning in, she imagined herself offering her neck and him...

When she'd been with Brooks in high school he'd taught her thrilling things about her own body. About what she wanted to do with a man's body.

But she wasn't in high school anymore. The mysteries of the sexual universe were solved, and she didn't need to be taught. She knew exactly what she wanted to do to him. And what she wanted him to do to her.

And she couldn't escape the fact—no matter how much she wanted to—that she regretted never having slept with him. That when she'd been facing down the prospect of her whole life with James, she'd regretted never having been with another man. That she'd regretted never having been with Brooks.

Because it left all this space for *what if.*

What if being with Brooks was more mind-blowing than anything she'd ever experienced with James?

Fundamentally, everything she'd done with Brooks had been better, but she didn't know if that was because they'd been seventeen and desperate and she'd been afraid of getting caught or what. If it had felt intense because she'd never had an orgasm or if it really had been that intense.

And now she was thinking about him sniffing her neck. And wondering. Really wondering.

She wasn't here for that kind of wondering. She wasn't here for anything of the kind. She was supposed to be getting her life back to what she wanted. Detangling from what her parents wanted, from what James had wanted.

She went into the kitchen and retrieved the first batch of fudge she'd made, which was cooled already, coming back in and holding it high. "Don't you feel guilty now?"

Her friends did not seem to feel guilty, and Hope stalked up the stairs, down the narrow hallway, and into the small bedroom she was staying in.

The bed was neat, small, with a brass frame, and honestly, even if there wasn't a rule against hooking up in the house, the very idea of one of them doing it here was sort of ridiculous. It was not made for that sort of carry-on. It was a sweet room. Fussy. With lace curtains and an old tatted rug. She could no more bring Sullivan Brooks into this room and—

She pushed it out of her mind. She collected all of her comfy clothes and went down the hall to the bathroom where she drew herself a bath in the large, deep claw-foot tub that was made for soaking, and that could only be filled once in an evening before the water heater was done for the night. That meant her friends would be hauling buckets of hot water up the stairs from the stove top if they wanted to have a wash tonight. Hope didn't feel at all bad.

She marinated there in the tub until the confusion of the day had been washed away, and then she got out and dressed quickly, heading down the stairs to see Kit, Pru and Charity looking at her fiercely. Pru was holding the jar.

"You've broken another rule."

"I have not," she said. "All I did was take a bath."

"You left your dishes."

"I was going to do them."

"You went upstairs and took a bath, and you did it because you wanted to take all the hot water because you were mad," Pru said, in a maddeningly patient tone. "And you left the dishes so you could do that. You're lucky we're not making you draw two slips of paper."

"I'm not drawing another slip of paper, and this is silly," she said. "It's all silly. Really, what are we even doing? We're grown women who have been living in cities and doing big jobs, and we are here sharing a farmhouse with no cell phones taking dating advice from an old magazine.

And so far all it's done for me is put me in the path of the one man I absolutely shouldn't be dating."

"Slip," Kit said, pointing into the top of the jar. "The universe is calling."

"This isn't the universe. This is you!"

"Acting on behalf of the universe," said Kit. "You can't leave your life up to fate selectively, Hope. That's not how it works. It's all or nothing."

Granted, the first tip had brought her into contact with Brooks, which felt a lot like fate. But the idea of this had been a lot funnier when it was Kit having to cry a tear and Pru having to wear a wedding gown on a street corner.

Less so when it was her getting *smelled*.

"You're mean," Hope said, huffing. "I thought this was all to *help* me."

"Sometimes," Charity said, "you have to reset a broken bone so that it heals correctly, and it is very painful. But that doesn't mean it doesn't need to be done. And it doesn't mean that anyone is mean."

"Mean," Hope said, taking another slip of paper out. *"No,"* she said.

"What is it?" Pru crowed.

"I have to wear high heels now? 'High heels are much more attractive than flat shoes,'" she read. "'It has a slenderizing effect on the legs.'"

"It is true," Kit said. "High heels are sexy."

"Paralysis of the feet isn't sexy," Pru said.

"I'm with Pru on this one."

"Come on," Kit said. "You can't tell me you don't wear high heels. I know you did back in Chicago."

"I'm not going to wear them on the main street of Jasper Creek."

"You will. With perfume."

And just like that, Hope's fate was sealed. And one thing was for certain, she was about to have a very fancy day in the candy store tomorrow.

CHAPTER FIVE

"HOWDY THERE, GARRETT." Brooks hefted the heavy crate filled with maple syrup out of the back of his truck, lifting it with ease, before slamming the bed of the pickup shut.

Garrett Roy was standing out on the street, staring toward what used to be his grandmother's yarn store. It had closed down a number of years ago, and had just been sitting there, filled to the brim with everything she hadn't sold before her death.

"You look happy," Brooks commented.

"Don't like it. Those girls are in there...changing things."

"Yeah, I expect they are. I'm doing business with Hope."

"Hope Marshall?"

Yeah, given that he had just filled Garrett's ear with poison on the subject of Hope Marshall, he could see why the other man was looking at him a bit skeptically now.

"Yeah. Hope Marshall. Turns out I want to line my pockets a hell of a lot more than I want to spite my face. Or whatever."

"Suit yourself," Garrett said. He shook his head, putting his black cowboy hat on his head. "I don't like it at all."

Since the former bull rider had breezed back into town with a chip on his shoulder after his grandma's health had taken a bad turn, Brooks had gone for a drink with him from time to time though he wasn't sure he'd call them friends. But then, he wasn't sure who Garrett Roy would call a friend. Or who *he* would call a friend for that matter.

He tipped his hat to Garrett and then continued on to Hope's candy store. He stopped at the door. It was bright red, painted over layers of other colors. The building itself was made of worn brick and through the antique windows he could see...

Hope Marshall's ass.

She was bent over one of the display cases and he liked very much what he saw.

"You going to let me in?" he asked as he tapped the window with his elbow.

Hope startled, and practically fell out of the case. And that was when he noticed that the woman was wearing... high heels.

A little flowery summer dress and high heels that were just begging for a man to lift her and set her up on that counter, step between her legs, and let her lock her heels behind his back while he lost himself inside of her.

She tottered over to the door, the shoes making her take deep, deliberate steps, her hips swaying slightly.

Damn.

She opened the door and looked up at him. "Good morning." She smelled like flowers. Or vanilla. Or both. And as she wafted away from him, everything in him went hard.

"Yeah," he said, stepping inside and closing the door behind him. "Where do you want this?"

"Oh," she said. "Back here. There's a small kitchen area..."

He followed her into a cubby that was behind the wooden counter in the front. She wasn't kidding.

"You're right. This is small."

"It's good enough for my purposes. Anyway, I've made

some fudge. The girls tell me it's great, but I need a second opinion."

"Is that a request for me to taste it?"

The question lingered between them and she looked away. "Only if you want to."

"Sure."

Hope reached into the pan and popped two squares of fudge out. She took a bite of one and handed the other to him. She closed her eyes. "It's so good. But I'm really not the best judge because I have no limit to my sweet tooth, and I am...you know, I'm kind of done with restraint."

"Right. This is on the theme of yesterday. And your cheese wedding cake."

"Yes. A cheese wedding cake. Not to be confused with a cheesecake for a wedding."

"Got it."

Her eyes connected with his and he felt the sizzle go through his blood. "Done with restraint," he repeated.

"I am."

He took a bite of the fudge and just about groaned out loud. "Hope, that's better than good."

"Well, if you like it then it must be good because you don't like me."

He huffed. "It isn't that I don't like you..."

"It's just that you don't like me."

"You don't really like me."

She let out a long, slow breath. "You broke my heart, Brooks."

He just stared at her, at that beautiful face that meant more to him still than he'd like to admit.

"Not before you broke mine."

"You didn't love me. How can I have broken your heart?"

He gritted his teeth. "Never mind all that."

"Right. Um… Help me pick out a perfume, will you?" she said, the sudden change of subject throwing him off.

"What?"

"I said, I need you to help me pick out a perfume. Vanilla is on the left, lilac is on the right." With her index finger she pointed to the hollows on each side of her neck just beneath her jawbone. And then she drew closer to him and for the first time in his memory, Sullivan Brooks wasn't exactly sure what to do with a woman.

OH, SHE WAS doing it. She was just doing it. She was stretching up on her toes, which she still had to do even in heels because Brooks was a mountain of a man, and she was leaning in, her neck bared.

What she wanted was his mouth right there. What she wanted was his teeth. He was some kind of a vision in that white cowboy hat, one she told herself she didn't actually want.

Hadn't she told herself that for years?

After he'd hurt her, she'd taken all the criticisms her parents had lobbed at him during her relationship and instead of pushing them away, she'd owned them. Held them. Used them as a shield.

She didn't like *cowboys* anyway. Didn't want to take up with a *damn redneck* when she could have a man that had some *class*. Had some *style*.

But wow, right now she wanted this redneck. And she wanted to be in his truck again. She could remember that night vividly, when they were kissing and rubbing all up against each other, seventeen and out of breath. Trembling with the desire for more. And he'd slid down onto the baseboards of the truck, flipped her dress up and put his mouth right over her white cotton panties. And then he... Well, he'd absolutely blown her mind.

And to this day, no other man had ever done that to her.

James didn't like it. He liked other things—namely, her going down on him. He just didn't like to reciprocate. And the sex had been fine and all, it just hadn't been...

Why was she thinking about sex while she was doing this? Why was she doing it at all? Kit, Pru and Charity would never know if she didn't ask Brooks to smell her.

Though, she knew that Pru was going to ask the minute that she saw her later today. Because that was just how Pru was.

"Vanilla," she whispered, angling her head.

A muscle in his jaw jumped and he moved closer. Her heart started to beat erratically.

"Good," he said, his voice hard. "Not too different from the sugar I smell all day."

"Too common?"

"Your skin makes it different."

He said it rough. He said it hard. And it shouldn't be sexy, not in the least. Only it was. A pulse beat hard in her throat, and echoed at the base of her thighs.

"Lilac," she said, angling her head again, and offering him the other side of her throat.

"I think I like the sweetness," he said. "It's you." He moved his head back slightly, but their mouths were only a breath away.

"Brooks..."

Then he moved away quickly and Hope felt lost.

She didn't know what she wanted from him in this moment, but her body was telling her what it thought it needed.

"Not a good idea," he said, his voice rough.

"So what?" she asked.

"So what? You know, I've had twelve years of thinking about you. I don't need twelve more."

Suddenly, Hope's throat went tight, her eyes filling with tears. And she couldn't stop them. She was just overwhelmed by it all. By the reality of what had almost happened.

"I almost married him," she said. "And do you want to know the deepest shame that I have, Brooks? That I wished I'd had sex with you. It haunted me. *You* haunted me." She thumped his chest. "And I… I think you did it on purpose."

"Do you?"

"I do. I think you did it on purpose because you were just…spiteful. Because you didn't want me to marry a rich man. And what you yelled at me when I said I was going to go to college? That I was just going to find myself one of those fancy men that was fancy like me? I thought about that all the time. You made me feel like I had betrayed you somehow when you were the one who… You were the one who said you didn't love me."

"What good would it have done, Hope? What good would it have done to love you?" There was something raw in his eyes that hurt her. "You already had one foot out the door, sweetheart. That was it. You were leaving. You didn't give me any kind of promise to stay. You didn't give me any kind of hope you might come back. I was just making it a clean break."

"It wasn't a clean break, though, was it? Because though we haven't talked to each other in twelve years, we just fall right back into it, don't we? And doesn't that tell you that neither of us ever really let go?"

"I don't know about that," he said.

"*I* do," she said. "*I* know about it. We never released each other. Not really. And the worst part…? The worst part is that you were right about me. I got my head turned by all these things that didn't matter. My parents were excited about my life for the first time ever. And that felt good. I felt like I was succeeding and the deeper I got into that life, the more I felt it. And I almost married him. I almost married him and I… I get more turned on thinking about making out with you in the back of a truck than I ever did having sex with him. And what's that? What *is* that?"

"Justice maybe," he said.

"What about you? How about all the girls who've paraded through your bed in the years since you last touched me? Did they do it for you?"

He gritted his teeth. "I prefer them blonde. And I prefer to be a little drunk. Because then I can't see quite so clearly. Leaves a lot of room for fantasy."

"You're just as messed up as I am. So how about it? Don't you think maybe…maybe we should…?" She took a step forward but her high heel caught on the wood floor and pitched her forward, right into Brooks's solid chest. And suddenly, she was breathing hard, her heart hammering wildly. Maybe she should have been embarrassed. Maybe it should have been the kind of slapstick moment you'd see in a romantic comedy, sort of like what had happened the first day they'd seen each other. But it wasn't funny. Nothing about it was funny.

Because he was warm and solid in all the ways that she remembered, but more so. Because he had changed. Because the sun and his cares had worn new lines into his skin, and his beard was heavier. Because his dark blue eyes held more cares than they had when he was seventeen. Because they were different people, but the same ones all at once, and it was all the more compelling for its complication.

And he was Brooks, that was the thing. It would always be the thing. He was Brooks, and she was Hope, and that was the thing. Because across years—twelve, to be exact—the two of them still had a connection. She hadn't spoken to Sullivan Brooks since the day he'd told her he didn't love her. Since she'd stood out there in the rain in front of his father's house and he wouldn't let her in, and she'd been weeping and asking why he couldn't love her.

Why he was so afraid that her saying she loved him was a lie.

That was the last time they'd spoken. And each and every word from that conversation was scratched deep into her heart. She felt it every time it beat. She had felt shame, and then triumph, when she'd first found another man. When she'd gone on a date with James. Yes, she had felt it then.

And then she'd told herself that Brooks was right and it was fine. That James was everything Brooks wasn't, and it was a good thing, because she and Brooks really were too different. Because they could never, ever be together—not the way she'd fantasized.

Back when she'd been young and foolish and drunk from his kisses.

But she was a woman now. Not the girl she'd been the first time she'd kissed Brooks, and not the girl she'd been when she'd first stepped away from him.

Now she had scars from Brooks, but she had scars from James too—from her parents, for that matter—and she wasn't sure how she felt about it.

Right now she just wanted…she just wanted to go back and do it over. With everything she knew now. To go back to him, knowing everything she did now.

As the woman she was now.

The woman who knew that a kiss didn't mean true love, and didn't have to.

That was the problem.

When she and Brooks were seventeen, it had been forever or nothing. And even when she had turned twenty-one and she'd met James, it had felt like being with him was a step toward forever. And it almost had been.

But if she kissed Brooks now, it could just be a kiss.

Just a kiss...

And she realized, with a blissful sort of satisfaction that there was no chance of her phone interrupting them. There was no chance of anything stopping them now. And so she looked up at him, and she slicked her tongue over her top lip.

And she knew. She knew she had him.

His mouth crashed down over hers and they ignited.

She had never forgotten those lips. They were hard and perfect against hers and it made her want to sob because a kiss hadn't really been a kiss since Brooks.

Brooks tore the sky away, made her see things she had never imagined might be there. A world of need, desire, and want that she had never experienced before.

And he was doing it now.

Even for thirty-year-old Hope, and that was a miracle all on its own.

She had kissed him so sure of the woman she had become. The woman who might meet him on equal footing in a way she never could have before. But as soon as their lips touched, that thought was gone. It wasn't about equal or unequal footing.

It was just them.

It wasn't about James, the past, or any other kind of

thing. Just Brooks and Hope. Impossible and perfect as they had ever been.

Too soon, he pulled away.

"I imagine," he said, his voice rough, "that you don't want me stripping you naked here in your store."

She sucked air in between her teeth. "Well…"

"Hope…"

"Okay. Maybe not. Especially because all the stores have a shared basement, and honestly, Pru could pop up at any moment with a pressing feed question."

"A feed question?"

"She has a feed store. Never mind."

"My place. Tonight."

"Yeah. Okay." She was too dizzy to say no.

And in only a few moments, he was gone, and she was left standing there, feeling featherheaded and wobbly on her high heels.

SHE SPENT THE next few hours practically floating on air, and she couldn't even feel how badly her feet ached in the stupid high heels. She made good progress when it came to setting up the store, which was a good thing because the centennial was edging ever closer and she really wanted to be in a position to have a soft opening before then so she had an idea of what people liked about the store. So that it didn't feel like such a hard deadline and a drop off a cliff into success or failure.

If they didn't get the shops successfully opened, the rent would go up so sharply they would never be able to afford it, and all of this would be for nothing.

Her parents had told her that this town wasn't what she wanted and for a while she'd thought it must be true. But she didn't agree. She just didn't.

She'd made her very best friends here. Grown up walking down Main Street. Summer to her would always be the Fourth of July barbecue. Christmas would always be white lights and a big tree with a redbrick building behind it.

Clear skies with diamond-dust stars and the smell of lilacs on the wind.

Jasper Creek wasn't a place to escape from. It was home. And it had taken the very real possibility of never calling it home again for her to realize that.

She was finding the life that mattered to her here. Not the life that mattered to other people.

And she had a feeling that her friends and family would have opinions about that. But all of their opinions were currently in her phone, nestled in a safe below her feet. She couldn't access them even if she wanted to.

What mattered was what was around her: the shop, the smell of the candy, the joy she took in creating different confections.

Her friends who were here.

And Brooks…

Well, she *wanted* Brooks.

That was clear to her.

As clear and real as Main Street.

At the end of the day, Hope stepped out of the store, just at the same time Pru, who looked sweaty and angry, Charity, and Kit stepped out of their stores too. They looked at each other, smiled, and put their keys in the locks, turning them nearly in sync.

"Ready for some dinner?" Pru asked.

"Very much," Hope said, reaching into her purse and pulling out some Skittles.

"You'll spoil your appetite," Charity scolded.

"It's an aperitif," Hope said, rattling the candy around in her hand. "A sugary one."

She was absolutely not maintaining the figure that she had cultivated for the wedding. The figure that she had cultivated to be good enough to be James's wife. And Brooks didn't care. Brooks wanted to see her tonight. Brooks, for all that the two of them were complicated, was attracted to her.

And honestly, it was a relief to have something like that be quite so simple.

Shouldn't it be?

It should be, really. It didn't have to be a big deal.

"How did the high heels go?" Kit asked, as they all headed down the street where they had parked this morning.

"Oh, not so bad, really. I might actually… Maybe you guys should go out tonight. And I'll stay in and reheat some salmon."

"You don't like salmon," Charity said, narrowing her eyes.

"I don't," she said, trying to make her eyes large and solemn. "I don't like salmon at all. However, the salmon is my responsibility. I visited it upon us. Unless the three of you have magically managed to off-load…"

"I am considering a grand opening incentive. Also, maybe you should look into salmon candy?" Kit asked Hope.

"No. It's wrong to foist the salmon on all of you. Or on customers. I need to take care of it. Myself."

"You are up to something," Pru said.

"*Me?* I'm not up to anything."

"Did you complete your tasks?"

She hedged. "Yes."

"Ah ha!" Pru said. "You did. You let him smell you.

And you're wearing high heels. And you're seeing him to-night, aren't you?"

"I… I might be."

"No hookups," Kit reminded her.

"I feel like that was just in the house."

"Your feelings are not facts," Pru said.

"And your revisionist history isn't either, Prudence. Anyway, I thought you all wanted me to be happy. I thought you all wanted me to have a little bit of romance in my life after my great tragedy."

"Not Sullivan Brooks," Charity said. "He devastated you."

"I remember that. But I'm not exactly in the market to fall in love right now, so he's not really a danger to my well-being at this point."

"He's…" Charity waved her arm somewhat frantically. "Complicated. He's complicated, and you can't be wanting complicated."

"What I want," Hope said, "is something that feels good. What I want, is someone who makes me feel good to make me feel good. About myself. Because I really don't. And I haven't for a long time. And he does that."

She swallowed hard. "James was…he really hurt me. Not by breaking up with me. By being with me. He made me feel wrong, wrong in my body. In my skin."

"I hate that guy," said Pru.

"So much," said Kit.

"If he needed the ER, I'd step over his body on my way to a coffee break," said Charity.

"And I appreciate that. This has been… I'm myself again. Candy and small towns and things I was told I shouldn't want, things I thought I didn't want. And Brooks was one of those things. And maybe it's a little bit crazy, and maybe it's not a great idea, but I threw myself at the mercy of the slips and they seem to be intent on bringing me Brooks. I know there are plenty of fish in the sea, but I seem intent on catching the same one twice..."

"As long as the fish you're catching isn't salmon, who cares?" Charity asked.

"Oh, come on," Kit said. "You don't have to lie about salmon. Salmon-related lies are now specifically against house rules, and are more dishonorable than all other lies."

"I'll draw another slip," Hope said. "I promise. But I need to go home and put on different underwear."

"Fair," Pru said nodding.

"And then we will expect details," Kit said.

"I can do that."

And while the girls headed to June's Kitchen, Hope went to her car and back to the farmhouse. Tonight felt like an opportunity: to step into the future, she was going to have to come to terms with her past.

And Sullivan Brooks was definitely the way to do that.

CHAPTER SIX

As THE MINUTES ticked by, and the sun began to sink behind the mountain, Brooks started to think she might not be coming. That she had pulled a patented Hope Marshall move and had somehow found a way to trick him into believing that she wanted him, only to balk when it came down to the ultimate intimacy.

But then, just as he was about to give up, drink a shot of whiskey and head to bed alone, he saw headlights out in the rosy dusk, heading up toward the house.

He got up and went out onto the porch.

Like a damn dog. Standing at attention just because Hope Marshall had come to him. Did things really never change?

Maybe we are doomed to repeat our same mistakes until we can put them to bed, so to speak, he thought.

Well, he had every intention of putting this particular mistake to bed once and for all. Tonight.

But right then he had a flashback of another time.

The night Hope had come to his house, something he'd never wanted her to do. The night she'd stood in his driveway in front of the shack where he lived and begged him to make promises while she was getting ready to go out to some fancy-ass college in Chicago. While she was standing there in a pair of jeans that were probably worth more than every electronic device in his house combined. While she was just *her*, all pretty and polished and everything that Hope Marshall had ever been, looking at him like *he* was the monster for saying they didn't have a future together when he already knew she was never coming back.

And here she was again.

So who's the fool now?

He gritted his teeth and walked down the steps.

He folded his arms over his chest and watched, waiting for her to park. Waiting for her to get out.

And she did, in that same pair of high heels and that pretty summer dress, her blond hair loose around her shoulders.

She looked…shy.

Which was silly. They weren't seventeen, and there was nothing to be shy about.

"Hi."

He huffed out a breath, then crossed the space between them, pulling her into his arms, his whole body getting rock hard at the feel of her soft curves flush against him.

And then he kissed her.

He kissed her with the memory of her standing out there in the rain all those years ago pounding heavily in his brain. He kissed her with every bit of that pent-up desire that had been inside of him all this time.

Because it was her, wasn't it? It always had been. He'd admitted it, much to his shame. He'd admitted it *to her*. That his very favorite hookup was a little bit blurry. So that he could think of her.

He'd never had a relationship—not since Hope—and he was thirty years old. That was messed up. And he could pretend all he liked, but that was the truth. He was low-class, like his old man, like his mother who'd run off, like everyone in town had ever thought he was. That he'd been born in the mud and he'd damn well stay there.

But the thing was…

It was Hope. And it always had been. All this time.

So he kissed her. Kissed her like she held the answers to the universe somewhere on those pretty lips, and if he searched hard enough, long enough, she might impart them to him.

And even if she did, he didn't know what he'd do with them.

The secrets of the universe would be wasted on him.

It was warm out, in spite of the fact that the sun had sunk behind the mountains and suddenly, he was gripped by what he really wanted.

"Come with me."

He took her hand and led her down the trail toward the sugar shack where he had parked his truck.

She stood back, her eyes wide and glowing in the dim light.

"What's going on?"

"I figure we've got some unfinished business."

She nodded slowly. "Yeah, I figure we do."

He walked over to the truck and opened the cab, pulling out a folded blanket. He walked around to the truck bed and laid it down across the hard, ridged surface. All right, maybe it wouldn't be the most comfortable, but if they'd done this in high school, this is how they would've done it.

Outside. Away from the lives that had made them who they were.

Away from the houses that marked him as the wrong kind of boy, and her as a sweet little rich girl—him as a boy with no real future and her as a girl with the bright light in front of her. Anything and everything she could want to be.

Yeah. Their houses had always been a barrier to what they felt. Had always been a bit too stark and clear when it came to revealing just how wrong they were for each other. But out here, under the stars, they were just two people who wanted each other. That was what he'd always liked about the time they'd spent in his pickup truck way back then.

Because the only thing between them then was desire, and they'd spent a whole lot of evenings running a heated race to nowhere in particular. Just touching and kissing and bringing each other pleasure without ever…

He'd never been inside her.

And he wanted that.

Craved it.

He was a man who had made an art form out of casual sex—hell, he made a whole rodeo of it—but right here, right now, with Hope, he couldn't pretend that sex between them could be anything like casual. Not remotely. Because it mattered. Because that final part when they would join their bodies together…it mattered.

And all the years in between melted away, all the people that had come since the two of them had first kissed in his truck. They didn't matter. Nothing did.

Nothing but this.

They put the tailgate down and he climbed up in the back, taking hold of her hand and lifting her up into the bed with him. He pulled her soft body down over his and kissed her.

"Outside?" she asked, breathless.

The sky was becoming that dark inky blue all the way down to the tops of the mountains, erasing the last vestiges of the sun, stars piercing through the coming darkness.

"It's how it would've gone, right? Back then."

She only stared at him.

He felt suddenly exposed. Hell, he wouldn't have felt this exposed if he'd been naked. He didn't give a shit about being naked in front of a woman, but those words had been revealing. This entire thing was revealing, and he didn't have the mind to care. Or turn away. Or change what was happening. Or take back what he'd said. The only thing that mattered was this moment.

The *only* thing.

He shifted, lying on his back, bringing her firmly over the top of him. She kissed him, her blond hair falling down in a silken curtain. He pushed his hands through it. So soft. Just like he remembered. She straightened and took her dress off, removing her bra quickly along with it.

And there he was, staring at Hope Marshall's breasts for the first time in twelve years.

"I used to write damn poetry about those," he said.

"What?"

"You had the prettiest body I'd ever seen." An uncomfortable laugh felt forced from him. "Hell. You still do. You're even prettier now." Later, he was going to have to do this with her in the broad, blinding light of the bedroom where they would have hours and a soft mattress, not just the cover of stars and the bed of the truck. But he needed this right now. *They* needed this.

He reached up, cupping her breasts, sliding his thumbs over the tightened buds. She gasped, letting her head fall back, her hips wiggling over where he was hard and aching for her. He kept teasing her, toying with her, until her breath was shaky, fractured and broken.

"Brooks," she whispered.

"Is this where you tell me that you're a good girl and you can't go all the way with me yet?" The question was strangled. His throat was tight.

She looked down at him, and he swore he could see a wicked smile curve her lips.

"I'm not a girl anymore."

His breath escaped in a rush.

"Thank God for that," he said. She pushed his shirt up over his head, and then he reversed their positions, growling as he worked her panties down her legs, leaving her in nothing but the high heels. "Those are ridiculous, you know that, right?"

"I'll explain," she said, panting. "But not right now."

"Yeah, not right now," he said. "Because if I do my job right, in a few minutes you're not going to be able to think."

CHAPTER SEVEN

THIS WAS HAPPENING. She was lying in the back of Brooks's truck and he was…

He was going to do exactly what she'd fantasized about for the last twelve years.

He kissed the divot by her hip bone, and then down her thigh. She began to shake.

He was the only man that had ever done this to her. And the thought of it kept her up at night. Invaded her dreams. Made her wake up tangled and sweaty in her sheets and caught between wanting to beg James to do it instead, and wanting it to be a fantasy about Brooks and Brooks alone.

You were never all in with that relationship.

You wanted to keep Brooks the whole time.

That stark truth poleaxed her because it was true. She had been angry because there were times when it had seemed like James had had one foot out the door—and of course abandoning her at the wedding proved it.

But she'd never given her whole self to him.

She'd kept pieces in reserve—memories and desires and fantasies that had only belonged to Sullivan Brooks.

And that was why. That was why he'd come to her in her dreams because it was all still there.

And then she couldn't think about it at all. Couldn't second-guess herself or marinate in her emotional realization even if she wanted to, because his mouth was on her, slick and perfect and bringing the kind of white-hot pleasure she'd only ever experienced with him.

Sure, she'd had orgasms, but that was just release.

This was something else.

Something all-consuming, all-encompassing. Blinding. Something that reached down deep and made her feel like she wasn't herself anymore. And yet somehow more herself all at the same time. Like she was teetering on the brink of something out of control and overwhelmed with need.

She clung to him as his lips and teeth and tongue played a symphony over her body that left her breathless. He moved his hand down between her legs, sliding one finger inside of her, then another. She gasped, bucking her hips up off the truck bed, whimpering as he pushed her further, higher, faster.

It was twelve years ago, and it was now. It was everything.

It was Brooks.

Brooks.

And when she shattered, it was complete. Utter and total decimation. A wave of pleasure that held her captive, made her feel like she was in danger of being dashed on the rocks, but it held her fast and brought her back down into his arms, into safety.

And before she could catch her breath, he was undoing the belt buckle on his jeans, and pushing them down his thighs. She reached toward him, and he made a low growling sound.

"What?"

"We're not playing around."

"But you have no idea…" She looked at him, at that most masculine part of him, thicker and stronger than she remembered, and oh so enticing.

"I think about this. About the way you tasted…"

"And I am not a man to say no to a blow job, Hope. So you can definitely owe me one. But we've done that."

"So you get to taste me and I don't get to taste you?"

"Damn straight. I want to be inside you."

The intensity in his voice, the roughness in his tone, undid her. Because when had James ever been desperate for her? Never. That was the answer. Never. Neither of them had ever once been desperate for each other.

Her eyes suddenly stung, the emotion overwhelming her. Brooks reached into the pocket of his jeans and produced a condom, protected them both, and then returned to her, kissing her hard and deep. Then she felt him pushing against the entrance to her body.

And then he thrust home.

She cried out with a mixture of pleasure and deep emotion she hadn't expected. He was still for a moment, and she looked up at him, barely able to make out his features in the dark. But she knew it was him.

Brooks.

She might as well have been seventeen again for all that she shook. For all that she felt this was new. Like nothing she'd ever experienced before.

Because it was him.

It wasn't sex she'd been afraid of. It was Brooks.

And she'd been right to be scared.

Because now she couldn't imagine leaving him. Not ever again.

You idiot. You just got out of a nine-year relationship, an almost-marriage.

And she had fallen right back into Sullivan Brooks's arms because…

Because they were the arms she'd been running *from* all this time.

Because this was the thing she'd feared more than anything. Wanting something this much and not being able to have it. She'd told herself that she wanted all those things in Chicago. She'd told herself that those friends and that position mattered. But it didn't. It never had, and deep down she'd never believed it. And that was why it had been easy.

Easy to cut out sugar and get lilac bridesmaid gowns and conform. Because it hadn't mattered if she failed.

But what if she couldn't be what Brooks needed? Being his girlfriend when she'd been in high school had been the most wonderful, devastating experience of her life. Underneath it all, there had always been a distance to them. And it was that distance that had scared her. The way he'd held her at arm's length from his life. The way he'd acted like she was always going to run.

And then you did.

Yes. She had. But he'd said he didn't love her and…

Like you didn't know he was just afraid?

She'd been seventeen. She shouldn't have had to know.

He shifted his hips, growled, and blinding pleasure shot through her, making it impossible for her to think. And so she let it all go. She released the past, and the future, to luxuriate in the present. In the feel of him, thick and hard inside of her. In the way he was above her, the way he held her, the way he growled as he found his pleasure inside her.

In the way her own pleasure shattered over her like glass, or like stars in the night sky, leaving her spent, breathless, certain she couldn't possibly handle any more, but desperate for it all the same.

They lay there, in the bed of the truck, her head on his sweat-slicked chest, feeling the steady rhythm of his heart.

And she just wanted to cry. What if they'd done this *then*?

What if she'd been brave enough?

"You want to go back to the house?" he asked, his voice filled with grit.

"I…" Suddenly, she couldn't breathe. Suddenly she needed…

She needed her friends.

"I have to go. We have…a curfew. And house rules."

"What?"

"Uh, we're not supposed to let men…take precedence while we're here. Rah-rah girl power and stuff."

"Umm…" he said, "what the hell?"

"It's a pact." He just stared at her and she wanted to scream. "*You're a boy.* You wouldn't understand."

She felt ludicrous and seventeen but that wasn't stopping her from scrambling out of the truck bed, hunting around for her bra and her dress, both of which she found easily. But her panties were… She had no idea.

"It's the shoes. And the perfume. There are penalties when you break house rules. I can't explain it right now but I need to go. And…thank you."

"Are you running away from me?"

"Maybe." She made a sound that was a little bit too much like a sob. "Maybe." And then she turned tail and fled back to her car, underwear be damned.

By the time she stumbled into the farmhouse, disgraced and miserable, she felt like she'd made a terrible mistake. Except, she wasn't sure which thing the mistake was: running from him or sleeping with him in the first place.

Her three friends were sitting in the living room. Charity was angrily stabbing at a ball of yarn, and watching Charity angrily do anything was almost enough to jerk Hope out of her sadness.

Though it had to be said that sometimes she wondered about Charity. Her friend seemed so placid and organized, but she'd left medicine and hadn't really explained why. And every so often it was like some rage that lived deep inside her escaped by accident.

The three of them looked at her, Pru from the game of solitaire she had spread out on the coffee table, and Kit from her romance novel, which she was reading while sitting sideways in a floral chair, both legs slung over the arm.

Charity moved her knitting needle twice more, creating a massive tangle, and then let out a deep howl the likes of which Hope had never, ever heard from Charity. It filled the room and Charity chucked the yarn ball onto the floor. "It's dumb! Yarn is dumb!"

"Okaaaaay," Hope said, edging slightly out of the room.

"Wait," Pru said. "Details."

"I can't talk about it." Hope went into the kitchen and opened up one of the painted green cabinet doors. She pulled out a teacup and turned the kettle on, then opened up the fridge, digging around the salmon until she found fudge.

Honestly, *screw all the salmon*.

She started eating the fudge straight out of the pan.

She looked up and saw her friends clustered in the doorway, staring at her. "Sex is stupid," she said.

"Oh." Kit put her hand on her chest, her expression one of horror. "Please don't tell me that Brooks is the kind of man who leaves a partner unsatisfied, because that is deeply disappointing."

"Oh no." She shoved another piece of fudge in her mouth. "He's a god," she said around the candy. "I don't think I'll ever walk straight again. I am ruined. For all other men. All other penises. All other sex. I… I…" Tears started to slide down her cheeks. "What's wrong with me?"

"Oh dear," Charity said, racing toward the kitchen table and pulling out a chair, which Hope sank down into gratefully.

"I'm an emotional disaster. And I keep thinking about how everything fell apart for us twelve years ago. And I… I didn't love James. I didn't love him. I almost married a man I didn't love. I… I never felt as much in bed with James as I did simply kissing Brooks and doing all the third-base stuff we did in high school. And now I… Now we did it. *We did it.*"

"You…went all the way?" The fact that Pru didn't even make fun of her for sounding like a high school girl was testament to how pathetic Hope knew she must look.

"Yes," she said. "And I feel like crying forever. And I feel like I'm in love with him. I can't be in love with him. I dated him twelve years ago, and then was with another man for nine years. *Nine years!* That's how long it took for me to get anywhere near an altar with James. To forever. To commitment."

"But you didn't love James," Kit said matter-of-factly. She walked over to where Hope was sitting and stole a piece of fudge from the baking dish. "You know that. It's clear to you. So why couldn't it be equally clear that you love Brooks?"

"Because that's not how it works," Hope insisted. "That's wishful thinking. That's… It's…unhealthy behavior. I should be single." She held a piece of fudge aloft. "I should be single and not in love and…finding myself."

"Maybe you did," Charity said softly.

"That isn't feminist, Charity," Hope growled, taking another bite of fudge. "I can't find myself by having sex with my high school boyfriend."

"Well," Charity began pragmatically, all the rage that seemed to have been simmering in her over the yarn tucked away again to wherever it was she kept her feelings. "You didn't know you didn't love James. Now you do. You have feelings for Brooks that this seemed to uncover. And things maybe seem a little bit clearer to you, so, I mean, feminist or not, it seems like it happened."

"This isn't one of Kit's romance novels." Hope scowled.

"The greatest lie ever told," Kit said gravely, "is that romance novels are unrealistic. They're not. They might sometimes happen over a compressed length of time, but I assure you that love is real and the sort of sex that brings clarity, intimacy, and screaming pleasure exists."

"You say this as a woman in possession of all those things?" Hope asked.

She was being mean now. She didn't care.

"I don't have to have experienced it to believe in it," Kit said.

"That just seems too easy," Hope said.

"Except it's clearly not," Pru pointed out. "Or you wouldn't be struggling with it, and it wouldn't have taken you this long to get here."

"And it's not done yet," Kit said.

This was why she'd needed them. Because they were right. Each of them.

"I guess I have to actually talk to him."

"What broke you up the first time?" Pru asked.

"He didn't think he was good enough for me. Or he didn't think I thought he was. And I... I was afraid that the real problem was that he didn't want *me*. My parents made it clear they wanted me out of here, at a good school where I could meet the right kind of man. But part of me just wished that…that Brooks would tell me not to go. That he'd ask me to marry him at eighteen and I'd just know. That he was right. That *it* was right. But he didn't say that. And I wasn't brave enough to take a risk. If he didn't want me, I couldn't disappoint my parents. Who else did I have?"

"You know we like you no matter what," Pru said.

Hope nodded. "I know, Pru. I do. It's amazing how you can take that for granted. Though what does it say about my family that I trust in the unconditional love I get from the three of you in a much deeper way than I could ever trust theirs?"

"I don't know what it says about them," said Charity, her eyes glossy all of a sudden, "but it says a lot about our friendship."

Kit put her hand on Hope's shoulder and Hope sniffed loudly, her breath catching in her chest. "It seems silly now, but back then I didn't know who I would be if I didn't do all the things my parents expected of me. I didn't know if I could be special enough to be the girl that Brooks wanted. I didn't know how to be…*everything*. To everyone."

"And then you went to Chicago and got sucked right into that trap," Pru said. "Lilac bridesmaid dresses and all."

Hope sighed heavily and leaned back in her chair. "This is all a little bit too much insight into my stuff, thank you very much. And I need a break from it."

"Understandable," Pru relented.

"I guess I have to draw a slip."

"You are released," Kit said. "You're miserable enough."

"Wait, she gets off scot-free and I had to wear a Band-Aid on my face as a man lure?" Pru asked.

"She's not scot-free," Kit said. "She's sad! And it was hookups in the house only. We were just being petty because we don't have hookups happening."

"And I had to wear a Band-Aid while hefting boxes, and the man who asked me about it was *Grant Mathewson*. If that's not misery I don't know what is."

Pru—who in Hope's opinion was protesting too much about Grant—was outvoted by Charity and Kit, and Hope remained un-slipped.

But slip or no, Hope realized that she was going to have to talk to Brooks. Really talk to him. And actually sort some things out. She was not looking forward to that.

But she'd found some kind of honesty with herself, whether she'd wanted to or not.

She'd thought that self-actualization might come when she was ready for it. Or maybe on the kind of schedule that would feel a bit more acceptable.

But none of it was waiting for her to be ready.

Sullivan Brooks had just burst into her shop.

And it didn't matter that she had a previous relationship she was healing from...

That's a lie. You don't care about James. You were always running from Brooks.

Always. He's the thing you never healed from.

She lay down on her bed, and she let herself be overwhelmed. Let herself give in to not being able to breathe past all the revelations that were swirling around inside of her.

CHAPTER EIGHT

BROOKS WAS IN a powerfully bad mood the next day and he was ready to go ahead and carry another torch of anger for Hope for the next twelve years when she called and asked him to meet her at the store.

"You could not go," he said to himself. He didn't have to go just because she'd called.

Except he was already in his truck. Already on the way. With a bunch of maple syrup, though he didn't know if that was why she wanted him there.

He could see her through the door, standing there surrounded by boxes of candy. She was, regrettably, not in high heels.

He pushed the door and found that it was unlocked. Hope watched him enter, her expression wary.

"Good morning," he said.

"Yeah," she said, looking away, her cheeks flushed pink.

"Are you...embarrassed?"

He wasn't going to lead with that. It wasn't kind. But then, he wasn't exactly known for being a bastion of kindness and compassion. Why start now? Why start with Hope? The person that he credited with his sunny personality.

That's not fair.

She cleared her throat. "Yeah, I have to say, doing... that in the back of a guy's pickup truck is not exactly in my repertoire."

"Well, it is now."

"Ten points to me. But… I don't know. It was just a lot. I'm sorry. I'm…going through some things."

He huffed a laugh. "Who isn't?" He'd meant to be funny but it was a little too close to the truth.

"I don't know what I'm doing here," she said. "I'm supposed to be finding my bliss, or something? Like *Eat, Pray, Love* but on a budget…and back in my hometown. And, you know, I should do it by myself. Or something. I should… I don't know. Maybe I just thought that by going back to the beginning I could figure out where I went wrong." She touched the gold compass necklace she was wearing.

"Is that what I am? You retracing your steps?"

Anger burned in his chest. He'd told himself this any number of times since running into her a little over a week ago, that this was about getting closure on something that he obviously didn't have closure in.

"No. That's the thing, it wasn't retracing my steps. I had a lot of feelings. I have…regrets. I'm having a hard time wrapping my head around all the regret because I've been ignoring it for more than a decade. I didn't love James, and I really thought I did. While I was in it. I convinced myself that was what I wanted. Maybe because you told me it was what I wanted."

"You can't blame me for your shady fiancé."

She laughed. "Okay. You're right. I can't. I'm sorry. I can't blame you for what happened in my life. I can't really blame anyone, and I guess that's the problem. I mean, I could tell you that so much of this has to do with what my parents wanted for me, but they're snobs, and on some level I know that. But I convinced myself that what I was doing was different, and I wasn't just trying to please them. But… I guess I was. I guess, as an only child, with parents who were so… The things they cared about were not the things I care about. But I *do* care about it. I do. I… I don't know how not to care. But nearly propelling myself head-long into a life that would've made me miserable has gone a long way in curing it." She looked around the shop. "And they're not here. My parents aren't here. Pru, Charity, and Kit are here, with me, trying to make sure that I'm happy. And that just makes me think that maybe I was a whole lot closer to where I was supposed to be way back when, and this was all just…"

"It can't be wasted time," he said, his voice rough. He didn't know why. He didn't know why he particularly found himself wanting to soothe her. Except that some guy had treated her badly for the last nine years and that enraged him. Down to his soul. There was never an excuse for that.

Some jackass had made her feel like she wasn't beautiful. Like she wasn't enough.

He had never worried about Hope being enough. No, he'd worried that *he* wasn't enough for *her*.

"So, enough about me," she said, kicking a box of wax-wrapped fruit candy to the side. "What have you been doing for the last twelve years other than making syrup?"

The abrupt change of subject threw him off for a second and he didn't really know why he was indulging her. Except, he couldn't…not.

"Right. Well, I got a job on a ranch. Dave McAllister's place. He died a few years back and he left me quite a bit more than I would have ever expected, and it set me up to get my own place. I was being a dick when I told you it was all down to hard work. It was, but I also got lucky. You don't work your way up to buying a piece of property like mine by being a ranch hand. You have to have something go really well for you. And I did. He was more father to me than my own ever was." He frowned. He didn't like talking about either man all that much.

"And your father?" she pressed.

"Also dead."

Her face infused with compassion and she said, "I'm sorry, Brooks."

"It's not a surprise. He was pickled by spite and alcohol in the end, and it was only a surprise that it didn't keep him going longer. But he went out walking in the back of his property and had an accident. Fell off the walking path over a ravine."

"Brooks," she said, her expression contorting with sympathy.

"He wasn't a good man, Hope. You know that."

"He was still your dad."

He nodded. "He was."

He thought about the years he'd spent getting angrier and angrier in the Rusty Nail, yelling at Garrett Roy and anyone else who would listen about Hope Marshall and her many sins, and he had to wonder if, much like Hope, his particular apple hadn't fallen far from the toxic tree.

"I never wanted you to see where I grew up," he said. "You know that, right? That's one reason I was so pissed off when you came that night."

"Oh, the night that…"

"Yes. I was ashamed, Hope. That wasn't what your house was like. It didn't smell like alcohol from out on the porch. Didn't have a ton of trash all in the yard."

"Yeah, but my house wasn't actually that great. My mom and dad were always jetting off to the next thing and they expected me to be good. To take care of myself. To be a reflection of who they were in a positive way, but not actually need their intervention. And I just wanted… I wanted their approval. You were a detour from that. And I can admit that. You were a little bit of a rebellion, and at the beginning I never intended for you to be more. But in the end, Brooks, I really did love you. And I want you to know that. Not because I want to hurt you, just because it was real. And I think that's what got to me last night. I can't stand here with you now and not think about then too."

"Yeah, I know." He felt the same. There was no getting around it.

"I don't want to live for my parents anymore. For a vague idea that someday they might be proud of me."

"I was never living to make him proud of me," Brooks said. "Just to show him that he could have done better if he'd wanted to." The words hurt coming through his throat. "I think he liked to believe that the world was out to get him. That the world was out to get the whole Brooks family. And he was going to sit there and wait until the good Lord or Mother Nature or whatever the hell realized that it owed him a living. I was never going to do that. But I'm not as different from him as I would like to be." A reluctant smile curved his lips. "Bitter is bitter, even if it's in a nice house."

"You don't taste bitter to me," she said, stepping over one of the candy boxes. "You taste pretty sweet. And I know sweet."

And then Hope was kissing him, soft and gentle, and it was more than he deserved.

She reached down, curving her fingertips through his belt and jerking him toward her, and he growled a laugh against her mouth because Hope taking charge was adorable. And sexy as hell.

Then she pushed her fingers up underneath the hem of his shirt, and his growl turned into a groan. Yeah, he was ready to have her, here and now on top of that pink taffy in the box down by their feet. Wherever. Didn't matter.

They'd already done way too much talking for people who should have been doing this for the past twelve years.

He'd missed her.

That hit him like a bolt of lightning.

He didn't hate her. He *missed* her.

He gritted his teeth against that. Anger was so much easier.

Anger was a hell of a lot easier.

But this swollen, aching feeling in his chest…he didn't like it at all. Not at all.

"Hope, could you…?"

They broke apart and turned around, and were faced with a wide-eyed Charity. "You know what? Never mind…"

"Charity," Hope said.

But she'd already scurried off.

Hope groaned. "I guess it's a good reminder that we are standing here with everything unlocked. I mean, the store's not open and it's early in the morning, but Charity has access through the basement."

"Right. So, did she not know about this?"

"No, of course she did." He was staring at her. "What? They're my friends. *Of course* they know."

"That's not really how it works with dudes."

"You don't talk about your hookups?"

"Hookups, sure. Not girlfriends." He realized what he'd said, and saw the color rise in Hope's cheeks. "I mean, you *were* my girlfriend."

"Right," she said. "You don't talk about the size of…" She held her hands out in front of her chest.

He recoiled in horror. "Why the hell would we do that? You can *see* them."

She howled, and he did not think it was funny enough to merit the level of laughter that the statement got.

She was hooting, in fact, wiping tears away from her cheeks. "Oh that's ridiculous. I don't even know why I think it's so funny. It's just…" She looked at him, her eyes shining. "Nothing has been funny for a really long time." She let out a long, slow sigh, that ended on a hum. "I missed my life, Brooks. And I didn't even realize it. And I almost… I almost went and lived a whole other one."

He looked at her for a moment, something inside him shifting.

"Well I'm glad you didn't," he said, his voice rough. "I'm glad you're here."

"So am I. I really am. I feel like I just woke up. In a candy explosion, which is fantastic. But yeah, last night… it's just a lot. And I shouldn't be in a relationship."

"Yeah. No," he said, ignoring the sharp sensation in his chest.

"I mean, I have the store to set up by the centennial. And I really would like everything to be ready for a soft open before then. There's no reason I can't have something going before the end of August. And it would be easier if I could so that I could get it kind of up and running and get everything started so that we don't… Well, if we can't get the businesses going by the centennial then the rent goes up. Like, sky-high up."

"Wow."

"I know."

"Well…" He looked around the space. "What can I do?"

CHAPTER NINE

SHE AND BROOKS were doing a pretty terrible job of *not* being in a relationship. The funny thing was, they didn't actually have sex again. The timing was difficult, and she was living in a farmhouse full of women, and she'd missed her friends.

Everyone was going through their own thing, and it required lots of intervention, and talking, and board games.

Friendship was essential.

She hadn't seen the girls as often as she would have liked. With Kit in New York, Pru in California, and Charity all the way in Seattle, they'd been relegated to texts and video chats more often than not, and it just wasn't the same. As much as she wanted Brooks, the chance to get her head on straight and focus on the candy store was important.

Instead, she and Brooks were spending a lot of time talking.

She couldn't escape the fact that when they were younger they hadn't done that.

He talked about his mom leaving but couldn't look at her while he did. About how his old man had got more and more drunk over the years. About how the house got more and more dilapidated. About feeling like there wasn't much he could do about the situation.

A whole lot of things had clicked into place as he spoke about that.

He talked about Dave McAllister and how he was the first adult to believe in him, to show him that maybe he could make something of his life. He talked about how much that had changed him.

She was lost in her thoughts about Brooks so much so that she broke another house rule, and incurred the wrath of the slip jar. In fact, they'd all been found in violation of the rules, which Hope owed to Pru being a Category 5 on the Pru-ricane scale.

But she wasn't even mad, because she knew exactly the man she'd be using the slip on. She'd protested, obviously, because if she hadn't they'd have found another way to punish her.

And somehow they all ended up deciding to go out to the Rusty Nail with those slips in hand.

"I don't have a handkerchief," had been Hope's only protestation.

It was Kit who produced one. A proper handkerchief with flowers embroidered on it.

"I found it in the house," she said.

"I swear one of these days we're going to find a magic extra room. Like a Room of Requirement or something," Kit said, as they all piled into her car. "I feel like I'm always finding new artifacts and nooks and crannies."

"It's a magic house," Charity said.

"I think it's haunted," Pru said. "Sometimes I swear I smell cookies baking, but there are no cookies baking."

"And I think windows open by themselves," Charity added.

"Well," Hope said, from her position in the back seat, "there are four of us living in the house and it's very difficult to figure out who's doing what at any given time."

"Sure," Kit said, "be an enemy of magic and joy."

"And ghosts," Pru added.

"I will happily go on record as an enemy of ghosts," Hope said, fussing with her seat belt. "And salmon."

"Seriously though," Charity muttered darkly. "We have to get rid of the salmon. I have a plan for the Fourth of July picnic. We'll give it to the town."

"Good God," Pru said. "Are you actually trying to poison the entire town before we can open our stores and have them buy our wares?"

"It's not going to poison anyone," Charity said. "It's been in the freezer."

"I'm suspicious."

"Well, then you don't have to make the salmon mousse."

Kit made dramatic gagging sounds and slumped over the steering wheel as she pulled up to the curb.

They all got out of the car, Kit at least thirty seconds behind because she'd been so deeply committed to her feigned horror, and went into the bar.

It was like a festival of gorgeous cowboys. That was one thing Hope had always appreciated about her hometown, and one thing she had secretly missed. Though she tried to pretend she was immune to that down-home charm, she was not. Or Wranglers. It was in her blood. There was something about Realtree camo that got her excited, and she'd never known quite what to do about that or how to reconcile it with the new life she'd created in Chicago.

There was something about a country boy. And she couldn't deny it.

But there was something in particular about Brooks.

And Brooks was currently at the bar with Garrett Roy. Hope's stomach went tight. She was about to go over to him when Pru rubbed her hands together, her eyes gleaming. "Okay, who's going to do a shot with me?"

Shockingly, it was Charity who volunteered. "I will."

"*You* will?"

She shrugged. "I've never done a shot before. It's time I learned how."

Pru linked arms with her. "Atta girl." The four of them walked over to the bar. Pru ordered the shots, and Hope and Kit opted for "weak-ass baby lady drinks"—Pru's words.

Pru nearly collapsed in a fit of laugher trying to show Charity how to take a shot, and Charity nearly collapsed in watery-eyed misery once the whiskey had gone down.

"That's terrible," she croaked.

"I know," Pru agreed.

Hope was still feeling agitated about Brooks and getting away to see him.

"Hey, Pru," Hope said over the din of an old '80s country song. "Isn't that your brother?"

"And some Mathewsons," Kit added, as they all looked across the room at the pack of handsome men. "Can you tell them apart?"

Pru dialed up the storm in her eyes. "Yes."

"And is one of them your little helper?" Hope asked. "No, don't answer. I can tell by the look on your face that he is. The one talking to Beau. Wasn't he at our graduation party?"

"I don't remember," Pru said—a clear and blatant lie.

"Oh!" Charity pushed her shoulder. "You should ask him to dance."

Charity was Hope's unlikely savior, and Hope's next words to Kit were lost in the flurry of activity.

"How penalized will I be if I hook up?" Hope asked.

"Very," Kit said, her smile lacking any kind of sincerity.

"Well, I guess I'll take it. I'm not dropping a handkerchief for any reason other than to have that man look at my ass."

Kit smiled. "Good for you."

"He likes it. And doesn't think that I need to quit eating candy."

"Don't let anyone ever tell you how much candy you should eat," Charity said, as Pru was propelled toward Grant Mathewson. "That is nobody's business but yours."

"Thank you, Charity. I always knew you were a good and supportive friend. Now, I'm off to drop a handkerchief. Pru has fulfilled her slip. Better get cracking, ladies."

She had a feeling that there were going to be any number of shenanigans happening tonight, and she was sort of sorry to miss them. But she had a mission, and that mission was Sullivan Brooks.

He saw her and got up from his position at the bar. As he made his way toward her, his dark eyes smoldering beneath the brim of his cowboy hat, she turned away and slowly walked with catlike steps over to the jukebox. Then she reached into her purse, lifted up the handkerchief, and held it high before letting it flutter down to the bar floor. The bar floor was disgusting, and she had not thought this through adequately. But she smiled anyway, vaguely in Brooks's direction, and then bent at the waist, caught the white fabric between her fingertips, and pushed her hips out behind her, before picking it up again.

She wondered if that was what was supposed to happen with a dropped handkerchief. Maybe it wasn't supposed to be about showing your ass. Maybe the man was supposed to pick it up for you? Oh well. This was not 1945.

"What are you doing?" he asked, a slow, lazy smile on his lips.

"Fulfilling my challenge. And look, it worked."

"Yeah, is this what you were alluding to the other night

when you left my place? Something about...slips and consequences?"

"We've all been following dating advice from the '40s and '50s on how to land a husband."

He jerked back and she realized what she'd just said.

"Obviously we are modern women of the world who are not using it to catch husbands."

"Oh, obviously."

"Would you like to know what my challenges have been?"

"What I would like to know is if you've been using them on other men?"

"No, I haven't. Well, the funny thing is, my first one was that I was supposed to fall down, and a gallant stranger would come help me up."

"Did you fall to...get my attention?"

She laughed. "No. I actually fell. And there you were. But anyway, that got me out of the first one. Then I had to wear high heels, and ask a man's opinion on my perfume."

A slow grin spread over his face. "Yeah. I remember those."

"And tonight I had to drop a handkerchief."

"Okay. How is any of that supposed to work?"

"You're here, aren't you?"

He leaned in. "Yeah, but that's because of you. Not any other reason."

She felt restless all of a sudden. She really was falling in love with this man. And she didn't know what to do about it. Didn't know if there was anything she could or should do about it except...fall. She'd been too afraid to fight for him twelve years ago and she was...well, she was scared now.

But she'd lost herself for way too long.

And this was what she wanted. Charity was right. There

was no point in making it about ideals or what was supposed to be or not supposed to be. It wasn't about that.

It was about Brooks. And it always had been. She just hadn't fully realized what she needed or why.

But he made her feel more like herself than anyone else ever had. Anyone except her friends. And if there was a man who made you feel as comfortable as the very best friends you'd known all your life, plus you were wildly attracted to him and wanted to kiss him all the time, wasn't that something real?

She'd never felt comfortable with James. She'd always felt like she was auditioning for something, and the reason she'd thought that was right was that it was how she'd always felt with her parents.

And on some level she felt like that was a family.

It wasn't.

Pru, Kit, and Charity were family.

Brooks was her heart.

She wanted to be family with Brooks.

Marry him. Be his wife.

Have his babies.

She wanted that. She ached for it in a way she'd never ached for James.

But now, here in the Rusty Nail, in Jasper Creek, Oregon, she was standing there holding a handkerchief she'd just plucked off the ground explaining the particular brand of insanity she'd been embroiled in for the last few weeks and he didn't even seem to think she was crazy. Instead, he was looking at her like she might be magical.

"I had Skittles for dinner," she announced.

"Okay…?"

"I'm just telling you. That's who I am as a person."

"I like who you are as a person."

So she kissed him. In the middle of that crowded bar. Because why not? Because what else was there to do?

She kissed him until neither of them could breathe. Until they were sneaking out the back door, laughing like kids.

"I don't really want to have you in the back of the truck again. How about we go back to my place?"

"Wow," she said, suddenly feeling shy. "The two of us in a bed. That's a little bit wild, Brooks."

"I think I'm ready for that kind of wild with you."

THEY DROVE BACK to his place in silence, and he kissed her out of the truck, up the front steps, into the house, and back to his bedroom. Kissed her all the way down onto that soft mattress.

"How many other girls have you brought here?"

"I'm a class act," he said. "I take my hookups to Gold Dust." Gold Dust was a crappy little roadside motel just outside of the main drag of Jasper Creek.

"You do not," she said.

"I do. Because I think I've been trying to prove that I'm a particular sort of hillbilly trash for the last several years. That I was everything you should've run from." He looked down at her, his eyes intense. "Maybe you should run from me now."

"I'm not going anywhere. I ran from you for years. I don't like where it took me."

"I want you," he said.

And in her heart, she wished he'd said *I love you* instead. But she would take want for now.

He kissed her and kissed her, stripping away her clothes, stripping away her inhibitions. Brooks's hands were magic. His mouth was a revelation. His body, strong and thick inside of hers, made her want to weep.

And finally, she did, a broken cry of pleasure that mixed with his own.

"I love you," she said. She hadn't meant to say it. She really hadn't. "I love you, Brooks. I'm not seventeen anymore. You can't just send me away. I know who I am. I left once already and I'm not doing it again."

He said nothing. He just wrapped his strong arms around her and held her.

And she was not young enough or foolish enough to think that it was an agreement. That it was an *I love you too*.

That it was anything other than a mounting disaster like the kind they'd experienced twelve years ago.

CHAPTER TEN

HE SHOULDN'T HAVE done it. He kept telling himself that
while he poured his morning cup of coffee, still half asleep.
He'd let her say that and he hadn't said a thing in reply.
He'd let her spend the night in his bed, had turned to her
multiple times during the night, and he hadn't said a thing.

And this morning it ate at him like a beast.

I love you.

But she couldn't. She'd run right out of here to Chicago.
She'd been with another man for nine years. She'd nearly
married him. And now what? She was retracing her steps.
That was what she'd said. He was just…what she knew.
What was comfortable.

It wouldn't end well. It just wouldn't. It was all the same,
that was the problem.

People didn't change. People couldn't change. He knew
that. Not really. You could change everything around you,
but you were still you. Hadn't he spent the last twelve years
proving just that? While he *got* better and *did* better and
shoved it in his old man's face, they'd both grown angrier
and more bitter and it didn't solve a damn thing. Hadn't he
proved it every night he'd gone out drinking in the bar, pretending he was a better man than his father, raving about
the woman who'd left him? Just like his dad.

He wasn't different.

And Hope was still too good for him, and too fancy for Jasper Creek. She wouldn't stay. She would leave.

His own mother had left him. Why the hell wouldn't she?

Love.

People said it all the time. She must have said it to the man she was going to marry. And then she'd looked right at him and said she'd never loved that guy. It came and went that fast, that easy.

What they had now was great. It was great sex. But that didn't mean it was love.

He should have said that last night. He shouldn't have let her stay.

His bed was still warm and it smelled of her, and all he wanted was to go back upstairs and get into it. But he shouldn't have let her stay. He shouldn't let her stay now.

He heard footsteps in the hall, bare feet on the wood, and he knew it was her.

"Good morning," she mumbled. She was back in the clothes she'd worn the night before, so maybe she had a sense for what was coming.

Guilt and pain gathered at the base of his spine and spread upward, making his limbs feel heavy, making his chest feel like it was made of lead.

"Yeah."

"All right. Okay. I recognize this Brooks. I hoped that you making love to me for the entire night might mean that we were going to have a different conversation this morning. But I was afraid of this."

"Afraid of what?"

"You have that same look. That look that says we need to say goodbye. I know that look, Brooks, because it's seared into my brain, because the last time you told me you couldn't love me is still branded inside of me, and I really don't need to hear you say it again."

"Yeah. Well."

"You know, the difference is that back then I didn't fight for us. That's the difference. You're the same. Standing there completely closed down. I was awake all night, by the way. If you thought I was sleeping you were wrong. I was lying there waiting for you to say something. I wasn't going to turn you away when you needed me. I wanted to show you that I'm all in. I'm not a seventeen-year-old girl anymore. I've been out, and I've been back again. I've been in a city. I got engaged to that fancy man you told me I was going to find and there was nothing there. There was nothing behind it. Nothing against fancy men. If I'd loved him then it would have been fine. Well, also if he hadn't have been a cheater who liked to make me feel bad about myself. But that aside, he wasn't you. He never was. I was trying to prove something to my parents and to you all at once. And you know what, I never asked him to go down on me because I wanted that to just be you, Brooks. Something that *we* shared. Something I got from *you*. I didn't try to fix our attraction or make it better because I wanted…because I was hanging on to you. Don't you get that? I was hanging on to this place. I wasn't me there. I'm me *here*. In the back of the truck, under the stars. Laughing with my friends and going to the Rusty Nail. And in my little store, surrounded by sugar. And who gives a damn about adrenal glands? I don't even know what they do."

She took a deep breath. "I want an over-caffeinated, over-sugared, quaint, small-town life. And if my parents think I'm not living up to their expectations of me then that's too bad because their expectations have not made me happy. I can't live for them. I can only live a life that makes me happy. And it needs to have you in it. It has to."

He felt like he was clinging to the side of a cliff and her words were an outstretched hand. But if he let go to reach for her…

He might lose his grip altogether.

"Look, I get what this is. You're having a whole emancipation situation. You're reclaiming things, and that's great, but I can't get dragged into it because the fact remains that you're you and I'm me. Hope and Brooks. And it was never going to work. Not twelve years ago and not today."

"No. That's bullshit," she said, stamping her foot. "It's bullshit that we told ourselves because we were scared. Because we couldn't step far enough away from the situations we were in to make a new one. But we can do that now. We're not kids. We're thirty years old. We don't have to live a life decided for us by our dysfunctional parents. You hated where you grew up so why would you keep on living there."

"Woman, look around. I don't live in that shithole. I live here."

"You haven't left. You haven't left, not in your soul. You're still there and it still controls you. So what does it matter if you live here or there? It's the same."

"Yeah," he said, his voice rough. "You're right. It's the same. And that's the problem. I'm the same." As soon as the words left his mouth, he felt them hit hard.

"You've spent the last twelve years blaming me, haven't you? You figured I was going to leave anyway, but here's the thing, Brooks. I came back. The only reason I left is that when I was seventeen I wasn't brave enough to stand up and tell you that I loved you while you told me you didn't want me. And you've gotten to live this comfortable, angry life back home, convincing yourself that it was *me*. That *I* was the one who was going to destroy us eventually. That you just lobbed a preemptive strike. That if I'd really wanted you I would've stayed. It was *you*."

That last word fractured, and her calm along with it, but she kept on going. "All along it was you. Because here I am." She flung her arms wide. "Here I am and I'm throwing myself at you. I love you. I know how the world works. I love you, and you can't tell me that I don't understand the way of things. That I would be happier if I was in a city. That I would be happier if I was married to a rich man. That I don't understand what makes the world go round and I don't understand what a life with you would be like. You can't write me off this time, and because of that it's all obvious now. You were the one who was running scared, and you were the one that was going to destroy us, not me."

"Hope," he said, his stomach clenched tight. "You don't know what you're talking about."

"At least own it. *You're* the one who's scared. You're the one who can't do it. It's not me. Am I not good enough for *you*, Brooks? Is that it? Because it seems like you just want to push that off on me. Like I think I'm special or something, so what is it? You think you know how the real world works and I'm just so soft and coddled? Is that it? You think you're better because you know the way of things?"

"No," he said. "I will never be good enough for you, and that's the damn truth. And I don't see why I should try."

"Stop telling me what I want! Because let me tell you something, I was with a man who thought he was too good for me. It didn't do me any favors. And at the end of the day, good is relative. Yeah, all right, so you don't look good on paper. You're a little bit of a disaster. But you're *my* disaster and I would really like to be yours. I have a litany of flaws, Sullivan Brooks. If I didn't, I wouldn't have gone to

Chicago and gotten engaged to the wrong man. I wouldn't have walked away from you that first time. I wouldn't have flung myself headlong into the abyss of trying to please my parents. But I did. So there you go. I'm flawed."

She shook her head, her eyes dewy with unshed tears. "I did think, well, maybe Brooks is right. Maybe I do deserve a man who could buy me nice things. A man who can make me feel important. A man who can elevate me in the world, give me a big house and a flashy car. I thought all that. So maybe I'm not as good as you think I am. But I would really like to be your mess. The woman who knows that she isn't happy without you. The woman who went out and tried fancy. Who tried all these bright and wonderful things that people tell you can make a happy life. And I found nothing there. It was hollow, because you weren't there. So I already know. I already know, and I have no claim on being too good for anyone or anything. But I think I might be just right for you. You bitter, cantankerous asshole."

"I can't do it," he said, watching as his words hit her across the face like a slap, as she recoiled from him. "Because you're right. Things don't change. I'm my father's son."

"And what? You can't love?"

"Or won't. Doesn't much matter."

The words scraped him raw as they exited his mouth. Hope's eyes filled with tears. It might as well have been raining, just like the first time they'd done this.

But it was for her own good.

She would only end up unhappy.

"Don't you think you should spend some time on your own?"

"Yeah, I thought that," she said. "But I'm living for me, and that's what counts now. And the fact of the matter is,

Brooks, I spent twelve years without you, and that's already twelve too many."

That cut. Deep.

"You know, if you knew you were going to do this, you shouldn't have touched me," she said, turning away from him. He didn't have any response to that because she was right. Because he already knew that, and he'd already called himself ten kinds of asshole over it. She disappeared into the kitchen and he could hear her say a few words, then slam his old-school phone back down into its cradle. Then she ran out the front door, and she was gone, and it was like he hadn't learned a damn thing. Like he was still seventeen and swinging his own fists at himself.

Because why?

Because then you know when the hit's coming.

Because it's better to make them leave when you're expecting it.

Because eventually they'll leave anyway.

Because if there was one thing he knew about men like his father, it was that they couldn't be enough for the women they loved, and then those women left.

His mother hadn't taken him with her, so wasn't that proof enough? Was that proof enough that he would lose Hope too?

Well, you lost her anyway. So congratulations.

He stood there in his big-ass house that he'd been using to prove something to her. To himself.

And realized none of it mattered because she saw who he really was.

And who he was just wasn't good enough.

CHAPTER ELEVEN

SHE DIDN'T TELL her friends what had happened. Charity had picked her up at the end of Brooks's driveway and hadn't asked for details. And in the days since, she'd kept quiet on what had happened.

She'd even had a whole conversation with Pru and given her grief about not sharing her issues, but for more than a week she hadn't said a word.

She thought it would get better, but it only got worse. She was morose all through the day, and all through the Fourth of July picnic. She'd tried to banter, but it had been halfhearted at best and it wouldn't be long before they all noticed.

They'd failed to off-load a meaningful amount of the salmon, even when fashioned into salmon mousse with endive by Charity's capable hands, and the fact that they were returning to the farmhouse with it—and without Kit who had gone off with Browning West on the back of his motorcycle—seemed apt in some way.

Kit had been forced to attend the parade holding a hatbox—another slip—and had caught herself the biggest man-whore in all of Jasper Creek.

It was unjust.

"Okay," Pru said. "What's wrong?"

"Oh, everything imploded again," she said angrily, taking the entire Tupperware tray filled with salmon and dumping it into the trash.

"Hey!" Charity said. "That's my Tupperware. And also, I made that."

"And no one wants it," Hope said, storming off into the living room. "It's not about your cooking, Charity. It's my symbolic salmon. And you know what? It's symbolic in all the wrong ways because it's just pieces of a life that I don't want, pieces of me that I don't want. And maybe it's part of why Brooks still doesn't love me." She'd told herself she wasn't going to do this. She'd told herself she wasn't going to be pathetic. And here she was, on the verge of weeping quite pathetically.

"Oh no," Charity said.

"That's it!" Pru announced. "We're getting the salmon and we're putting it in his truck."

"No," Hope said. "I don't want to salmon his truck."

"Well," Charity said, trying to keep her tone delicate. "You have salmoned the house. Throwing it in the trash was maybe not the best idea."

"I don't care. I was stupid, wasn't I? Expecting a different result with the same guy. But I had it all built up in my head that it meant something to me, that it mattered. It felt like...finding a piece of myself, and I thought that it was the same for him. But it was just him getting in my pants because he never did in high school. And he's the same dumb idiot that he was back then, talking about how he can't be what I need. But he doesn't know what I need."

"What do you need?" Charity asked.

"A life that will make me happy. Not what will make anyone else happy. And I need everyone to quit telling me what I want. I tried all the things my parents wanted. I don't want them. I want him. I want this store. I want to be with you guys. That's what I want. It's not actually that complicated."

"So why do you think he's intent on telling you otherwise?" Pru asked.

"Because he's a yellow-bellied, lily-livered coward." Dumb cowboys deserved cowboy insults.

"Sure. Granted," Pru said. "But why?"

Hope closed her eyes. "His mom left him. And his dad was a piece of work, and I just… I just wonder if he can't accept that we could be happy. That I won't leave. I think he was testing me all those years ago and I failed."

"That's not fair," Charity said. "You were kids."

"Yeah, but we're not kids now."

"No," Pru agreed. "You're not. So I guess you just have to hope that he steps up and starts acting like a man and not a boy."

"I guess so. And in the meantime, what do I do?"

"Well, you have us."

"Not Kit. She's a traitor. All it took was a motorcycle and the promise of Browning West's hands."

"In fairness," Pru said, "they are very nice hands."

"It will only end in heartbreak," Hope said. "Men are evil."

Charity looked thoughtful. "You have a point. But also, they are attractive."

"Cowboys are the worst."

"No argument here. But," Pru said, "you love him, so I know you don't actually think that."

"But what is the point of love in this case, *Prudence*? What is the point?"

"It's your chance to stay. It's your chance to stay and prove how true it is."

"You mean my chance to be pathetic?" Hope asked.

"No," Pru said, a storm in her eyes. "I think pathetic is marrying a man you don't love. I think pathetic is telling the woman you do love that you don't love her because you're scared. I think pathetic is living your life for another person. Nothing about you is pathetic, Hope."

Hope blinked. Her eyes felt gritty. "Thanks."

"What do you want?" Charity asked.

"I want to do well here. To have a place that's mine. A place that I'm passionate about."

"And you have that. You can't control what he does. But we're here for you. And we'll help you."

CHAPTER TWELVE

HE WAS MISERABLE. That was a fact. And that was how he found himself wandering the same trail his dad had been on when he'd fallen to his death. It was morbid, and he knew it. But he wasn't here because he had any kind of death wish. It was because he wanted to argue with a ghost, and as much as he knew that was pointless...

"So why were you such a prick?" he asked the pristine air around him, the tall green fir trees, and the mountains beyond.

There was no answer, which was probably fair. The mountains probably hated his dad as much as he did.

It had always seemed like a blight to him, that shack he and his father had lived in on this property that was so beautiful. Like some kind of metaphor for his family and the way they stood out in town.

"Did she hate you so much that she had to leave me too?" he asked. "Or did she hate us both? You're dead and I can't ask you. I never could. Because you just...committed to that. To that meanness. And you spilled it all over everything, including me."

It was right there, pushing against the walls of his heart, and Brooks knew it, but it made him so damn angry that he didn't want to confront it.

It was just a choice. His dad had made a choice. To embrace bitterness and alcohol when he could've embraced his son. When he could've done something to make up for the choices his wife had made. To be there for his son. He hadn't made those choices. He'd leaned in to the bad parts of who he was, and Brooks had…well, he'd spent a lot of years doing the same thing. Being motivated by anger. And by…

Fear.

Because that was the thing, wasn't it?

The real problem was if you tried to change, if you thought it might be possible, then someone could still reject you. And the thought of that was what killed him. If he tried and he still failed… If he gave all of himself…

Then what?

"Yeah, then what?" he asked nothing. Nothing. Because his father hadn't been here to ask when he was alive, and he sure as hell wasn't hanging around now he was dead to help his son.

His dad had never given a damn. He'd never done a damn thing for him and here was Brooks, still trying to show him, still letting him decide what he was.

Dave McAllister had seen more in him than his own father. He'd seen a kid worth investing in and why the hell did a father who'd done nothing have more say in who he was than that man did?

Than Hope did.

He knew what twelve years of his life was like without Hope.

Even her name… It nearly made him laugh. He was living a life without *hope*—in all the ways that applied—and what was the damn point of protecting himself, of hanging on to his pride? Using anger as a shield gave him nothing in the end. She still wasn't here. He'd still lost.

He would rather cut himself open and bleed all over

everything. He would rather have nothing left, no pride, no stone left to turn over in the dark recesses of his soul.

He would rather have *her*.

And if that meant risking himself, if that meant risking everything, then he would do it.

Before he could stop himself, he was in his truck and driving toward the old Gable house. Because he had to find her. He had to.

And since the woman had no phone, he couldn't call her.

He parked his truck and went up the front steps, knocking firmly on the door. It opened, and three faces, none of whom belonged to Hope, were staring at him.

"What do you want?" Pru asked.

"To see Hope," he said.

Kit flicked her scarf, wrapping it around her neck imperiously. "She's not here and even if she were, she wouldn't want to see you."

"Because you're a dick," Pru added.

"Yeah," said Charity.

"Where is she?" he asked.

"You've not earned the right to ask about the whereabouts of our friend," Kit said.

"Not remotely," Pru added. "You broke her heart. We don't approve."

"Not at all," Charity said.

"Yeah, that's the thing. I don't approve either. I broke my own damned heart, so I just want to fix it. I just want to fix this."

"I'm not sure if you can," Kit said.

"You're not sure if I can?"

"Nope," Pru said. "Love is dead."

"Love," Charity repeated, her eyes getting large, "is dead."

"Not if I say it's not," he said.

They looked at each other, then back at him.

"You want to fix this?" Charity asked.

"That's what I've been saying!"

They exchanged another glance.

"You broke a house rule," Pru said.

He frowned. "I don't live in the house."

"Doesn't matter," Kit said. "We'll tell you where she is but you have to pay the penalty."

"Fine. What's the penalty?"

"You have to draw a slip," Kit said.

He heard rustling behind them, and then Charity produced a large glass jar.

"Wait, are those the finding-a-husband tips?"

"This is a new modern era," Pru said. "What's good for the goose is good for the gander."

"You really want me to draw one of these?"

"Yes," Kit said, smiling in a way that made him think she would lose no sleep at all over eviscerating him with her gleaming white teeth.

"Fine." He drew a slip. "Happy now? Where is she?"

"The candy store, dumbass," Pru said.

And they slammed the door, leaving him there on the porch. He looked down at the slip and he laughed.

A good grovel never goes amiss.

Well, fine.

He was out of pride anyway. So that was just what he would do.

CHAPTER THIRTEEN

EVERYTHING WAS READY. Everything was beautiful. The candy was gleaming like jewels in its bins, along with her fudge and other hand-created concoctions.

And she felt dead inside.

Great. Sullivan Brooks had managed to ruin candy for her.

No. She wouldn't let that be the situation. He didn't get to do that. This place was her true north.

She touched the compass necklace that hung around her neck. This was home, and in her heart she felt like she'd been led back to where she was supposed to be. She really did. And she wasn't going to let Sullivan Brooks and his inability to deal with his emotional baggage decide that for her. She wasn't going to let him make her feel different.

As if her bitter thoughts had conjured him, she looked and he was there. He was outside the door, all sexy in a black T-shirt and black cowboy hat.

How she wished that she could be immune to him. That she could look at him and feel nothing. But she didn't. Her heart nearly burst with love and she couldn't do anything to stop it. She couldn't even really be mad.

But fundamentally, there was a difference between being left at the altar by a man you didn't even like that much, and being pushed away by a man you knew felt too much. She knew he was afraid. But he was here. He was here.

She ran to the door and opened it, breathless as she caught his scent, all hard work, maple, and man.

"What are you doing here?"

A smile tipped the corners of his lips, and then he dropped down to his knees in front of her, right there on the step of her candy store.

"What are you doing?"

"I'm sorry," he said. "I'm so sorry. I was wrong, Hope. And I was afraid. I thought that if I pushed you away first, that if I didn't try to be anything better, then I would be safe. That I couldn't be devastated again. Because, you know, having my mother walk away, having my father disappear down into a bottle instead of stepping up to be the man he should've been…you don't walk away from that without scars. You just don't."

The rawness, the honesty in his pain broke through all of Hope's defenses. This was Brooks. And it was all she'd ever wanted from him.

Not the boy with ten-foot walls around his heart pushing people away before they could push him away, but a man. A man who felt deep, real pain.

"I thought that maybe I could just…" He sighed. "I don't know. I thought I could just build a wall up around myself and that I wouldn't love you. That I wouldn't miss you. I made everything I felt for you turn to anger and resentment, but you were right. It wasn't you who broke us. If you'd stayed, it would've been me. Maybe not that year, but some year. Because I wouldn't have been able to break down all those walls for you. But time and distance and twelve years without you, twelve years without hope, showed me what I need to do. What kind of man I need to be. Pride be damned, I love you, woman. More than anything. And I have since I was seventeen years old, but I was too much of a coward to say it. Too much of a coward to do a damn thing about it. But I'm here now. I'm asking, I'm *begging* you, to forgive me. To let me try and be better. I don't know if the best I can be is good enough for you, but I will spend every day of my life trying to make it good enough. More than good enough. Because you're everything, Hope. You're so bright that it blinds me. And your love is so precious to me that the idea of trying to be worthy of it…"

Hope crouched down in front of him, taking his hand in hers. "You never had to try to earn it, Brooks. It was just there. And you…you disrupted me. My life. My plans. You're the reason my compass points back here. I know you are. Otherwise the girls and I could've gone to any town. It could be a candy store anywhere. But it's not home if it's not with you."

She tumbled forward into his arms, and they both fell back onto the sidewalk. She laughed.

"Now we're both on the ground. Who's going to pick us up?"

"We'll pick each other up. Forever. Always." But they didn't move. They only stared at each other. "I have a confession to make," he said.

And then he produced a slip of paper.

"What?"

"I was told that I had broken a house rule and I had to take a slip. They wouldn't tell me where you were otherwise."

"They're the best. But is that the only reason you came here? Because the slip said you had to grovel?"

"No. It just happened to be the exact thing I needed right when I needed it. I feel like all the slips have kind of been that way."

"I don't think I needed to prance around in high heels and have you smell my neck."

"Maybe not, but I didn't mind it."

"Well," she said, "of course you didn't. That doesn't make it magic."

"I don't know," he said. "I think there might be a little magic. A little farmhouse magic. And a lot of magic between the two of us."

She smiled. "I love you, Brooks. I always have."

"I love you too," he said. "And every time I sat in that bar and told Garrett Roy that I hated you, that was what I meant."

"Did you really do that?"

"Oh yeah. I was bitter as hell. But you know what, it was just me trying to pretend I wasn't ruined for all other women because of you."

"Were you?"

"You know I was. I love you. Whatever you need, I'm going to be there for you."

"Good. Because what I need is help getting all our stores open. Otherwise we're going to lose them, and I might have to go find other work."

"Well, that's not going to happen."

"Grant Mathewson is helping Pru clear all the junk out of the corner store of hers. It's a lot bigger than mine. But still, we need some help. Some muscle."

"You have my muscle. And all the free maple syrup you could ever want."

She cocked her head to the side. "Does that make you my sugar daddy?"

"I guess it does."

"What do you know? I had to come back home to get one of those too. And it was you all along."

"That's the truth. It was you all along."

"I love you a lot, you know. But I can't move in with you."

His brows shot up. "Why not?"

"Not until we're done getting the stores set up, not until we're done with our time at the farmhouse."

He smiled. "The way you and your friends care about each other is part of you. It's part of what shows me that when you love, you love forever. If I'd been less of an idiot back then, I might have seen that. Anyway, we can sneak around for a while."

"I'm more than okay with that. It's fun, bringing a little bit of the past into the present."

He smiled. "That should carry us into the future just fine."

She touched the compass necklace, and she gave thanks.

Thanks for the old pact that had brought them all back home, for the farmhouse that had sprinkled on that extra magic dust, and for Brooks.

And most of all, for love.

Love that didn't grow weaker with time, or shaky with trials, but love that strengthened.

Between her and this town, between her and her friends, and between her and her man.

Here in her shop, he wasn't a boy from the wrong side of the tracks and she wasn't a poor little rich girl. Right now, they were just Hope and Brooks.

Like always. Like forever.

* * * * *

HOW TO WIN HIM

Caitlin Crews

To the other three points on my Jasper Creek compass,
thank you for being you.

CHAPTER ONE

Kit's Story

KIT HALL HAD never had the slightest intention of returning to Jasper Creek, Oregon, for anything more than a quick holiday visit.

In fact, she'd always been actively opposed to the very idea. She'd assumed that the life she would be leading at age thirty would be so objectively brilliant that the topic of the pact she'd made with her three best friends a million years ago would never come up.

Or, if it did, that it would apply to her friends but not to her. Never to *her*.

She'd dedicated most of her life to making sure of it.

And on paper, she'd succeeded. Even her father thought so. And Lawrence Hall—who'd spoken truth to power (his take) as the editor of the local paper since before Kit's birth yet preferred to be known for his true passion (his words), *The Jasper Creek Chapbook*, which featured seasonal volumes of poetry, vignettes, and worthy essays (all written by him, of course)—was the self-appointed arbiter of all things intellectual in this corner of rural Oregon.

Kit had departed this little town, which sat in a largely overlooked state that no one who wasn't from here ever pronounced correctly, like a comet. She had started getting ready for greatness there and then.

She'd insisted on being called by her legal name, Katherine, before her plane had touched down on her way to Princeton. Because Princeton was serious and Kit intended to be serious right along with it. And after she'd gotten herself an Ivy League education, she'd taken it a step further. She'd followed up her summers of interning at Carriage & Sons, publisher of possibly the most nose-bleedingly literary masterpieces ever committed to paper, by becoming an editor of said masterpieces.

If anyone had told her, back when she'd first walked through the doors of the iconic Manhattan building where Carriage & Sons had been housed since the nineteenth century, that she would end up out of publishing, back in Oregon, and spending the summer in a farmhouse with her three best friends, Kit wouldn't even have laughed. It would have been too absurd to laugh at.

But there was no denying that was exactly where Kit was.

Out on the front porch steps of this sweet old farmhouse, looking out over the deep green hills that could only mean she was home. With the three people who knew her best.

For better or worse.

She clutched the compass necklace they'd all worn since childhood like it was a talisman.

Because it *was* a talisman.

"I go by Katherine now," she had told her friends in Chicago the last weekend in May, on the morning of the canceled wedding that had started all of this.

Because they'd apparently needed constant reminders.

"Do you, *Kit*?" Pru, who Kit thought should have been an ally, given how much *she* hated her full name, had smirked at her.

Kit had already been uncomfortable in her bridesmaid's

gown, in a horrific shade of lilac that made her look jaundiced. She obviously preferred her adopted Manhattan uniform of all black, all the time, with perhaps a gray T-shirt to mix it up when she was feeling spicy.

"Since college, actually," Kit had replied, not exactly under her breath.

Charity's placid doctor's smile from within the embrace of her own lilac horror had not been remotely supportive. "I love how when people at the rehearsal dinner asked Kit where she went to college, what she said was, 'I went to school in New Jersey.' Then waited. Everyone else on earth names the college they went to when asked. Except Ivy League people. Why is that?"

"You know why," teased Hope, their bride-to-be. The bride-to-be-that-wasn't—though at the time they'd been in the last moments of not knowing that. Of not knowing that what should have been a happy occasion would instead see them all shacked up together in Jasper Creek, having tossed their old lives aside. "They don't want *you* to be embarrassed that they are so finely educated."

"Katherine is actually my name," Kit had continued to murmur to the receptive audience of her lilac monstrosity. "It's literally on my driver's license."

"Let me guess." Pru had rolled her eyes, grinning. "Everyone in *the city* calls you Katherine on command."

"They do. Because people in New York know that it's my *actual name*."

"You've been Kit since we met in the cradle." Charity had waved a hand. "Everybody in New York City can call you whatever they want. You'll always be Kit to us."

In a way, that had been foreshadowing. And Kit had run with it.

Katherine Hall, a senior editor at the haughtiest of all

the publishing houses in Manhattan, certainly couldn't quit her job and break her apartment lease on a whim, move back to the Pacific Northwest, and decide to open what would certainly be considered the trashiest of all the trashy bookstores.

Kit, on the other hand, had started sneaking her grandmother's romance novels when she was twelve. One of the finest days of her life had been discovering that her mother had long been doing the same. Theirs had always been a quiet rebellion, conducted under Kit's father's nose—which he would've lifted in disdain had he known that the literary halls of his home were thus polluted by popular fiction of any type.

But especially, *especially*, romance novels.

Everyone she knew either was or would be appalled to discover that Kit had, long ago, dreamed of opening a cute little bookshop that sold the books she actually liked. And that she was now, thanks to her friends, launching herself straight on into that dream. Kit couldn't really believe it herself.

She heard the farmhouse's screen door open behind her, followed by footsteps across the porch, and then Charity settled in next to her on the top step.

Kit lifted her coffee mug in tribute. Charity grinned sleepily and did the same, though her mug was filled with tea.

For a moment, Kit stopped thinking about her New York dreams and the fact she'd given up on them. For a moment, she sank into the easy, casual intimacy she'd missed.

Charity didn't have to say anything. They'd been involved in the same long, comfortable conversation for most of their lives. All four of them had. It was tempting to say that they were like sisters, but Kit knew people with sisters. They never seemed to get along the way she and her friends always had, whether they chose to use her legal name or not. It didn't matter how long it had been since they'd talked, or had seen each other. They all slotted right back into place again, the way they always did.

That was why all four of them still wore their compass necklaces.

And why, if she was honest with herself, they'd all felt they could admit they weren't happy in their lives and had come back here—no matter how much they might have preferred to pretend it was all an act of solidarity with Hope.

So even though Kit could have said a thousand things, what she did was sit there, pressing her bare toes against the rickety top step of the porch until it squeaked. She and Charity watched the sun climb up over the rolling hills of a green Oregon summer, fresh and bright and bursting with flowers and birdsong.

"Who drank the last of the coffee but didn't start a new pot?" came a grumpy voice from behind them. Hope.

Kit didn't bother craning her head around. "Was it so fancy in Chicago that you forgot how to make coffee?"

"All I know is that you appear to have coffee, and I do not. No fanciness involved."

"You snooze, you lose," Charity singsonged.

There was the sound of even louder footsteps behind them, heralding Pru's arrival. They called her *Pru-ricane* for a reason.

"Pru, there's no coffee. Yet both Charity and Kit have some," tattled Hope.

"I have tea," Charity clarified.

"A clear and egregious violation of the house rules," Pru judged.

Kit turned around, then stood to face her other two best

friends through the screen. They'd added to the original house rules they'd made when they first arrived here, but she would have remembered if there was a coffee amendment. "You don't get to randomly decide that something is a house rule just because you're cranky in the morning."

"I think you'll find that house rules are house rules, *Katherine*," Pru said loftily. "You agreed when we made our new pact. No cell phones, weekly meetings in the living room, being social, no unauthorized seafood and especially no salmon—"

"I swear the salmon is reproducing," Hope said darkly. "Every time I look at it, there's more."

Charity frowned at her. "Why are you looking at the salmon?"

"Why didn't you leave the salmon in Chicago with the remains of your wedding feast instead of transporting it across the country?" Kit asked at the same time. "That's a better question."

"And," Pru said as if none of them had spoken, "not being the kind of questionable roommate who leaves an empty pot of coffee sitting on a hot burner, like a taunt."

Kit sighed. "I'll remember this ruling, Prudence."

"I would have made more coffee," Charity offered as she got to her feet. "But I didn't realize Hope and Prudence were baby ladies."

"Didn't you?" Kit asked.

She briefly wished she had her locked-away cell phone, because she would have loved to take a snapshot of the look on Hope and Pru's faces, then threaten to post it. They'd all agreed to spend the summer without their phones, mostly because that way their previous lives couldn't haunt them. Hope's in particular.

What Kit found funny was how *not* awful it had been so

far to be without the phone that was usually welded to her hand. Who knew she didn't actually *need* it? And it also provided a handy excuse for why she wasn't calling anyone now that she was back. Like her father.

They all cheerfully called each other shocking names on the way to the kitchen where Kit made a theatrical production worthy of Broadway out of putting on another pot of coffee. After which they moved into the living room to watch Kit accept her punishment.

This was part of the pact they'd made. They'd come to this farmhouse for the summer to make good on their childhood notion that the four of them would run darling little shops along the main street of Jasper Creek, like the games they'd played when they were little. With leases being practically handed out by the mayor, as long as the shops could be ready before the town's centennial in early August, how could they refuse? They couldn't. They hadn't.

Charity had done all the research. The particular corner of Main Street where the shops stood had been derelict for ages. When the tourists had started to discover Jasper Creek, they'd found the old brick buildings charming despite their condition and were forever taking pictures in front of them. That was part of why Kit, at least, felt certain they'd be able to make a go of things. If the buildings drew in tourists without any shops in place, imagine what would happen if there were things there to buy?

But the summer was about more than darling dreams. It was about happiness. Hope's happiness after her wedding disaster, specifically, which they'd decided meant she had to meet people and date…someone. And since they were all single—another reason they were all up for this adventure—they would date too. Kit liked to tell herself that this was yet another example of what an amazing friend she was to

Hope, but the truth was, she'd long since grown tired of what passed for dating in New York City. She was all app-ed out. And she couldn't help thinking that the last time the idea of boys had really truly been *fun* had been in high school with her best friends. Why not re-create that?

Besides, she figured it was low risk. This was Jasper Creek. How many single men could there be? Much less, single men who didn't find her *too much*.

They'd found some old magazines from 1945 in the living room of the farmhouse and had taken the husband-hunting tips in them as their guide. Pru had written out all the tips and thrown them in a jar, to use as punishments. And challenges.

But mostly punishments.

Because they were funny.

They were funny when it was happening to everyone else, that was. Kit found the whole thing significantly less amusing when it was her; but still, it was nice to have to walk around town with a *reason* for being an oddball. Instead of being one because she didn't fit in with anyone but her three best friends.

Which was pretty much the story of her childhood.

Kit scowled when she read hers. "I can't do this."

"I believe that's another violation right there, Katherine." Hope blew on her coffee. Serenely. "Are you refusing to accept your slip?"

Kit rolled her eyes so hard they hurt, and found herself glaring around the pretty little farmhouse living room. Because that was better than looking at her friends' smug faces. She glared so hard a book fell off one of the bookshelves and she was more than happy to go and pick it up while rearranging her not-a-team-player expression before she was called out on it.

Sometimes she thought this farmhouse was a little bit magical, but she didn't dare say that out loud. The mockery might end her.

No matter how many times they got back from a day in town to find the ancient Victrola playing old Andrews Sisters songs, it was easier to pretend they thought one of them had done it instead.

"I accept the call of the slip," she said when she could do it without rolling her eyes. "But I don't see how I'm going to tell the guy I have coming today how to build my bookshelves when I'm supposed to be..." She eyed the slip in her hand again, but it hadn't changed. And she counted herself lucky that she didn't have to wear a wedding dress in public the way Pru had. This was much better. "Letting a single desolate tear fall down my face while standing in a corner."

Pru snorted at that. Hope took the slip from Kit's hand and cackled. "I like that it's a desolate tear. As if a single but somehow happy tear would ruin the whole thing."

"Are single tears ever anything but desolate?" Charity asked. "Because if you were laughing so hard that you started crying that would be a lot of tears, not just one."

"I prefer no tears," Pru muttered.

"And like you don't know who *that guy* is, Kit." Hope shook her head. "Like somehow, with all your time running around New York City, you somehow forgot Browning West."

Browning West. A man who had always been his whole name, even when he was a kid.

"I didn't forget him. But I didn't remember him, either. Specifically."

"That's a lie," Pru said. "Nobody *doesn't specifically remember* Browning West."

"Do you remember when he was dating Chelsea Mackavoy?" Charity asked dreamily. "And they would make out in the chemistry lab?"

"I don't know that I would describe what Browning West did in high school as *dating*," Hope countered.

"The way he would put his hand in the back of her jeans…" Charity trailed off.

They all sighed…because they all remembered. Kit certainly did. Browning West was one of a handful of brothers from a ranching family, all sons of the marvelously named Flint West, and all possessed of names relating to firearms. It was a story Kit had dined out on both at Princeton and in New York. The older West brothers had been either too stern or too taken or both, but Browning had been far too good-looking, as well as cheerfully promiscuous, as a teenager.

He'd been breathtaking. A car crash waiting to happen.

But oh, what a glorious ride first.

"Let's get real," she said now, because she had done no *riding* of any kind in high school and certainly not with him. "A guy like Browning West was on a downhill slope even back then."

"But his *hands*," Charity murmured.

Kit ignored that. "Look. He was a whole thing in high school, I grant you. But none of us are in high school anymore. Everybody knows that the kind of guy who peaks as a teenager has nowhere to go but down. And fast. Into despair."

"That's the saddest thing you've ever said to me, Kit Hall," Hope declared. "The entire point of Browning West is the fantasy. I think you know that."

"I'm just saying that we might need to adjust our expectations. I'm expecting a beer belly, a receding hairline, a face like a map of regret and, possibly, a slew of baby mamas. The prom king gone to seed, in other words."

Pru eyed her. "You're a ruiner."

"If the hand situation is still stellar you can always take the rest on," Charity said hopefully. "Like another renovation project."

"The bookstore is more than enough," Kit replied. Severely, because it was true, the hand thing had been epic and she needed to get her head out of that gutter.

They disbanded then to get ready for their mornings as shopkeepers—with shops that were still in varying degrees of disarray. Kit caught a ride into town with Pru, and they were too busy listening to music turned up far too loud, the way they always had in high school, to continue poking at each other. Both being their favorite pastimes.

"What are you doing with your face?" Pru asked as they parked around the back of their row of shops and climbed out of the car, coffee from the cute little coffee cart in hand.

"If you must know, I'm attempting to produce any moisture at all, much less one single, desolate tear." She tried again. Harder.

Pru did not look impressed. "You look constipated."

Kit did not dignify that with a response. Instead, she walked to the back door of her shop and forgot all about tears, desolate or otherwise, because there wasn't much she liked better than pulling out the key to her very own shop.

Her shop.

She let herself in, switching on the lights and then smiling around at the walls and rooms that were now hers. *Hers.* She could fill this place with books she loved. And talk to others who loved them too and, like her, would have given anything for a shop that catered to their private addictions. No boxes of Gram's books here, hidden out of sight, but all those bright and happy covers cheerfully displayed.

Kit was lucky because her shop, with its two big bay

windows that looked out over the street, hadn't been in quite the rough shape that some of the others were. All four shops shared a common basement—which housed the safe where they'd locked away their cell phones for the duration—but Pru's feed store couldn't even begin to take form until she finished clearing away all the old stuff that was packed in there. All Kit had needed to do was sweep and scrub, then throw out a few boxes of debris.

Which was why she was ready for bookshelves a week into her new life.

She could see it all so clearly in her head, as if she'd been doing nothing but planning to open a shop like this for years instead of shuffling back and forth between work and her tiny studio apartment, never quite taking advantage of all the magic and mystery New York was supposed to have on offer. It did, but there was never time. She was always tired. And there was always more work to be done. More manuscripts to read, more editing to do, more endless meetings to sit through.

The first time she could remember reading a book for fun in years had been on the plane back from the horror of Hope's wedding. She'd agreed on the spot that it was time to activate the pact, but she hadn't thought they'd all go through with it. Surely it had simply been talk to get Hope through. But then she'd grabbed a big, fat paperback romance from the airport bookstore and hadn't tried to hide what it was from her seatmates. And she'd been so happily diverted all the way home that she hadn't even noticed that air traffic control had them circling New York for an extra hour before landing.

She'd taken it as a sign.

Then acted on it.

The reality of an actual store that she had to fill with

books she would then need to sell was a little more daunting. But Kit figured that as soon as she got shelves in and books to put on them, everything would fall into place. Because she knew what she would want if she walked into a romance bookstore, and she assumed that other readers would feel the same way.

She unlocked the front door, then opened the windows wide, letting in the sweet, cool breeze of the summer morning.

Sighing happily, she went into the back room, where she would put used books so folks could trade in books they didn't want and try out new authors more cheaply. She was standing in the middle of the room—imagining it filled with books and happiness and possibly a cat of some kind because bookstores needed cats, obviously, or were they even real bookstores—when she heard the unmistakable sound of cowboy boots against her hardwood floors out in the bigger front room.

And despite all her talk about downward slopes and high-school peaks, Kit felt something in her belly twist.

Because Browning West hadn't simply been the most dangerously charming boy in school. He'd been half-feral with it, so good-looking it should've been a crime, and that was before he'd flashed that wicked grin of his around. Long after she'd left Jasper Creek, Kit had spent a lot of time thinking about what she wanted in a man and it had always been the polar opposite of a Browning West type. She hadn't spent all these years pining for the high-school Lothario; she'd just been using him as an example.

Of what *not* to look for.

Accordingly, she'd dated weedy, noticeably intellectual types in New York. Men with pointy wrists and unexciting hands who could talk at length about the latest exhibit at MoMA, debate arcane points of philosophy, and make erudite comments about the importance of things like eclectic jazz ensembles. Men who chose not to have televisions, called themselves aficionados of black-box theater, and were personally appalled by the gentrification of Brooklyn neighborhoods they didn't live in.

Men who could never be confused for redneck country-boy cowboys.

Men who were not Browning West, the epitome of redneck country-boy cowboys. Deliciously dirty, maybe, but not the kind of guy she could bring home to Dad.

Her mom, sure. But not her dad, who wanted better for his only child than *rural Oregon*, as he'd said approximately twenty million times a week while she was growing up. Another reason she was glad he couldn't call her and force a conversation she wasn't ready to have.

Kit was already mourning the loss of beautiful teenage Browning, his cheekbones as sharp as his saunter was lazy, as she arranged her face into an approximation of a smile and walked into her front room.

And then stopped dead.

Because there was a cowboy standing there, all right. Sunlight poured into the room and bathed him in light as if it too was a silly teenage girl as obsessed with him as the rest.

There was no hint of a beer belly or any maps of regret. He wore a cowboy hat but Kit knew, somehow, that male-pattern baldness was not a challenge this man faced. He was dressed in a black T-shirt and jeans, plus the requisite boots, but it was the *way* he wore them that made her mouth go dry.

She felt a strange heat wash over her, so sharp and sudden that she dimly figured she was having some kind of heatstroke. Even if it was only June. And not at all hot.

He took another step closer, so she could see his face. God help her.

The Browning West she'd known in high school—in the sense of having seen him from afar, like everyone else, since as an awkward younger girl who was more bangs and braces than the sort of beauty Chelsea Mackavoy flung about so easily, she was beneath his notice—had been lanky. Beautiful, yes, but still a boy.

This Browning West was a man. A grown man, and he'd filled out. His shoulders were wide, his torso a tapered wonder. His legs looked strong in a way that made that heat roll through her again.

And his face looked like a fallen angel's.

A wave of some kind of impossible, unwieldy emotion washed over her then, and Kit was seized with the sudden, horrible fear that she was about to burst into tears.

But then she remembered that she was *supposed* to burst into tears.

So she let the odd wave of emotion and his face wreck her, told herself it was because she was one step closer to her dream coming true and it was *fine*, and cried.

When she never cried.

And not one single, desolate tear, but a whole lot of them.

"I'll be damned," came Browning's amused voice in a drawl like whiskey that felt like a bonfire, and all that heat made her cry even harder. "That's not the reaction I usually get."

CHAPTER TWO

MOST MEN WOULD turn tail and run for the hills at the sight of a sobbing female.

Browning West wasn't most men.

He didn't mind tears. They were part and parcel of what he liked to call his deep enjoyment of women and all their various moods and facets. His brothers, all four of them—even Smith who barely spoke—liked to call his lifelong appreciation of all things feminine other more cynical names, especially when they'd had a few. If Browning were the sort of person who allowed the opinions of others, including his own family, to influence his behavior that might have smarted.

But Browning never had been much for external validation. He liked what he liked and was generous with his gratitude. Could he help it if that gratitude was so often enthusiastically reciprocated in kind?

The woman before him wiped her face, and then she stared at him with a sudden, solemn directness that took him back when he couldn't remember her name. Had he written it down? He doubted it. Browning would have expected a woman who'd started sobbing like that, quick and out of the blue, to come over all fragile once the tears stopped. She'd be soft and fluttery and instantly in need of a big, strong arm to hold her up, which was usually the purpose of tears on command—but not this one.

She looked like she might bite his arm off if he extended it in her direction.

He had no idea why that made him smile.

Browning studied her with specific interest then. Not only as one of the current tenants of his sister-in-law's farmhouse that he'd come to help out today, who happened also to be pretty. She had glossy dark hair that hung down to her shoulders and was cut into dead straight bangs across her forehead, so she was all big blue eyes the color of faded denim and, currently, a frank stare that was beginning to feel accusatory. She was luminously pale, indicating that even though his sister-in-law Keira had told him this particular tenant was a local girl back home, she was clearly not from the kind of ranchers or farmers around here who spent time outside. Though he could see a few freckles across her nose that suggested the June sun had gone ahead and had its way with her whether she liked it or not. She had the kind of bone structure a man wanted to cradle between his hands and, best of all, that mouth.

Sulky and ripe, it tempted him to take a taste before he introduced himself properly.

More fascinating, she did not smile at him.

At all.

In fact, if he didn't know better—based on a lifetime of experience that suggested there wasn't a woman alive who didn't like to smile at him, big and bright and sometimes with a flush that suggested she couldn't help herself—Browning would've described the way she was looking at him as downright unimpressed.

Like he'd done something to her when he was sure he'd never had the pleasure.

"I expected you to be puffy and dissipated," she blurted out.

Also not a typical reaction.

"It's early yet," he replied lazily. "I was planning to head down to the diner for lunch and get good and puffy. And I usually save the hard-core dissipation for nightfall."

He waited for her to apologize, or backtrack. Giggle, flush, look embarrassed. *Flutter, damn it*.

She did not.

Instead, she kept right on staring him down.

Browning could not for the life of him understand why such a pretty girl would put so much effort into making herself look...well, not ugly. That wasn't possible. But so *serious*. There was the aggressively blunt hair, but there was also what she was wearing. She was dressed like a black shroud.

As if she was in mourning, which, now that he thought about it, would explain the spontaneous crying. "I apologize," he said, keeping it polite. And not thinking about her mouth. Too much... "Has somebody died?"

She blinked. "You mean...in general? I think someone has always died."

"You look like you're grieving, that's all." Browning reminded himself that he was doing a favor here for Keira, his sister-in-law, which meant he was also doing a favor for his brother Remy. And in the West family, it was always good to have a few favors to pull out when needed. So he smiled wider than he might have otherwise. "I don't mean to intrude."

"Why would you think I'm *grieving*?"

"You look like you're dressed for a funeral. And you burst into tears when I walked through the door."

"Oh." She looked down at her outfit, which looked to him like an oversize black dress—possibly a small circus tent—with some sort of black scarf thing thrown over it. It was all oversize and slouchy and yet somehow, he was still aware of the fact that she was slender and delicate beneath it all. "Because I'm wearing black?"

"A lot of black."

"I'm wearing a dress and a scarf. Two garments. Hardly *a lot*."

"Why are you wearing a scarf? It's summer."

She looked at him like he was a lunatic. "Um, it's a summer scarf? Obviously."

"Obviously." Maybe he really was a lunatic. But Browning was surprised to discover that wasn't a deal breaker. His body was communicating its interest in unequivocal terms, and not only because she was the most entertaining thing he'd seen in some time. "I know I'm going to regret asking this, but the tears?"

She stared at him, deadpan. "Allergies."

"I'm afraid to ask what you're allergic to. Me?"

She folded her arms over the front of her shroud of a dress and her summer scarf, tilting her head slightly to one side to size him up. "That has yet to be determined."

Browning only grinned. "Do you want me to go get my tools? Or would you rather I stay here and see if it brings on anaphylaxis?"

"Do you spread allergens wherever you go? That is *not* what it said on the bathroom stall in high school."

Browning threw back his head and laughed. "It sure didn't."

"How would you know what it said? It was the *girls'* bathroom."

"I know what it said." He grinned at her. "I wrote it."

He left her and headed outside then, shaking his head slightly as he walked to his truck. He paused as he was getting his tools because there wasn't much better than a summer morning here in Jasper Creek and Browning never passed up an opportunity to indulge himself—in women, work, whiskey, or the sweet goodness of a perfect morning.

Browning had been lucky enough to get himself born and bred right here in this part of Oregon, and he was wise enough to appreciate that stroke of good fortune. The West ranch had been a fixture in this community for generations and, unlike his father, Browning had four brothers to help shoulder the responsibility. This land was stamped deep in him and he liked it that way. He liked the pretty little town, done up in old brick and ignored for a generation, but now cared for by its concerned citizens. He liked the mountains that framed the valley, the rolling foothills, the deep green forests, and the rich fields.

Home, in other words. He'd always liked being right where he was.

He had his own property out on the family acreage that he hadn't seen fit to build on yet, though he would one day. Meanwhile, he got to work the land with his best friends who he occasionally wanted to kill, given that they were his brothers. His parents could be challenging, but Flint and Annette West made up for it by always, always treating their sons like men. The West family was known for its intensity, sure, but Browning had always liked to distinguish himself.

He was happy-go-lucky no matter what, no matter that even his family were tempted to consider him less serious about things when they should have known better. And he was still the one who Remy had called to help Keira's tenant out because he was dependable. Colt and Smith, the oldest West brothers, were too overset with responsibility or incapable of carrying a conversation, respectively. Parker, the youngest, was more likely to get in a fistfight than lend a hand.

Browning didn't mind if they dismissed him. Just like he didn't mind what the people of Jasper Creek liked to say about him both to his face and behind his back, because he didn't do shame. He was who he was, take it or leave it.

But he found himself wondering about the girl in the shroud who was standing there like a rain cloud in the middle of an empty, sun-drenched shop. And why she remembered his name on a bathroom wall when he didn't recall ever laying eyes on her before.

He would have remembered that face.

On his way back to the shop, he tipped his hat at old Mrs. Kim, sitting there on her favorite bench. *She* smiled at him. As he walked he cast a critical eye along the row of four old Western-style storefronts that had been sitting there, falling apart, for years now. He couldn't think why four friends who hadn't even lived in town in recent memory would want to take on a project like this.

And he said as much when he got back inside to find his little shroud waiting for him. She still had her arms crossed and she was still *this close* to a full-on scowl, but she'd moved to stand behind the counter like she was warding him off.

Good luck with that, Browning thought.

"Moving back here and opening four brand-new stores in the course of one summer seems like more than I'd want to bite off," he said.

"I understand. It can be hard to think outside the box."

Was that an insult? She kept surprising him. When was the last time someone had *surprised* him? "That's me. Always right in the center of any box that's around. I meant taking on a new business; it's a risky proposition anywhere, but especially in a small town. Nothing to sneeze at, I would've thought." He grinned at her lazily and a little hotter than the situation called for. "Particularly given your allergies."

"We did actually grow up here," she said, sounding faintly disapproving. He tried to remember her name. Kathy. Kelly. Something like that, but Browning knew that it was never appropriate to ask a lady her name. No matter the situation, she was always going to think he should already know it. "My father's Lawrence Hall."

She said it like that was supposed to mean something to him, so Browning considered it for a moment. "You mean that guy from the paper?"

"The editor-in-chief of the *Jasper Creek Gazette* for the past thirty years or so? Yes. That guy. He also puts out the *Jasper Creek Chapbook*, so."

Browning had started to measure but now he stopped pretending he wasn't watching the show. "What's a chapbook?"

"A chapbook," she said slowly then sighed so hard it made her bangs flutter. It was amazing how much Browning would have liked to brush that whole blunt edge back and set his mouth to the top of her frown. "It's like a poetry magazine. Although in this case, it's not only poetry, of course, but essays and observations."

"Jasper Creek has a poetry magazine?"

"This part of Oregon is actually filled with creative energy."

"Is it now."

Her cheeks were getting red, finally. He didn't hate it. "There are any number of artists around here. I personally think it's all the green—the forests, the hills. It promotes creativity in a way concrete can't."

"Here I thought it was all pickup trucks and country songs in these parts."

It occurred to Browning as he drew out his drawl there that he was playing up the redneck in him. And more, that she was having absolutely no trouble believing it.

This sharp-edged woman with her elegant hands and her summer scarf and her bathroom wall thought he was a yokel.

Browning found he was happy to play the part.

He took his sweet time measuring her walls and her floor space and everything else.

"I want to accentuate the exposed brick rather than hiding it," she said, following him around. "I'm expecting that the books will provide their own colorful decor."

"Why do you keep calling the bricks *exposed*?" he asked. "Are they feeling particularly vulnerable all of a sudden?"

She looked at him for a moment as if he wasn't speaking the same language. Then she laughed a little. "Oh. Sorry. I just mean the brick walls."

"When I mean a brick wall, I say *brick wall*. I find it clears up any confusion about the emotional state of stones."

They were standing in the back room, maybe a little too close. But if she didn't notice that, Browning wasn't about to tell her. Especially because, for a thunderous shroud of a woman, she smelled a lot like lavender.

Turned out he liked lavender. A lot.

"In New York, they say *exposed brick*, probably because that indicates that it's an older building," she told him. "Prewar, meaning before World War Two."

He got it then. The mention of New York was what did it. And that tone she used, like she couldn't help herself, like she *had* to deliver that information to him or she might die. That, plus her father and his paper, made the pieces come flush. She was Kit Hall.

Browning still didn't remember her from high school, but he remembered hearing about her afterward, when the fact that she'd gotten into a fancy East Coast school had been the talk of the valley. Meaning, people had talked about Kit's college plans to his mother, who had then complained about it to the whole family.

Life is free, Annette had drawled. *But by all means, pay out a fortune for a fancy degree for all the good it will do you.*

In retrospect, Browning wondered if it was Kit's father his mother had an issue with, given how many folks around here went off to college without inspiring any commentary from Annette.

"Jasper Creek is filled with old brick buildings, also prewar," he said. "That being the Civil War."

She frowned again and looked as if she was about to say something but didn't. Browning might not know a whole lot in this life—he was conversant on cattle, and he liked a drink and a decent burger—but when it came to women, he was an expert.

And it didn't take an expert to see the moment it occurred to Kit Hall, Princeton graduate, that she was standing much too close to him. In the back room of her empty shop that looked out over a deserted parking area. Where anything at all could happen.

Browning watched her blue eyes widen. She swallowed, hard. He waited for her to back away, but instead, she gave him a regal sort of nod.

"Don't let me distract you," she said, as if she was doing him the favor.

"You're not distracting me. Thank you for the opportunity to do something other than ride fences. They don't come along every day." He smiled. Slowly. "Truth is, I've always been good with my hands."

The most fascinating stain of color washed over her then, while he watched. It made her glow. It made her vibrate.

"I'll be out front," she said, curtly.

And then she swept from the room, leaving the scent of lavender behind her.

Browning finished his measurements and then ambled his way back out to the front room, where she was standing behind her counter again, looking stiff and mutinous. And if he wasn't mistaken, staring at his cowboy hat like she'd never seen one before.

He set his pad of paper down on the polished wood between them and didn't look at her again while he sketched out his ideas. His grandfather was the one who'd taught him how to build things. Browning's three older brothers had always been in the midst of one squabble or another, meaning the two youngest had spent extra time with their grandparents while their parents handled the hellions. Parker had considered it torture. Browning had loved his long weekends out in the shop with Grandad, learning how to take things apart, put them back together, and if he was patient enough, make it art.

When he got around to building his own house, he had big plans for his own shop. He would build things using the tools his grandfather had given him two Christmases ago when the old man had finally accepted that his arthritic hands had betrayed him for good. It was like having a memory of the life he knew he would have. It felt that real, that right.

"Are you…an artist?" Kit asked, with a note of interest in her voice. And astonishment. Too much astonishment, certainly, but he concentrated on the interest. Given it was the first she'd shown since he'd walked in.

"I can draw."

"I wish I could. I can't even draw a stick figure." She wrinkled up her nose and it was so cute it made his ribs hurt. "They always come out looking like I accidentally murdered them. Their heads are always wonky and the hair is just tragic."

"Do you spend a lot of time drawing stick figures?"

She paused. "I have been known to attempt a doodle or two, yes."

Browning put his pen down. He was leaning against the counter on one side and she was leaning in from the other, and he wasn't going to be the one to change that. "Why do you sound like you're making a confession?"

"Oh. It's not that, it's just..." She shrugged. "I know doodling is frivolous."

"Frivolous." Browning did not reach across and test the sharp edge of her bangs. Or acquaint himself with the line of her jaw. And he felt he deserved a parade for his restraint. "That's a real fancy way of saying *fun*."

She jerked like he'd slapped her, and instantly scowled.

Browning found her charming when he knew, objectively, she had so far been about as charming as a wet cat.

He did not make the obvious *Kitty* joke and, again, felt that continuing to refrain from antagonizing her when he easily could have, should have resulted in applause at the very least.

None was forthcoming.

"The point is, no, I'm not an artist," she said flatly, when that blue-jean gaze of hers was anything but flat. "Hence my career choice of books. First editing them, now selling them."

He pushed his pad over to her with his quick sketches of where he thought shelves could go and she grabbed it like it was a lifeline. Then glared down at it, hard.

"I don't want to burst any bubbles," Browning said. "But you know Jasper Creek already has a bookstore, right?"

She didn't look up. "No. I've never been on Main Street. I thought I'd swan in and open up a shop on the main drag without at any point looking to see what other businesses were here."

Wow. "This isn't New York City. Jasper Creek is a small town. You really think we can support two bookstores in two blocks?"

Kit made an impatient noise, still looking at the drawing. "We won't have the same clientele."

"You're both going to sell books, right?"

She raised her head then and it was all very serious bangs. "This is going to be a genre-specific bookstore."

Browning didn't know what was wrong with him that the more New York she sounded, the more it made him grin. "Genre-specific, huh?"

"Romance novels." She rolled her eyes. At him, clearly. "And before you feel compelled to make any commentary on that, I should tell you that these walls are a contempt-free space. There will be no maligning of romance novels here. Period."

"I'm not a big maligner," Browning drawled. "The bathroom wall should have made that clear."

"Romance is about hope, not bathroom walls," she said fiercely. And sure enough, that flush was back. Browning liked that. Way too much. But then, passion was passion. "Hope and happiness and redemption. Who doesn't need those things? And before you wind yourself up to say something you think is funny that I can promise you will not be, I would challenge you to read a few."

He eyed her from across the counter for long enough that she shifted on her feet and he was pretty sure the color in her cheeks was no longer about books. And more than that, she was as aware of how close together they were standing as he was.

"And here I would've sworn that you don't think I know how to read," he drawled.

She got even redder. "I have...never had so much as a passing thought about your literacy."

"Haven't you?" He tapped his finger on the pad between them. "You can keep this. Look it over and make any changes you want. I'll come by tomorrow and we can talk materials."

"Materials," she echoed. She cleared her throat, then frowned. "I'll probably have a lot of changes. Is that going to be a problem?"

Browning had the strangest sensation then. It was a lot like the way he felt when he imagined his future shop and his grandfather's tools.

He knew that Kit Hall and her very serious bangs were already a problem.

But he wasn't ready to think about the ramifications of that, so he didn't. He grinned instead, because that was easier. Always. "I don't believe in problems."

She sniffed. "I'll keep that in mind."

"But I will take you up on your challenge."

Did he imagine that she looked faintly alarmed?

"Challenge? What challenge? I didn't challenge you."

"You did. You challenged me to read romance novels. Then we discussed the challenges of literacy in rural communities and, frankly, grew closer for it. I'm wounded you don't remember, especially because it was twelve seconds ago."

Kit was vibrating again. And breathing a little bit fast, which was all the parade he needed.

"Fine. I'll bring you a romance novel tomorrow. And will eagerly await your critique."

"You don't sound eager. You sound annoyed." He shook his head. "I have to wait until tomorrow?"

She searched his face and Browning, always sure about women and what they saw in him, found himself wondering what *she* saw. It was a disconcerting sensation. He straightened then swiped up his hat as he stood.

And when he realized he was rubbing absently at his chest, because it was tight, he dropped his hand.

Kit mumbled something that sounded like *damned hands*. Then she reached down behind the counter and came up with a fat paperback. She slapped it down between them.

"Here," she said.

"That looks used."

"It is *loved*, Browning. Deeply. It's one of my favorites and if you can't handle it—"

She made as if to take the book back, but he snagged it first.

"There's not a lot I can't handle, Kit."

Her mouth fell open slightly. "You know my name."

"I know your name." He considered her a moment, and that bright glow that didn't seem to fade from her cheeks. The longer he looked at her, the brighter she got. It made that ache in his chest seem to pulse straight through him. "And I have a challenge for you in return."

"I didn't agree to any challenges. I agreed to lend you a book. Note the word *lend*. I expect it back in the same condition, by the way."

"I'm not an animal."

"The exact same *pristine* condition."

"Fine." He put his hat on and thumbed the brim. "For every romance novel I read, you have to do something fun."

"I don't need a *fun intervention*, thank you. I have fun all the time. My life is a nonstop carnival ride of fun. Ask anyone."

He ignored her. "You won't decide the fun thing. I will."

She scowled at him, her hands on her hips, which he appreciated, because thanks to the shroud, he hadn't been entirely sure she *had* hips.

"I don't know why you think I'm interested enough in whether or not you stunt read good books to commit myself to some horrifying *barter situation* with you, but let me hasten to assure you that I really am not. At all."

"Come now, Kit," Browning chided her. "There's no need to lie. I think we both know you're interested."

And then he took advantage of the stunned look on her face and sauntered out the door, grinning all the way.

CHAPTER THREE

"GIRLS WHO WHINE stay on the vine," Hope singsonged at Kit.

"I'm not whining. I don't whine." Kit did not care for the round of sniggers that greeted her protest. She glared balefully around the farmhouse kitchen at her friends. "All I'm saying is that I actually *like* salmon. Or I did. Now that love has been trampled. Abused. Mashed into whatever it is you're making, Charity."

"Salmon mousse in endive leaves," Charity said brightly, her attention on the mixing bowl in front of her.

"We need to get the salmon out of the house." Pru's voice was serious, her gaze even more so. "By whatever means necessary."

"Terrific. Now we're not only the weird friends who moved into June Gable's farmhouse *as a group*, unmarried and resoundingly unloved." Kit was sitting ramrod straight in her chair at the farmhouse table, her arms crossed, glaring at the green cabinets. She was fine. *Fine.* "Now we're also the ones who crash potlucks with salmon appetizers."

Hope sighed. "Salmon *mousse* in *endive leaves* is clearly an hors d'oeuvre. I would think somebody from the—" She was clearly about to say *the city* and win herself a trip to the slip jar, but stopped herself. "From *New York* City would know that."

Kit glared at the tray of leaves Pru was assembling.

"Hors d'oeuvres are merely appetizers with performance anxiety. Whatever city they're from."

"Are you…projecting?" Pru asked.

"Certainly sounds like projecting to me," Charity said. To her mousse.

Hope was also seated at the kitchen table, though she was not participating directly in the current salmon operation as she was flipping through one of the ancient magazines. Hence her whining comment. "Rule number forty-three. Do not room with a girl who's a sad sack as she'll only drag you down with her."

Pru whistled at that. Charity bit back a laugh. Hope cackled.

"I'm not whining. And I'm not a sad sack." Kit glared at her friends again, expecting them to jump in with soothing remarks. They did not. She felt herself falter. "Am I?"

"Of course you're not a sad sack," Charity said loyally. Into the silence.

Hope shrugged. "Not all sacks can be happy, can they?"

"It's not so much that you're a sad sack." Pru eyed her critically. Kit deeply regretted asking the question in the first place. "But you do dress like a sad sack. Like, literally, you're wearing a sad sack right now."

"It's called a balloon dress, Pru."

"It's July. The Fourth of July, in fact, and it's hot, Kit. Why are you wearing a balloon anything?" Pru shook her head. "I would give you a pass on a water balloon. That's how hot it is."

"I find balloon dresses darling," Kit said. Through her teeth.

"No one else does," Hope muttered. She looked up as if she could feel the way Kit gaped at her. "What does Browning think?"

Browning. The last thing in the world Kit wanted to think about was Browning West, the things he could do with lumber, the way he grinned, his *hands*, and…anything else to do with him, ever.

Therefore he was the only thing she thought about.

"Did I not mention that the first day he came into the shop he asked me if I was grieving?" Kit didn't know why she was giving them that detail. It was like throwing blood in the water and sure enough, the sharks came for her at once.

In the form of three pairs of very solemn, very concerned eyes.

"You know you didn't tell us that," Charity said chidingly, putting down her mixing implements.

"Because if you had," Hope said in the same tone, "we would've made you change your clothes."

"I know you think that you're the most fashionable of us all," Pru chimed in, sounding faintly impatient. "Because you were geographically adjacent to actual fashion houses, but you're not in Manhattan anymore."

"And you're not an editor anymore, either," Charity added. Then, like Hope, she reacted to Kit's glare. "I thought it was your *editorial uniform*, or something."

"You're in Oregon now," Pru said briskly. "It's time to stop wafting around the streets of Jasper Creek like you're that woman."

"Audrey Hepburn?" Kit supplied. Tartly.

Pru smirked. "You wish."

And that was how Kit found herself in cutoff shorts and a skimpy little T-shirt at Jasper Creek's annual Fourth of July potluck lunch some hours later, following the extra-special centennial parade through the (few) streets of town. She had succumbed to the indignity with very little grace.

"I have very sensitive skin that does not care for direct sunlight," she'd snapped at her merciless friends.

"And I have this amazing new invention called *sunscreen*," Hope had snapped right back.

While Pru had muttered something beneath her breath that sounded a lot like *princess*.

Kit insisted on wearing her own sandals. She did not care that the platform wedges were entirely too high for a picnic that took place on the lawn outside the historic city hall building. She would walk across the grass in these shoes if it killed her. She would not mince, or tiptoe around, or appear to even notice that she was walking over uneven ground in high heels for no apparent reason.

"You're really showing us," Charity said from beside her as they waited for Pru and Hope, who had been tasked with delivering the latest salmon offering to the potluck table—though Kit doubted the assembled throng was going to go for *mousse and endive* over Mrs. Kim's pigs in a blanket.

"I'm glad you appreciate the statement I'm making," she said airily.

"It's a statement all right."

"I don't like your tone, Doctor."

Kit whirled around, preparing to storm off in mock high dudgeon but instead slammed into a wall.

A vast brick wall of the male variety.

Browning.

Exactly who she didn't want to think about. Much less *touch*. His hand shot out to grip one elbow like he expected her to pitch forward, and God help her...*his hand*. Her shoes gave her four extra inches, which should have helped, but she still had to crane her head back to look up at him.

"Careful," he rumbled at her, in that way he did. "You're going to break an ankle in those shoes."

"Why are you so obsessed with my shoes?" she demanded, far more breathily than necessary, but his hand was still on her and her heart was drumming and how was she supposed to *breathe*?

"Can't say that I consider myself obsessed so much as appreciative."

Browning took his time looking down toward her feet. A long time, with a lot of detours along the way, and Kit had never in her entire life felt so…exposed. And not in a brick-wall sort of way. The thing about balloon dresses and various other floaty layers and shrouds and all the rest of the things she liked to wear was that they were all smoke and mirrors. They floated about, this way and that, hiding most of her from view. She liked it that way.

Pretty girls worry about the prom, her father had always told her, peering at her over the stacks of dense, important books in his study. *Smart girls worry about Princeton.*

But she had been bullied into wearing skimpy little shorts that barely made it to the middle of her thighs. And a T-shirt that she'd claimed was pornographic the minute she'd pulled it on.

"I think what you mean is that it fits," Hope had said.

Pru had nodded. "Turns out you're not shaped like a balloon."

But neither the shorts nor the T-shirt *felt* as if they fit. Not with Browning looking at her the way he was. Everything felt too tight. Kit was much too hot. She told herself it was sunburn, the heretofore unknown *rolling* kind that swept over her from her head down to her toes and made her feel like she was melting from the inside out.

Browning finally dragged his gaze to hers again. And sadly, dropped his hand. "Deeply appreciative, Kit."

"I'm going to take a hard pass on this entire interaction, thank you."

Kit did not glance down at her elbow to see if he'd left scorch marks behind. She could feel them.

"We made a deal," Browning said then.

She had come to realize in the weeks that this man had taken over her life, that his grin was not the happy-go-lucky celebration of sloth and sin she'd always imagined it was. It was steel straight through. How did no one else seem to see that?

"We made a deal and I've upheld my end of it."

He had read two books of her choosing. He had delivered his verdict on both, proving himself irritating, male, and wrong. Still, he'd read them. Which meant Kit had subjected herself to his brand of fun on two occasions.

She had been expecting something shocking. Or dirty. Adult truth or dare, maybe.

"I'm not in high school," he had told her when she'd foolishly said something like that in the store one morning. "This isn't the girls' bathroom, Kit."

And then he'd forced her to eat watermelon with him while sitting on the back of his pickup truck so that they could have a seed spitting contest.

"That was disgusting, not fun," she'd pronounced afterward.

Browning had only grinned, hot and wicked. "You just hate that you lost."

The second so-called fun excursion had involved tequila shots in the Rusty Nail. Kit and her friends had been there anyway, forced to act out the usual ridiculous slips they'd pulled from the jar on the way out that night. Hers had been to laugh wildly at anything a man said in her presence, because *men like girls who do not challenge them, but find them funny.*

"I don't think you need tequila," Browning had said when he found her at the bar. "But it sure is fun."

"Everybody needs tequila," she'd retorted. Then she'd remembered herself and had laughed uproariously.

Until he'd shaken his head, laughing too.

And Kit knew that if not for the slips, she'd have spent that entire night in a corner, glaring. The slips allowed her to be silly. The truth was, they gave her an excuse, because all she knew how to do was be overly, endlessly serious.

The rest of that night had gotten a little blurry, though Kit distantly recalled that smile of his. And the way his hands had felt—those *hands*—when he'd rested them at her waist out there on the dance floor.

If she thought too much about the fact she'd been out on a dance floor at all, she might swoon, so that was one more thing she wasn't thinking about. *Active amnesia*, she liked to tell herself. *Use it and love it.*

"I don't owe you anything from our deal," she protested now, squinting at him in the Fourth of July heat. "The bargain was very specific. You have to read another book."

"I stayed up late last night finishing that book," he said, sounding vaguely offended. "You're going to have to explain the appeal of a biker to me. I don't really get it."

"What's not to get?" Kit frowned at him, then frowned harder when he grinned. "He's an outlaw who makes his own rules. Obviously that's universally appealing, or neither one of us would be standing here in Oregon, a state that was pretty much settled by rule breakers who refused to stay put back east."

"That's certainly one take on the Oregon Trail."

Kit drew herself up, fully entering what her friends

called her Lecture Mode. "Whether or not you personally relate to an outlaw biker is neither here nor there. He fulfills a need in the heroine. He can't be tamed, but he lets her hold him, all the same. She can't trust the world she lives in, but he lives in his own world and protects her. It's beautiful, Browning."

"If you want a ride on my motorcycle, Kit, you can just ask. You don't have to make it a whole thing."

That...made everything stop. "You have a motorcycle?"

She tried to envision that, something that was entirely too easy, God help her.

"Wow. You're actually not scowling at me for three seconds. Be still my heart."

"I guess that makes you a weekend warrior," she said, in a desperate attempt to get her balance back. "Isn't that the phrase?"

"It is not," he replied. "At least, it's not the phrase you should use when you owe me an adventure."

Kit realized she'd completely forgotten the fact that they were standing there in full view of the entire assembled population of Jasper Creek. She knew her parents were around here somewhere, though she'd been doing her best to avoid them. Well. Not her mother, who she snuck over to see sometimes for lunch, but her father. She could scent Lawrence Hall's disappointment on the summer breeze so there was no need to subject herself to the close-up version.

Once again, she was happier than she'd ever imagined she could be that she didn't have her phone...though she was starting to wonder if she was the one avoiding her father or if he was the one avoiding her. Her stomach twisted at that. Normally he would have sat her down so she could regale him with *tales from civilization*, as he liked to call it. She kept telling herself that if she had her phone, he would have called a million times already instead of listening to her mother's secondhand updates.

But what if he hadn't? What if he was watching her right now, along with everyone else, wondering how she'd turned out to be such a disappointment?

Kit swallowed, hard, because it almost felt like she might sob.

She focused on Browning. Maybe a little ferociously.

"I thought, for fun, we could attend this annual potluck," she said, and shifted her body backward. Just to put a bit of space between them. "The good news is, we're already here."

"I have a better idea."

He didn't say anything else. Instead, he looked at her. Very strangely, she thought.

"What?"

"Is that...a lasagna, or something?"

Kit followed his gaze down to her own hand as if she'd forgotten that she was carrying a hatbox.

Because she had, in fact, forgotten it.

Yes. A hatbox. Because of her *perfectly reasonable* objections to her friends' insistence that she wear perky little shorts that left her thighs hanging out *as well as* the skintight T-shirt that could easily have won a wet T-shirt contest without being the faintest bit damp, she'd been forced to march downstairs and take a slip.

Carry a hatbox.

"Oh, sadness," Kit had drawled after she'd read it out loud. "I must have left all my hatboxes in New York."

They'd all jumped at the sound of something hitting the floor, loudly, in the next room. It was not the first time the farmhouse had come over a little strange. They'd all walked together, in a knot, over to the entrance of the dining room and peered in.

What should appear to their wondering eyes, but a freaking hatbox in the middle of the floor? Having levitated itself off the top of the china cabinet, apparently.

Kit had not spent a lot of time looking at hatboxes in her lifetime, magical or otherwise. Still, it was clear to all of them that was what the glossy pink-and-coral round box was. Complete with the sassy leather handle.

"Obviously it's not a lasagna," she said now. "It's too hot for lasagna, and even if it wasn't, who would carry a lasagna in a pink leather box?"

"I don't think you should be looking at me like I'm the weird one here. You're the one wandering around with a round box in one hand. I thought maybe it might be a small tuba, if it wasn't a lasagna."

She frowned at him. "It's a hatbox."

"You're not wearing a hat, Kit."

"If I was wearing a hat, why would I need a hatbox?"

And this was the problem with Browning. Every morning she would arrive at her shop, braced for the day ahead. She was ordering books. She was setting up accounts with the local distributor and its warehouse in Roseburg. She would be ready to open in August.

But then he would appear at some point or another. And he was...

Annoying.

That was the word she'd settled on.

He teased her. He confronted her. He was simply *there*, gleaming and beautiful and sometimes lounging around in her bay windows until every female in Jasper Creek seemed to stop and giggle and pay entirely too much attention to a store with no merchandise in it.

All annoying.

But the real trouble with Browning was that she had chosen not to enlighten him as to why she did ridiculous things like carry a hatbox for no reason, or laugh wildly at his every utterance. And he...rolled with it.

As if he found her eccentric, sure, but charming.

Kit had never been *charming* in her life. *Charming* was right up there with *frivolous*. Intellectuals were serious, not silly.

But Browning West didn't know she was an intellectual. He had no evidence to support that. She was a woman who was opening a bookstore. A romance bookstore, filled with the only books that literally everyone felt perfectly comfortable sneering at. Openly. That was what Browning knew about her—that she liked *those* books. He was not impressed with her college degree, how many times she'd pretended she'd read *Ulysses*, or which *luminous works of stunning prose* she'd worked on. Those topics didn't come up.

To Browning, Kit was a weird girl who had cried when she met him and was currently staring at him as though she didn't understand why every other woman outside city hall wasn't carrying her own hatbox.

And he likes you anyway, a voice inside her whispered, as he grabbed the hand that wasn't holding the hatbox and started towing her across the field.

He didn't seem to care that they were on display. That a tidal wave of *whispers* rose up and followed them as they went.

Kit thought that maybe she should offer up some kind of token resistance, if only to feel better about herself. But his hand was wrapped around hers and the last thing she felt was resistant.

"Where are we going?" she asked.

He looked down at her, and if she thought that looking at the sorts of things he did with his hands back in high school had been almost too much for her heart to bear, feeling his *actual hand* on hers was worse. Or better.

Worse! she snapped at herself. *Much worse!*

But all she could see was that fallen-angel face of his. That wicked grin on his lips, the too-bright light in his eyes.

"I told you," he said, with exaggerated patience that seemed to set off a chain of fires inside her. "I have a motorcycle. I'm betting you've never been on one before."

"I've done a great many things, actually, *Browning*, and you don't know—"

"Have you, Kit?"

Her breath shuddered out of her. She told herself it was because his hand was so *big*. So deliciously calloused from what she assumed was a lifetime of all that hardy ranch work. And hot to the touch so that it shivered all the way through her.

"No," she whispered. "I've never been on a motorcycle." She cleared her throat, though it did not require clearing. "They're very dangerous. The statistics—"

"Kit." There was so much heat in his gaze then that she was fairly certain the town was not going to need its usual fireworks display. She could do it herself. She was doing it, right here on the grass as they walked. She was surprised no one had called in the fire department. "You're going to be fine, I promise. All you have to do is hold on."

CHAPTER FOUR

BROWNING WAS SURPRISED to discover that he liked romance novels.

His brothers had been horrified when he'd started whipping them out during their lunch breaks out on the ranch.

"You're not really reading that?" Parker had sounded alarmed. Deeply alarmed. *"Why are you reading that?"*

"You should try it," Browning had drawled, kicking back in the bed of his pickup. "Word on the street is, you could use a little instruction."

But his surprising enjoyment of love stories paled in comparison to his appreciation for Kit Hall.

Who was not wearing her customary shroud today.

He hadn't understood the sensation that had stampeded around inside of him when he'd first seen her on the lawn after the parade. All those long, absurdly un-sun-kissed limbs, as if she'd been living in a cave belowground. She was blinding in the heat and sun, but it turned out, Browning didn't mind being cauterized by the sight of her. The little red T-shirt she wore not only *clung*, it flirted with the top of her gloriously short shorts. So that every time she breathed, he got a glimpse of the soft strip of her belly between the hem of her shirt and the top of her shorts.

And God help him, her legs.

She made a man feel something like religious.

Browning had stood there, completely ignoring whatever it was his sister-in-law Keira and her cousins were talking about—something about dogwood trees and their late grandmother—because he was fairly certain he'd been struck upside the head and been made a born-again virgin. Just by *looking* at Kit.

He had half a mind to check himself for the pimples that had disappeared along with that long-ago state, but he caught himself just in time. He'd mumbled his excuses to Keira and her family, nodded at his brother—while ignoring Remy's smirk—and had made his way directly to Kit's side like he was a boomerang.

Browning had never been whipped or anything close to whipped in the entirety of his adult life. He would've strongly objected to the term if anyone else had said it in his presence.

And yet when Kit's sulky eyes had met his he was sure he heard the crack of one, echoing sharply in his ears. Stranger yet, he didn't mind.

There were the shoes. An absurd pair of wedge things that should have had her face-first on the ground, rolling around without the use of either broken ankle. Or her hair, still hanging darkly around her as if, despite actually wearing reasonable summer clothes for a change, she wanted to get her shroud in where she could.

He had spent more time than he cared to admit imagining what it would be like to gather up all that dark, silky hair in one hand, press his mouth to the nape of her neck, and taste her some.

For starters.

The fact that she was carrying a hatbox, whatever that was about, made it better.

She was an odd little thing and he felt a powerful need

to get inside her. Her body, yes. But inside that head of hers too.

He tugged her with him to the street, where he'd parked the Harley he'd been tinkering on for years—mostly to irritate his brothers with what Colt liked to call *Browning's fake hobby*. He handed her a helmet and watched as she buckled it on, that hatbox hanging from one wrist. Then he climbed on and nodded to the space behind him.

And waited, because one thing he knew about Kit Hall was that she never, ever did something without overthinking it first. He liked to watch the way her blue eyes sharpened. The way her brow furrowed. The way her *thoughts* were louder than whole bars he'd frequented in his time.

She considered him for a long while. Then she tottered closer in those shoes—seeming to be alarmingly comfortable walking on what were basically stilts—and climbed on behind him.

She wrapped her arms around his chest, that bizarre hatbox now sitting on his lap.

Browning would have carried twenty-five hatboxes like a circus clown if it meant she'd hold him like that. Behind him, she fought the natural position of her body on the seat for a moment or two before breathing out, hard, and then sinking into him.

He usually spent the annual picnic enjoying the many potluck offerings—not all of them the edible kind. Not when so many local women tended to think he'd be an excellent way to celebrate their patriotism. But he barely gave the assembled townsfolk another thought. He gunned the engine and took off, heading out of Jasper Creek and up into the hills.

He hadn't thought much of the biker hero in the last

book she'd given him, it was true. But he certainly got the appeal of a motorcycle and an open road.

It was a perfect summer's day. The sun beamed down and the trees were green and lush. There were flowers everywhere—from carpeted fields covered in wildflowers, to beautiful displays on the front porches of the happy, tidy houses they passed in the valley. They wound their way through vineyards and farms, to the tops of hills with views that stretched in all directions. He took them back down to chase the river through the center of the valley, in and out of the shade of manzanitas and willows, past proud lines of cottonwoods and near enough to hear waterfalls tumble over the rocks on their way to the sea.

Finally, he stopped in the shade of a particular oak tree he'd always liked best, on the shore of a bright blue unspoiled lake hidden away from the rest of the valley on the land he was going to make his home one day.

"This is so beautiful," Kit said softly in his ear when he turned off the bike, and she didn't let go.

It seemed to take her a moment to get her bearings. To remember that she was melted there against his back, so he could feel every inch of her torso and those sweet thighs bracketing him. He wasn't about to hurry her along. His head spun a little, like she was alcoholic, and he welcomed the opportunity to drink deep.

The way he had that night he'd danced with her in a crowded bar, when she was sloppy and silly and laughing like a loon for no good reason. Too sloppy and too silly to do anything but dance with her a little and regret the feel of her, too perfect in his hands, before packing her off into the care of her friends.

But he hadn't slept much since then, because his dreams were too vivid with all the *what-ifs*.

He regretted stopping the bike at all when she moved, swinging her leg off and then taking a few steps toward the lake. She kept her back to him while she fumbled with her helmet.

And if he wasn't mistaken, hit herself in the face with her hatbox.

Why couldn't he get enough of this woman?

It didn't do much for his ego that he could not only not answer that question, but needed a moment or two to handle himself before he followed her. When was the last time he'd reacted to anyone like this?

But he knew the answer. Never.

He took her helmet and the hatbox, and placed both on the bike with his. Then he returned, standing next to her as she looked out over the stretch of mountain-fed freshwater lake that had always been his favorite spot in the world. No houses. No cars. No speedboats or overenthusiastic paddle-boarders or grumpy fishermen in the weeds.

Just the blue of the water, the green of the hills, the even brighter blue of the sky. In the winter the mountains were dusted in snow. In the spring the flowers and trees rioted with color. There was no season he didn't love in this place.

And she was the only woman he'd ever brought here.

"Someday I'm going to build a house over there," he told her, and he was horrified to hear those words come out of him. He sounded like the man he'd never pretended he was. Had never wanted to be. The kind of responsible grown-up who did things like plot a life that would involve building houses. Settling down.

In the back of his mind, he'd always assumed that he'd start thinking about those things right about the time he found the person he'd share them with. And he'd always known what kind of girl that was going to be. Cheerful.

Easygoing. Happy-go-lucky, just like him. Undemanding, uncritical, and really, more a beam of sunshine than a person.

Not a walking shroud who thought he was kind of dumb.

He was definitely not thinking about that. Not now. Not here.

Kit slid a look his way, then looked back across the lake toward the open field that was begging for that house he wasn't thinking about. "I don't think I realized we were on the ranch…"

"We are and we aren't. This isn't the working part of the ranch. This is just my acreage."

He never said things like that. That sounded way too much like his parents, always talking about land and water rights and all kinds of other things Browning pretended he didn't understand.

He lived in one of the bunkhouses near the main house where he could have his independence and also be on hand for the twenty-four-hour duties that came with ranching. He'd figured there would be time enough to bore others with his every last opinion on the water table.

"You're lucky," Kit said.

Browning had never heard that note in her voice before. He'd heard her rant passionately about books. He'd heard her on the phone, sounding professional and in charge. He'd heard her with her friends, the four of them sounding the way he thought he and his brothers must, sometimes. That was what happened when you knew people for a lifetime and liked them all the while.

But he'd never heard her sound wistful before.

"I suppose I am," he agreed. "It never feels that way, does it?"

Her mouth curved into that wry smile that made him

lose his place in the world. "I couldn't say. No one's offered me an acreage or two."

Browning acknowledged that with a nod. "Everybody is used to their own kind of normal, whatever it is. We each got to pick out our fifty acres on the day we turned eighteen. And I'm fourth, so I already knew what my older brothers took and it seemed pretty clear to me that they all got the better bargain. Colt took most of the hill right across from the ranch complex because he'll be running it one day. Smith took the furthest possible chunk that he could, way out where our property backs up into BLM land, where he can hermit it up as he likes. Remy chose a good plot but he works his wife's land these days. And I could have picked working land, but I chose this instead. Because it's pretty." She was the only person alive he would dream of saying that to. He shrugged it off to compensate. "They've all made fun of me ever since for picking a vacation home, not a ranch."

Kit's gaze held his, serious and direct. "Why do you need your own ranch? You already have one."

He found himself grinning. "My feelings exactly."

There was the blue sky and the blue water, then the blue of her eyes, and the shade of the oak tree did precious little to take the edge off any of it.

"I'll admit," Kit said, turning her face back to the water, "I didn't expect to like that motorcycle so much."

"Everybody likes motorcycles, Kit. Or there wouldn't be any."

"Thank you," she said, her voice soft. But when she turned back to him, the look in her eyes…wasn't. And Browning stopped thinking about half-formed dreams of *someday* he'd never thought would arrive and concentrated on *this* day instead. "That really was fun, unlike the disgusting spitting contest."

"The bike wasn't our adventure." He grinned. "That was only the transportation."

"You distinctly said that it was the motorcycle ride."

"If you cast your mind back, you'll find I didn't. I asked you if you'd ever ridden a motorcycle before. I didn't say that riding one would be the thing."

"The clear implication was that it was the thing."

"It's not."

He'd grown deeply invested in watching this woman fume. The way it made her eyes seem to change color, taking on the whole of the summer sky. The way she could keep her face so serious, so solemn, while she blushed everywhere and gave herself away.

"If you want to go back on your word…" Browning drawled.

"I do not." She folded her arms over her chest, a gesture which was very, very different when she was wearing a skimpy little red T-shirt. Normally there were summer scarves and billowing shrouds. Today, he could see her perfect curves, the compass she wore around her neck, though he doubted Kit Hall ever allowed herself to get lost, and better yet, that tempting swath of belly.

He was going to devour her whole.

"Well?" she asked dryly. "What fun thing do you think we can do here at this deserted lake, off in the middle of the West ranch, where no one will ever find us?"

"This isn't a horror movie. I'm not planning to build a creepy summer camp here."

"That's a comfort."

"This is going to be much more fun. Everybody loves skinny-dipping."

She stared back at him for so long, he would've thought

she hadn't heard him if he hadn't seen the evidence all over her body.

He reached over and traced the burst of red he could see down one arm. "Every single feeling you have is written all over your skin. You know that, right?"

"I don't like the heat," she bit out, jerking her arm back an inch, which did nothing to get rid of the goose bumps. "What you're seeing is a physiological response to too much sunlight."

"Are you trying to tell me that you're a vampire?" He laughed. "Let me guess. The sparkly kind."

"You'll have to excuse me," she said, glaring at him. "The heatstroke is getting to me. Because I actually thought you said that you brought me here to go skinny-dipping."

"I did."

He lifted a brow and waited. And Kit...sputtered.

"We can't go skinny-dipping!"

"Why not?"

"Let's start with the most obvious reason. It's illegal."

"How is it illegal?"

"I believe they call it public indecency, which I'm guessing you're more than passingly familiar with, given your various exploits over the years. On and off bathroom walls."

"That's hurtful, Kit." He nodded toward the water. "It's my lake. My land. Private, nonpublic, and definitely not illegal."

"Is this the Browning West experience I heard so much about in high school?" She made a huffing sound. "I do not mind telling you that I find this very disappointing."

"I don't think you do."

"Is this really what your playboy reputation has been about all this time?"

"I have a *playboy* reputation? Who uses that word?"

"This can't be your thing. You drive vulnerable women out to secluded spots and demand they *skinny-dip* with you?"

He laughed. "Is there a vulnerable woman in the vicinity? I think you might have scared her away."

"It's not that *I* feel remotely scared. I expected magic, that's all. *As promised* on every bathroom wall and from every starry-eyed teenage girl you ever looked at twice."

"Kit. Please. I took you on a motorcycle ride, which you loved. And I asked you if you'd like to go skinny-dipping with me. You can say no."

"Well. Then, obviously—"

"But if you do, you break our deal." He shook his head sadly. "Penalties will have to be assessed for that."

She scowled. "What penalties? We didn't agree on penalties."

"There are always penalties for breaking sacred vows, Kit. Everybody knows that."

"We didn't make a blood pact, *Browning.*"

"No. We made a deal. If you renege on that deal, there'll be a price to pay. You can't be surprised by that."

"We didn't agree on a price."

"That's because I thought you could be trusted to keep your promises." He made a tsking sound. "If you can't, seems to me I get to decide the prices involved."

She stared at him for another long simmering moment, then made the kind of noise that he associated with the teen girls she'd mentioned.

"Fine. Let's define our terms, then."

"Is skinny-dipping the kind of thing that's confusing in New York? Because here in Oregon all that's involved is taking off your clothes, then getting in the water. No definitions or terms necessary."

"There will be no touching," she said, her scowl deepening.

"I won't touch you, if that's what you want." He grinned lazily. "But you can touch me all you want."

She pointed a finger at him. "You will turn your back. You will not turn around again until I tell you that it's okay to do so. When I am ready to get out of the water—something I will decide, not you—you will once again turn your back. You will stay in the water, back turned, until I am fully clothed and tell you so. Do you understand the terms and conditions?"

Kit was scowling at him like he'd asked her to haul manure, her gaze stern and that finger wagging at him. And all he could think was that he might actually die if he didn't get his mouth on her. And soon.

But despite all appearances to the contrary, Browning had always been a patient man. Perfectly content to wait for what he wanted, because that made sure what he got would be perfect.

"I think you're missing the point," he observed. He wanted to catch that finger with his teeth, but he didn't. "Which is, in case you forgot, *fun*. Not a legal contract on a pretty summer's day."

She sniffed in that snotty way of hers that, like everything else about her, he liked way too much. "If you do not agree to these terms and conditions as I've laid them out, that puts you in violation of our deal. That means I get to decide the price."

He let his mouth curve into something much too hot to be his typical, easy grin. "It's okay, Kit. You can build all the walls you want to hide from the fact we're about to get naked together. I think we both know the truth."

"You mean that I'm calling checkmate on your shenanigans?"

"If it wasn't a big deal to jump in the water with me, you wouldn't freak out and get all Supreme Court over it, would you?"

He didn't wait for her to sputter at him over that. No need to rub it in. He kept his gaze trained on hers.

Then peeled his T-shirt off his body and tossed it aside.

He watched, delighted, as she turned even more glorious shades of red. She defied nature. She was a human torch and he wanted to burn them both to a crisp.

"What…what are you doing?"

For once, she didn't sound like snooty, Princeton Kit by way of New York. She sounded…hot and bothered and sweet straight through.

"Skinny-dipping, Kit," he said patiently.

Her eyes widened. "You can't… I mean you're just… You're standing right in front of me!"

"I don't care if you watch me get naked, baby. In fact, I prefer it."

"Okay. *Okay.* I… I'm not your baby."

"That feels cruel, I don't mind telling you," he drawled. He kicked off his boots and moved his hands to his belt buckle. "Especially while we're getting naked together."

She stared at his hands. Then she made a high-pitched sound of sheer feminine frustration. She whirled around, presenting him with her back and gripping the trunk of the oak tree like she needed it to keep her upright.

"Are you backing down?" he asked her softly.

"Certainly not."

"You look like maybe you're backing down."

He could see every part of her trembling, and questioned the wisdom of his course of action here. He wanted her too much and he'd promised to keep his hands to himself—unless she didn't.

And he couldn't recall ever having those two things happen to him at the same time before.

"If all your twenty thousand other conquests could jump in that lake with you, Browning, I certainly can," she said. Briskly.

Browning wanted to say something funny about conquests as he stripped off his jeans and boxers and kicked them aside. But there was nothing funny about standing there naked, looking at her beautiful body. He wanted to roar until the sky fell down. He wanted to drop to his knees behind her and lick his way up to the ragged hem of her tiny shorts.

He wanted to possess her, totally.

"I've never brought anyone else here," he told her gruffly. "Only you, Kit."

He heard the soft, needy sort of sound she made then. It about broke him.

But he was a man who kept his promises, so he made himself step back when it was the last thing he wanted.

Then he marched himself to the lake and dove straight in to cool himself off before he lost it.

And while he was at it, figure out what the hell he'd been thinking.

CHAPTER FIVE

KIT HEARD A splash and carefully turned around from the tree she'd been gripping for dear life, afraid of what she might see.

Liar, she chided herself. *You're not afraid at all.*

And she wished so hard and so deep that she had her cell phone, so she could text her friends and share this impossible scenario with them. It actually made her ribs ache.

She had spent her whole life obsessed with finding the precise correct word to describe any situation or scenario and yet she didn't think there existed a proper word in any language to describe how she felt now.

That motorcycle ride with the wind snapping all around them, her arms tight around him so she could feel his ridged abdomen, her body pressed into his back so they moved as one with every turn...it had amazed her how intimate it could feel to be hurtling down a road like that, wrapped around him like a clinging vine, like it had always been supposed to be that way.

She didn't understand anything that was happening, the tumult inside her, the strange emotion that seemed to swirl around them when Browning spoke of houses he might build and the future he planned to have, right here on the shore of this lake he'd only ever showed to her.

Only her.

Kit told herself that had just been a line. He probably used it on everyone.

But deep down, there was a sweet, sharp kick of pure joy at the idea that she might be special to this man in some way.

Anyone could have a crush on him. And many did. But he'd brought *her* here.

Now he was out in the water and there was nothing fair about that. Browning fully clothed was a problem. Browning standing there in the lake, grinning at her while water coursed all over that beautiful body of his...

Kit wondered if she was actually having the vapors.

"Turn around," she ordered him.

Maybe she had to say it a couple of times, because her voice didn't seem to be working the way it should.

"I heard the rules, Kit." He shook his head at her. "I'm not the one who wanted to go back on the deal we made."

"Says the person who's not turning around."

He laughed, then made a little production of turning his back to her.

She felt a shot of something that was a little too close to shame. That she wasn't cool enough, like the girls he knew. Like Chelsea Mackavoy, back in high school, who had been so sure of herself. So at ease in her body when all the other girls were awkward disasters.

"He probably thinks you're a Puritan," Kit muttered to herself.

It was sheer temper and bravado that had her stepping out of her shoes, then shucking off the shorts and the shirt and everything beneath. She would do this. She would prove, once and for all, that it wasn't that she didn't know how to have fun. It was that she'd *chosen* a more serious path. Because she liked it. Because it was satisfying, and worthy, and had led to all of her dreams coming true, as planned.

That line of thought got her all the way down to the water. She stopped there for a minute, breathing too hard because Browning's beautiful back was right there before her. And she was stark naked, standing out in the open for any passing creature to see.

Her heart was thudding so hard and so loud she was surprised it didn't rip its way right out of her chest. And it was more than simply *beating*. It was sending pulses all through the rest of her. It charged through each limb, turned into something knotted in her belly, and became a long, slow lick of flame between her legs.

Kit wanted to burst into action—either race back for her clothes or quickly throw herself into the water and submerge herself to her chin—

But she made herself stop.

Because she had never done anything like this before and was very unlikely to do it again. So she...breathed it in, this bizarre moment. She could hear birds, loud and gossipy in the trees. There was a faint summer breeze, rustling the leaves and dancing all over her bare skin. It felt a lot like the way Browning's fingers had, moving over her arm.

The sun felt like his laughter, bathing her in all that light.

For a moment, just a moment, she didn't think about what she *ought* to do. She didn't sort every sensation and feeling into what was serious and what was frivolous, then govern herself accordingly between the two.

She tipped her face toward the sun. She took a deep, shuddering breath. And for a moment, she simply enjoyed being in her own skin beneath the endless summer sky.

For a moment, she enjoyed everything.

When she looked at him again, Browning hadn't moved.

He still stood out there in the water, his lower body hidden from view, and waited.

As if he could wait forever. And would.

Kit believed he would.

She started into the water, cautiously at first. But it was a hot day and the cool embrace of the lake felt like another caress. After a few steps, she sank down into the water herself, dunking her head, and then swimming a bit.

And it was…a marvel.

The water was silky smooth and, feeling it everywhere, with no barrier, was a revelation. She thought of all the romance novels she'd read in her lifetime, too many hundreds upon hundreds to name, and the wonder of it was that she wasn't sure she'd ever understood the meaning of the word *sensual* until now.

She swam farther out, feeling as if her body was being held aloft, wrapped up in the water and the sky above, until she could hardly tell whether she was faceup or facedown, swimming or flying.

When she stopped, she was facing Browning from a few feet away. And Kit thought her face might break apart at the force of her smile.

She braced herself then. For the jokes. The banter. The usual Browning response to anything and everything. Her heart seemed to pick up speed, because she couldn't tell if that was what she wanted. Or if she wanted…this, instead.

The suspension of everything she knew. Nothing left but skin and water and sky, and the two of them caught right in the center of it.

But Browning didn't crack a joke. He didn't even smile.

A different kind of shuddering began to work its way through her, a kind of deep shaking she knew, instantly, was changing her. The very foundation of who she was, while she stood there, caught.

Because the way he was looking at her wasn't funny. Or wicked, in that way of his.

His eyes were a dark blaze of heat. His beautiful face was all fallen, no angel, and there was nothing to distract her from the stark beauty of his features. He was all male, and if she wasn't mistaken, as caught in this moment as she was.

She stretched her toes down to press into the sand beneath her, as if that would help ground her. But the water caught her anyway. It was easier to float, and she forgot that she should've been guarding herself. Making sure that the parts of her that needed to stay private were beneath the water.

It was like…being in the water changed everything.

"You're going to want to be careful," he said after an eternity or two, lost in the heat between them. In the tugging need she could feel all over her, making her nipples hard and the core of her slick. Making her skin feel oversensitized by its own nudity and the water against it, reminding her. "You keep looking at me like that…"

"And what?" She'd intended it to be stern. But it came out like an invitation. "If you do anything at all, you break the rules. And then you pay the price."

"It would be worth it."

Kit agreed.

Rules and deals and prices seemed like the sorts of things she'd left onshore with her clothes. Everything that had happened since Hope's terrible wedding day seemed to have been leading her here. Right here, to this lake.

To Browning.

Because it had been easy to tell herself that she was

a good friend. That she could honor the pact she'd made with the others, because it was fun. And she *was* fun when she wanted to be, damn it. Kit had told herself that, even as she'd thrown herself into the opening of her bookstore the same way she'd done everything else in her life: with a humorless drive and single-minded focus that was exhausting, which was often what her best friends used to make fun of her. It was also the reason Browning had made this bargain in the first place.

And sure, she'd achieved her dreams. But somewhere along the way, she'd decided that dreams were only worthwhile if they were all about hard work, dedication, sweat and tears and an endless grim march forward.

Maybe all of those things were necessary. But Kit was opening a bookshop that celebrated love. Passion. Women and men who took a clear-eyed view of facts and figures and then threw themselves headlong into raw, aching vulnerability anyway.

She'd approached the shop the way she'd approached getting into Princeton, or her editing career in New York: grim marches in all directions, when surely the part of life that mattered most was the brightness. The joy.

Anyone could march grimly. It was joy that was so fleeting. It was joy that people would truly kill or die for, in the end.

And Browning West—*the* Browning West—was in this lake with Kit, not Katherine.

Kit, who he seemed to like no matter how strangely she behaved around him. When she'd whispered things in his ear at the bar. Laughing uproariously at everything he said. Or that stupid hatbox. Even the crying.

He'd taken all of that in stride. And still, here he was.

It was a national holiday today. Kit decided that maybe, just maybe, she ought to take a holiday too. From herself.

She moved a little closer, aware of the exact moment the bright sun up above dimmed in comparison to the heat in those dark eyes of his. And all over his beautiful face.

"Careful, Kit," he said, his voice low and scratchy, rough and deep.

She stopped before him and tipped her head back. Then did what she wanted to do, not what she thought she ought to do.

Without analyzing the *oughts* and the *shoulds*, she threw herself at him.

Browning caught her, easily. And then it was all wet skin and his hard, gorgeous body. His arms went around her and his hands gripped her as she wrapped herself around him.

Just the way she had on the bike, except this time, from the front.

And it was…better.

"I don't want to be careful," she told him.

Then she tilted her face up and tugged his head toward hers with one hand. She was kissing Browning West at last.

He did not hesitate.

There was nothing tentative, nothing pointy-wristed, about the way he kissed her. She was the one holding on to his head, but there was no doubt about it when he instantly took control.

Everything inside her hummed, loudly, then melted straight through.

His arms tightened around her and he pulled her closer, so that her breasts were pressed against his chest, and he kissed her.

Again and again.

Kit could feel how much he wanted her, that unmistakable length of steel against her belly.

But he didn't hurry them along. He didn't catapult them into something more.

He just kissed her.

Not lazily and not like he had an agenda.

But as if he was perfectly content to taste her like this forever.

She knew when that kiss shifted from a noun to a verb, because then it became a tasting. A deep, necessary tasting. As if they were trying out each other's shape and need and longing, discovering the contours of all that heat.

And all the while the water moved around them, the sky arched above, and she was sure that they were flying together. Flying or swimming or both, over and over and over, until it was all part of the same thing.

It was so beautiful it hurt.

She pulled back right at the critical moment when she thought she might never pull back at all. Ever. He rested his forehead against hers while they both panted, out there in the middle of this marvelous nowhere that felt like theirs.

"You taste even better than you look," he said, there against her mouth. "I would've sworn that was impossible."

"You taste like magic," she whispered back.

He shifted her in his arms so he could move one arm and slide her hair back from her face. Then, while she tried to keep her heart from exploding, he leaned closer and pressed a kiss to her forehead.

Then, while she frowned to make her heart ache less, he pressed another one between her brows.

Kit was laughing a little, though she couldn't have said what was funny, when he kissed her on the tip of her nose too.

Browning West, known for his sexual exploits, who was huge and hard and pressed against her, was kissing her.

Sweetly.

That shaking inside of her was a wrecking ball, she was sure of it. There was nothing left of her but wishes in smithereens.

And the mad notion that she'd fallen off a cliff without realizing it.

Her feet weren't even on the ground, and still she felt the world fall out from beneath her.

His hand moved, running over her slicked-back hair.

"Hey," he said, quiet and low, even as his gaze seemed to burn with the same fire that raged in her. "This is supposed to be fun."

"Fun. Right."

Kit thought it might actually wound her, to the point of scarring, but she pushed herself off that impossibly perfect body of his and swam back a foot or two, still holding his gaze as if they were both free falling off the edge of that same cliff. As if they'd both lost something that they knew there was no unknowing.

She slapped her open palm on the surface of the lake and splashed him.

When he stood there, staring back at her in astonishment, she did it again.

"This is supposed to be fun, Browning," she managed to say.

Then she had to dodge when he splashed back at her.

And she lost herself as best she could in the splashing back and forth until both of them were laughing again.

Laughing almost too much.

Because you know, now, something told her, feeling

more like a prophecy than it should, *and you can't go back from that*.

Kit shook that off and laughed.

Because that was better than crying over the ache inside her that grew and grew and that she knew, somehow, was never going to get any better.

CHAPTER SIX

LATER, BROWNING SAFELY delivered Kit back to the old Gable farmhouse outside of town.

It was tipping over into evening. The sun was less fierce, spilling gold all over the green hills and bright fields. He rolled up near a pretty dogwood tree and took the helmet Kit handed him once she climbed off.

He watched the way her hips moved in those ridiculous shoes as she walked toward the porch, her hatbox still dangling from one wrist.

He enjoyed the view a good long while.

Then he lifted his gaze to where all three of her friends were waiting, poker-faced, on the porch. He nodded at them with only slightly exaggerated courtesy.

"Ladies," he drawled.

He grinned all the way home.

But, starting that day, anytime he finished a book, he took her to his lake.

Sometimes they swam. Sometimes they didn't.

Browning was becoming addicted to the feel of her wet skin beneath his hands. He dreamed about kissing her like that, deep and wild and thrilling, because the last time he'd just *made out* with someone had been so long ago he couldn't remember who it was or when. He dreamed about it, then he did it, and all that kissing was making him feel half-drunk.

But then, Kit made him feel a little blurry whether they were kissing or not.

It was taking him over.

Nights he would normally spend throwing back a beer or two with his brothers and friends, he found he would much rather spend with her. He finished the bookshelves in her shop, then took it upon himself to excavate the apartment that sat above the bookstore and had been, as far as he could tell, little more than a storeroom for the past decade. One night she'd gone off with her friends and he'd told her he was going to finish up, then go meet his.

"I guess you need a key then," she said, with studied indifference.

"I guess I do," he replied. With a grin.

And when she slid an extra key off her key ring and handed it to him, neither one of them had commented on the fact that she'd clearly anticipated the moment and gone to get a duplicate made. No need for commentary when Kit was blazing red, telling him everything he needed to know.

Browning never made it to the bar. He stayed in the shop all night, working on the plumbing in the apartment bathroom upstairs so it would work perfectly when Kit arrived the next morning. Because that was perfectly normal. That was what all volunteer handymen did.

"Missed you last night," his brother Parker said the next morning while they were heading out into the upper pastures. "All the usual suspects were there, but you weren't."

Browning shrugged. "I'm very mysterious, Parker."

"Since when?" Parker retorted, with a laugh. Browning aimed the pickup truck for the biggest pothole in the dirt road, just to jostle him for that. "There's nothing mysterious about a man-whore."

"I'll thank you not to slut shame your older brother,

Parker," Browning said, and grinned the way he normally would have.

But that grin was starting to feel more like a prison sentence and less like his favorite expression of the carefree charm that seemed to be deserting him these days.

He made sure to take the rest of the dirt road a little too fast, so Parker had to hold on and curse him, which was a whole lot better than him talking about Browning's man-whore ways.

Man-whore ways that had deserted him since he'd met Kit Hall.

But before he could think a little too much on that particular topic, he stopped himself. Decisively.

Because no good could come of it. He knew that.

And still, there he was in the apartment above her bookstore day after day, fixing it up for God knows what purpose. Today he'd arrived to find her surrounded by boxes of books in the back office, looking so happy and edible it should have been illegal.

He'd grunted something even he found unintelligible and had removed himself. Before he couldn't.

Now he heard her footsteps on the stairs and looked up from where he'd just finished painting one of the walls.

"Are you looking for a place to live?" Kit asked, leaning against the door that opened onto the small landing and the spiral stair that led down into the bookstore's small, cozy office. "Is that why you're renovating this apartment?"

"Aren't you looking for a place to live?" Browning squatted back on his heels and peered at her. He told himself there was no reason he should feel it like a kick to the gut when she stared back at him like she didn't understand what he was saying. "You're opening a shop, Kit. In Jasper Creek. Or are you planning to run it from New York?"

"Of course not." She blinked, then scowled. "We're all staying in the farmhouse for the summer."

"Funny thing about seasons," Browning drawled, flashing that grin again, and again felt trapped by it. "They don't last forever."

Kit looked like she wanted to argue, but she didn't. Today she was wearing pearls and a pretty black dress—one that was not seventeen sizes too big for her body. It had cute little sleeves, a rounded neckline, and skimmed over her gently rounded belly that he could almost always now feel pressed against him, even when it wasn't. Not to mention the acres and acres of those legs of hers that he already knew felt great wrapped around his back.

Browning wanted to experiment with that position in a more horizontal fashion.

Not here, dumbass, he growled at himself. *Not now.*

She had told him loftily that she liked to take her time and had frowned at him, clearly expecting an argument. He figured he could probably change her mind, and easily, but he knew he didn't want *her* commentary on his man-whoring ways, thank you.

He concentrated instead on the elbow-length gloves she was also wearing today. Another in a long line of strange things this woman did that he should have seen as evidence of the fact she was unhinged.

Instead he thought it was cute.

Disastrously cute.

"I guess I haven't really thought much beyond the farmhouse," she said after a moment. "Everything happened so fast."

He'd finished painting the wall, so he busied himself with the mess of brushes and paint cans while she drifted further into the big room and looked around as if she was seeing it for the first time. The fireplace at one end, the big bay windows at the other, like the ones in the store below. There was a kitchen and a dining space, high ceilings, and hardwood everywhere. But what he was really focused on was that strange feeling inside him, standing there in an empty apartment with this woman because it felt a lot like they were sizing it up themselves.

A notion that would have had him running for the hills, historically.

But this was Kit.

You need to stop, he ordered himself.

He was having trouble with that. Browning was having trouble all around, as a matter of fact, and it had Kit's name written all over it.

"It's been almost a month and a half," he pointed out. "Not exactly the speed of light."

"It still seems too fast to me," she said, laughing a little as she drifted over to the bay windows and looked down at the pretty street below. The sun was setting, or thinking about it, and all the brick buildings were lit up in preparation for a long summer night. "At the end of May I had an entire life I would've told you I was happy with. *Delighted* with. New York City, interesting books to edit; everything was in its place."

"Can't have been too much in its place if you came back anyway."

She took her time turning to face him; this was happening more and more lately. That same feeling that had about taken him to his knees when he'd held her in the lake that first time, naked and connected. When they looked at each other, it was almost as if—

Stop, he ordered himself again.

"It was for Hope," Kit said softly. She was wearing her

usual compass necklace beneath the pearls and she toyed with it as she spoke. "We made a pact when we were kids that we would all come back here when we were thirty if our lives weren't going according to plan. Then Hope's wedding blew up and it was obvious we needed to uphold that pact. It felt good to be able to tell ourselves we were doing it for her. Concentrating on Hope made it easier to ignore the fact that we were all doing it for ourselves too. I know I never would have done it on my own. I'm not that brave."

A month and a half ago, Browning would've shrugged that off. He liked his life. Always had. He had fun, he liked his work, he had no complaints.

But these days he wanted things. And he wanted them now.

He wanted that house out by the lake. He wanted something more than *the usual suspects* Parker had mentioned.

He wanted a woman who looked at him like he was the only thing in the world while he was looking at her the exact same way.

A lot like this, he thought now, facing Kit across an empty room that smelled like paint and turpentine and already seemed to be full up with the life she was going to live right here.

Because she had to live right here.

Because the only woman Browning could picture any longer was her.

"I guess it's been easier not to think too far ahead," she said.

He felt that like a slap. Like she was reading his mind when he knew that though Kit Hall was good at a great many things, telepathy wasn't likely one of them.

"You might want to think about drawing up a business plan," he offered dryly. "I hear they're all the rage."

"It's a really nice apartment." She looked around again, shaking her head slightly like she was dazed. "I didn't even think about the fact that it was here and I could use it. I don't know what I was thinking, to be honest. We can't all live together in a rented farmhouse forever, can we?"

But she wasn't looking at him when she asked that. It felt like she was deliberately not looking at him.

"Kit..." Browning said quietly.

Too quietly.

It was like this too often these days, as July waned toward August. Ripe and almost painful and he was sure that this would be the time—

But down below, the bell she'd put on the shop's front door jingled. Kit jumped as if someone had slapped her.

"Oh," she breathed, while her whole body turned red. *His* red, Browning liked to call it. She cleared her throat. "I thought I locked the door."

He had a powerful urge to catch her by the waist as she brushed past him, but he didn't. Because he didn't want to seduce her. Not her. Not Kit.

He didn't want to play a game.

Browning wanted her, fully and totally. He accepted that. But most of all, he wanted her to want him in the same incapacitating, life-altering way.

He wanted that so much it hurt.

He took his time following her downstairs, washing his hands, getting a grip, then getting a better grip when the first one failed. Only when he was in control of himself again did he head down that spiral staircase that was almost laughable for a man his size. He would be better off with a ladder, he sometimes thought. Something he'd think about changing—

But he didn't have any reason to change things in this

building, he reminded himself harshly. He was lending a hand to his sister-in-law's tenant. No more, no less.

If there *was* anything more than that, he needed to view it as a happy summer gift then let it go.

Why couldn't he get that through his head?

He could hear Kit talking when he made it down into the office, though there was a strange note in her voice. He moved to the door, looking out to see Kit standing in the middle of the store.

His shelves looked fantastic, if he did say so himself, but they looked even better with all the books she'd put on them. She'd divided the shelves into different sections to honor the different romance subgenres, which she'd lectured him about extensively, and which he could now discuss fairly knowledgeably because of those adorable lectures.

But what he liked best about them was how cheerful they were—all those brightly colored covers giving the bricks and the hardwood floor a kind of glow.

Just like the books would give their readers the same glow.

That's the entire point, Kit had said, grinning widely at him, when he'd said something like that to her.

And as he was on record as liking the way *she* glowed when she was in this building, doing her thing, he noticed real quick that tonight, she wasn't.

He studied the man who stood there, taking Kit's glow away, and it took him a moment to place him. Older. Bearded, in that particularly Pacific Northwest way. And with a long-suffering look on his face.

Then it clicked, and Browning liked it even less.

It was her father.

Lawrence Hall, editor of the local paper, the valley's

greatest intellect according to himself, and all-around snob, according to Browning's mother.

It's not a question of liking or not liking Lawrence, his mother had told him when Browning had oh-so-casually brought him up after a family dinner a week or so ago. She'd given him an amused, considering sort of look, but hadn't pressed him to tell her why he was suddenly interested in the local paper's infamous editor. *It's a nonissue with someone like Lawrence. He either deigns to acknowledge you or he doesn't, but he makes the determination based on how smart he thinks you are. And he isn't shy about telling you. Imagine how I feel about that.*

Browning didn't need to imagine it. Annette West had yet to suffer a fool in the whole of her life, as far as Browning was aware. And if there was a greater fool than a man who underestimated her intelligence, *to her face*, Browning would have said he doubted such a creature could live long enough to prove it.

Yet he wasn't particularly surprised to discover that the man standing in the middle of Kit's store, clearly causing her agitation, was precisely that kind of fool.

He wasn't wearing a shroud, but he looked like one all the same. While Browning had found Kit's circus tent wardrobe entertaining, he found her father's put-upon demeanor nothing short of insulting.

Kit was waving her hands and talking excitedly about potential customers and plans, but eventually trailed off.

Browning felt every muscle in his body tense when all Lawrence did was let out a long, weary sigh.

"You should be proud of me, Dad," Kit said—bravely, Browning thought, which made him feel...edgy. "You always said this valley could use more bookstores."

"You'll have to walk me through this, Katherine," her

father said with another sigh. "Because I'm having trouble connecting the dots."

Browning stayed where he was at the office door, the name *Katherine* echoing around his head. *Like hell*, he thought.

His Kit was sleek in the water, kissed like a dream, and rubbed that body of hers all over his until he thought he might die from longing. His Kit got intense about her favorite books, waved her hands in the air when she got excited, and laughed so hard he sometimes thought she'd fall over. Someday he bet she would, and he couldn't wait to catch her.

He didn't know who *Katherine* was.

But he could guess.

"There are no dots to connect," Kit replied coolly.

"My Princeton-educated, literary-novel-editing, Manhattan-based daughter has not only returned to rural Oregon, she has a store filled with pointless trash called Happy Ever After Books, if I read that tacky pink sign correctly." Her father blinked as if he had never been confronted with such a ghastly horror in all his days. "Am I missing any of the baffling choices you've made in the past few months?"

"Dad."

"What can you possibly be thinking?"

"I'm thirty years old," she said, with an earnestness Browning didn't think her father deserved. "And I spent all these years doing what you wanted me to do. Don't get me wrong, I wanted to do them too. I really did. But I thought it might be fun to do what *I* wanted for a change."

Fun was doing something gross like spitting watermelon seeds for no good reason, *because* it was gross and for no good reason. It was not the word to describe the passion he'd seen in her when it came to her books, and it didn't sit right with him that she felt she had to downplay how she really felt for her father.

"And *this* is what you want to do?" Lawrence scoffed at her. He rubbed a hand over his face. A soft hand, Browning noted. No work on that hand that he could see, unlike his own. "I need you to tell me where I went wrong, Katherine. How could you throw away all you've achieved like this? And to what end?"

"I like romance novels, Dad." She blew out a breath. "And I'm sorry to tell you this, but Mom likes them too."

Browning tensed, because Kit did. She held herself like she'd just thrown a bomb at her father and was waiting to see what exploded.

But all her father did was sigh. Again.

"I love your mother," Lawrence replied. "But she's not a serious thinker, Katherine. She's not an intellectual and I wouldn't want her to be. I expected better from you."

"I don't have to choose between having an intellect and enjoying a book," Kit shot back.

Her father drew himself up as if he was in pain. "I suppose you don't. I suppose you can dedicate your life to frivolity and yet secretly, somewhere deep inside, maintain a fierce intellectual rigor. But how likely do you suppose that is, Kit?"

Browning saw Kit jerk at that. He didn't need Kit to walk him through her relationship with her father to understand that switching *Katherine* to *Kit* was a deliberate jab.

"I wish you could just be happy for me," Kit whispered.

Her father shook his head. "I'm not going to do that. Because I love you enough to want the best for you, as I always have. You had a big life and, for no reason that I can discern, you chose to shrink it down into this. Small and squalid, and, frankly, embarrassing."

"You don't have to shop here, then," Kit shot at him, but Browning could hear the emotion in her voice. He wanted to take Lawrence Hall apart with his hands.

He settled for coming out of the office and standing behind the counter, grinning with lethal amiability in Lawrence's direction.

"Evening," he drawled. "It's beginning to sound a little ignorant up in here, if you don't mind my saying."

Lawrence looked at Browning, then looked back at Kit. Then did something with his face that made him look as if he'd just stepped in something deeply unpleasant.

"I see," he said, in a chilling sort of tone. "I imagine this is my fault. I pushed you too hard as a child and you never rebelled then. You've chosen to rebel now, when all you're going to do is ruin your own life. *Romance novels*, I ask you. And Browning West, renowned throughout the valley for his faithless alley-catting about. You've accomplished your mission, Kit. Congratulations. I'm heartily ashamed."

Lawrence didn't look at Browning again; his judgment was clear. He merely turned and walked out of the store. The bells jingled, sounding out his departure, but he didn't slam the door. It was quiet. Awful.

And Kit was still standing there, those proud shoulders of hers slumped forward, her head bent.

Browning didn't think. He moved out from behind the counter and went to her, turning her around so he could look at her face.

So he could assess the damage. Then fix it, whatever it took.

He expected tears—and they were there, making her eyes glassy and brilliant. But her mouth was mutinous.

"Kit," he said, with an urgency he didn't entirely understand. "You have to know that everything he said—"

"You know what, Browning?" She sounded both like herself and nothing like herself at once. She sounded wild and a little bit dangerous. He felt his hair try to stand on end, and he was hard. Instantly and always, for her. "I'm tired of talking. It's time for—"

"Fun?" he supplied.

"Fun is not enough," she said, something dangerous moving over her face. "I intend to get good and frivolous. Surpassingly frivolous, until it hurts."

Then she threw herself at him, the way she always did.

He caught her, the way he always would.

And when she kissed him this time, it was fierce and it was wild. Perfect.

Browning had to think for exactly three seconds about the fact Kit clearly thought he was as *frivolous* as her daddy did, but then he kissed her back like the starving, obsessed, straight-up whipped man he was, and let her blow them both apart.

CHAPTER SEVEN

THERE WAS NO THINKING, only sensation, and it was glorious.

Browning held her easily and that made everything that much hotter.

His mouth was on hers and that was all that mattered. Not her father. Not that hollow place in her chest that Kit thought she'd long ago outgrown.

The more Browning kissed her, taking her mouth boldly and sweetly at once, the more that hollow place seemed to fill with the hot fire that crackled and burned between them.

And for the first time in her life, Kit abandoned herself completely. No overthinking. No thinking at all.

Just this beautiful man, the wildfire sensation between them, and the way her heart pounded—as if to tell her that there was nothing else on earth that mattered but this. Him.

Them.

He would wash away everything and anything that wasn't this magic between them.

And he did.

She didn't realize they were moving until he was setting her down, breaking the kiss so she could take a look around and realize that they were back in her office.

"I guess it makes sense not to give the entire town a show," she acknowledged, because that sounded like an adult, reasonable thing to say.

But the truth was that she didn't care.

"I've given the town more than enough shows in my time," Browning said, with a certain intensity that made her breath go shallow. "Tonight, Kit, it's just you and me."

"Perfect."

And when she drew his head back down, she was… different. Less desperate, in a certain sense. And in other ways, so desperate she was surprised she didn't shatter into a million pieces.

They set about stripping each other of their clothes. The ridiculous gloves and pearls she'd had to wear today because of behavior deemed too cranky this morning. Browning removed the necklace and each glove carefully, then set them all aside the same way, making something in her tremble.

Kit tugged at his T-shirt because she had a deep thirst for him now. That marvelous chest, dusted with hair and ridged in ways that made her belly flip. She couldn't seem to stop kissing him, laughing a little bit because it wasn't enough. It was never enough.

He was laughing too as they both sat up, wrestling to get closer on that couch, stripping away layer after layer until finally they were naked.

And this time, neither one of them was soaking wet.

Finally, Browning took his hands and his mouth to the whole of her body. He was somehow reverent and dirty at once, making her arch up against him. He took his time, finding his way over her curves until he could get his mouth in all that heat and need between her legs.

When Kit broke apart, crying out his name, he let her shake.

Before she came down all the way, he crawled back up

the length of her, then filled her with a deep, perfect thrust that made her break apart all over again.

Then everything got even better, because Browning began to move.

She'd wanted fast and wild, but that wasn't what he gave her.

That dark gaze of his pinned her as surely as his body did. And as he set his rhythm, everything seemed to… change.

It was flesh and heat, but it was so much more than that. As if they were held together, wrapped up so tightly in each other that it was impossible to tell which one of them was which.

Kit felt scraped raw in the most magical way, and she couldn't contain it. It raced through her like a new kind of sensation. Bigger than need or want. Brighter than joy.

Love, something in her whispered.

And she wasn't thinking, or analyzing, or any of those things she'd always considered the very heart of who she was, so there was nothing to do but pour herself back into him.

Love. Light. No matter who was who.

He was inside her, but she felt as if she was in him too.

This time, when she shattered, Browning came with her.

And Kit didn't feel awkward or uncomfortable as she slowly began to feel like herself again. Instead, she felt *more* like herself than before. Nothing to prove, nothing to hide, just the two of them tangled up in each other.

Browning lifted his head and grinned at her.

That crooked grin that was all hers. "Not bad. Let's do it again, just to make sure."

She laughed. "If you believe in yourself, I guess I do too."

But she could feel that he was already ready. She sighed

as he pulled out, then swapped out their protection, watching her watch him do it like this was a part of it.

She had to repress a shudder. "*And* you came prepared."

"I've been prepared since the day I met you, Kit," he said, and there was that thread again in his voice. The one that made her tremble all over, and got worse when she tried to stop herself.

But there was no stopping anything tonight. There was only tumbling into it, head over heels, and this time, it was fast and wild and a little bit edgy.

Kit buried her face in his neck to keep herself from screaming so loud that someone might come in off the street to investigate.

Afterward, she was so wrung out that he had to dress her. He did it with that grin on his face and too much heat in his eyes.

"I can't believe I'm going to say this," Kit said as he rolled her gloves back up her arms. "But if anything, the bathroom stall underestimated you."

"I aim to please."

Browning tugged her second glove into place, but then he kept her hand in his. He played idly with her fingers.

"You know that everything your father said to you tonight was bullshit, right?"

Kit blew out a breath, lifting her free hand to her chest because she expected that ache to come back at her.

But it didn't.

"There's no point talking about my father," she said after a stunned moment. "That's just the way he is."

"Seems to me that if you disappoint him, you should take that as a compliment."

Kit kept her gaze on their fingers. On the difference between her white-gloved hand in Browning's big, calloused male fingers. She acknowledged that the way even his fingers moved filled her with pure delight.

Even now.

"I'm not going to pretend he didn't hurt my feelings," she said softly, trying to hold on to the delight. "He always does. Normally it would send me into a dark spiral. I would analyze my entire life, trying to see how I could make it better. How I could please him. But I knew when I came back here that this would offend him on every level. He's known I was in town this whole time, and I think he waited until the store was *this close* to opening before he came in to do his rain cloud impression all over it."

"He's an idiot."

"I used to think he was the smartest man in the whole world. And I liked that he thought I was like him, not Mom." She frowned at Browning then, not wanting him to get the wrong impression. "They really do love each other. She thinks he's funny and he finds her endlessly charming and I suspect there's a physical component I don't want to think about. He saves his disappointment for me."

"Baby, the way he talks to you isn't okay."

"No," Kit agreed, and she wished Browning knew how revolutionary it was for her to say even one word against her father. To mean it. Could that have happened before she'd met him? Before he'd looked at her, grinned, and liked what he saw—everything he saw, no matter how nutty? "I've spent a lot of time making sure that he had no reason to be anything but proud of me. I figured the first interaction would be the hardest. And it has been." She smiled at him, though she felt a little more fragile than was strictly comfortable. "I'm glad you were here."

"Because I'm frivolous?" he asked, and he wasn't grinning back.

Kit felt her own smile falter. "In all the best ways."

She went to tug her hand away, but Browning didn't let go. Instead, he turned toward her, once again pinning her with that dark, ruthlessly intimate gaze of his.

"I like fun, Kit. You know this. And your dad's not wrong; I have a reputation. And maybe, just maybe, frivolous is a good enough word to describe my social life. Not one I would choose, mind you."

"It's my father's favorite put-down. It doesn't mean anything."

Browning reached over and ran his hand over her jaw. Kit couldn't tell if he was caressing her or holding her so she couldn't look away from him.

Either way, she trembled.

"It does mean something," Browning said. "To you."

Kit fought to keep the tremble from her voice. "I thought this was supposed to be fun."

"Aren't you having fun?" But his voice was rough. His gaze was dark.

"I just…"

She didn't know why she felt like crying, suddenly. There was a pounding thing inside of her that wasn't as simple as a heartbeat.

Or she did know, but her brain was working again. So she shoved it away, though this time, it was harder to do. She shoved and shoved.

"Kit," he said, not shifting that gaze from hers. "I think you know this isn't just fun."

"Browning…" She wanted to get up and run. Sitting still—staying where she was, stuck firmly in place, and so *seen*—felt violent. She couldn't bear it. "Don't."

"Too late, baby." His mouth curved. "I'm in love with you."

The words fell through her, connecting to that brutal storm inside. Making her want to howl.

Kit couldn't take it a moment longer. She pushed herself away from him. She threw herself off the couch and stumbled across the room until she made it to the office door.

And she couldn't help but look back.

Browning stayed on the couch. He lounged there, every inch of him the perfect cowboy fantasy.

All he did was watch her, but it felt like a rebuke.

"You can't." She bit off the words, hardly recognizing her own voice. "You can't love me."

"And yet here I am." He shrugged. "Still in love."

"You can't love someone you barely know. I think your brain is a little bit addled because we had sex."

"Really?" He laughed at that. Though even when he laughed, there was that particular intensity in his gaze that didn't change. "I don't think I'm addled, baby. I think you're scared."

"Don't be ridiculous."

"Ridiculous. Frivolous." He got up then, with that male grace of his that made her feel…fluttery. "My brother called me a man-whore the other day. Your father said the same, but with fancier words. But none of that matters, Kit. What do you think?"

"I… I don't know what you mean."

It was only when she realized that he was walking toward her, and she was backing up, that she stopped.

But now she was out in the main room of the shop. The lights were on and the street outside was dark, so all she could see were romance novels everywhere she looked. Love. Vulnerability. Hope and happiness.

And Browning West, moving toward her with a lazy accuracy that made her understand, maybe for the first time in her life, how easy it would be to topple right over into a full-on swoon. How preferable it would be to…this.

"I think you know exactly what I mean," Browning said quietly. "The difference between you and me is that I don't care what anybody thinks about me. But you do, don't you? You care a lot."

She tried to find her temper. She wanted desperately to ride the flare of it. "If you mean that I don't like disappointing my father, I think you'll find that's not an unusual way for a daughter to feel. Everyone has family stuff."

"Now you're frowning again. Ready to argue. Emotions are scary, right? But if you can scowl at something, chop it up into little pieces, think your way around it, that's when you really feel good. In control. Safe."

She took another step back, no longer caring if he saw her shaking. "Stop it."

"I love you, Kit," Browning told her, resolutely. "And yeah, it's fast. I've always known, my whole life, that one day I was going to meet the right woman and that would be that. I'll admit I wasn't expecting snooty Miss Princeton with her summer scarves and weird obsession with black. But here we are."

"Browning. You can't…"

Kit felt like she was having a panic attack. She couldn't think of any other explanation for the chaos happening inside of her. "Why are you doing this? Everything was fine, and fun, and now—"

"Now what?" Though he didn't get loud, or cutting the way her father did, Kit understood that the storm in her was in him too. "You think you can argue me out of my feelings, Kit? Is that how your father does it?"

"You don't understand. You don't understand *me*. You don't—"

Browning's dark eyes blazed. "I understand you perfectly. And I like every prickly, funny bit of you, Kit. I like the shrouds. I like when you frown and get into your lecturing mode. Hell, I like the lectures. I like how unafraid you are of confrontation when you can use your words to dive right in. I love that you're the kind of person who would hold on to old friends, honor a twenty-year-old pact, and when it came down to doing it, not half-ass your way through the promises you made."

He looked around the store, and opened up his hands as if he was trying to hold it—and her—between them. "I like these books. They're proof that no matter how much black you wear, how sharp and blunt you cut those bangs, how many big old vocabulary words you use, at heart you're sweet inside."

Kit felt like she was some kind of melted, sugary thing all right—and he'd left her out in the hot summer sun.

She couldn't seem to breathe.

But Browning wasn't finished. "I know what makes you smile. I know what makes you sad. I know the difference between the way you flush when you're mad and how bright red you get when you want a taste of me. Don't tell me I don't know you, Kit. I've done nothing but study you since the day we met."

The storm inside her howled, raging through her until that was all she could hear, even while his words seemed to punch through her like bullets.

"I don't want to hurt your feelings," she threw at him, though she was shuddering. And she couldn't tell if she only felt like she was crying, or if she actually was. "You've been nothing but kind to me and I love that, I do."

"Is this the part where you patronize me? The fun never ends."

"I've spent my entire life being serious about things," she hurled at him. "Deeply, deathly serious. And the store is one thing, but you—"

She had to stop, because her voice was too loud. She hardly knew if she was standing upright any longer. Everything hurt, and the worst part was that she could see she was hurting him too.

"Say it," he invited her, and broke her heart.

"Browning," she whispered. And hated herself. "You're not serious about anything. Especially not me."

Before he could respond to that—before her heart could abandon her too, before she let her sobs take over—she turned and flung herself out the front door, into the summer night.

Away from him.

Away from *love*.

Away from what she'd said to him and that look on his face.

Away before she did the stupidest thing yet, and stayed.

CHAPTER EIGHT

WHEN KIT MADE it back to the farmhouse, still in pieces, her heart sank when she saw the lights on and all her friends sitting in the living room.

It was okay, she told herself. She would sneak in, head upstairs, and avoid the inevitable grilling that would occur if her friends caught sight of her.

She took off her shoes and tiptoed up the stairs of the front porch, then eased her way in through the door. From there it would be easy enough to move quietly to the stairs, head off to shower, then hide beneath her covers for the rest of her life. Or maybe just hurry up and hide, and worry about showering later.

But as she set off for the staircase, the floorboards in the front hall, which had never made a single creaking sound since she'd arrived, suddenly burst forth in a symphony of noise, drowning out the Bing Crosby record on the Victrola in the living room.

"Stop it, house," she muttered.

In response, a book that had been sitting on the hall table seemed to catapult off for absolutely no reason and hit the floor. Loudly.

Kit swore under her breath, and froze.

But it was too late.

"Kit? Is that you?" came Hope's voice from the living room.

"It had better be Kit," Charity said dryly, "because otherwise, there's an intruder situation that we should maybe investigate. You first."

"Bite me, Charity," Hope suggested in a syrupy tone.

"It's me but I'm going upstairs," Kit called. "I need a shower."

She bent down and swept the book up, because she was constitutionally incapable of ignoring a book, even a supernatural book like this one clearly was. And when she straightened, she found herself face-to-face with Pru, who was coming out of the dining room that led into the kitchen holding a bowl she could smell from where she stood. It was homemade caramel-covered popcorn.

Her favorite. Damn it.

"Nice try," Pru said, eyeing her a little too intently. "You're not going upstairs."

Kit tried to summon her umbrage. "I'm a grown woman and I will go where I want, Prudence."

"You're a disaster, *Katherine*," Pru replied. She jerked her chin toward the living room. "Go on. Get in there."

Kit didn't bother to argue. Maybe, secretly, she was glad she'd been caught. Still, she turned dramatically and made her way into the living room, very much as if she was walking a plank. And because it made Pru roll her eyes—very nearly audibly.

Charity and Hope were sitting on the floor on either side of the huge coffee table with what looked like every board game in the house arranged in front of them.

"We can't decide what game to play," Hope said. "So we're playing them all."

Kit sniffed. "I don't really like games, so."

"You like games just fine," Charity said reprovingly. "What you don't like is losing."

"Who likes losing?" Kit demanded. "Why does everyone say that like somewhere out there, swathes of people are sitting around thinking, *what I'd really like to do tonight is lose a game that only the winners will find fun*?"

She realized she'd yelled that in a potentially unhinged manner when Hope and Charity finally looked up from the board game smorgasbord and stared at her.

"I'm fine," Kit muttered.

Beside her, Pru snickered. "Yeah, you're fine. You seem fine."

Kit surrendered. She let Pru not so subtly nudge her further into the room, then made her way over to the couch and flung herself across the cushions. Possibly like an opera heroine.

"Kit's fine," Pru announced. "Perfectly fine, as you can see. She said."

They all looked at her in a considering sort of way that made Kit feel even more aggrieved. "My father dropped by to share with me that he does not approve of the bookstore or, you know, my life."

Hope shrugged. "I thought that that was the entire purpose of the bookstore. You knew perfectly well he was never going to be happy unless you opened a chapbook stand."

"Don't be ridiculous," Kit muttered. "That's far too commercial."

Hope rolled her eyes. "A fate worse than death!"

"If Lawrence Hall approved of a romance bookstore, that would be a clear sign that the world was ending," Pru said. "He's a snob. He's always been a snob."

"I think your father always imagined a different life for himself," Charity said. With far more compassion in her tone than the other two. Kit didn't know how to feel about that, because she wasn't sure *she* wanted to feel compassionate toward her father just then. "He made you think that was the only path. And if it made you happy, that would've been great. But it didn't, did it?"

Kit sat up from her full-on opera sprawl. "I wasn't unhappy. Really. It was that I wasn't—"

"Happy." Charity arched a brow. "I know."

Kit leaned forward and grabbed a handful of the gooey, buttery caramel corn then shoved it all inelegantly into her mouth. It was sublime, as always. A couple of hours ago she would've said there was nothing on this earth that could possibly taste better than Pru's freshly made caramel corn.

But that was before she'd tasted the full glory of Browning West.

Great, she thought morosely as she chewed. *Now everything is ruined.*

"So," Pru said, biting back a smirk. "Why is your dress on inside out, Kit?"

While the other two made delighted sounds and squinted at her in a way she did not like, Kit glared balefully at Pru, taking her sweet time licking the caramel off her hand. She almost wished she hadn't peeled off her gloves in the car, or she would have thrown one at her so-called friend and possibly demanded a duel.

"Oh," she said, in the most bored New York voice she could muster. "I had sex with Browning. Twice."

"Oh my God," Hope breathed. "Please tell me he lives up to his reputation."

"He surpasses his reputation entirely." Kit found she couldn't hold on to the whole pretending-to-be-blasé thing. "Like…entirely."

Charity studied her. "Then why do you look so unhappy?"

"Because he ruined it." Kit thought her face crumpled,

maybe, and that was horrifying. But there was nothing to do about it but push on. "He told me he loved me."

"Bastard," Pru said loyally.

"I don't think Browning West runs around telling people he's in love with them," Hope pointed out carefully. Her tone suggested that Kit really did look broken. "If he did, there'd be a parade of women prancing around behind him at all times instead of sighing at him from afar."

Kit rubbed at her sad face, wishing she could regain her equilibrium. Since when had she *felt* so much? "He's confused."

"He is?" Pru tilted her head to one side. "Or you are?"

Kit scowled at her, then at Charity and Hope too, just to spread it around. She opened up her mouth to light into all of them.

But nothing came.

She was definitely broken.

"I've never known you to giggle much about a boy," Hope offered. "Browning makes you giggly. When you came home after that motorcycle ride you were silly for hours."

"You went skinny-dipping with him," Charity chimed in. "You literally peeled off your clothes and hung out with him naked. You. Who, until this summer, I would've said probably had sex in full body armor behind blackout curtains."

"No body armor," Kit muttered, while her heart careened around inside her chest in a manner she was sure had to be medically unsound. "Just, you know, always under the sheets. Like a lady."

They all hooted at that, and Kit felt herself flush. Which reminded her of what Browning had said about all the different ways she flushed and blushed.

Which made her think about the way he'd moved inside

her, his gaze so intent, like he'd been waiting his whole life for this.

For her.

She fought back a shudder.

"Your father has always made you think you're not good enough," Pru said. "And let me guess...he doesn't think much of Browning, either."

Kit opened her mouth, but again, nothing came to save her. No sharp, cutting remarks that might make her feel better. She blew out a breath instead. "He's *Browning West*. He belongs on bathroom walls. He might not have a parade marching behind him but he does nothing to stop all that sighing, either. What does he even *do* besides waft around his family's ranch and *grin* at people in bars?"

"Kit," Hope said gently. "I love you. We all love you. But you can be such a snob."

"Hey!" Kit glared at her, then at each one of them in turn, because no one was leaping to her defense. In fact, her three best friends in the entire world looked like they were...in full agreement. "We were all a lot nicer to Hope. Isn't this supposed to be some girl power thing? Aren't you supposed to grab the wine and the ice cream and shout about how amazing I am?"

"That's when someone hurts you," Charity said apologetically. "I don't think having someone tell you he's in love with you—something you should've already known because since when does *Browning West* hang around *doing chores* and *reading romance novels* when he could be notching up his bedpost—counts as him being mean to you."

"Tough love doesn't come with ice cream, Kit." Pru shrugged. "I don't make the rules."

Kit scowled at her. "You make a lot of rules, actually, *Prudence.*"

"We all know the kind of man you imagined you were going to end up with," Hope said. She started counting on her fingers. "Smart. Educated. Possibly in possession of his own hidebound volumes of careful, finely-wrought, handwritten poetry."

Kit swallowed, hard. "That is worryingly specific."

"Because that's what you wrote down every time we decided to make lists of our future husbands' attributes," Pru reminded her. "Every time, Kit. But if you wanted that guy, I feel like they must have been thick on the ground back East."

"You came home instead," Charity pointed out. "Where there's only one person around who really meets that description, and the truth is, Kit, he's not very nice to you."

It was amazing how much that hurt when Kit knew it was true. Hadn't her father proved it tonight?

"Browning, on the other hand, gets you to ride motorcycles. And loves what you do. And looks at all of this—" Hope waved her hand *at* Kit, "all of you, all of what makes you *Kit,* and likes it."

"Have you all been discussing this?" Kit demanded, outraged.

Or maybe she only wished she was outraged. That would be far better than being called out because she was terribly afraid they were right.

"Obviously we've been discussing it." Charity reached for the popcorn bowl, sounding deeply unconcerned with this betrayal. "Literally every second you're not in the room. You're welcome."

"Great," Kit said miserably. "I'm a snob. My friends hate me. I don't know my own mind and—"

"Do you love him?" Pru asked, in her matter-of-fact, direct way. "Because if you don't, that's that. But if you do…"

Kit looked at each of her best friends in turn, and then, miserably, looked away. She couldn't tell what was happening to her. She was too hot. She thought maybe she was crying. Then she knew she was when a tear splashed down on her hand as she stared down at her lap much too fiercely.

Much too desperately.

And her friends left her to it. They settled around the fifteen board games on the table and launched back into what must have been the mostly good-natured argument they'd been having before she arrived. The Victrola played on.

Kit shifted her position then realized she was still holding that book that had betrayed her in the hallway. She picked it up to squint at the cover but it fell open.

Whoever had read this book before—a big, thick romance novel, if she wasn't mistaken, and when it came to romance novels she was never mistaken—had underlined a sentence on the page.

How can you love another person if you're not sure whether or not you love yourself?

It was that sentence that haunted her when she finally left the living room and went upstairs. She stood in the shower, the line still echoing in her head. Then she lay awake in the darling little room that had been hers all summer. She pulled the patchwork quilt up to her chin, though it made her too warm, and stared at the whitewashed ceiling, waiting to sleep.

But she didn't.

The next morning, she woke up after maybe fifteen minutes of sleep, grumped her way through coffee, and somehow managed to escape the house without having to pull three or four slips as rightful punishment. She suspected that was her friends' version of the wine and ice cream they hadn't offered her last night. And as she busied herself with the store inventory, she found herself waiting for Browning in a wild mix of anticipation and apprehension.

But he didn't come.

He didn't come and it made her feel hollow.

She walked to her parents' house a few blocks over at lunchtime, smiling when she saw her mother where she always was on warm summer afternoons—out on the front porch in the swing, reading a romance novel with a cover as bright as the hanging baskets overflowing with geraniums.

"You look glum," her mother said, without appearing to glance in her direction.

It was mama magic, and Kit loved it.

She sank down next to her mother on the wide seat then she laid her head on her mother's shoulder like she was still ten. They sat like that for a long while as the summer wore on all around them. The birds made a racket in the trees all around the tidy little house where Kit had grown up. She'd played in this yard, and could almost feel the grass beneath her feet. She'd tried to capture tree frogs, had helped her mother in the vegetable garden, and had built secret forts with her friends beneath the porch.

"Mom," she said when she felt a bit steadier, "why does it sound like someone's banging around out back?"

"That's your father," her mother said. "I've invited him to move into that shed he made into a man cave a few years ago."

"I thought that was his office."

"Some men have fishing lures or power tools. Your father has his poetry. But still, a man cave is a man cave."

Kit sat up. "Wait. Like *moving out*, moving?"

Judy Hall smiled serenely. "I've invited him to spend the

rest of the summer ruminating on his behavior. And I used big words so he'd be certain to understand me. If he can't read enough from my romance collection to conduct himself appropriately in romance bookstores, he can stay out there forever. Between you and me, it gets cold in winter."

Of all the things her mother might have said, Kit had not expected…that. "This wouldn't have anything to do with his visit to me last night, would it?"

"It has everything to do with that visit," her mother said, her expression suddenly fierce. "I didn't mind your father pushing you as long as it was what you wanted too. And how could any parent not be bursting with pride at all you've accomplished? If you wanted to wander barefoot through that desert in Nevada for the next ten years—"

"Do you mean Burning Man?" Kit blinked. "How have you even *heard* of Burning Man? And also…no."

"My point is, whatever you choose to do with your life makes me happy, Kit." Her mother sighed, but not in the way her husband did. "You know I love your father. I love the arcane things that come out of his mouth, the funny things he thinks and does that no one else ever thinks or does. I love his poetry and those chapbooks and how deeply he cares about his journalistic integrity in this sleepy valley. There isn't a single part of him I don't love." Her blue eyes flashed. "But if he can't support my daughter, he can sleep in the shed."

Kit wiped her suddenly damp eyes, and smiled at her mother. Judy wrapped her arm around Kit's shoulders and for a moment, they stayed that way.

Eventually, Kit took a shaky breath. "You really think he'll stay out there until winter?"

Her mother cackled, a knowing sort of look on her face.

"He won't last a week. Believe me. You can look forward to an apology in about two days."

When Kit opened her mouth to ask her mother how she knew that, she stopped herself. Because she understood that look on her mother's face; it was just wicked enough. She knew that she really, really did not want to hear her mother's answer.

"I don't read romance novels to escape my marriage," Judy said, her gaze gleaming. "I read them to help celebrate it."

"I support that," Kit said. "And also, please do not say another word."

"You come from a happy marriage between two people who've loved each other a long time and plan to keep on loving each other forever, sweetheart," her mother said with a certain intensity that spoke of more of that mama magic. "Your father dreamed of Ivy League schools and prominent jobs, but I don't care about that. I have only one expectation of you. That you never, ever settle for anything less."

Kit walked back to the store, her head spinning and her heart making a nuisance of itself. When she got there, she stood out in front for a moment. She looked down the row of brick buildings that were dreams she and her friends had made real.

Dreams they'd built on the strength of their friendship, together.

The Jasper Creek Centennial was still a couple of weeks away. But as far as she could tell, they'd already done it: all four of them, back in Jasper Creek and committed to this madness they were all making work.

She lifted a hand to hold the compass that hung around her neck and always would. From Seattle, California, Chicago, and New York. From dating slips to house rules to making these abandoned shopfronts their own. Whatever road the four of them took, it always led them home.

Because they'd made themselves their first, best home long ago.

"What are you doing?" Hope asked, coming up beside her. She squinted at her own shop, handing Kit a lemon bar from the bag she was carrying. Because of course she was carrying a bag of lemon bars. Kit took hers immediately. "Are you having second thoughts about this thing we're doing?"

"Not a single one," Kit said.

And she meant it.

Pru appeared in the open window of her feed store. "Are we loitering on the sidewalks today? Because some of us have work."

"Oh," Charity said, flinging open the door to the knitting shop. "I was hoping you were the delivery guy. I have a big yarn shipment coming."

"Are those lemon bars?" Pru demanded. "Why does Kit get one?"

Hope smiled. "I was going to give you one, Prudence, but I don't like your attitude."

"Does that mean I get hers?" Charity asked brightly.

"You guys," Kit said. She smiled wide, and not because she'd stuffed that lemon bar in her face and was now riding a sugar high. Or not entirely because of that. "You realize… this is our life now."

"Ew, Kit," Pru said, though she was grinning. "Too sentimental. Too earnest."

She moved back from her window. Charity shook her head, looking up at the sign on the front of her shop, with that folksy Z they were all getting used to. Or trying to get used to.

Hope slung an arm around Kit's shoulders and grinned.

But when Hope and Charity went back inside, Kit stayed where she was.

Her mind was still spinning, her heart was still a riot, and she was beginning to understand that neither was a bad thing.

Quite the opposite.

"You're *supposed* to feel things," she muttered at herself.

Then she had to smile mildly at Mrs. Kim, who was passing by and looked rightly suspicious of the weird woman talking to herself in the street.

And then, following an urge that seemed to sing out from deep inside her, she didn't go inside the bookstore.

Instead, Kit got in her car, and headed for the West ranch.

And Browning, at last.

CHAPTER NINE

BROWNING HAD JUST finished pounding the life out of the fence post he was replacing when he heard a vehicle approaching.

He didn't even look because he was sure it was one of his brothers, and he wasn't in the mood.

Epically not in the mood, in fact—something they'd all noticed earlier this morning and had piled on him anyway. Because that was the West brothers' way. He'd left them all back at the barn and had headed out into the great, wide spaces of the far pastures where he could nurse his battered heart at his leisure.

And without any brotherly mockery.

He heard a door slam and waited until whoever it was had walked up behind him.

"Not in the mood," he growled. "Thought I made that clear."

"That's not what it said on the bathroom wall," came the reply.

Kit.

Kit! something in him roared.

Browning had been working on a pretty decent helping of righteous indignation since she'd run out of her shop and left him there last night. It had beat at him all along his drive home. It had kept him company while he nursed his feelings over a bottle of whiskey in his bunkhouse.

It had not in any way helped his hangover.

He threw his tools to the ground, took his time straightening, and then he turned to get an eyeful of her.

She didn't wear shrouds any longer. Today she was wearing a pair of cutoffs that made his brain short-circuit and a tank top that made him want nothing more than to take it off to see whether or not she was wearing anything beneath it. Her dark hair was swept up into a knot on the back of her head and her sunglasses took up most of her face—pretty much everything but that sulky mouth that he had no hope of getting over.

"You've got a lot of nerve," he observed with as much drawl as he could manage in the face of such provocation. "What did you come here for, Kit? Do you want to shove the knife in a little bit deeper?"

He expected her to flinch. To go pale and fluttery.

But this was Kit. She showed no particular reaction, because of course she didn't. Until, as he watched, one brow arched.

Why did he find that almost unbearably sexy?

"I came to apologize," she said in that deliciously snotty way of hers that made him want to eat her alive. "But I certainly don't have to if you'd rather brood at me."

Browning had actually never experienced something like this before. He was usually the one extricating himself. The one navigating the land mines of someone else's feelings.

He had no idea how to handle himself.

"I told you I loved you, Kit," he gritted out. "And you told me I was basically nothing but an airhead, then ran away."

She still kept looking at him with that poker face. "I can't deny it."

Browning felt like growling. So he did. "If you're going

to stand here and get your intellect all over me, at least take off your sunglasses."

"What? It's the middle of summer. The sun will blind me."

"Off," he commanded.

Her scowl intensified.

And sure enough, he loved that too. It was beginning to irritate him.

Kit lifted up a languid hand to slide her sunglasses back onto her head, and confirmed everything Browning already thought.

Those faded blue-jean eyes of hers made him feel like melting.

"Satisfied?" she asked.

"Not yet."

He wanted to put his hands on her—maybe he always would—but he didn't. Because he had no intention of making this easy for her. The way he'd made everything easy for her.

The way you intend to always make things easier for her, a voice inside him said.

But not today.

He crossed his arms, arched his own brows, and waited.

Kit cleared her throat. "Well. Like I said, I wanted to apologize."

Then she waited, like that would do it. He could see her expression get hopeful and he let out a bark of laughter.

"What sucks for you, baby, is that you made me read all those romance novels. And if you think you're getting away with a few stilted words when we both know it's time for a big old speech, forget it." He tried to fight his grin and failed. "I want a little groveling."

That was when she turned his favorite shade of red.

"You can't really think…"

"I'm not kidding, Kit."

She floundered. He watched her mouth open, then close. She was bright red and maybe a little bit miserable, and she should be.

He waited.

"I'm sorry," she said, fast, like the words left marks on the way out. "You scared me, Browning. All those things you said to me. You *see* me, when no one else ever has. No one but my friends. They accept me and tease me in equal measure and it never crossed my mind that a man could possibly *like* me like that. Much less love me, at all." She blew out a shaky breath. "It's been pointed out to me, by three people who love me enough to tell me the truth, that I'm a terrible snob when I want to be. Just like my father."

Browning frowned at that. "Let's not get carried away."

But she rushed on. "I hate that he said terrible things to you and not only did I not defend you, I piled on…when I don't even think it's true. Because I know you too."

Kit moved closer then. She reached out her hands so she could put them on his arms, carefully. And when he didn't jerk away, she curved her palms over his forearms so she was holding on to him.

Just like that, everything was better, but Browning didn't crack.

Not yet.

She tipped back her head, and there was no trace of a smile on her face then. Not even a scowl.

There was only…this.

Them.

And the pounding of his own heart, so deep and loud that Browning thought he should use it in place of a hammer on the next fence he touched.

"You showed me so much more than a lake in the place where we're going to build a house someday," Kit said solemnly. "You pretended it wasn't serious, but it was. I knew it then, and I pretended I thought it was nothing but fun. I knew better, Browning. It was your heart."

He hadn't realized she was going to kill him.

It was only his pride that kept him on his feet.

"I bruised it," she whispered. "And the only reason I did that was because I was scared. How could you be everything I wanted? How could you handle all the silly challenges I had to do with my friends—hatboxes and too much laughing and *opera gloves*, for God's sake—the same way you held me in the water? The same way you kissed me. Like you could do it forever?"

"Because I could," he said. He meant he would, but he bit that back.

He was going to have to ask for more details about her "challenges" later because for now she was still talking.

"Everybody knows the legend of Browning West," Kit said, her gaze and her voice intense. "But they don't know you. How kind you are. How sharp. Smart enough to play dumb and not interested in proving yourself to anyone. You know what you want and you get it, don't you? Always."

"Don't go telling everyone, baby." He was cracked into pieces, but he liked it. There was so much more sunlight that way, like summer was right here, between them and in them. "They like their legends to stay the way they left them."

"You've taken care of me since the moment we laid eyes on each other, when I was sure I didn't need anyone to do anything of the kind. You make me laugh. You make me cry. You make me want all the things I was trying to tell myself weren't practical, and you make me believe we can do it. And will."

"We will," Browning managed to say. "I promise."

"I don't know how to ask you to forgive me," Kit whispered. "But I will never, ever fail to stand up for you again. I swear it."

"It's already done. I forgave you before you showed up here today. It's kind of irritating, if you want to know the truth, how little I want to stay mad at you."

He went to pull her closer, but she stopped him.

"No." Her gaze was solemn. "I think it's going to take a long, long time to adequately apologize, Browning. I said you weren't serious—"

"Kit." He tugged his arms free and brought her close, looking down into her perfect face. The face that haunted him even when he was looking straight at her. He hoped it always would. "I can be unserious about a great many things, but you? I'm never going to be anything but serious about you."

She smiled then, wild and heartbreaking and beautiful.

Kit was all of those things and so much more.

But most of all, she was his.

"I'm going to make it up to you," she said. "I'm committed to it. And you know me. When I put my mind to something, nothing can stop me."

He smiled back, slow and sure. "About how long are you thinking?"

And as he asked, he felt the world shift around them. Not an earthquake, but more of a *becoming*, because this was how it was going to be. They were going to live in that apartment over her shop that he'd been fixing up like he'd known it was theirs all along. Then he was going to build them a house, and they were going to live there together, looking out over that lake where they'd found each other.

It was like he could see it all laid out before him.

She was going to have his babies. They were going to raise them up together and have each other while they did it. There would be more laughter than tears, if he had anything to say about it. He'd even win over her father if it took him the rest of his life. She would do the same with his mother, because Annette wouldn't see Kit coming.

Sometimes they were going to hurt each other, mostly they would love each other, but it would always come back to this.

To them.

The beginning and the end of everything.

"I'm thinking, to start off, a lifetime," she said, smiling wide. "Just as long as you forgive me."

"Always," he drawled. "We can start by moving into that apartment. Labor Day?"

"Don't be ridiculous." Kit sniffed. "I'm not *moving in* with someone three months after we start dating."

"Halloween, then."

"How is that better?"

"Thanksgiving," Browning said. "But that's my final offer."

"I love you, but I am not going to—"

"Stop," he told her. "Say that again."

Kit was scowling, of course. She blinked, then her face smoothed out, tipping right over into a big, bright smile. "Didn't I mention that part?"

"You did not."

She looped her arms around his neck and arched herself into him. They both sighed at the contact.

"I love you, Browning West," she said, her gaze on his.

Her smile went a little giddy, though he could see she was trying to get that scowl back. "But I am absolutely not moving in with you until the New Year."

"I love you too," he told her, because that was the way a good happily-ever-after worked.

And then he showed her, right there in the sweet grass, that happily ever after was only the beginning.

* * * * *

HOW TO HOLD HIM

Jackie Ashenden

To my yarn stash, which has been the brightest, most joyous thing in the whole of this 2020 nightmare.

CHAPTER ONE

Charity's Story

CHARITY GOLDING STOOD outside the vintage brick storefront of Jasper Creek's old yarn store and contemplated the name for a moment, frowning. Knitting and Thingz.

It was a bit…old-fashioned, especially with the *z* at the end of *things*. Just like the store itself in many ways. A bit musty. A bit dusty. Lots of doilies. Nothing that would appeal to a younger crowd, which was a mistake given how lots of younger people were getting into handmade crafts. Yet it was perfect all the same.

She'd used to come in here when she'd been a teenager, overwhelmed by the pressure of needing outstanding grades so she could get into med school. She hadn't known how to knit or crochet, or even sew on a button, and though part of her had been attracted to the thought of learning a new craft as a stress reliever, she hadn't quite mustered up the will to try.

School had been hard enough to cope with and the thought of learning something new had brought its own stress, and so she'd contented herself with just standing in the store and looking at the brightly colored yarn. That had been enough to make that horrible choking sensation go away.

After the disaster of Hope's canceled wedding, Charity,

Pru, and Kit had been desperate to help their friend, and so she'd suggested that the four of them spend the summer doing up the four vacant shops in Jasper Creek. It had always been a place of peace for her, so Charity had really hoped that none of them would choose the yarn store.

She hadn't told the others, but in the last few stressful months of work, she'd been thinking about that yarn store more and more. And when her father had finally decided on a move to Florida, and she'd helped him pack up and leave, she'd found herself driving past the store and stopping. And just…looking at it. Wondering what her life would have been like if she'd stayed in Jasper Creek and opened up a store just like it. Whether things would have been different if she had. Whether she would have been happier.

Hope's wedding being canceled had certainly been awful, but it had given Charity a moment of clarity. She could turn that awfulness into something better, into something positive, and since they'd all once dreamed of opening stores on Jasper Creek's main street, why shouldn't they make that dream a reality?

Certainly this was her moment to get a taste of what life would have been like if she'd stayed. If she hadn't gone into medicine to make her father happy. If she'd stayed put in Jasper Creek, and opened up a yarn store, and filled her days with fiber instead of the shouting, screaming chaos that was a hospital ER.

Well, now she could. This was her chance.

She almost gave herself a little hug right there in the street, but managed to stop just in time. No reason to get carried away. She wasn't going to be quitting medicine for good. This was just a…small reprieve rather than a big life change. A couple of months of stress leave and then she'd be back in the usual grind in the hospital in Seattle.

But until then she could enjoy some time in a small, peaceful place, making decisions that weren't life or death, where the most challenging thing was going to be rehabilitating the old yarn store in time for Jasper Creek's centennial celebrations in a few months.

And the first thing to be rehabilitated was the name. That was definitely going to change.

She reached into the pocket of her jeans for her phone to add *change store name* to the store to-do list and then muttered a curse when she found the pocket empty.

Dammit. She didn't have her phone. The annoyance lasted only a second though, since it had been her idea for them all to be without their phones for the entire three months they were in Jasper Creek. She'd thought it would be good for them not to be distracted by calls and texts and emails, and to do things the "old-fashioned way." Certainly if she wanted to de-stress herself then not having her phone had to be a part of it. She didn't want any calls from her colleagues or from the hospital, and the constant buzzing of text messages and notifications kept her on edge, making her feel like she was constantly on call.

No, she was glad she didn't have it with her, and she'd been fine when Pru had taken the whole phone thing one step further, as she always did—they didn't call Pru's little storms Pru-ricanes for nothing—and made everyone put their phones in the safe in the shared basement below the shops.

That was where her phone was now, in the safe in the basement with all its many to-do lists, reminders, and all her preset alarms.

Charity dismissed the slight anxiety that the thought of her phone brought her, and reached into her back pocket for the pretty notebook she'd bought herself from the cute little bookshop along Jasper Creek's main street the day she'd arrived, along with the lovely pen that matched it. She scribbled down *change store name* on the clean white pages, then made a mental note to tell Kit that she should sell nice stationery in the bookstore she was rehabilitating, then tucked both pen and notebook back into her pocket once more.

Getting out her key, she unlocked the front door of the yarn store and stepped inside.

Definitely dusty and a bit musty, and the carpet on the floor was worn and old. Most of the yarn and other store stock that had once been there was gone, but there were boxes here and there on dark wooden shelves that lined the walls as well as old needlework samplers, a few shawls on hangers, some lacy doilies, and a few old-fashioned baby matinee jackets tacked to the dark, gloomy walls themselves.

It was the same as she remembered—the antithesis of stress and pressure—and for that reason alone, she loved it.

She'd been in Jasper Creek a month already—she'd wanted a bit of downtime before she started the project properly—and had been into the store a couple of times to take a look around. But most of June had been spent with her laptop in the old farmhouse she was staying in with the others, browsing different yarn stores around the country, seeing how they were set up. Research was always her first step when taking on something new, especially a new business proposition, and this was no different.

However, now it was July and Jasper Creek had just celebrated the Fourth with a picnic. It was time for Charity to get stuck into the hard work of actually getting the shop ready.

She pulled out her notebook again, taking a look at the

ideas she'd jotted down about a store spruce-up. She would definitely lighten up the walls and the shelves, and rip up the old carpet to expose the wooden boards underneath. She'd thought paring everything back and going simple would look good given the old brick and glass of the storefront. A light, airy space painted white to show off bright yarn colors and knitted pieces was definitely the way to go. Then again, it could be a bit antiseptic and she didn't want the place looking like a hospital.

Ugh. No, definitely *not* like a hospital. She wanted no reminders of the ER while she was here, that was for sure. What she wanted was yarn and lots of it.

"Hey," a deep, very male voice said from behind her. "Are you the new owner?"

Charity froze for a second, then turned around sharply.

A man stood in the doorway of the store, very tall, very broad, almost filling it. Worn jeans and a faded dark blue T-shirt. Boots and a black cowboy hat. Thick, short black hair, glossy as spilled ink. And eyes the color of a new minted silver coin. They stood out in his handsome tanned face—so bright, couldn't miss 'em.

Couldn't forget, either, those hard, beautifully carved features she'd sat across from at the kitchen table in the little house attached to her dad's medical office every Tuesday after school. A face she'd tried not to stare longingly at as she'd helped him with his homework. A presence she'd missed with all her teenage heart when he'd subsequently dropped out of school and disappeared off the face of the planet.

All the girls had swooned after Browning West, but Charity had only had eyes for Garrett Roy, the baddest boy in school.

He'd been all brooding and hot, with a tragic backstory

to match. His mother had run off when he was six, then he'd lost his father, a famous bull rider, in an accident when he was ten. He'd been brought up by his grandmother and even though Charity had no memories of her own mother, who'd died when she was a baby, she still liked to imagine the loss gave her a certain…kinship with him.

She felt that same kinship now, despite all the years that had passed. That stupid heart of hers gave a little leap, because apparently it was still seventeen and in love with a boy it could never have.

"Garrett," she heard herself say breathlessly, the way she used to do whenever he arrived for their weekly tutor sessions. "Oh my God, it's you."

And then immediately she wished she hadn't spoken, because she wasn't that breathless seventeen-year-old anymore, but a hardened ER doc who dealt with emergencies on a day-to-day basis, and whose job depended on her ability to remain calm and in control.

It was too late now, though, and to make matters even worse, she was grinning like a lunatic and clutching her special compass necklace for luck, while he betrayed exactly zero recognition, shoving his hands in his pockets and eyeing her instead.

Perhaps he didn't remember her, which would come as no surprise. He hadn't wanted to be tutored by her and he'd made that obvious every minute of their time together.

Charity dialed back on her smile, turning it cool, and took a step toward him, letting go of her necklace and holding out her hand. "Sorry, I know it's been a while. I'm Charity Go—"

"I know," he interrupted. He did not take her hand.

Charity lowered hers, surprise that he'd remembered

her only just edging out her awkwardness at holding out a hand he hadn't wanted to take. "You do?"

"Sure." His gaze was sharp and very level. "Every Tuesday. Math and English."

She blinked, shaken for some reason. "Oh," she said, because she couldn't think of anything else to say.

"Look, I won't beat around the bush," Garrett said in that same abrupt way. "I got word that you'd bought the lease on this store so I wanted to come and check it out. This place used to be owned by Emmeline Roy, my grandma, and I want to know what kind of plans you have for it."

Charity opened her mouth. Then shut it.

Garrett had never been friendly toward her, and it seemed like that hadn't changed. He'd never been rude, but she'd always had the impression that he didn't like her much. It had wounded her back then because of the crush she'd had on him, and she'd never understood what she'd done to earn that dislike.

She'd thought it might have had something to do with one Saturday afternoon when she'd made a visit to the yarn store and she'd seen him working behind the counter. Instead of his usual scowl, he'd been smiling at one elderly lady and chatting to her about something, and that smile of his had lit a fire in her heart that had never gone out.

She still had no idea why. But she'd thought that if he smiled at her like that one day then she'd die happy.

Of course, then he'd realized that she was in the store and watching him, and that scowl had returned with a vengeance. As if she'd caught him doing something he hadn't wanted her to see.

She'd got it—the town bad boy being caught in the yarn store being nice to old ladies wouldn't exactly do wonders for his cred. But still. Seeing him smile wasn't a heinous crime, was it?

Anyway, right now his deep voice didn't sound overtly confrontational, but there was a definite...edge to it. And that glitter in his gray eyes was just as friendly as it had been all those years ago—in other words, not at all.

What was his problem? Was it the fact that she was the owner? Or was he just worried she might do something awful to his grandma's shop?

Whatever it was, it was clear that reminiscing for old time's sake was not going to be happening.

Charity kept her professional smile tacked firmly in place and told herself she wasn't disappointed about that in the slightest. "Oh, I'm still thinking about the details, but I plan to keep this going as a yarn store, so don't worry."

"I'm not worried." His gaze had narrowed even further to slits of brilliant silver, suspicion radiating from him. "Grandma passed a couple of years ago, but she owned this place a long time and it was pretty much an institution. People would not be happy if you decided, say, to open a clothing store instead."

"I'm sorry to hear that," Charity said sympathetically. She hadn't known Emmeline, but Garrett must have been close to her. "That would have been very hard."

He stared at her, his expression enigmatic. "Well?" he asked, not acknowledging her sympathy one iota. "What are you planning on doing with the place?"

Okay, so he'd lost his grandma, and that had to be rough. But still, his manner could use some work. Especially when she'd been perfectly pleasant. What had she ever done to him except help him with his homework?

She was tempted to tell him she was going to turn it into a nightclub, just to see if that stony expression on his handsome face would change, but it certainly wouldn't help matters.

"Well," she said, holding tight to her usual calm. "All I'm planning on doing is refreshing the interior—painting the walls and ripping up the carpet, polishing the floorboards and giving them a coat of varnish. Then I'll get some new stock in." She gave him her best "I'm a doctor and I'm here to help" smile. "Honestly, the only thing I'm going to change is the name."

SHE WAS ABSOLUTELY not going to change the name.

Garrett stared at the woman standing in front of him, shock still reverberating through him. He knew he was being unfriendly and difficult, and he didn't give a damn.

"You are not changing the name," he said.

Charity Golding, the daughter of the town's doctor and the girl who'd once haunted his dreams back when he'd been a senior in high school, kept that calm and vaguely patronizing smile on her face. "Oh, don't worry, I've got a really lovely alternative. It's—"

"You're not changing it." He could hear the flat note in his voice, knew he was being a dick, but he couldn't seem to help himself.

His morning had started out badly with yet another phone call from his uncle trying to manipulate him into selling the ranch, only for things to get worse when he'd arrived in town and realized he'd left his wallet at home, which meant he couldn't buy the fencing materials he'd come into town to get. Then it had descended into extensively crappy with the discovery that the new owner of the yarn store—which he'd decided to poke his head into just out of interest—was not only Charity Golding, but she was also going to change the name of a business that his grandma had poured the last thirty years of her life into.

Charity Golding, who just happened to be as cute and sexy as she'd been thirteen years ago, all bouncing red curls, adorable freckles, eyes the same color as the delphiniums that his grandma kept in a vase on the kitchen table, and a body curvy enough to fuel a man's fantasies for an entire month of Sundays.

That body was outlined now in a pair of tight-fitting faded jeans and a loose cotton blouse almost the same shade as her eyes, and he was *not* happy about the way his blood pumped a little harder at the sight of her. Not happy at all.

He'd put her and the ridiculous crush he'd had on her firmly behind him the day he'd dropped out of school. And that had been years ago, for God's sake. He should not be getting all worked up now and the fact that he was, was just damn irritating.

He'd spent years as a bull rider traveling the circuit, getting high on adrenaline, fame, money, and all the women who'd thrown themselves at him. Until he'd given it all up to take care of his grandmother. And he hadn't looked back, not even once. He'd stuck to ranching, unlike his old man. He'd kept his eyes on the straight and narrow, which did not include one pretty redhead he still had the hots for.

And most especially not when said pretty redhead was changing the name of the yarn store.

It was a little thing, maybe, and in the normal scheme of things he might have let it go. But he was in a bad mood and his gran had loved the store, and he was absolutely not going to stand for it.

Charity opened her lovely rosebud mouth. Closed it. Smiled. Then raised her hands in a calming gesture. "I hear you. And I'm open to discussion."

Garrett had never been a fan of being placated and he got the feeling that she was placating him now. It irritated the hell out of him.

"Here is the discussion," he said. "The name stays."

A crease appeared between her brows and she tilted her head, examining him carefully as if he was an unexploded bomb that might go off at any second. "It means a lot to you, doesn't it?"

Since leaving the circuit and coming back to Jasper Creek, Garrett had put his past behind him, but there were still people around who muttered that he had too much of his father's wild streak to settle into ranching. He'd worked hard to stop those mutters by keeping his head down and his eyes forward, and not letting himself get riled.

But Charity's soothing tone got under his skin like poison ivy, making him itch.

He tried to ignore it.

"My grandpa named the store," he said, keeping his tone hard and flat. "Gran loved it. It was a memorial to him and you can't just change it on a whim."

The crease between Charity's brows deepened. "Okay, I get that it's important. But I'm not changing it on a whim. I put a lot of thought into the new name."

"I don't care how much thought you put into it. Knitting and Thingz is what it's called and it's staying."

"Well," Charity said with a patience that was starting to grate, "with all due respect, it's a little old-fashioned, don't you think? Plus, it would be good to have a clear distinction between the past owner and the new one." She smiled again. "The new name isn't quite as...obvious."

If he'd been in a better mood, he might have found her smile adorable. Now, it was patronizing. "Obvious is good. Obvious tells you exactly what the store is about."

"Sure and I totally agree. But I wanted something more evocative."

"Evocative?" he echoed. "'Knitting' is evocative. And so is 'things.'"

"Things with a *z*." Her smile held gentle amusement.

She wasn't making fun of it, he got that, but right now he wasn't in a place for gentle amusement. Not with her standing there, her blue eyes sparkling the way they had all those years ago when she'd had to explain a math problem to him and was trying to get him interested. And all he'd been interested in was the way her breasts pushed against her T-shirt and how her eyes were so blue they didn't seem real.

They still didn't. And her breasts were still just as distracting as they had been when she was seventeen.

"There's nothing wrong with a *z*," he growled, really starting to get annoyed now, both with himself and her. "Grandpa was specific about the *z*. He said it added a point of interest."

Charity examined him once again in that careful way, which in turn only worsened his annoyance. It didn't help being very aware that his gran would have been appalled at his grumpy behavior. She'd always been a stickler for manners.

"I'm sorry," Charity said with what looked like absolute sincerity. "I shouldn't have said that. But do you want to hear my alternative?"

"No."

She ignored him. "I was thinking of calling it A Simple Thread."

"A Simple Thread," he repeated, wanting to hate it and being even more irritated that he didn't. "What's that evocative of? Not knitting."

"It does indicate yarn, though."

"The store was about more than just yarn. There were… things too." Great. Now not only did he sound incredibly rude, he also sounded like a complete idiot.

Charity opened her mouth, no doubt to say something calming and placating again, but he was done. He had to get out of there before he said something really stupid.

"You're not changing it," he said. "And that's my last word."

Then, before she could respond, he turned around and walked out.

CHAPTER TWO

CHARITY CARRIED A tray of drinks into the living room of the sweet old Jasper Creek farmhouse that she, Hope, Pru, and Kit had rented for the summer, trying to keep a lid on the irritation that had been simmering inside her all day.

It was time for their weekly meeting, where they shared their progress on their collective store rehabilitation projects. She was debating whether or not to complain about Garrett Roy and his extremely irritating objections to her changing the name of the yarn store.

On balance, and considering that though his manner could have used some work his objections were completely fair, she decided she wouldn't complain. It seemed petty.

Not to mention that it's not really his objections that you find so annoying.

That was true. It was his hotness that had really annoyed her. That was the problem. He was all tall, dark, and muscular, filling the yarn store with a raw, masculine energy that had made her breathless and giddy.

And it had seemed that the calmer and more soothing she was, the more that energy radiated from him. It had been kind of addictive, if she was honest…as if some part of her had liked making him angry, which couldn't be true, surely. Not when she hated conflict. Still, that had been better than the complete indifference he'd shown her years ago, even though she really wasn't supposed to care about that now.

"So how's the yarn store going?" Kit asked as Charity put the tray of mojitos, made with mint from the farmhouse's herb garden, down on the coffee table.

"It's fine." She sat down in the armchair near the fireplace. "I just didn't realize that knitting could be so fraught."

"Fraught?" Kit raised a brow as she reached for a mojito. "How?"

Charity was annoyed with herself. Why had she said that? She hadn't been going to mention him. "Oh, nothing." She pasted a smile on, waiting until Pru and Hope had taken their drinks before she reached for hers. "Just, you know, the usual…yarn difficulties."

"What usual yarn difficulties?" Pru asked, leaning back against the couch next to Kit. "Is there something problematic about wool?"

"No." Charity sipped on her drink, trying to think of something to say that wouldn't prompt a whole lot of questions. "I just…had a visit from Garrett Roy. Remember him?"

"Oooh, the bad boy you used to tutor and who you had a giant crush on?" Hope looked at her with big eyes. "That Garrett Roy?"

Charity could feel her cheeks getting hot, which was extremely annoying. "I did not have a crush on him."

"Sure you did," Kit said, looking elegant and delicate in her usual black. "It was a well-known fact."

Calm. Be calm.

Charity ignored the whole crush discussion. "Whatever. He came into the store today to tell me he didn't like the new name and he didn't want me changing the old one."

"Huh." Pru took another meditative sip of her drink. "Why not? I thought the name was great."

"So did I," Kit agreed.

"Ditto," Hope offered.

Charity had told them her plans for the new name the day before and she knew they'd all liked it. Their support should have warmed her but for some reason, tonight, it didn't. All she could see was Garrett's stupidly handsome face and his stupidly mesmerizing silver eyes, telling her in that hard, flat tone, leaving no room for argument, that she couldn't change the name. And quite frankly, the only warmth she felt was the cleansing fire of anger.

But anger wouldn't help and it only made things worse, so she forced it away.

"The store was his grandma's," she said, trying to keep her voice measured, "which I'd forgotten. Apparently the name came from his grandpa, so I guess he feels some ownership over it."

"Yeah, but he's not the owner now," Pru said. "You're the one holding the lease, not him. You can do whatever you want."

It was true. Garrett's grandma might once have owned the store, but she wasn't around anymore. It was Charity's store now and she had every right to change the name if she wanted to. And it wasn't as if she was going to change it to something awful, so really, his hostility was a tad out of proportion. Especially when she hadn't been rude.

You did enjoy making him mad, though.

It was true, and that seemed a bit petty and wrong now. Still, a part of her had liked the silver glitter of irritation in his eyes, a sign that she'd gotten to him on some level, though why that should matter after all these years, she had no idea.

The crush she'd once had on him was well and truly dead, and the flutter of her heartbeat when he'd walked into the store had simply been an autonomic reflex—her female body responding to his male one. Nothing to do with *him* at all.

Anyway, she wasn't here to get all hung up on him again. She was here to get the yarn store up and running, and have a couple of months of peace and quiet before she returned to work.

"I guess so," she said. "You think I should go with the change then?"

"Duh, of course." Pru rolled her eyes.

"But his grandmother…" Charity couldn't stop herself from saying. "I don't want to dishonor her memory."

"Look, if you were going to turn it into a sex shop then that might be dishonoring her memory," Kit pointed out. "But you're not. You're keeping it a yarn store. All you're doing is changing the name."

Hope's blue eyes gazed at her from over the top of her mojito. "Don't go being all nice, Char. You put a lot of thought into that name and besides, like Pru said, it's not his store. It's yours."

Again, true. Yet the urge to smooth things over the way she always did when it came to conflict tugged at her again. It made her even madder.

She was always the peacemaker, always pouring oil on the troubled waters, a habit ingrained in her ever since she'd been a kid and trying not to be any trouble to her father. Her mother had died when Charity was a baby, so her dad had brought her up, and she knew she'd been a lot of work for him. He had always been very busy with his medical practice and would sometimes get stressed, so she'd made sure she was always calm and never a bother to him.

That ability had come in useful in her job, and her colleagues had valued her talent for remaining calm in the high-stress environment of a hospital ER. It had certainly been a good way of coping with the near-constant state of conflict that was an ER doc's working life, and it had come in handy with her friends when it came to keeping the peace too.

But sometimes, just sometimes, it would be nice if she didn't have to be the calm one all the time. If she was allowed to be angry and difficult the way the others sometimes were.

You chose that role for yourself, remember?

Oh yes, she was well aware. Which was part of the problem.

"I'm not going to be all nice," she snapped, adding an immediate, "Sorry," that didn't help her mood.

The others were silent a moment, all of them regarding her with varying degrees of curiosity, mostly because she never snapped.

"What?" She tried not to sound irritated.

"Sounds like someone needs to have it out with a certain bad boy," Hope murmured.

"Indeed," Pru agreed.

Charity glared at them, her irritation climbing from a light simmer to a full-on boil. "Garrett's got nothing to do with it."

"Sure he hasn't." Kit was staring very pointedly at her mojito.

"You should go and talk to him," Hope said. "And don't apologize for once, for God's sake. Just tell him you're changing the name and that's final."

"I don't want to talk to him." Charity fought not to sound cross. "I can keep the name, it's no drama."

"If you do, please don't leave the *z* on the end of 'things,'" Kit murmured and sniffed. "It offends me."

"Except that you don't want to do that, either," Pru said. "We all know what you really want is to go and stare into Garrett's dreamy eyes, and you're really annoyed about it."

Charity felt her cheeks get even hotter than they already were. "No, I don't. In fact, I'd be quite happy to never see him again."

"Uh-huh," Kit tutted. "No lying is a house rule, remember?"

The other two grinned.

"The jar is over there." Pru pointed to the mantel where the jar full of scraps of paper with old-fashioned dating advice on them stood.

They'd all decided that if any one of them broke a house rule, they had to take a slip from the jar...and use it. Hope had thought the idea a fun one and despite privately finding the rules annoying, Charity didn't complain. It made Hope happy and her friend needed some happiness after the disaster of her canceled wedding. Plus, complaining would only get her another slip, and she really didn't want that.

"You can use it on Garrett," Hope said, clearly delighted at the prospect.

Charity, feeling cornered, debated simply getting to her feet and leaving the room. Which of course would give away far more about her feelings concerning Garrett Roy than she wanted to—not that she had any feelings concerning Garrett Roy, but still. No point in giving her friends any more ammunition.

"Fine," she said. Calmly. "I don't mind."

"Sure, sure," Hope said. "Take a slip, girlfriend."

Charity put her drink down, gathered what dignity she could, rose from her seat, and went over to the jar that sat on the mantel. She put her hand inside, grabbed a slip of paper, and drew it out. Then she opened it with a certain amount of ceremony.

They all looked at her expectantly.

"'Point out to him that the death rate of single men is twice that of married men,'" she read out. Okay, so it could be worse. She could have got the Band-Aid on the cheek that Pru had drawn.

Hope and Pru grinned, while Kit nodded approvingly. "Perfect," she said. "I feel you can inform Garrett of this while you're telling him you're changing the name come hell or high water."

Charity opened her mouth to say that she would not be informing Garrett of anything, because she wasn't going to be seeing him again. Then shut it. Arguing about the dating advice was another house rule and besides, they'd probably then demand she use it on some random stranger, which also wouldn't be happening.

"Fine," she said, trying not to snap, since snapping wouldn't help.

"Tonight," Pru added.

Charity frowned. "What do you mean tonight?"

"I mean, go and tell him tonight."

Well, this was getting better and better. Charity wanted to tell Pru that she wasn't going tonight, or even tomorrow, and possibly not even the day after that, but she knew that doing so would only put off the inevitable.

"I would go tonight," she said levelly. "If I knew where he was. But since I don't—"

"He'll be with Brooks at the Rusty Nail," Hope interrupted.

"Oh really?" Kit glanced curiously at Hope. "And are you going to be joining him yet again tonight?"

Hope colored. "I couldn't possibly say."

"That's the third night in a row," Charity said, relieved not to have the spotlight on her.

"Don't change the subject." Hope dismissed the question with a wave of her hand. "Pru will lend you the keys to her truck, won't you Pru?"

"Sure." Pru gave her a pointed look. "We'll be expecting an update, okay? So no weaseling out of it."

Clearly there was going to be no escape.

Her friends could be relentless when they wanted to be, yet Charity knew it was coming from a place of love. As much as they teased her about Garrett, they wouldn't want her stewing about it, which she would—not a good thing when she was supposed to be getting less stressed here, not more so. Perhaps they were right. Perhaps dealing with it quickly and amicably was the answer.

She might as well get it over and done with and do the stupid dating advice thing too, then have more of a discussion with Garrett about the name change. Get him to see it her way.

"Okay," she said, like it was no big deal. "And don't worry, there will be no weaseling."

"There'd better not be." Kit gazed sternly at her. "Remember to hold your ground. You're a strong, capable woman who doesn't need a man, right?"

"I believe the exact phrase is, 'don't need no man,'" Hope pointed out.

"Whatever," Kit waved away the correction along with the bad grammar. "You know what I mean."

She did. It was something they'd told each other over the years, through each heartbreak and heartache, and she appreciated the reminder. Because she *was* strong and she *was* capable. Even though having to take stress leave from her job made her feel like she wasn't, and even though she felt guilty for not telling her friends about it.

She hadn't told anyone about it, most especially not her father.

They were all so proud of her and it wasn't that she thought they wouldn't be understanding or would think any less of her if they knew about her difficulties. It was more that she wanted to be the person they believed her to be. The "mom friend." The calm one, the one who had her life together. If they knew, she wouldn't be that person anymore, and she didn't want to lose that like she'd lost the faith she had in herself.

But she wasn't going to think about that now. She was here in Jasper Creek to find the thing that had been missing from her life for too many years to count: happiness.

And that happiness had absolutely nothing whatsoever to do with Garrett Roy.

GARRETT WAS ALLOWING himself a single beer and very much enjoying it after his crappy day, when the door to the Nail was pushed open and Charity Golding walked in.

Every muscle in Garrett's body tensed.

Brooks, sitting opposite him in the booth, frowned. "Something up?"

Garrett didn't hear him. He was too busy staring at the woman standing in the middle of the bar, her red curls shining and looking so pretty and wholesome it ought to be downright illegal.

Goddamn. He'd only just managed to stop thinking about her and now she'd just waltzed in like his fevered imagination had somehow conjured her up.

What the hell was she doing here?

Perhaps she's looking for you.

Garrett ignored his hopeful brain. No, he didn't want her to be looking for him. Didn't want to see those dark blue eyes and that gorgeous, red pouty mouth turned in his direction, curving in that damn patronizing smile that if he'd had any sense, he'd have kissed from her face at the earliest opportunity.

Except he shouldn't be thinking of kissing. These days he was a good boy, and he didn't date women from Jasper Creek. The place was too small and he didn't want to mess around with anyone who might get hurt. When the urge took him, he went to the next town to scratch the itch.

He just wished that itch wasn't itching now and he most especially wished it wasn't itching because of Charity Golding.

Man, she better not be here to argue with him about the name of the yarn store again. He'd been pretty clear about his thoughts on the subject.

You were also pretty damn rude.

Yeah, he had been, and unfortunately for Charity, he didn't feel any less rude now. Denial had never suited him.

"Well," Brooks said, clearly noting her presence. "Look who's here."

At that same moment, Charity turned her head, her deep blue gaze locking with Garrett's, making something deep inside him charge with a familiar heated electricity.

Dammit to hell. He'd really been hoping that chemistry in the yarn store earlier in the day had been an aberration. Clearly, it wasn't.

Annoyed, Garrett leaned back in the booth and held her gaze, putting a touch of insolence into it in the hope that would be enough to make her walk away.

It wasn't. Instead, a determined look crossed her face and she started walking purposefully toward him.

"If it isn't your favorite yarn store owner," Brooks murmured with some amusement, having listened to Garrett's rant about the name change only a few minutes before. "What a coincidence. Doc Golding's daughter, right? Isn't she the one who used to tutor you back in high school?"

"Yes," Garrett said through clenched teeth.

"What did you do to piss her off?"

Garrett opened his mouth to tell him not a goddamn thing, when Charity finally arrived at the table.

"Hi, Garrett." Her voice was cool, her gaze still determined. "I hope you don't mind me interrupting. Could I have a word?"

Brooks stood up before Garrett could say anything. "Hey, Charity."

"Nice to see you again, Brooks." Her smile was much warmer and more natural for Brooks than it had been for him, Garrett noted.

"You too." He nodded his head toward the bar. "Can I get you anything?"

"No, thank you," she said politely.

Brooks nodded again, shot Garrett a pointed look that Garrett ignored, before heading toward the bar.

Charity sat down in Brooks's vacated seat, absently tucking one red curl behind her ear, and Garrett found himself watching the movement, his gaze drawn to the elegant curve of her neck. Yeah, not good.

He scowled. "I didn't say you could sit."

She folded her hands on the tabletop, giving him that flat-out annoying smile again. "I'm sorry. It'll only take a second, I promise. I just wanted to talk to you about the… ah…incident at the yarn store this morning."

Damn, so she *was* here to argue with him.

His annoyance gathered tight. "What incident?"

A slight flush rose under her skin and much to his added irritation, it made her even prettier, highlighting the deep blue of her eyes and making her freckles stand out. He remembered those freckles. They'd given him a lot of trouble as he'd sat at her kitchen table, trying to puzzle out some math equation he wasn't interested in. He hadn't been able to concentrate, too busy wondering what she'd do if he kissed those little freckles one by one. Then, when she'd looked up shyly from the equation, she'd blushed.

That was when he'd known he couldn't have her tutoring him anymore. He'd never pushed himself on anyone who didn't want him, and he wasn't about to start, but if she did want him... That had been the straw that broke the camel's back of his control.

She'd always been so sweet and shy, the doctor's daughter. She had serious written all over her, and he'd had his head full of dreams of being a bull rider like his old man, and no time at all for sweet and shy. He hadn't wanted to hurt her, so that day he'd walked out her door and he'd never come back.

And he hadn't thought of her again until today.

Until he'd discovered her standing in the middle of his grandmother's yarn store, the apparent new owner. Still sweet and sexy, though perhaps not as shy. Still just as much of a distraction as she'd ever been, and if he'd had his way, he would have been quite happy to ignore her all summer if he could.

But he couldn't. He'd let his grandmother down once before when he'd left for the rodeo, and he wasn't going to do it again. He had to protect her legacy somehow.

"You know what incident I'm talking about," Charity said. "The slight disagreement about the name of the store earlier today."

"It wasn't a disagreement. It was you telling me you wanted to change the name of the store and me telling you that you couldn't."

Her smile became rather fixed. "I know you did. And I totally understand where you're coming from. Change is hard and it's only natural to be afraid of it."

Garrett narrowed his eyes. "I'm not afraid of change."

"Of course you're not." Her hands lifted slightly as if she wanted to pat the air around him in a soothing fashion. "Adjusting to new things takes a while and it can be uncomfortable, I get it."

Was she messing with him? She had to be. No one could be that patronizing and mean it. Back when she'd used to tutor him, she'd been shy and sweet, not this...fake calm crap.

"Do you say this bullshit to everyone?" he asked, not caring how rude he sounded. "Or is it just me?"

Her smile disappeared, the glint in her blue eyes getting dangerous, which only made her even prettier. Some people didn't suit the old cliché of being beautiful when they were angry, but Charity Golding sure did.

"You're kind of an asshole," she said. "You know that, right?"

She's right. You are.

Okay, so he was. But maybe that was a good thing if it got her to go away.

He stared belligerently back and for a second the air between them seethed with a tension that shouldn't be there. It made him very conscious of how much he'd like to make her eyes bluer and her cheeks pinker, and all the ways he could go about doing just that...

Something hot clenched tight inside him, which was a very bad sign indeed. Because that hot, tight feeling was a sensation he only got on the back of a bull. It was raw and addictive—part adrenaline high, part the thrill of a challenge—and he'd always liked it far too much for his own good.

He should not be feeling it now.

Then again, he wasn't nineteen anymore. He'd made promises to his gran when he'd come home from bull riding to take care of her; he'd said he would put some much needed attention into his father's ranch. Perhaps even one day settle down. He wouldn't do what old John Roy had done, spending half his life riding bulls and neglecting what he had. Including his own son.

Yeah, Garrett wouldn't be following his old man's path. He was a solid rancher now and no one was going to distract him from it, still less one pretty redhead.

"I'm sorry," Charity said all of a sudden, looking contrite. "That was uncalled-for."

Not expecting it, Garrett gave her a suspicious look. "You're sorry? What for?"

"For what I said about you being an asshole." She was giving him that forced smile again, though anger still glinted in her eyes. "I'm not here to make this into some big thing, or to disrespect your grandmother's memory."

"What's with the smile?" he asked before he could think better of it.

"What smile?"

"The one you're giving me right now. It's patronizing as hell."

Color washed through her cheeks. "It's not meant to be patronizing."

"Then what is it meant for? Because it sure comes across as patronizing."

The smile vanished once more, her gaze full of hot blue

sparks, and he felt that heat and anticipation sweep through him again, making his breath catch.

Perhaps arguing with her was a bad idea.

Yeah, he really shouldn't have.

Charity took a breath, obviously making a monumental effort not to snap at him. "Okay, look, all I wanted to say was that I appreciate that your grandmother had a history with the yarn store, and perhaps we could come to some compromise over—"

"No," he interrupted, furious with himself for sitting here and talking to her when if he'd had any sense in his stupid head, he'd have got up and left the moment she'd walked through the door. "There will be no compromise. Knitting and Thingz is the name and—"

Charity abruptly slapped her hands down on the table. "Right. That's it. I've had it. You don't run the store, Garrett Roy. I do. And I will be calling it A Simple Thread." Her gaze was furious, her cheeks burning, her hair flaming like a sunset, and he couldn't look away from her. "Do you understand?"

Oh, he understood all right. He understood that all he wanted right now was to reach over the table, slide his fingers into all that silky red hair, pull her to him, and get a taste of her anger. Let it wash the both of them clean away.

Which would be one hell of a mistake.

"No," he said flatly. "I don't."

Charity's eyes became electric, the patronizing smile a memory. One glossy red curl had come loose from its position behind her ear, grazing her jaw, and he wanted to pull on it, to see what she would do.

She'd probably punch you in the mouth.

"Tell me something, Mr. Roy." Her jaw was tight, anger rolling off of her. "Are you single?"

Mr. Roy, huh? Oh, he'd definitely gotten to her.

"Yeah. Why?"

Her gaze sparked like cut electrical wires. "Did you know that the death rate of single men is twice that of married men?"

Garrett frowned. "What's that got to do with anything?"

She leaned forward slightly. "Stay. Single." Then she pushed herself up and walked out of the bar without another word.

CHAPTER THREE

CHARITY WAS STILL furious a few days later as she poked through boxes on one of the shelves in Knitting and Thingz. Her attempt to solve the issue of the store's name had ended in disaster and that was solely due to Garrett Roy being an intransigent, stubborn ass.

She'd ranted about it at length at various times with her friends, detailing Garrett Roy's various faults, including and not limited to his complete and utter disregard for the fact that she'd apologized to him—which she hadn't needed to do, as Kit had pointed out—as well as her attempt to calm things down by being understanding of where he was coming from.

Her friends had all been shocked at her temper, which she supposed was fair since she rarely got angry. But somehow the fact that they were shocked only made her even angrier, because really, why shouldn't she get annoyed about stupid Garrett?

After they'd all gotten over the surprise of Charity actually raising her voice, Pru had wanted to know whether she'd used the dating advice or not, and so Charity had told them what she'd said to him. They were all very admiring of how she'd used it as an insult, though Hope had told her that wasn't the point of the advice. Charity had told her that she didn't care. She wasn't going to be dating Garrett Roy, and in fact, she sincerely hoped she never ran into him again.

Not wanting to see him again didn't stop her from going over the night in the Rusty Nail again and again though. Dwelling on how he'd leaned against the back of the booth, all long, lean, and muscular, staring at her with that insolent silver gaze. Telling her that he hadn't asked her to sit. That she was being patronizing. That the name of the yarn store was staying...

She didn't understand why he was being so stubborn about a simple name change. Had she offended him somehow? And why should her wanting to change the name of the store be such a big deal? He didn't have to be so rude about it.

He *really* didn't need to be so incredibly sexy, either, though maybe that was just her and her terrible taste in handsome, silver-eyed bad boys.

Picking a box up off the shelf, Charity carried it over to the counter and put it down. Then she got out her notebook and pen, and began going through the box, noting down what was inside. She wanted to see what stock there was in the store already before she went out and ordered anything, because there was no point in ordering things she didn't need.

But it was difficult to concentrate with her brain replaying Garrett's deep voice asking her whether she said "this bullshit" to everyone or whether it was just him.

The ass. If "this bullshit" meant her trying to be understanding then yes, she did say it to everyone. And everyone liked it. They found it calming and reassuring—or at least that's what all her patients had told her.

Why are you getting so angry about it? Does his opinion matter that much?

No, of course it didn't. She'd long since gotten over the massive crush she'd once had on him. He'd ignored her back then, and since time had clearly not improved him, she cared not one iota about his opinion now. She was here to de-stress and take some time out, not get into horrible arguments with terribly attractive men.

Finishing up her list, Charity put her pen down then lifted the box again in preparation for putting it back on the shelf. The damn thing was heavy and she was busy trying to get a good grip on it, so she didn't notice when the front door opened then closed, or hear the sound of a footstep behind her.

Oblivious, she turned around and ran straight into a hard, male chest.

She gave a little gasp of shock, and then two large hands covered hers where they gripped the box, helping her retain her hold on it. Inexplicable heat raced through her, and she glanced up into a pair of familiar gray eyes.

Garrett.

For a second neither of them moved, tension humming in the air.

She was very conscious of his hands covering hers, of how large and warm they were, how strong they were too. It was disconcerting in the extreme, and to make matters worse, she could feel her cheeks start to get hot.

Irritated at herself and her reaction, not to mention him, she took a step back, wrenching her hands away from his and almost dropping the box in the process.

Garrett muttered something under his breath and before she could protest, he'd taken the box away from her entirely.

"Hey," she said crossly. "I was carrying that."

"No, you weren't. You were dropping that on your foot." He moved back to the counter with the box.

"Don't put it there," she snapped, irrationally annoyed

with him and at her own reaction to him. "It has to go back on that shelf."

"Which shelf?"

"That one." She pointed. "Though don't put yourself out. I can manage."

He ignored her, moving over to the shelf she'd indicated. She tried not to notice the way the black T-shirt he wore pulled tight over the powerful muscles of his shoulders as he bent over the shelf, or how his biceps flexed as he put the box down.

Her hands where he'd covered them with his tingled, her heartbeat gathering speed. She was very conscious of the fact that he'd never touched her before.

She really hadn't wanted him to touch her now, either, especially if this insane physical reaction was the way she responded when he did.

It made her *so* mad.

Mad that he was here. Mad that her body wouldn't act normally when he was around. Mad that she was even thinking about him when thinking about him was the last thing she wanted to do.

"You startled me." She tried to make it less of an accusation and more of a statement of fact, though she didn't think she'd succeeded.

He straightened and turned around, giving her an impenetrable look that somehow made her blush yet again. "Sorry." He did not sound sorry in the slightest.

Restless and twitchy, she pushed an errant lock of hair behind her ear. "What are you doing here?"

He kept on staring at her, making the heat in her cheeks get even worse.

"Look," she said when he didn't speak. "If you're not going to—"

"I owe you an apology," he interrupted. "That's why I'm here."

Charity realized her mouth was hanging open. She shut it.

So. That was unexpected. And annoying, because she was full of irritation and was desperate to dump it somewhere. She didn't normally take it out on people, but for some reason she really wanted to take it out on him.

He eyed her. "You're still pissed at me, aren't you?"

"Of course I'm still pissed at you. You were incredibly rude to me that night in the bar."

"Yeah. I was."

Charity blinked, not expecting that. She shifted on her feet, the wind taken out of her sails. "Yes," she said lamely. "You were."

"I'm sorry." His voice was very level. "I was out of line."

There was no doubt he meant it; she could see it in his face. But she didn't quite know what to say. Him coming in to apologize for his behavior was the last thing she'd expected.

"Well, thank you," she said stiffly.

A heavy silence fell.

Charity folded her arms, suddenly awkward and feeling like she needed to apologize for her behavior as well. "I shouldn't have said that about single men and their life expectancy," she offered. "Or about you being an asshole. That was offensive."

"I wasn't offended." There was something in his voice she didn't quite understand, an almost rough edge that made her breath catch. For some reason, she didn't want to look at him directly, which was just silly.

She braced herself and held his gaze. "So what exactly was the problem?"

He didn't answer immediately, a silver glint in his eye. Then, strangely, one corner of his beautiful mouth turned up into a ghost of a smile. "You are the problem, Charity Golding."

A small burst of shock went through her.

"Me?" she asked blankly. "What do you mean me?"

"You really don't know?" He raised one straight black brow. "No idea at all?"

"No, why would I?"

He let out a breath and then glanced around the room as if he was searching for an answer in the shelves around them. "I guess not then," he muttered.

This was getting weird. Why would she be a problem? And in what way? It was apparent she was missing something vital.

"What do you mean 'I guess not'?" She stared at him. "You guess not what?"

His gaze came back to hers, oddly intense. "Why are you here, Charity? What are you doing back here in Jasper Creek, I mean?"

The question wasn't one she'd expected him to ask, because a) she didn't think he'd be interested in why she was here, and b) the Jasper Creek jungle telegraph was usually pretty efficient and surely he would know by now.

Obviously a) he was, and b) he didn't.

"I'm surprised you haven't heard," she said. "Me, Hope, Pru, and Kit are here to—"

"Yeah, I know about the four of you and the store thing. But why are *you* here. You specifically."

Oh. Right. That.

There was no reason not to tell him—at least the same superficial reason she'd given her friends. "I wanted to take a break from medicine. Spend a few months doing something different, something a bit quieter and more peaceful than being in the ER anyway." She nodded at the shelves. "I've always loved the yarn store so I thought it would be the perfect place to start."

He nodded slowly. "So, you're planning on going back?"

"To Seattle? Eventually. But not soon." She stopped, not wanting to think about going back right now. "Why?"

"Why do you think?" The look he gave her was suddenly very intense. "Because you're too damn sexy for my peace of mind and I can't start anything with you, no matter how much I want to."

"START SOMETHING WITH ME?" Charity repeated, her blue eyes wide. "What are you talking about?"

Garrett knew that broaching this particular topic wasn't likely to be a great idea, but he didn't see much point in lying, most especially not to himself.

The last few days since Charity had stormed out of the Nail had been pure torture. He hadn't been able to stop thinking about her. He'd stalked angrily around the ranch, throwing himself into some of the tougher physical tasks in order to let off some steam.

She'd got him good and riled, and it didn't help that he damn well knew it was all to do with his own unwelcome physical reaction to her and nothing at all to do with the yarn store.

Which left him with two options: he either pulled himself together, put the attraction to one side, and got over it. Or he had it out with her.

He'd initially gone with the first option, since having it out with her had the potential to lead to all kinds of disasters, and besides, he'd wanted to prove to himself that she hadn't gotten under his skin as badly as he'd feared.

Then he'd walked past the damn store and seen her inside, and he just hadn't been able to stop himself. Something he hadn't been able to fight had pulled him inside.

He should have announced his presence in some way, but he hadn't, so she'd turned around with that box and almost walked straight into him. He'd had to put his hands over hers before she dropped it, and then she'd looked up, her eyes wide with surprise and so very blue.

She'd felt warm, the light coming through the windows glossing her pretty red hair, the spark of attraction in her gaze undeniable.

He should have let her go and escaped out of the store, gotten away from her while he could. But he hadn't. So many years had gone by since that day he'd first looked into her eyes and seen the spark of desire, but it was still there, still burning.

He'd decided then and there that all he could be was honest with her, because while letting her think she'd offended him somehow was great for pushing her away, it was also a dick move. And he wasn't supposed to be a dick these days.

So he'd told her the truth.

"I think you know what I'm talking about." He shoved his hands into his pockets, trying to ignore the warmth lingering on his palms. "You. Getting under my skin."

She blinked then looked away, her cheeks rosy, the freckles dusting her nose standing out. She was in jeans again today and a plain white T-shirt, and he could see the shadow of her bra underneath it, the vaguest hint of lace. It made him think very bad thoughts.

Perhaps he should go. Perhaps being honest hadn't been a good idea after all.

"Why tell me that?" She looked out the front window of

the store, very pointedly not at him. "I mean, why would you think I'd need to know?"

"Because I think you feel the same way."

Her head snapped around, her blue gaze clashing with his. "I do not."

He held it. "Of course you do. You think I don't know when a woman wants me?"

"That's incredibly arrogant. You know that, right?"

He ignored her. "Tell me I'm wrong, then."

"You're wrong," she shot back.

"Really?"

"Of course you're wrong." Her cheeks blazed almost as red as her hair. "Why on earth would I want you?"

"I don't know, you tell me. But I can see the way you look at me, Charity. And I can feel the tension between us. That's chemistry, whether you like it or not."

Her gaze turned furious, sparks glittering in it. She looked so pretty standing there, ruffled and radiating outrage, and all because of him.

It made him think about how they weren't seventeen anymore, and he wasn't the angry teenage boy with his father's wild streak who, by the time he was sixteen, had gotten a name for himself for underage drinking and stealing cars. And she wasn't the good doctor's young daughter, the apple of her father's eye.

They were both consenting adults and—

You should leave.

Yet Garrett found himself rooted to the spot, unable to take a single step toward that door.

"Chemistry?" She said the word like she found the taste of it unpleasant. "What are you talking about?" She started toward him, closing the space between them until she stood right in front of him. "Well? Where is this chemistry you speak of, Garrett? Because I'm not feeling it."

Her face was upturned to his and her eyes were the same blue of the summer sky over his ranch. She looked angry and adorable and her mouth was made for kissing. She smelled of honeysuckle and she was way too close, and he didn't know why he was still standing here, not moving.

"No chemistry, huh?" His hands were out of his pockets and he'd pushed one of those errant curls behind her ear, his fingertips brushing over her cheek before he even knew what he was doing. Her skin felt just as soft as he thought it would. "Then why did you shiver just now?"

Because she had. He saw it, plain as day.

"It was not a shiver." She scowled. "It was a shake of complete distaste." And then, bizarrely, given said distaste, she took a step closer. "Here. I'll prove it to you." And before he could move, she lifted her hands, took his face between them, went up on her toes, and pulled his mouth down on hers.

It was an angry kiss and it hit him like a bolt of lightning, pure electricity shooting straight down his spine and grounding through his feet. He couldn't move. Could barely breathe. He was conscious of nothing but the softness of her lips and the warmth of them, the feel of them on his. How her honeysuckle scent surrounded him. The heat of her palms on the side of his face...

Then, as desire surged inside him, every sensation narrowed into one bright shining thought.

He had to have more.

He reached for her, his palms settling on her hips and pulling her curvy little body against his. She didn't protest. Her hands crept up around his neck, and she went up onto her toes, arching into him, her mouth hungry and desperate.

It had been a long time since he'd had a woman. He'd been too busy working to pay off the last of his father's debts, getting the ranch back on track like he'd promised Gran he would. He wasn't selfish and irresponsible the way he'd once been. He wasn't like his father.

But he was tired of working hard all the time. And Charity Golding had occupied far too much of his brain for far too long. Finally, she was kissing him and it was just as good as he'd imagined it all those years ago, sitting at her kitchen table.

Better, even. And she tasted like the kind of reward he deserved after a long, hard day working. Softness and heat and pleasure.

He didn't want to let her go.

But as suddenly as she'd pulled him down for a kiss, she pushed herself away. The look on her face was shocked, as if she hadn't expected the intensity that had blossomed between them, and it was all he could do not to reach for her again and pull her back to him for more of that astonishing kiss.

He didn't though, because she was glaring at him as if he'd personally insulted her, all flushed and gorgeous, her blue eyes glittering.

"There," she said hoarsely. "You see? No chemistry whatsoever."

Then, before he could argue, she turned and walked straight out the door.

CHAPTER FOUR

CHARITY CHARGED DOWN the sidewalk, barely conscious of where she was going. Her heart thumped, her pulse raced, and her lips felt seared, as though she'd pressed them against a hot coffee cup. In fact, her whole body felt seared, as though the imprint of Garrett Roy's hard torso had been burned into hers.

She'd been incensed at his claim of chemistry. Absolutely furious when he'd told her that she wanted him. She wasn't exactly sure why she'd been so furious, she just was, and proving him wrong seemed to be of the utmost importance.

With your mouth.

She gritted her teeth, ignoring someone's cheery greeting as she charged on.

She never lost her temper. She never got mad. She hated confrontation. She didn't want to hurt people, she hated yelling at them, and she didn't like it when people were mad with her.

But apparently none of that mattered when it concerned Garrett Roy.

And not only had she lost her temper, she'd done it in the most ridiculous way possible, by trying to prove they had no chemistry with a kiss.

She didn't know what she'd been thinking. She'd just gotten...angry. He'd stood there looking so arrogant and gorgeous, talking confidently about their chemistry like he knew anything about her. And she'd wanted to do something—anything—to shake him as badly as he'd shaken her.

A kiss had probably been the least intelligent thing to do and it had backfired on her in a spectacular fashion. Far from proving they had no chemistry, all it had done was prove the opposite.

God, she was an idiot. Where the hell did that leave her now?

She came to a stop, breathing fast, the echo of that kiss reverberating throughout her entire body, only to realize something else: she'd walked out of her own shop and left her purse behind.

Ugh. She was going to have to risk meeting him again by going back to get it, or she would have to walk aimlessly around Jasper Creek until he left the store.

Charity reached into her back pocket for her phone, since talking to her friends seemed vital in this moment, only to remember that of course she didn't have her phone. It was in a safe in the basement.

She cursed under her breath. So, it was either humiliation or wandering aimlessly.

Then someone said from behind her, "Charity."

The voice was deep, male, and it made every cell in her body sit up and take notice.

Charity closed her eyes. Of course it was Garrett. Of course.

She didn't want to turn around and face him; it was too humiliating for words. But if she didn't, she'd be acknowledging that he'd gotten to her.

Isn't it a bit late for that?

Sadly it was. A totally unnecessary kiss before escaping out the door had more than acknowledged that.

So much for opening this yarn store being the perfect escape from stress.

Fighting for composure, Charity slowly let out a breath, opened her eyes, then forced herself to turn around.

He stood behind her, so tall and dark and gorgeous that she had to catch her breath. His gaze was completely impenetrable, that hard mouth she'd just kissed looking like it never smiled.

She couldn't stop looking at that mouth. She couldn't stop looking at him.

She'd kissed him. She'd kissed Garrett Roy and it had been so very good.

Had he liked it? Had it affected him as badly as it had affected her? She thought it might have since he'd pulled her against him, but maybe not. It was difficult to tell.

Why does it matter? You were proving a point, nothing more.

Of course it didn't matter. And as for her point, well, the less said about that the better.

The beautifully carved planes and angles of his face betrayed nothing. She had no idea why he'd followed her.

Then he held out her purse. "You forgot this."

Right. So he'd come after her, but only because she'd forgotten her purse.

Not because he liked the kiss. Not because he wanted more.

Color burned in her cheeks for absolutely no reason. No, it was good. She didn't want more. She didn't want anything from him at all. In fact, it would be better all around if she never saw him again. Maybe she could dig a hole in the ground and go live in it for the foreseeable future.

"Thank you," she said stiffly and reached for the purse.

But he held on to it, fire glittering in his silver eyes. A heat burned into her, stealing all her breath. "I'll be at the Nail tonight. If you want to join me for a drink."

For a second, Charity wasn't sure if she'd heard him right. Then she opened her mouth to double-check that was what he'd said, but he abruptly let go of her purse and stepped back. He raised his hand, tipped his hat, gave her one last searing look, then he walked away, leaving her staring after him.

What had just happened? Had he really asked her to join him for a drink? And if so, why? Was it a date? What?

Heart still thumping, Charity walked slowly back in the direction of the yarn store, deciding that for the rest of the day, she was *not* going to think about Garrett Roy.

Unfortunately, though, her brain wasn't taking commands. It didn't matter what she did, it kept replaying that ill-considered kiss over and over again. Making her feel hot and restless and shooting her concentration all to hell.

She wasn't going to go and meet him. Of course she wasn't. Was she?

Later that afternoon, she got home to the farmhouse to find everyone else already there.

Pru was on cooking that night and she stood at the stove looking critically into the pot of whatever she was stirring, blond hair stuck to her forehead, while Kit sat at the table dressed in one of her black "New York fashion" sacks and peeling potatoes. Hope leaned against the counter, sipping on a mug of tea and offering unwanted advice.

They all looked at Charity as she came in.

"What happened?" Kit asked immediately, putting down the potato she was peeling.

Dammit. So much for her game face.

Charity pulled out a chair, sat down at the table, and looked at her friends' expectant expressions. She knew there was no way she was getting out of this one. She was going to have to tell them the truth.

"You really want to know?" she said. "I kissed stupid Garrett Roy."

There was a silence.

"Wow," Hope murmured. "I approve."

"I was going to ask why," Kit said. "But then it's obvious why. He's hot."

"He's annoying," Charity said crossly, full of renewed anger at herself. "And he was being arrogant in the store today and he said we had chemistry so I had to prove that we didn't."

"So of course you kissed him." Pru glanced up from the stove. "I'm sure that worked out well."

Charity sighed. "Pretty much as well as you'd expect. And then he said he was going to be at the Nail tonight if I wanted to join him."

Kit picked up her potato and examined it with a critical eye. "That sounds very much like an invitation to me."

"Hell, yeah," Hope agreed, pausing to glance in Pru's pot. "You know what would go very well with that?"

"If you say salmon I'll hit you with this wooden spoon." Pru kept her gaze on the pot.

"I think threatening to hit someone with a wooden spoon is a violation of the house rules," Hope said, frowning.

Charity ignored them, the restless feeling inside her making her want to get up and pace around the kitchen. Normally she'd take a few calming breaths and go through her mindfulness exercises until the feeling passed. But it wasn't passing. In fact, if anything, it was increasing.

Aggravated, Charity gave in, shoving back her chair and

getting to her feet, pacing over to the counter and then back to the table again while her friends looked at her in surprise.

"I don't want to join him," she said. "I didn't come back to Jasper Creek to get it on with someone. I came back to reopen the yarn store and that's it."

Kit raised a brow. "And what's wrong with getting it on with someone?"

"Nothing. But it's a stress I don't need right now." Briefly she thought about telling the others why she'd taken a couple of months off. About the panic attacks and the anxiety that threatened every time she stepped into the ER. But she couldn't face it, not after having to field questions and possible recriminations about stupid Garrett.

Hope turned her mug carefully in her hands. "It doesn't have to be stressful. I mean…do you want to get it on with him?"

Automatically Charity wanted to say no, of course she didn't want to get it on with him. But something stopped her. Because it wasn't true. She really *did* want to get it on with him. She wanted more of that kiss. More of that hard body she'd felt pressed to hers. More of his hands on her hips, touching her. More of that hot mouth on hers…

She'd been dreaming of him ever since she'd been seventeen and now she had the opportunity to have what she'd always wanted…

"Oh yeah," Pru said. "She really does want to get it on with him."

Charity flushed. Hell. No point trying to deny it now.

"I didn't want any complications getting in the way of me opening this store." She turned and paced over to the counter once more. "All I wanted was to set up the shop and open it with you guys and not…" She stopped.

"What's complicated about banging a hot guy?" Pru

waved her wooden spoon for emphasis. "Casual sex is a thing."

Hope was still frowning. "Have you ever had casual sex, Char?"

It wasn't really the conversation she wanted to be having with her friends right now, but then she was the one who'd started it with her ill-advised confession about Garrett.

"No, she hasn't," Kit said before she could reply.

"Hey." Charity glared at her.

Kit's eyes went wide. "Did you see this, guys? I think Charity is actually angry with me."

Great. And now they were going to have the "Charity never gets angry" conversation, were they?

"Can we not talk about this?" she snapped, pacing over to the table again.

"What else did you want to talk about?" Hope said. "You having casual sex with Garrett Roy?"

"I am not going to have casual sex with Garrett Roy," she insisted.

"Why not?" Kit stared at her from over her potato. "He's hot. You kissed him, and presumably it was good, otherwise you wouldn't be blushing like that. And he must have enjoyed it too, otherwise he wouldn't have told you to join him for a 'drink'—emphasis my own."

Charity gritted her teeth, turned, and paced back to the counter, trying to figure out exactly what her problem was. Because now she thought about it, there didn't seem to be any reason why she shouldn't take this further with Garrett.

Yes, he was unreasonably arrogant and extremely annoying, but how much of that was frustrated chemistry? He'd basically admitted that she was a problem for him, so maybe the most logical thing, for both of their peace of minds would be to sleep together and deal with it.

Yeah, really good plan. Nothing like sex to make something less complicated.

Charity ignored the doubtful thought.

"Um, I hate to be a downer," Hope said, "but doesn't casual sex come under the 'no hookups' rule?"

Kit gave an airy wave of her potato peeler. "I think this can be an exception. Emergency hookups are allowed."

"Oh really?" Pru looked up from her sauce, narrowing her gaze at Kit. "And why are you deciding this suddenly, hmm?"

"It's okay." Charity held her hands up peaceably, the way she always did when she was trying to calm a situation. "I'll take a slip. Rules are rules."

Hope sipped at her tea. "I guess that means you're going to sleep with him then."

Charity wanted to tell her that she hadn't decided yet, but of course that was a lie. Now the possibility of casual sex with Garrett had been raised and fully justified in her head, she literally couldn't think of anything else.

Her only relationships had been serious ones, and only with other doctors, because no one else would put up with the crazy hours. She'd liked both men, but in the end the relentlessness of the profession had gotten to her. Going out with another doctor meant she could never escape medicine, and sometimes escape was what she wanted, even though she felt guilty about it.

Garrett wasn't a doctor. He had nothing whatsoever to do with medicine. And despite what she'd been trying to prove earlier, they *did* have chemistry. A *lot* of chemistry.

Now was her chance to have the hot bad boy so why was she even hesitating?

She turned toward the kitchen door and strode out into the hallway, going into the living room.

"She's getting a slip, guys," Pru called out. "Girl means business."

Charity reached into the vase on the mantel, pulled out one of the pieces of paper, then went back to the kitchen and paused in the doorway.

"You sure you want to do this?" Kit put her freshly peeled potato in the bowl beside her. "You're risking some truly terrible dating advice in return for casual sex?"

Charity thought about Garrett. About the kiss. About his hot mouth and his large hands, and the hard feel of his body against hers.

Oh yes, she absolutely did.

She opened the piece of paper. "'Stand on a busy street corner with a lasso.'"

Pru laughed. "Oh boy. The sex had better be phenomenal to be worth that."

Charity had a feeling it would be. And how.

"No problem. I'll do it tomorrow." She folded the slip up and put it in her pocket. "Now, I'd better—"

"Go see a man about a lasso?" Hope finished, grinning.

"I wouldn't mind seeing that particular man's lasso," Kit murmured.

"You mean, Browning West's lasso," Pru said.

Charity didn't wait around to listen to Kit's response.

She had better things to do.

GARRETT SAT IN his truck outside the Rusty Nail, staring balefully at the saloon doors and wondering just what the hell he thought he was doing.

Telling Charity to come and meet him at the bar had been a mistake. He should have handed back her purse then walked away, pushed that kiss to the back of his mind, and forgotten about it.

Except he hadn't. His brain had been too full of the sweetness of her mouth, making him think about what she'd look like if he did more than kiss her. If he touched her, if he had her beneath him in bed.

And once that was in his head, all his common sense had flown out the window and he'd asked her to join him for a drink. Even though a drink wasn't what he wanted and he thought she probably knew that.

Yeah, a mistake. But it was too late to drive away now, and besides, was working out this chemistry with Charity really a problem? It was only sex, and she wasn't the doctor's good-girl daughter any longer. Hell, she said she'd be returning to Seattle too, so it wasn't as if she'd be hanging around town permanently or anything.

He'd just be up-front with her, tell her that casual was all he had to give. She could make her own decision about whether to sleep with him or not, and no problem if she didn't. He'd be disappointed, but there were plenty of other women he could find as an alternative.

It didn't have to be her.

Bullshit, it doesn't.

Garrett ignored that particular thought. Opening the door of his truck, he got out.

A long twilight had fallen, Jasper Creek's pretty main street full of flowerpots and flags all lit up with the pinks and golds and oranges of the sunset.

But none of those colors were as brilliant as the curls of the pretty woman approaching the doors to the bar now, a blue dress hugging her curves.

Charity.

A surge of satisfaction gripped him. Especially when she turned her head at his approach and her eyes gleamed as if finding him there was exactly what she'd been hoping for.

She looked so lovely, her red curls turned to fire by the long twilight, shifting on her feet and obviously nervous.

He liked that she was nervous. He liked that a lot.

"Oh, uh…hi," she said, her fingers shifting on the strap of her purse.

He came to a stop and looked at her.

Pretty Charity Golding and she was here for him, John Roy's no-good son.

"You want to get a drink?" he asked.

Her gaze flickered away from his and then came back again. And stayed there. "You don't really want a drink, do you?"

He looked into her blue, blue eyes. "No, I don't. What I'd really like is to take you to bed."

She colored. "Ah."

He held her gaze, feeling the tension build between them. "Don't get me wrong. I'll take a drink if that's what you'd prefer. But you have to know that's my final aim."

She gave a little nod then stood aside as another couple entered the bar. "You said earlier that you didn't want to start anything with me," she murmured as the door banged shut behind the couple. "What changed your mind?"

He could have said many things to that. Flirtatious things that meant nothing. Or ignored her completely and pulled her in for a kiss then and there. But he didn't.

"You did." He had to give her the truth. "That kiss… I couldn't let it go."

She flushed. "I'm sorry about that, I was only trying to—"

He lifted a hand and laid a finger across her lovely mouth, silencing her. "Don't apologize for that. Don't ever apologize for that." Her lips were as soft and as warm against his finger as they had been against his mouth earlier, and he could not wait to taste them again.

She nodded and he took his finger away, though reluctantly. "I didn't want to be attracted to you, Garrett," she said after a moment. "You have to know that. I didn't come back to Jasper Creek for anything other than to open the yarn store and be with my friends."

The imprint of her lips burned against his skin. "So why did you come to meet me?" It felt important to know, though really, her reasons didn't matter. Only the fact that she was here did. But still, he didn't take the question back.

"Well…" She hesitated a second then went on, "I came back to Jasper Creek to get away from medicine for a while. To have fun, to just…be happy. And honestly? You're a problem for me like I'm a problem for you, so maybe we can deal with it like consenting adults."

He almost grinned at the serious look on her face. "By having sex?"

"Yes." She'd gone pink. "It's quite logical when you think about it."

Oh, he'd thought about it. A lot. And if she was going with logic to justify sleeping with him then who was he to argue? It was certainly a lot better than his own reasons.

"I agree wholeheartedly," he said, his gaze lingering on the soft hollow of her throat, where her pulse raced.

"Okay." Her voice had become breathless. "Just be aware that I'm not…very good at casual s-sex."

Interesting how she stumbled over the word. Interesting too how it made things below his belt suddenly get a hell of a lot tighter, which it really shouldn't. He was the king of casual sex and he'd never cared why his partners had chosen him or what their own experience was. As long as they both got off, he was good.

But her confession and the serious look on her face told him that casual sex was not something she did a lot of. And that choosing him to have it with meant something to her.

He meant something to her.

It was a dangerous thing to think though, so he ignored it.

"Luckily, *I* am," he said. "Want to go back to my place?"

"Yes." Her mouth curled in a tentative smile that reminded him all of a sudden of the shy tutor she'd once been, and it made his breath catch hard. "I think I'd like that very much."

CHAPTER FIVE

JOHN ROY'S OLD place was about twenty minutes out from town—though perhaps she should be thinking of it as Garrett's now—and Charity dreaded the drive. She felt self-conscious and weird, like she didn't know what to do with her body. Didn't know how to hold herself. Didn't know what to say.

It felt like she was seventeen again, sitting in the kitchen with Garrett on a Tuesday afternoon, her heart beating furiously as she worked out a math problem with him sitting beside her, leaning in to watch her work. She'd been so conscious of him, of the muscular length of his body, his heat, and his scent of hay and sunshine and musk. It had made her mouth go dry, made her completely unable to concentrate.

She wished she'd had the confidence to say something then, but she'd had zero confidence when it came to boys. So she'd sat there, burning with need, saying nothing. Doing nothing.

If only she'd known then that years later she'd be sitting in his truck as they drove back to his ranch to have casual sex, and that she'd still be just as tongue-tied and awkward as she had been at seventeen.

Then again, perhaps it was better that she hadn't known. At least then she'd have had the comforting illusion that one day she'd be an adult and magically all of this would become clear.

Except it wasn't clear, and she found herself frantically trying to think of something to say, anything to relieve the suffocating tension in the truck, but every time she thought of something it seemed lame and boring and cringe-inducing.

She felt sweaty, like she had back in the ER the time of her first panic attack when a normal night shift full of overdoses, drunks, and assault victims had turned nasty. A guy had pulled a knife on her and security had been called; she'd gone into the bathroom to calm down and get herself into doctor mode and found she hadn't been able to. The thought of going back out into the ER had made her heart beat way too fast, made her feel cold and shaky and sweaty.

She'd thought the feeling would go away in time, but it hadn't. It had only got progressively worse. Really, the cancellation of Hope's wedding couldn't have come at a better time, because it had given her the perfect excuse to get away, to take some time out.

Perfect, except that she was on the verge of having a panic attack in Garrett's truck right before having sex with him for the first time. How humiliating.

"Hey," Garrett said quietly after a good ten minutes had passed. "You can relax. We don't have to do this if you don't want to."

Oh great. So he'd picked up on her anxiety. She'd almost ruined her career and now she'd probably ruin this too.

She smoothed her dress. "I do want to do this. I'm just… nervous."

He glanced at her in a flash of silver. "Why? It's supposed to be fun, remember?"

Of course it was. But she could also feel a certain familiar pressure weighing down on her. The same pressure she used to feel whenever she sat down for an exam or had to hand her report card to her father. It was the pressure to do well, to live up to the expectations her dad had of her.

"I know." She let out a shaky breath. Should she tell him the truth? Would he want to know? Would he laugh and tell her she was ridiculous? Would it ruin everything if she did?

"Just…performance anxiety," she said, going for a casual tone. There, that would do it. Just a little performance anxiety, no big deal.

Garrett sat there, the very epitome of laid-back and relaxed, one hand on the wheel, the other resting negligently on one powerful thigh. He didn't laugh. He didn't even smile.

"Yeah, fair," he said, treating her confession with absolute seriousness. "But you don't have to perform for me, doc. Why would you think you had to?"

Charity looked down at her dress, the blue fabric all creased by her nervous fingers. "Probably because most of my life has been about performance. That's what a lot of medicine is at least, being calm and in control all the time. Having to look like you know what you're doing even when you don't."

He nodded. "Well, sure. But this isn't medicine. You're not saving me from death or anything. Though," he added, "I'm not sure that kiss of yours wouldn't have brought a man back to life."

Charity felt a smile tug at the corners of her mouth. The tension in her shoulders slowly began to unwind and the cold feeling in the tips of her fingers and toes receded.

"In fact," Garrett continued. "You don't have to do a damn thing. I'll do all the work, while you just lie back and enjoy it."

A heated image came to her of doing just that, relaxing back on his bed and letting him take control. Letting him make all the decisions, working to figure out what was wrong and what treatment she needed. What he could do to make her feel better.

She could be the patient for once and let someone else take care of her...

Need unfolded inside her, aching and desperate. "Yes," she said thickly. "I think I'd like that."

She could feel him watching her, but she didn't look at him. She felt a little too exposed for that.

"Okay," he murmured in that quiet, deep voice. "That I can certainly do."

The tension in the truck stayed taut, but it wasn't a difficult tension now. It was more anticipation than anything else, and by the time they'd pulled up the gravel driveway to Garrett's house, the anticipation had turned into a charged excitement.

Garrett got out of the truck, came around to her door and pulled it open. Then he took her hand, his fingers enfolding hers, warm and strong, and led her from the truck to the front porch and up the stairs.

Once they were inside, standing in the spacious, high-ceilinged hallway, he took her face between his hands and all her remaining uncertainty vanished as his mouth settled on hers.

Charity met the kiss with her own hunger and a desperation that felt too strong to contain, as if she'd underestimated just how much she'd wanted him. As if years of longing had built and built without her knowing, and now it was all flooding out of her and into him, all that desperate teenage desire she'd never quite managed to leave behind.

He tasted hot and rich and decadent, and she kissed him back, chasing his taste, putting her hands on his hard chest and spreading her fingers out, testing the feel of him. His hands moved to her hips, pulling her close the way he had earlier in the yarn store. It felt like leaning against a hot iron stove.

She arched into him, her mouth opening beneath his, letting him in. He accepted her invitation and deepened the kiss. He tasted so good she couldn't stand it.

He smoothed his hands over her butt, fitting her hips to his. She could feel how aroused he was through the denim of his jeans and she felt a little burst of pride at how she could make a man who'd been the baddest of boys want her so very much.

She pressed herself against him, flexing her hips against his, and he made a low, rough sound in his throat that excited her. Then he broke away abruptly and before she could protest, he'd swept her up into his arms and turned for the stairs.

"I should probably walk." Her voice was breathless, her mouth burning from his kiss, her heart thundering.

"No, you shouldn't." He carried her up the stairs as if she weighed nothing at all. "I told you I'd do all the work."

She rested her head against the hard muscle of his shoulder, glancing up at his beautifully carved profile. "Should I just lie back and think of England then?"

He glanced down at her, and a smile turned his mouth, so wicked it stole her breath completely. "Don't think of England. Think of me."

Charity quivered. Oh, he was so gorgeous. And for tonight he was hers, all hers.

Garrett reached the top of the stairs and her heart began to thump harder as he moved down a short hallway to the doorway at the end. It opened onto a big room with a window overlooking the back of the house and a massive wooden bed. The bed was covered in a beautiful handmade quilt of blues and greens, and as he carried her over to it and set her down on the mattress, she ran her hand over it.

"This is beautiful," she murmured. "Where did it come from?"

He raised an eyebrow. "I'm about to give you the night of your life and you're asking me where I got my quilt from?"

She blushed. "Sorry."

"You've got to stop apologizing." He knelt down on the floor in front of her, the most flat-out sexy smile turning his mouth. "You have nothing to be sorry for."

Something inside her relaxed at the sight of that smile and at the heat glittering in his eyes. She gave him a tentative smile back. "Force of habit, I think."

"Break the habit, doc. You're fine." He pushed a curl back behind her ear, letting his fingers trail down the side of her neck and making her shiver. "My gran made me the quilt."

Something strangely tender caught at her heart. Bad-boy Garrett Roy had the quilt his grandmother made him on his bed. But then…that was what had made her fall for him years ago, wasn't it? Watching him that day in the yarn store, helping out behind the counter and smiling at the old ladies, chatting with them. And then the times she'd spotted him in town with his gran, catching at her elbow to steady her as they'd walked down the street together.

The bad boy who lived with his gran and who obviously cared for her. The bad guy with the heart of gold…

She smiled. "You used to have such a terrible reputation. But you were never really all that bad, were you?"

He shook his head. "Don't go thinking I'm some kind of good guy because of this quilt, Charity. You know I dropped out of school and left Jasper Creek to go bull riding. Just like my dad. Caused my grandmother no end of grief."

Curiosity caught at her. "But, you're back now."

"Yeah, I am. And I have a lot of stuff to make up for."

"Oh, but—"

His hand firmed on the back of her neck, bringing her in for another heated, desperate kiss. "No more talking, doc," he murmured against her mouth. "There are a few other things I want to do."

And then he was kissing her again, his hands deftly stripping the dress from her, and then her underwear, until she was sitting there naked.

There was no self-consciousness, as if he'd stripped her inhibitions away along with her clothes, leaving only an overwhelming need for him to be naked too, so she could touch him, feel him against her the way she used to imagine all those years ago when she'd barely been able to imagine what making love to a man meant.

She reached for him but he'd already gotten to his feet, stepping away and getting rid of his clothes before joining her on the bed.

He was beautiful—hard and chiseled and powerful. A work of male art. And then she was under him, his hands moving over her, stroking her, teasing her, taking his time with her. His mouth burned at her throat and then lower, kissing down her body, lingering on her breasts, teasing each nipple with his tongue, before sucking gently.

Charity sighed and arched into him, the heat of his mouth inciting and inflaming her, pleasure moving like wildfire throughout her entire body. She touched him all over the way she'd dreamt of, stroking carved muscle and the oiled silk of his skin, his body all hard, flat planes while she was soft curves. She'd never been so aware of the differences between them. Never realized quite how arousing it would be, either.

Then his hand stroked between her thighs and the wildfire moved lower, became more urgent, more demanding, and she gasped, lifting herself against him, pushing into his hand.

He murmured into her ear, soft things and dirty things that made her moan against his mouth as he kissed her, that made her writhe beneath him as the pleasure wound into a tight, hard knot inside her. Then he did something with his hand even as he drew one hard nipple into his mouth, and she felt the knot inside her break apart, pleasure exploding like a bright light being switched on in a dark room, chasing away the darkness and turning everything brilliant.

She lay there, trembling and barely conscious of what was happening, as she heard him reach into the drawer of the nightstand beside the bed. There came the rustle of foil as he protected them both, then he was back over her, spreading her thighs with his hands and pushing his hips between them.

"Garrett," she whispered as he positioned himself, running her hands up his broad chest and feeling the slight prickle of hair and the smooth velvet of his skin.

He looked down at her, his eyes gone molten silver. His expression was taut and hungry, the wicked smile gone. He slipped one hand beneath her at the small of her back, tilting her hips, and then, still looking down at her, he pushed inside in a long, deep glide.

She groaned. He was big, but he felt so good, fitting her in the most perfect way. In fact, everything about this was perfect. It was a dream in many ways, a fantasy come to life. Yet so much better than any fantasy.

He settled deep inside her, his body like a furnace over

hers, and she loved it. She loved everything about it. She didn't have to do anything; it was all on him, just as he'd said. All she had to do was lie there and hold on to him, look up into his eyes and feel what he was doing to her.

He began to move, slow and deep, in a rhythm that made her breath catch and everything inside her pull tight in hunger. His hand was at her back, encouraging her to move and then she was, matching him, and it felt right. It felt perfect.

She stared up at him, mesmerized by the look in his eyes, by the pleasure she could see there, his gaze electric with it, burning like magnesium. He didn't look away, just stared down at her as he moved inside her, sharing the pleasure with her, pushing them both higher and higher, until she didn't think she could stand it.

Then his hand was down between them, touching her gently right where she was most sensitive. It was the lightest brush of his fingers, and she felt the pleasure rise like an ocean wave, unstoppable, inevitable, overwhelming.

She cried out his name as it crashed over her, drowning her, but his arms were around her, anchoring her, keeping her safe in the flood.

Dimly, she felt him move harder, faster, and then she heard his growl of pleasure as the climax came for him too, drowning him right along with her.

CHAPTER SIX

GARRETT HELD CHARITY'S trembling body against his and struggled to catch his breath. She was so warm and soft and silky, fitting against him so perfectly that he didn't want to let her go. It was a strange thing to think. He'd never wanted to hold a woman before, not like this. Mostly once the sex was over, he was done and out of there.

It was one of the reasons he hadn't ever brought a woman back to his place, so why he'd brought Charity back here, he couldn't fathom. It just felt like she deserved more from him than a seedy motel or the back of his truck.

He'd waited a long time to have her, after all, and now here she was, in his bed, beneath him, looking up at him, her deep blue eyes gone dark with pleasure, her cheeks rosy and her mouth full and red from his kisses. He felt no urge to leave as quickly as possible the way he normally did.

In fact, moving to the bathroom to get rid of the condom was almost beyond him.

However, he forced himself to move, shifting off her, kissing her briefly before slipping out of bed and into the bathroom down the hall.

A couple of minutes later he was back, gathering her into his arms as he slid beneath the covers again, her sweet, musky scent and the feel of her nakedness against him already making him hard again.

"You okay?" he asked, rolling over onto his back and

bringing her with him so she was sprawled over his chest. Her weight on him was delightful, the silky brush of her hair against his skin even more so. Hell, he wanted her again already while the aftershocks of the first orgasm were still echoing through him.

"Yes." Her expression was a bit dazed. "That was kind of amazing."

"Kind of?"

She smiled. "Okay, fully amazing. Wholly incredible."

He lifted one hand, toying idly with one of her curls, winding it around his finger. "I aim to please."

Her smile deepened. "You're still a little arrogant. Though after that, I guess you have a reason to be."

He laughed. "I'm not the only one with a reason to be arrogant. And I agree with it being amazing."

Her smile turned shy, a ghost of the smile he remembered from years ago. "I was so annoyed with you when you first turned up, you know."

"Really?" He tugged playfully on her curl. "I'd never have guessed."

Charity folded her hands on top of his chest and rested her chin on them. She had no self-consciousness to her now or even a trace of the anxiety he'd seen in her face earlier in his truck, which made him very glad. "I suppose it was obvious. I'm sorry, I should—"

"Hey." He tugged on her curl harder. "What did I say about apologizing?"

She rolled her eyes, which made him want to pull her in close for another kiss. "You were pretty annoyed with me too."

"Of course I was. I wasn't expecting my secret high-school crush to have suddenly bought my grandma's yarn store." Talking after sex wasn't something he normally did. But he was relaxed and it felt natural to talk to her like this.

Charity's blue eyes widened in surprise. "I was your secret crush?"

"Oh yeah." He let her curl unwind around his finger, then slowly wound it up again, enjoying the silky feel of it against his skin. "I was hot for my brainy tutor all right. You were so cute in your little skirts and knee socks. So sweet and earnest." He grinned at the shocked look on her face. "I felt bad because you were so desperate to help me and yet I was having the dirtiest thoughts about you. You shot my concentration all to hell."

She was blushing now, staring at him as if she wasn't sure whether to believe him or not. "No way. You never said anything to me."

"Of course I never said anything to you." He rubbed his thumb over the silky curl, looking into her eyes. "You were far too good for me, Charity Golding. And I thought at the time that if there was one decent thing I could do, it was to stay away from you."

She stared at him for a long moment, then her lashes descended, veiling her gaze as she concentrated on his chest. Then she said, "I thought you didn't like me."

He hadn't thought it would matter, not after so many years, but there was an edge in her voice that caught at him. Letting go of her curl, he reached for her chin and tipped it up slightly with one finger, so he could see her expression.

"That's what I wanted you to think." He studied her. "Because I didn't trust myself around you. And when I was seventeen and an idiot, that seemed like the best way to make sure you stayed away from me."

She let out a soft breath. "Well, it worked. It worked really well."

That almost sounded as if she'd been hurt, which he was surprised about. It had been a long time ago and surely whatever she'd felt for him, she'd gotten over it easily enough.

Yet, perhaps not?

"Did it really matter that much to you?" he asked, frowning.

Her lashes lifted, her gaze meeting his. "Yes, of course it mattered to me. I had one hell of a crush on you too. Didn't you know that?"

Garrett wasn't sure what the feeling was that swept through him, a curious mix of intense satisfaction and a very real regret. "I didn't know," he said quietly. "I mean, I suspected that you might, but I wasn't sure how serious it was. I thought if I pretended I didn't feel a thing around you, you'd forget about me."

"Why would you want me to forget about you?" she asked, as if the answer wasn't obvious to her. And clearly it wasn't.

He stroked the curl wrapped around his finger. "Think about it. You were Dr. Golding's daughter. Top of the class, with a bright future ahead of you. I was no-good John Roy's deadbeat son. Cutting class. Stealing cars. Drinking behind the bleachers. Shoplifting from the stores in town. There was no future ahead of me except a downward spiral. I had nothing to give you and so I thought it would be better if you stayed way the hell away from me."

Her gaze was on his, dark and curious. "I suppose. But why did you do all that stuff, Garrett? You weren't stupid. You could have gone to college if you'd wanted and I think you knew that."

The conversation had taken a turn that he wasn't keen on. He wasn't here to talk about the past. They were here for sex and that was all. Yet he didn't want to give her nothing. She'd always deserved better from him.

Instead, he looked at the curl wound around his finger. Even in the darkness of the room he could see the red in it, smoldering like embers of a banked fire. That was Charity, wasn't it? She was all banked embers. All it would take was one breath and she'd go up in flames.

"My mom left when I was six," he said after a moment. "I don't even remember her. And Dad was out on the circuit all the time. He was hardly ever at home—at least, I sure as hell barely saw him. Then he was killed in a bull-riding accident when I was ten, and for a lot of years after that I was just… angry. Angry that I never got any time with him, because he was never at home. Angry that bull riding was always more important than I was. When he was home, I tried to be the good son to give him a reason to stay. But nothing I did made any difference. He just kept on riding. Then, after he died, my grandma tried her best with me, but I was too angry to listen to her. And when I hit puberty I thought that since he was gone, there was no reason to try to be good enough anymore. So I wasn't."

She didn't say anything, her gaze full of sympathy and without judgment.

"Gran put up with me for a few years, but then she got sick of my behavior," he went on. Now he was talking, he couldn't shut himself up. "She told me that she'd raised me better than this and if I didn't start taking responsibility for myself, I'd be no better than my dad. It really stuck with me, what she said. And I decided I was going to be better than he was. That I wanted to be the best damn bull rider in the state. So I left school without graduating—I needed to be out of that environment—and I went on the circuit, and eventually, I did become the best damn bull rider in the state."

"So what made you come back here then?"

"I wasn't planning on it." He unwound and rewound her curl, trying to ignore the strange heaviness that sat inside him. The regret that always came with remembering the past. "But Gran had a fall. My uncle, who didn't show his damn face once after Dad died, called me to tell me, but when I offered to come home, he told me not to bother. He said it would be better if Gran was looked after by someone responsible and reliable, that I was too much like Dad to be a good caregiver." Tension crawled through him, his jaw getting tight. "I couldn't let that stand. So I gave up the circuit and came home."

Charity's brow creased. "Wow. So you gave up everything to come home and look after her? What about your uncle?"

"He wanted Dad's ranch and I think he thought that if he took over caring for Gran, she'd sign it over to him since she'd inherited it after Dad was killed. He didn't care about her. But I did. She'd raised me and I didn't want to leave her alone with a son who didn't give a shit about her."

Charity's gaze became soft. "That's a pretty amazing thing to do, Garrett Roy. To give everything up to come home and look after her."

He didn't like how she was looking at him, as if he were a goddamn saint, which he knew very well he was not. "It would have been more amazing never to leave in the first place. More amazing not to go chasing my father's ghost all over the damn state. Perhaps if I hadn't left, she wouldn't have had that fall."

Concern rippled across her face. "No, you can't go thinking like that. The important thing is that you were there when she needed you."

Part of him wanted to believe that, while another part of him wanted this conversation to be over. Because they weren't here to discuss the past, to have any deep and meaningful conversations about their lives. They were here for casual sex and that was it.

"Yeah, well, whether it was an amazing thing to do or not, I just did what needed to be done." He tightened his grip on her and rolled over, taking her beneath him. "Now, how about we have some more of this casual sex, hmm?"

Charity looked like she wanted to say something more, her gaze flickering over his face. But then she let out a breath and reached for him, drawing his mouth down on hers and ending the conversation.

CHAPTER SEVEN

A COUPLE OF days later, Charity bustled about the yarn store, moving the last of the boxes out in preparation for ripping up the carpet on the floor when the door opened.

She glanced up in time to see Garrett come inside, the door banging shut behind him. He was carrying two take-out cups, the rich smell of coffee filling the little shop.

Her heart did a strange leaping thing, which was aggravating, but it was probably due to the scent of coffee. Yes, it had to be that. Nothing else. Certainly nothing to do with the way those worn jeans of his fit, or how the black T-shirt he wore today molded to his wide shoulders and broad chest.

Gorgeous doesn't even begin to cover that man.

It really didn't.

Stupid doesn't even begin to cover your decision to keep sleeping with him, either.

Charity ignored her tiresome common sense. Because, really, what *was* stupid was thinking that continuing to sleep with him was stupid. She was back in Jasper Creek to find happiness and have fun, and so far, she was very happy and also having fun. And a large part of that was down to Garrett.

He'd been the one to suggest that they meet up again the following night and she'd been more than happy to do so. He'd said he had a few fantasies to work through when it came to her and she was very much okay with that, since she had a few of her own. It was all part of the "casual sex" thing.

So, for the past few days, Garrett had been picking her up from the store, helping her with buying the supplies she needed for the restoration, then taking her back to his place where they fell into bed almost immediately. Afterward, he'd make dinner and they'd sit in his big, open-plan farmhouse kitchen and talk. She'd tell him some of her ER war stories, while he'd return the favor with some bull-riding ones.

Of course, she'd had to endure some good-natured teasing from her friends, but that was a small price to pay for the nights she enjoyed with Garrett.

Much to her annoyance, Kit had found a lasso sitting on a box in the attic, which meant she'd had to waste a valuable fifteen minutes standing on Jasper Creek's main street holding it for absolutely no reason as her punishment for breaking the "no hookups" rule. She complained until Pru threatened to get a random passerby to take a picture, since all their phones were still locked in the basement downstairs.

Luckily Garrett hadn't been in town that day so at least she didn't have to explain that to him.

They hadn't talked again the way they had the first night, which was fine with her since it seemed like that had made him uncomfortable. If she was honest, it had made her uncomfortable too, though finding out he'd had a crush on her had given her the biggest thrill. She understood why he'd never said anything to her. Nothing good would have come of it, not when she'd had so much schoolwork to keep up with. Plus, he'd clearly had some issues in his life, his dad being one of them.

She was curious about that, just as she was starting to

be curious about most aspects of Garrett Roy's life, but she pushed that curiosity firmly to one side as he came over with the coffee. They were "casual" and she was pretty sure discussing his father's death did not fall under the definition of casual in any way.

"Caffeine," she said instead. "You must have read my mind."

"I kept you up pretty late last night, so I thought you might need something to keep you going." His smile got a wicked edge. "Especially when I plan on doing the same thing again tonight."

She grinned, taking the cup from him. "I could be persuaded."

His silver eyes glittered. "Can I start the persuading right now?"

Her heartbeat sped up, excitement gathering inside her. Oh, she'd love for him to start persuading her now. The centennial was still weeks away, which meant they could afford some time out, surely? Then again, she did have to start somewhere and there was still a lot to do to get it ready. It wouldn't do to get distracted.

She took a sip of the coffee. It was the good stuff, from the coffee cart that she'd discovered the first day she'd gotten in to Jasper Creek. She made a visit there every day; she'd always run on caffeine ever since she was a med student.

"I'd love you to, but unfortunately I have work to do." She looked around at the store which was still cluttered with things. "I need to start ripping up the carpet, which means moving all of this stuff ASAP."

Garrett took a look around. "You want some help?"

Her heart gave another of those stupid leaps, which she again ignored. "You really would?"

His gaze came back to hers, but she couldn't read it. "You sound surprised."

"Since you weren't happy about the name change, I kind of assumed you wouldn't want anything to do with a complete refurbishment."

A rueful smile turned his mouth. "I wasn't happy because I was still attracted to you and I didn't want to be. It had nothing to do with the name change."

Charity didn't know whether to be annoyed about that or not. "Oh. Right. So you're okay with the name change?"

He took a sip of his coffee, gazing at her from over the top of the cup. "Does it matter?"

"Of course it matters. I don't want changing the name to end up being contentious and I don't want to hurt anyone's feelings about it."

"You're very worried about upsetting people."

"I'm a doctor and doctors are supposed to make people better, not upset them." She changed her grip on the cup, the heat of the liquid inside burning her fingers.

Garrett hitched one powerful shoulder up against one of the shelves. "So when exactly are you going back to Seattle?"

The question was an uncomfortable one, mainly because the thought of going back filled her with the kind of heavy dread that made her feel like she'd swallowed a bag full of rocks.

But she didn't want to talk about it or even think about it right now. Not when she had a store to set up and casual sex to have. There would be plenty of time for that later.

"After the centennial," she said noncommittally. "Well, if you're going to help, you can start by taking some of those boxes down into the basement." As changes of subject went, it wasn't a very graceful one and she could tell by the pressure of his gaze on her that her answer hadn't satisfied him.

"What made you want to take a break?" he asked, not moving.

Charity turned away, going over to the counter and putting her coffee cup down then fussing around with the other boxes that were already sitting there. She didn't want to have this discussion yet, not when she hadn't even had it with her friends. They hadn't asked her what had made her take a couple of months off, obviously picking up on her "I don't want to talk about it" vibes, and she was grateful.

Talking about her ridiculous anxiety attacks and the general stress of her career made her feel like a failure anyway. Her father had so wanted her to specialize in emergency medicine; it had been his dream for her and she'd wanted it too. He'd sacrificed a lot to care for her after her mother had died, and so giving something back to him had felt important. He'd been ecstatic when she'd gotten into the emergency medicine training program and thrilled when she'd landed a job. And the thought that she then hadn't been able to cope with the demands of the position bothered her a lot. She didn't want to disappoint him.

Certainly she didn't want to talk to Garrett about it. Bull riding took determination and strength, and he'd been good at what he did. He'd only given it up because he'd had to look after his grandmother. But her? Stress leave because someone had pulled a knife on her. As if assaults by patients didn't happen in every ER every day. It sounded pathetic to her. Weak, even.

"Haven't we had this discussion?" She tried to sound dismissive. "You know, Hope's wedding was canceled and so we all decided to—"

"I know about Hope's wedding. Brooks told me all about

it. No, I want to know what made you want to come here. A couple of months is a long time to take out from a job for one canceled wedding."

Charity fiddled with one of the boxes, trying not to tense up. She didn't know why she was turning this into a big deal. What did she care if Garrett thought she was weak or a failure? It didn't matter, especially when she was going back.

She could tell him and he could think whatever the hell he liked.

"I had to take stress leave after I started having a few panic attacks," she said lightly, staring down at the dusty counter. "We had a security incident one night and some guy pulled a knife on me. It was fine; I wasn't hurt. He was drunk and worried about a friend…but still. It affected me. I found it difficult to come in for my shift the next day and it got worse and worse." She was pleased with how casual she sounded. "Then one day I couldn't even step over the threshold. I took a few days off here and there but then the thing with Hope's wedding happened and I decided it was the perfect time to take a couple of months off, so I did."

She straightened and forced herself to turn around and face him, to show him that it wasn't a big deal, no matter how it sounded. "And here I am."

His gaze was very level and it struck her suddenly that there was something very level about Garrett Roy, period. No matter that he'd been a wild kid when he'd been young, he was still the boy she'd seen helping out in this very store, smiling at the mainly elderly clientele and chatting easily with them.

A calm sort of guy.

Definitely not you, no matter how hard you try.

It was true. Calm was something she'd had to cultivate,

since it didn't come naturally to her, no matter what her friends liked to think. She felt everything very deeply, but doctors couldn't allow their feelings to get the better of them and so she constantly had to corral hers.

Garrett's silver gaze roved over her, and she had to fight the urge to shift on her feet, uncomfortable with how intently he was looking at her.

"I'm sorry," he said, and it sounded as though he genuinely meant it. "That sounds tough."

Charity lifted a shoulder, shoving the feelings of discomfort back up in her mental attic with all the rest of her emotions. "It was. But it's better now I'm here." She forced a smile. "You don't have to help me with the boxes if you don't want to."

Garrett pushed himself away from the shelf. "I'm here for your pleasure, doc. And if that means moving boxes right now, then I'm happy to do that for you."

He didn't push and he didn't bring up the subject again. And Charity wasn't sure if she was disappointed about that or not.

No, she decided. She wasn't disappointed. Not in the slightest.

GARRETT STACKED AWAY the last of the boxes in the basement under the yarn store, his head still full of what Charity had told him earlier about why she'd taken some time out from medicine. About the panic attacks. Her voice when she'd told him the story had been perfectly level but there had been a slightly defiant glitter in her eyes when she'd faced him. As if daring him to say something about it, though he wasn't sure what she'd thought he might say.

Taking a break after something like that had happened seemed reasonable to him. Sure, as a bull rider, you got injured, you got thrown, you just got back up on the bull and you tried again. Especially if you wanted to get paid.

But riding a bull was different from being a doctor in the ER. When you were a bull rider, the only thing you had to worry about was yourself. You weren't responsible for another person's life. Plus, when you got onto a bull, getting hurt was always a possibility and you knew that going in. As a doctor, on the other hand, you expected to save other people, not have your own life be threatened.

No wonder the attack Charity had described had affected her.

Clearly, though, by the way she'd said it, Charity was trying to minimize what had happened to her and that made him wonder why. Taking a couple of months off work on stress leave was a pretty big deal and sure, admitting that you couldn't handle something was tough. But it was nothing to be embarrassed about. Or was there more to it than simple embarrassment?

Why are you even thinking about it? What does it matter why? It's none of your business anyway.

It wasn't. Yet it was clear that she didn't like talking about her decision to take some time out. It was clear that something about it bothered her and he didn't like that she was bothered.

It made him want to help her. If she wanted something different, a break from medicine, then perhaps he could give that to her. He couldn't help with much else, but he could certainly help her relax and have a bit of fun. He was a good-time guy after all.

After checking he'd finished with the boxes, he then headed back upstairs to the yarn store.

The place was looking much less cluttered now, but she was still going to have her work cut out for her with dismantling the shelves then ripping up the carpet. She'd mentioned to him that she'd wanted polished wooden floors, and that was going to mean sanding and then varnishing... Yeah, it was going to take some time.

"That's the last of them," he said, moving over to the counter.

She was bent over it, writing something in a little notebook.

"What's that?" he asked.

"Oh, my plans for the store. Do you want to see?"

"Sure."

She pushed the notebook to him and he glanced down. The paper was covered with an illegible scrawl.

He shook his head. "I'm sure it's all great, but I can't read that."

She laughed. "Oh, sorry. Doctor's handwriting. It's always bad."

"Why don't you give me a quick rundown then."

Charity didn't need to be asked twice, launching into an explanation about how she wanted to paint the walls, pull up the carpet, and polish the floors. Then she was going to get in some new stock and maybe paint the shelves white to show off the yarn.

"You want to do all that? In time for the centennial?" He took a slow look around the store. "You might struggle doing it all on your own."

"Yes, I know. I'm behind in my schedule." She shot him a look. "Which is your fault."

Well, he knew that. And he didn't mind it one bit.

He gave her a wicked look. "Feel free to say no. At any time."

She flushed, glancing away from him then back again,

a smile curving her lovely mouth. "Maybe I should. Your ego is getting out of control."

It wasn't his ego. It was his desire for her, which showed no sign of abating. If he'd let himself think about it, it might have worried him. But he didn't let himself think about it.

You can't go getting involved.

He wasn't getting involved. He was only sleeping with her and offering to help out with the shop preparation. That was all. No big deal.

"Why don't you let me help out?" he suggested. "In return for getting you off track."

Charity gave him an enigmatic look, biting on her lip the way she used to back when they were teenagers. "Help out how?"

"I've done my fair share of painting and sanding. Had to, to get the ranch up to scratch after I came back from the circuit. I'm pretty handy with building and fixing too."

She frowned. "What about your ranch?"

He thought of his uncle and his opinion that Garrett's environmentally friendly approach to his ranching was evidence of his recklessness. He thought of his grandmother too, and how she'd left him the ranch, a demonstration of her belief in him. Both of them were very good reasons not to neglect it.

But then, he wasn't planning on neglecting it. And it wasn't like he was going back on the circuit again like his father had. He was only helping out a friend.

"I've always got ranching to do. But I can come over here in the evenings, if you like." He nodded toward the shelving units. "You'll need my help taking those down, and ripping up carpet and sanding floors is a hell of a job. So is painting. Plus, you'll need help going through the stock and seeing which things you want to keep and which to throw away."

Her frown deepened, but then she always frowned when she was thinking hard about something. It made him want to put his finger between her red brows and smooth the lines away. It also made him very aware of how much he wanted her to say yes.

Because he couldn't think of anything nicer than being in Charity's store and helping her get it ready for customers. And not because he cared about her customers, or her store, to be fair. It was Charity he wanted to spend time with.

She blew out a breath. "Well, I did want to do this myself, but I suppose you're right. I don't have a lot of time left. I don't want to impose though."

"You're not imposing. I offered, remember? And I'd be honored to work on this. It's my gran's legacy after all."

The frown on Charity's face eased. "When you put it like that, I can hardly say no. Okay, you have a deal."

He ignored the rush of satisfaction that shot through him. "Great. I'll come here in the evenings after I've finished at the ranch. How does that sound?"

She smiled, a spark glowing in her eyes. "It sounds good. I just… I want this to be a success, Garrett. The past six months have been really hard and I…" She stopped. "I just want a win. Plus, easy and fun and uncomplicated wouldn't hurt, either. Does that make sense?"

It did. Given what she'd just told him, it made a whole lot of sense. And it was all stuff he could help her with. Certainly the fun and uncomplicated part.

The success though… If she wanted a win that badly, it must mean that in some way she'd had a loss.

Perhaps it was those panic attacks. Perhaps she felt she'd failed in some way.

"It does," he said. "And I can help you out with all of that. But winning only matters if you've got something to prove. You know that, right?"

Color shifted in her cheeks. "Sure. But I don't have anything to prove."

"Then does it matter if it's a success or not?"

"I'm sure the mayor who gave us the leases would have something to say about that."

"I'm not talking about the mayor. I'm talking about you."

"Okay, yes. It matters to me if it's a success or not. I didn't like that I had to take some time out from my career. And it would mean a lot for me to have something to show for it in the end."

That made sense. She'd always been such a high achiever and he'd used to wonder back then what she was trying to prove, or who she was trying to prove herself to. Was it her dad? Given that she'd talked a lot about him and how badly he'd wanted her to succeed, that seemed likely.

It also seemed that, though she'd succeeded in doing everything she'd planned back then, she still felt the need to prove herself.

He wondered why that was and almost opened his mouth to ask her. But then he stopped, because it wasn't his business to ask. It wasn't his business to wonder, either.

Easy, fun, and uncomplicated, that was what she wanted. And that was what he'd give her.

He reached out and touched her cheek, letting his fingers brush over her skin. "You'll get that win, doc. I'll make sure of it."

CHAPTER EIGHT

CHARITY BARELY SPENT any time at the farmhouse over the following couple of weeks, since she had so much to do in the yarn store. But she shared gossip with her friends over the lunches they had together as the others got stuck into the hard work of restoration on their own stores, even though Pru complained the rest of them talked more about their men than they did about their stores. Hope was starry-eyed about Brooks, and Kit was all "Browning this" and "Browning that," and to be fair, Charity wasn't exactly blameless. She did mention Garrett rather often. But then, it wasn't as if Pru didn't stay quiet about Grant, either.

Privately, Charity wondered if there wasn't something going on there, but she didn't have too much time to think about it, because at the end of another day moving furniture or ripping up carpet or plastering walls, Garrett would turn up and she'd find herself staying until he'd finished whatever task she'd given him for the evening. Then he'd drive her back to the farmhouse so she could shower and change, before taking her home to his place.

They still hadn't talked about personal stuff, not since she'd told him about the panic attacks, and she was glad. She didn't need to talk about it. The sex was phenomenal and he made her laugh, his calm presence soothing something tense and aching inside her. One night he even taught her how to knit, which delighted her. She'd never have guessed that the sexy school bad boy knew how to knit his own socks, and the fact that he did and was quite matter-of-fact about it, charmed her completely. She wasn't very good at it and that bothered her at first, but then Garrett said that if there weren't any mistakes, then it wasn't handmade. She liked that thought enough that she stopped worrying about loose tension and slipped stitches. She was content to knit a scarf with lots of holes that she ended up loving anyway because she'd made it herself.

It was enough.

Almost enough to make her forget that all of this was temporary. That after the centennial, she'd have to go back to work. But since there was no immediate pressure to think about it, she didn't. She preferred to think about the easy, uncomplicated present with Garrett instead.

Toward the end of the week she did another of her mad dashes into the shower, before scrambling into a clean pair of jeans and a blouse of light green silk, then dashing down the farmhouse stairs, heading for the front door.

She and Garrett had just finished polishing the floor and the varnish was now dry enough to walk on, so they'd planned on sitting down and going through what stock needed to be ordered. It was still a working evening, but not one that was going to involve too much physical exertion, and she wanted to put on something pretty for him, hence the silk blouse.

It didn't mean anything. Only that she wanted to look nice. Nothing more. Though, as she dashed out the door, Kit called out from her place on the front porch, "Who is that strange woman who keeps helping herself to our shower? Any of you guys know who she is?"

"Sorry," Charity called back over her shoulder. "I have to get to the store."

"Who wants to bet it's not the store?" Pru said.

Hope said something else to that, but Charity didn't bother to stay to find out.

She had other places to be.

She got Pru to give her a ride into Jasper Creek and when she got there saw the strange glow through the windows of the yarn store, a warm, flickering light.

Puzzled, she pushed open the door and then stopped, her breath catching.

A rug had been spread over the newly sanded and polished floorboards, and a few cushions were scattered about. On carefully positioned pieces of newspaper stood candleholders with little candles burning cheerfully in them.

Plates had been placed on the rug too, with cheese and crackers, a salad, crusty French bread, and cold meats. Another plate held some delicious-looking chocolate desserts and a bottle of white wine stood open with a couple of glasses beside it.

Garrett was sitting on the rug. He looked up as she came in, meeting her wide-eyed gaze and smiling, the candlelight gleaming in his silver eyes. Charity felt her heart literally miss a beat.

The store was now freshly painted with pristine white walls and the floor was polished and gleaming. It was luminous. Light, airy, peaceful. A special place.

But not quite as special as the man sitting there with the picnic he'd clearly organized especially for her spread out around him.

Slowly, she shut the door and came over to where he'd spread the rug. The scent of varnish, new paint, and warm wax hung heavy in the air, and she knew that forever afterward, that would be the smell of happiness to her.

"Wow," she said, her voice not quite as steady as she

wanted it to be. "This is amazing, Garrett. What's the occasion?"

"I thought we should celebrate finishing most of the hard physical work." He patted the cushion next to him. "Come and sit. I'll pour you some wine."

She moved over to the cushion he'd indicated, her heart beating a little too fast for comfort. She couldn't remember the last time anyone had done anything this nice for her.

He poured the wine, handed her a glass, then picked up his own. "Here's to A Simple Thread."

Charity blinked. "I thought you didn't like the name?"

He grinned. "I changed my mind. I think Grandma would have loved it."

Her throat closed and she couldn't have said why. It was just a name after all, nothing worth of this sudden upwelling of emotion. And yet the fact that Garrett did like it after all mattered to her.

It shouldn't.

Well, maybe not. But she could get a little emotional about the fact that he appreciated the name she'd picked. It didn't have to mean anything if she didn't want it to.

"Thank you." She tried to keep her voice measured. "Thank you for your help. Thank you for…this." She nodded to the food and the picnic setting.

Heat glittered in his gaze along with something else she couldn't quite interpret. But all he said was, "No problem."

A small, hot ball of emotion sat in the middle of Charity's chest, but since it had no right to be there, she ignored it. It was just a few candles and some wine and food. A lovely gesture, but nothing worth getting emotional about. He was only helping her celebrate the refurbishment, that was all.

She swallowed past the lump in her throat and breathed past the weight in her chest.

"A Simple Thread," she murmured and clinked her glass with his. Then she took a sip of the wine, which was cool and tart on her tongue.

"So, what made you think of it?" she asked after a moment. "The food and candles, and the wine, I mean."

"I could have taken you out somewhere nice for dinner, but I thought you might prefer to have it here." The heat in his eyes glinted. "Plus, there is privacy."

She flushed. Clearly the man had plans and she liked it. "Very true."

Garrett held his wineglass in one long-fingered hand, a slightly wicked half smile curving his mouth. But there was a sharp look in his eyes, one that had nothing to do with desire.

"I wanted to ask you something. Why is this being a success so important for you?"

Great, so he wanted to talk about what she'd said the previous week about wanting a success. About needing a win. Damn, why had she said that? She felt like she'd given too much away.

"Why do you want to know?" she asked, taking another sip of her wine.

"Because I couldn't stop thinking about it. You said you wanted easy and fun, and yet this also needs to be a success. I just wondered why you're putting pressure on yourself, which doesn't seem to indicate easy and fun to me."

Charity fiddled with her wineglass. "I'm not putting pressure on myself."

"So you didn't say that you needed a win, then?"

Damn him. Why was he wanting to talk about this now?

"Does it matter?" she asked impatiently. "I thought we

were going to talk about what stock to order, not have a Q and A about my motivations."

If the sharp note in her voice bothered him, he gave no sign, pinning her with that relentless silver gaze of his. "Did you even like practicing medicine?"

Charity opened her mouth to tell him that of course she liked practicing medicine. That she loved it. You couldn't put all the years of training into it if you didn't love it.

But for some reason the words wouldn't come out.

Did you really love it? Or was it all just for your dad?

She ignored the thought, clearing her throat and forcing the words out. "Naturally. I wouldn't have put myself through all the time and expense if I hadn't. What makes you think I don't like it?"

"Because you don't talk about it. In fact, apart from telling me about the panic attacks, you barely even mention it."

Trying not to sound defensive, she asked, "So?"

"So, you talk about the yarn store all the time."

Charity drew her knees into her chest and wrapped her arms around them, her wineglass still held in her hand, discomfort twisting around inside her. She didn't want to talk about this, yet she also didn't want to give away that it bothered her. "What's that got to do with anything? You don't talk about your ranch nonstop. Anyway, it's not true that I never mention it. I told you some old ER stories."

"Yeah, a couple of old stories last week and that's it." His stare was very direct. "Why don't you like to talk about it?"

She shifted on her cushion. "I'm fine with talking about it. What about you? Did you love being a bull rider?"

Garrett didn't even blink at the abrupt change of subject. "I enjoyed the adrenaline rush. And the beer. And the money." A glimpse of a self-deprecating smile. "And the girls. So yeah, I loved those aspects of it. But after my uncle told me about Grandma, I realized that none of those things mattered. That people were more important."

The comment touched a chord inside her, making her momentarily forget her discomfort. He was a much more complex man than she'd thought, and he saw far too much, which was not the most comfortable combination.

But certainly people mattered to him. And they mattered to her too, but she knew deep down that wasn't why she'd gone into medicine. It was because the man who'd raised her had had such high standards for her. It came from a belief in her abilities, she understood that, but it also set such a tremendously high bar for her to reach.

Could you ever reach it? Were you ever good enough for the dreams he had for you?

He'd loved her, she had no doubt of that, and had believed in her. And she'd loved him too, which was why she'd tried so hard. But that love had ended up being such an enormous pressure, and here she was, still trapped in it.

"So it was easy to walk away?" she asked, not wanting to think about that thought. "You don't regret it?"

"No." The word was unhesitating. "I got to spend Gran's last few years with her and that was worth any amount of money or trophies. I couldn't have gone on for much longer anyway. Bull riding as a profession has a very limited life span."

"And now you're ranching." She sipped her wine, watching his face. "You ever miss it? The adrenaline rushes? The fame?" And then, because she couldn't help it, she added, "The girls?"

His eyes gleamed in the candlelight and something twisted inside her, something she didn't want to think was jealousy. "Sometimes," he admitted. "The money was good and yeah, I liked the adrenaline rush. But the ranch is where

I need to be. Gran left it to me and I wanted to do her proud since Dad neglected it so badly. Plus, my uncle wants to buy it from me because he disagrees with the way I do things. He thinks I'm not looking after it properly. And I want to prove him wrong."

There was determination in his eyes and his will was an almost palpable force. Charity found the combination almost unbearably attractive. She'd always liked a man who made decisions. Still, there was a certain irony in what he'd said.

"Is that why you keep asking me about what I have to prove?" she asked. "Because you have to prove yourself to your uncle?"

"I don't want to prove myself to my uncle. I want to prove him wrong." His grin flashed. "There's a difference."

"Why does he think you're not looking after it?" Charity asked, curious. Talking about him was much more interesting than talking about herself.

Garrett lifted one muscular shoulder. "I'm trying to do things in an environmentally friendly way and he doesn't like that. He thinks it doesn't work. Plus, he blames me for leaving Gran in the lurch when I went off on the circuit. He saw it as irresponsible. Too much like Dad, apparently."

"I'm sorry, Garrett," she said, not quite sure what else to say. She hadn't been expecting to have quite such a personal conversation. "That sounds tough."

"Well, I guess it was irresponsible of Dad to go off the way he did. But…he was only ever happy riding bulls." Garrett looked down at the wineglass in his hand. "He certainly wasn't happy on the ranch. So yeah, he neglected it. People said he was a bad father, but when he was home, he wasn't."

She could see it in his face all of a sudden, hear it in his voice. Garrett had loved his father. "Garrett, I—"

"When he died, I was angry," he went on, as if she hadn't spoken, clearly in the grip of some kind of memory he couldn't break out of. "I didn't want my gran. I wanted my dad. But she was so patient with me, even when I went off the rails. She wasn't happy with me going off chasing his ghost, but she knew it was something I had to do. So she let me go in the end."

Charity said nothing; she just let him talk.

"And I had a gift for it, like he did. But then Gran needed someone to look after her." A smile that had nothing to do with amusement twisted his beautiful mouth. "My uncle didn't want me to. He thought I'd do what my dad did with one foot in the ranch, the other in the circuit. That Gran would be left on her own. But I wanted to show him that I was better than that. That I was better, period."

He's not wrong. You're still trying to prove yourself too.

No, it was different with Charity. She wasn't trying to prove herself to her dad. He already thought she was capable of doing amazing things. It was more that she was trying to live up to what he wanted for her.

Or wanted for himself; there was no getting around that.

The thought sat uncomfortably inside her. That somehow her own career trajectory looked a lot like the trajectory her father had wanted for himself. Only, he'd never had it, because his wife had died leaving him with a small baby to care for.

You stopped him from achieving it, as well you know.

Yet, he'd never blamed her for what he'd lost. Her dad had been a good father, bringing her up with love and kindness. And she loved him very much in return. Which was what made her failure so much worse. He'd sacrificed so much for her and yet, it had all been for nothing…

Charity swallowed. "You're not like your father, Garrett," she said aloud, concentrating on him instead of the stupid thoughts that went around and around in her skull. "You made a choice to come home and stay home. For your grandmother and for the ranch. You're nothing like him at all."

Garrett's silver eyes held hers for a moment. "I thought I wasn't. But…there are a lot of things I should be dealing with at home, and yet I've done nothing the past week but spend time with you. And now I'm trying to figure out how I can spend even more time with you." He paused. "And that's a problem."

HE SHOULDN'T HAVE said it. He knew that the moment the words were out of his mouth and her eyes darkened. Talking about all of that wasn't what he'd set out to do with the candles and the little picnic he'd arranged. All he'd wanted was to celebrate what they'd achieved and to see her smile.

But he hadn't been able to kick his curiosity about her, and the more she didn't want to talk about herself, the more he wanted to know. So he'd mentioned his uncle and his dad in the hope she'd offer something, yet she hadn't. She'd only asked him questions, making him think about what was happening between them, reminding him of things he hadn't wanted to think about himself.

Like the ranch and how much time he'd been spending in this yarn store, time he'd been spending with Charity, and how much more time he wanted to spend with her. Which wasn't supposed to happen. Their affair was about being casual and fun. Neglecting his ranch in favor of being with her was neither casual nor was it fun.

He watched her face, feeling his chest get tight as she looked away, because he knew exactly what she'd say next. She was going to apologize.

"I'm sorry," she said, confirming it. "I didn't mean—"

"No," he interrupted, angry at himself for even introducing the subject. "I don't want you to apologize. It's not your fault."

"Okay." The candlelight played over her pretty hair, turning it to brilliant flame, and he wanted to touch it, to stroke the soft silkiness of it. "So...what can I do about it?"

"Nothing." He put the wine down, the tight feeling in his chest getting worse. "There's nothing you can do about it. The problem is me, not you."

He'd been telling himself a lot of lies over the past few weeks, he realized. That the tasks he had to do on the ranch could wait another few days, that he'd get to them eventually. That he didn't need to be there 24/7. That this thing with Charity wouldn't last that long since it was only sex.

Yet a couple of weeks had passed and being with Charity was still just as good now as it had been when they'd first gotten together—better even. And he couldn't see the end of it. He didn't know if he even wanted to see the end of it. Having her in his bed and in his house, laughing with her as he taught her how to hold a pair of knitting needles, talking with her about nothing in particular...

Small things. And yet they were starting to mean something to him.

She was starting to mean something to him, and that was a problem.

Caring in general was a problem, especially when he'd let down the only other person who'd meant anything to him.

His gran had brought him up with patience and love, even when he'd been a stupid teenager full of anger. Even when he'd been stealing cars and drinking and making her life difficult. And even though she hadn't wanted him to leave for the circuit, she'd let him go.

But he shouldn't have gone. He shouldn't have left her. She'd had a fall and he hadn't been there, and it had been a shitty repayment for all the years of care she'd given him. A shitty repayment after all the years of neglect from her own sons too.

It was a pressure, that care. It took up space and he needed that space for the ranch. That was where his caring needed to go, not to a person.

Then you know what you have to do, don't you?

The tight feeling inside him clenched like a fist all of a sudden. Because yeah, he did know. This thing with him and Charity had to end and the sooner the better, before either of them got in too deep.

You'll hurt her.

Garrett ignored that thought. She might feel regret, but surely not too much hurt. And after all, she'd never given him any sign that her feelings might be more involved than he thought. She was affectionate and warm, but he could sense the distance she was keeping between them; the whole conversation he'd tried to have about her medical career was a stellar example of that.

She wouldn't care that much if he called a halt, right?

"Is this...?" Charity stopped, her voice sounding a little husky. "Are you trying to say you don't...that you want to stop having casual sex?"

He studied her face, but apart from the soft husk in her voice, he couldn't tell if this disappointed her or not. "Yes," he said, because he had to be honest. "I think it might be better if we had a break. I'm sorry."

"It's okay." She smiled, but he could see how forced it

was. "I understand. This was always supposed to be casual and fun, remember?"

Oh, he remembered. He remembered all too well. The first day she'd turned up, she'd ignited his passion and now she was igniting something else inside him. A deeper, more lasting feeling. But ever since he'd gotten back to Jasper Creek, he'd been trying to make up for the way he'd left, and even though his gran was gone, that didn't mean he'd stopped trying.

Perhaps one day he'd eventually feel as though he'd done enough, but that day wasn't today. And while that was happening, he didn't have room in his life to care about anyone else. Even a woman as special as Charity.

Come on, you know the truth. You're not good enough for her and you never were.

His heart ached. Of course he wasn't. She was beautiful and fearsomely intelligent, and a high-flying ER doc. He was just a rancher. A guy who'd put his own wants above the needs of the woman who'd sacrificed her older years in order to look after him.

No, it wouldn't work. It wouldn't ever work.

Charity was still smiling that terrible smile, the one that looked like she'd cut it out of a magazine and stuck it on her face. He knew what she was doing, that she was trying to be understanding and make it okay.

But it wasn't okay, was it? She was hurt; he could see the glitter of it in her eyes.

"Don't do that," he said roughly, angry with himself for misjudging this because it was clear that he had. That she had feelings he'd missed. Or perhaps just hadn't wanted to see. "Don't pretend."

She blinked, red lashes fluttering in the light. "Pretend? Pretend what?"

"Pretend that you're not hurt."

Her smile looked even more forced and her voice was rigid with calm. "I'm not hurt, Garrett. I always knew this was casual. I never wanted anything more."

"Then why did you look like I'd slapped you just before?"

She blinked again, then looked away, pretty red lashes veiling her gaze. "I don't understand what you want me to say."

"How about giving me the truth?"

"I thought I did."

"No, doc," he said flatly. "You told me what you thought I wanted to hear."

There was a long silence. Charity stared at the floor as if she was looking down into it for answers.

"But then that's what you do, isn't it?" he continued on, not sure why he was pushing. "You'll do anything to keep the peace."

She was silent a moment, before suddenly looking up, her gaze meeting his. "And what's so wrong with wanting to keep the peace? How does getting angry ever help? It just puts needless stress on everyone."

"I'm not talking about everyone," he said before he could stop himself. "I'm talking about you, Charity."

Her fake smile had slid right off and now anger burned in her eyes. She was beautiful like this, burning with her own passion and not with that thin and brittle veneer of calm. "What about me?"

"You telling me that it's fine when it's not. You pretending you're not hurt. You giving me some bullshit about how you understand, how it's okay. That you were only ever after fun and casual. I don't want you to tell me that, especially because it's not true. I can see it in your eyes."

He thought she might look away at that, but she didn't. "So what would happen if I told you that I have feelings for you? If I told you that I wanted more than fun and casual? What would you say? What would it change?"

A pulse of electricity shot through him, though deep down he felt no surprise. She might not have given any sign that she felt anything for him, but some part of him had known.

And yet you carried on with her all the same.

Regret filled him, heavy and aching. He should have been more aware. He shouldn't have been so selfish. It was another example of why it had to end. He'd already let down one woman. He didn't want to let down another.

"You're right," he said clearly, because he had to be honest. "It would change nothing."

Something bright glittered in her eyes, then it was gone.

"I can't have a relationship right now," he went on. "The ranch is important to me and I have to give it my full attention. Besides, you're going back to Seattle after the centennial anyway."

"And if I wasn't?" She was sitting up very straight, her back rigid. "If I decided to stay here instead?"

He stared at her, shock rippling through him. "Why the hell would you do that?"

"I...don't know if I want to go back." With a certain amount of precision, she put the glass down. "I don't think I...ever made the decision to go into medicine. Dad made it for me. And I went along because, well, I wanted to make him happy." She paused a moment. "He always wanted to work in the ER. It was *his* dream, not mine. But I went ahead and made it mine too, because after Mom died, he had to stay in Jasper Creek and look after me. He didn't have a choice. He had to give up being an emergency physician because of me. And I…always felt that wasn't fair. That it was my fault somehow."

His heart contracted in his chest, a fleeting pain on her behalf for how she blamed herself. And for how love had set her on a path that wasn't of her choosing. Because that was obvious to him now. She'd sacrificed years of her life doing something she hadn't chosen for herself simply because she'd loved her father.

"It wasn't your fault," he said. "Your father made his own choices and he chose you, Charity. But you can't live another person's life, no matter how much you love them. I tried to live my dad's and it didn't work out. So now I'm trying to live my own. If you want to stay here in Jasper Creek, then that's what you should do. But you need to do it for you, not for anyone else."

"And what if I want to do it for you?"

He stared at her, his heartbeat thumping loudly in his head. "No. You can't. I don't want you doing anything like that for me."

"Why not?"

She didn't know. She didn't know what a selfish man he was. She didn't know how badly he'd let down the one person he wasn't supposed to. The one person who'd been there for him and yet, when she'd needed him, he hadn't been there for her.

He wasn't worth anyone's sacrifices, let alone Charity's.

Garrett held her gaze. "Why not? Because I'm not what you think I am. I'm not a good man, Charity. I'm selfish and though I'm trying to do better with that, it doesn't always work. You shouldn't stay for me, understand?"

She only stared at him. "Why on earth would you think you're not a good man?"

Dammit. He shouldn't have said anything. "Why do you

think?" he bit out. "My gran gave up a lot of years to raise me, years she should have spent relaxing and enjoying herself. Instead she was constantly bailing me out. Then, to make matters worse, I went off to do the same thing that got my dad killed. She didn't want me to go, but I didn't listen. I went anyway. And then she had a fall and I wasn't there. After everything she did for me, after all I put her through, I left her just like Dad did."

"You were eighteen, Garrett. You were a kid."

"What does that matter? I knew better even then." He held her gaze. "And I know better now. I don't want you doing anything for me, sacrificing anything for me. I don't want you changing your entire life for my sake. You did it once for your dad and I don't want you doing it for me. Because you'll regret it one day, Charity. Just like you're regretting it now."

More pain flashed through her eyes, like lightning. Bright one second, gone the next. "Okay," she said, her tone utterly neutral. "I get it. And perhaps you're right. Perhaps it would be for the best. I mean, I did come back here to leave behind the stress of medicine, and I really didn't want any complications."

She sounded so measured, so calm.

So goddamn fake.

Why does that annoy you? You don't want her to fight you. You don't want a relationship, remember?

It was true, he didn't. And this was a good thing. Her not fighting him was exactly how it should go.

He ignored the pain that sank into his heart and forced himself to smile. "I had fun, doc. I really did."

But her gaze when it met his was dark and she didn't smile back. And she didn't say anything for a long moment.

Then, abruptly she rose to her feet in a strange jerky movement. "I'm sorry, Garrett. I have to go."

The pain settled more completely inside him, but he didn't tell her to stay. It was better to do this now, before any deeper emotions had time to take root, before it would hurt her even more.

So all he did was nod. And he didn't follow her as she left him alone in the store, sitting among the detritus of his failed picnic.

The remains of what he thought might be a broken heart sitting in his chest.

CHAPTER NINE

CHARITY DIDN'T WANT to go back to the farmhouse, but she didn't have anywhere else to go. So, gripping her little compass necklace tight even though there was no luck to be had from it now, she got one of the low-rent cabs that sat outside the Rusty Nail waiting to ferry the drunks home, and all the way back, kept her jaw locked tight against the pain that was sitting right dead center of her chest.

He didn't want a relationship and she knew that. She'd always known that. Fun and casual was what she wanted too. At least, that was what she'd thought she wanted. Until he'd reminded her that he wasn't up for anything more, and all she could think about was how much she didn't want what they had going on to end.

How much she wanted to keep doing it, keep sleeping together, keep working on the yarn store together. Keep being together, period. She wanted his arms around her at night, wanted to wake up to his kisses in the morning. Wanted him teaching her how to knit, talking to her about the ranch, offering his calm, level viewpoint on her yarn store.

She just wanted him.

But he didn't want that. He thought for some insane reason that he wasn't worth making sacrifices for, and she didn't understand why. Oh, she could see he felt terrible about his gran, that he felt he'd let her down, but he was wrong about that, so wrong.

He was a good man. A steady and loyal man. And he was blaming himself for actions he'd taken when he was an angry kid who didn't know any better.

Maybe she should have stayed and told him that. Stayed and told him that she'd give up medicine and make a home here in Jasper Creek for him if she wanted to. That he couldn't stop her, but what would be the point?

He'd been very clear he didn't want a relationship and who was she to argue?

But he was right about one thing. She had sacrificed things for her father in order to make him happy. She'd sacrificed her own choices. In fact, she'd been living her father's life for so long, putting his happiness above everything else that she didn't know what she wanted for herself.

But Garrett couldn't do that for her. She had to work that one out alone.

When she finally got back to the farmhouse, she could hear the others in the living room sitting around talking and laughing. Shooting the breeze the way they'd all done with each other for years.

Normally she would have gone in and joined them no matter how badly she felt. She would have put her feelings to the side, pretended they weren't there, that everything was fine. But tonight that was impossible, so she went past the living room and crept silently upstairs to the room at the back of the farmhouse that she'd chosen for herself.

"Hey," Kit called as she went past. "You're back early."

Damn. She'd been hoping they wouldn't notice.

"Yeah, we finished early," she said over her shoulder as she went on up the stairs. "I've got a headache. Think I might just go to bed."

She didn't wait for a response, just went straight into her room and shut the door.

Then she crossed over to the bed and climbed under the covers, pulling them over her head, and turning her face into the cool cotton of the pillow. She closed her eyes.

No, she wasn't going to cry. It was good he'd broken it off now. Better than later, when she might have developed feelings for him. She certainly didn't feel anything for him now. Definitely not.

Yet her eyes prickled, tears starting in them, pain gathering tightly in her heart.

He didn't want a relationship and she got that, she really did. So why hadn't her heart got the message? Why did it persist in hurting like it was breaking apart?

Time passed—she wasn't sure how much—but then she heard a quiet knock on her door. She ignored it, curling up around the pain in her middle, hoping whoever it was would go away. But they didn't.

The door squeaked as it opened.

"Go away," Charity said, her voice muffled from the pillow.

There was no response, but she felt the mattress dip as someone sat on the end of her bed.

Charity didn't lift her head up. "I said, go away."

"What happened?" It was Hope. "Kit said you dashed up the stairs like the hounds of hell were after you."

Charity kept her face firmly in the pillow. "I don't want to talk about it."

"It's Garrett, isn't it?"

Oh great, so Pru was here too.

"No," she said. "It's not. Everything's fine."

"If it's so fine then why are you hiding under the covers and crying into your pillow?" Pru asked.

"I'm not crying."

"You are. Your voice is all scratchy and thick." Kit was here as well.

Wonderful. That was all she needed, the whole damn team.

And she knew them. They weren't going to go away unless she told them what the problem was.

Charity sighed and let go of the pillow, pulling the covers off her head. "Yes, it's Garrett. He said he didn't want a relationship and I agreed. And then he said we should end it. And I said that was a good idea. So it's over. Happy now?"

Hope was looking very concerned at the end of her bed, while Pru stood beside it, her arms folded. Kit leaned in the doorway, examining her critically.

"You don't look like you think it's a good idea," Kit said. "You're still crying."

"I'm *not* crying." Charity tried to ignore the tears streaming down her face. "It was fun and casual and now it's over. The end."

"Huh." Pru stared at her, frowning. "You're in love with him, aren't you?"

Charity put her hands over her face. The "no, of course not" was in her mouth, right there. Just waiting for her to say it. But it wouldn't come out.

Because somewhere inside, she knew it wasn't true. That somewhere, somehow, she'd fallen in love with Garrett Roy. Or maybe it wasn't that she'd fallen in love with him. Maybe it was that she'd never fallen out of it.

Maybe she'd always loved him, from the moment she'd seen him in the yarn store, helping out behind the counter. Or maybe even before that, the very first moment he'd walked into the kitchen in her dad's house that first Tuesday, full of insolent bad-boy swagger.

But he wasn't a bad boy. Not underneath. He was calm

and level and he was caring. People mattered to him. That was why he'd given up the circuit, because his gran had mattered more than money or fame or adrenaline rushes…

But not you.

No. Not her.

"Yes," she said hoarsely. "I think I do love him."

"Well, no surprises there," Kit muttered.

But Hope reached out and took her friend's hands in hers and pulled her in for a hug. Charity let herself relax into her friend for a moment, because a hug always made things better. "You need to tell him, Char," she said quietly.

"How will that help?" Charity pushed herself away, wiping her tears from her cheeks. "He doesn't want a relationship. He said he has to focus on the ranch and he doesn't want me choosing to stay here for him when I'm doing it to make him happy."

"He's got a point," Pru said. "I don't know if I'd want to have a relationship with someone who's only choosing to stay to make me happy. I'd want them to stay because they wanted to be with me."

Charity swallowed. "I don't know, Pru. I don't know if I want to stay."

Pru's gaze was uncomfortably sharp. "Are you staying, though, Char? I thought you just took some time off for a break."

It was clear that Pru had opinions on Charity's "break" and from the looks on the others' faces, so did the rest of them.

"I was getting panic attacks," Charity heard herself say, the words coming out of her before she could stop them. "Some days I couldn't even step into the ER. I'm on stress leave and I… I don't want to go back." Her voice, already thick, thickened even further. "I don't want to. I want to stay here. But if I don't go back, I'll be letting Dad down and you guys down and—"

"Char," Kit interrupted gently, stepping into the room. "You're not going to let anyone down. Why didn't you tell us what was going on?"

Charity wiped her face again, feeling dreadful. "I… didn't want anyone to know. I wanted everyone to think I had it together, because if you all thought I had it together then maybe I did."

Pru shook her head. "No one has it together. Everyone's a mess. You know that, right?"

"And you don't have to have it together for us," Hope said sympathetically. "We love you just as you are. And if you don't want to go back to medicine, then don't."

She shook her head. "I don't know. I don't know what I want anymore."

"I think you do," Kit said, quietly. "I think you know in your heart what you want. I think you've always known. That's why you left Seattle to come here. You came back for a reason."

Her chest felt hollow and sore, and her head ached. "I don't know what that reason is."

"You do," Hope said. "You came because you want to be happy. But that's a decision you have to make for yourself." An oddly knowing smile curved her mouth. "Don't be scared to make it, Char. It's worth it, believe me."

Charity stared at her friend and the hollow feeling shifted and changed.

Was it fear that was preventing her from making that decision? From making that choice?

Of course it is. That's why you never called your dad to

tell him you were having problems. You're afraid of what he'll say if you tell him you don't want to go back to medicine.

A wave of certainty went through her then as something inside her fell gently into place, like a key fitting in a lock, bringing with it a flood of relief.

No, she didn't want to go back. She never wanted to go back. What she wanted was to stay in Jasper Creek and open her yarn store. That was all she'd ever wanted to do. And she wanted Garrett Roy too. For herself, and no one else.

And yes, she was afraid of having to break the news to her dad. Afraid of disappointing him. But what Garrett had told her came back to her, that she had to live her life for herself, she couldn't go on living other people's and it was true.

She'd been telling herself a lot of lies about how it would make her dad happy. It wasn't that at all. It was because she was afraid that if she didn't do what he wanted, he wouldn't love her. Because of what he'd lost when she was born.

But if there was one thing she knew about her dad, it was that he also wouldn't want her to be unhappy. He'd want her to do what was right for her.

And what was right for her was Garrett Roy.

Charity threw back the covers. "Pru, can I borrow your truck?"

"Atta girl," Hope said, grinning.

Kit raised a brow. "Going to see Garrett, I assume?"

Charity was already out the door, not wanting to wait another second.

"Hey," Pru called after her. "You still haven't used that

slip I gave you in the bar the night you did shots. About asking for his advice."

Charity snatched the keys from the hallway table.

She already knew exactly what she wanted to ask.

GARRETT DIDN'T HIT the bottle even though he wanted to. He sat in the darkness of his living room and stared at nothing instead. There was an ache in his chest where his heart should have been and he knew what the issue was.

No matter how many times he told himself he felt nothing for Charity Golding, it didn't change the feeling in his heart. As if something had been torn out of it.

Her.

He'd told himself that ending it was the best thing for both of them. That she couldn't stay for him, couldn't change her life for him. That he wasn't worth the sacrifice.

But he knew that was a lie. And the biggest lie of all was that he didn't want to hold her every day until the end of time.

Every instinct he possessed was telling him to go after her, but he wasn't going to. She had to make the choice herself. He couldn't be around to influence it. And if she wanted to deny them both the chance at happiness, then who was he to convince her otherwise?

"Be happy, Garrett," his grandmother had told him once. "If you don't want to be your father, then the easiest way to do it is to be happy."

He hadn't understood that at the time, but now he did. Now he'd had a taste of what happiness meant.

So why are you sitting here in the dark? You have a chance at happiness. Take it.

But how could he? When he wouldn't ever know if Charity was staying for him or for herself?

Does it matter? That's just another excuse.

Garrett closed his eyes even though it was dark already; the truth overwhelmed him. Because of course it was just another excuse.

It wasn't about whether he would disappoint her, whether he'd let her down. Whether he was good enough for her or worth making sacrifices for. It wasn't even about her staying for him or for herself.

It was about love. He was afraid that somehow, his love wouldn't be enough for her the way it had never been enough for his dad. Not enough for him to give up the circuit. Not enough to make him stay.

He'd always left, and he'd always taken a piece of Garrett's heart with him.

And now he was afraid that Charity would do the same. That he would love her, but it wouldn't be enough to keep her. That eventually she'd change her mind about what she wanted and she'd leave. And he'd be left here with nothing. Again.

There was hammering on his door.

He was very tempted not to answer it, but the person hammering wouldn't stop.

Cursing, Garrett got up from the chair and went to the front door and pulled it open.

Charity stood on the front porch, the twilight shining in her hair.

Shock pulsed through him and he found himself gripping the door handle so hard it was a wonder he didn't crush it. "What are you doing here?"

Her chin lifted, her eyes blue as the sky, holding his. "I

need some advice. I'm in love with this guy and I want to tell him that I want to stay with him. That for a long time I've been living someone else's life, but now I've made the decision to live my own, and I very much want him to be a part of that. Except, I don't know if he'll believe me." She took a step toward him. "How do I make him see that I'm telling the truth?"

Garrett went very still, unable to move. Unable to breathe. "Charity." Her name was a harsh sound, scraped and raw, the only sound he could make. "Why are you here?"

She took another step. "I told you. I want to stay with you. And if you say no, if you don't want me, it won't be fine. It will be awful. And I'll shout and scream and weep. I'll do everything I can to convince you to take me back, and not because it's what you want to hear, but because I'm in love with you, and I don't think I can live without you."

Only his grandmother had ever chosen him. His mother hadn't and certainly his father had never turned up on his doorstep saying that he'd decided to give up the circuit and stay for Garrett's sake.

But here was Charity Golding doing exactly that. Telling him that she was in love with him, that she wanted to be with him.

He gripped the door handle even harder. "What about your career?"

"It was never mine. It was what Dad wanted for me and I just wanted to make him happy. But…he always wanted what was best for me too, and I think that what's best for me now is not back in Seattle." She took another step, coming so close he could feel her warmth. "It's here, Garrett. It's Jasper Creek. It's the yarn store. And it's you." She stared up at him, her soul shining in her eyes. "Will you have me?"

Garrett felt the hand that had clenched around his heart release, allowing him to breathe and his heart to fill with the feeling that had been there ever since he'd first looked into Charity Golding's blue eyes.

"Be happy," his gran had told him.

And because he wasn't his father and never had been, that was what he chose.

"Yes," he said roughly and opened his arms.

She walked straight into them and lifted her mouth to his.

A LONG TIME LATER, up in his bed, she lay beneath him, bright and beautiful and all his, under the quilt his grandmother had made for him.

"So what was your advice? You never answered," she said.

Garrett blinked, his head still ringing from the pleasure they'd shared. "What advice?"

"When I first got here. Remember?"

Oh yes, that.

Garrett smiled and pulled her close. "My advice, doc? My advice is that you stay here with me in Jasper Creek. That you live with me here on this ranch. That you open the yarn store. And that one day you marry me."

Charity spread her hands on his chest, her smile lighting up his world. "That's your advice, huh?"

"Sure. And it's backed up by science."

"Science, right." She pressed her palm against his heart that beat for her and her alone. "Give me one good reason, cowboy."

That one was easy.

Garrett looked down into her blue eyes, and though he

could see his past there, he could also see his future. And it was glorious.

He smiled. "Because I love you, Charity Golding."

* * * * *

HOW TO LOVE HIM

Nicole Helm

"Friendship is born at that moment
when one person says to another, 'What! You too?
I thought I was the only one.'"
—C.S. Lewis

For Maisey, Megan and Jackie,
who've never made me feel like the only one.

CHAPTER ONE

Pru's Story

"*THAT* IS A violation of house rules, Prudence Riley. Take a slip."

Pru opened her mouth to argue with her friend, but arguing about violations was cause for *another* violation, and Pru was about at the end of her rope for embarrassing encounters with the male species of Jasper Creek, and she'd only been home for two weeks.

So she kept her mouth firmly shut, stomped over to the big jar of truly horrendous vintage dating advice, and picked out a slip of paper. "'Wear a Band-Aid on your face. People always ask what happened.'" Pru threw her hands up in the air. "You *can't* be serious?"

"Oh, but we are," Kit said, smiling.

"I've got Band-Aids!" Charity zoomed off.

Pru tapped her foot, trying to keep her irritation at a low simmer. The slip idea had seemed like *grand* fun in theory when they'd first come up with it in an effort to cheer up Hope after her failed wedding, but enacting the stupid tips had turned out to be very *not* fun.

But she'd made an agreement. A *promise*. No matter how irritated she was, or how much she blustered, she'd never go back on what she'd agreed to. Pru would do anything for her friends.

And if she'd had any sort of thought that, like Hope, she'd let the universe take over, it had been quickly eradicated by the reality of the situation.

Besides, she *liked* to complain. It made her feel more in control of those mushy feelings of love and loyalty and junk.

"Here," Charity said, going so far as to unwrap the bandage for her, medical professional that she was.

"It has *flowers* on it."

"I know. Aren't they cute?"

"Not on my face they're not."

"Think of it like jewelry," Kit suggested.

Pru would *not* think of it like jewelry. The only jewelry she ever wore was the compass necklace, and only because of their childhood promise.

"It was bad enough when I had to wear Hope's wedding dress all day." Trying to work in a fluffy white monstrosity had been an exercise in pointlessness. And she was still mad about it and all the strange, jangling emotions wearing a wedding dress had brought up. "Why does mine always involve putting something on my body?" she demanded, slapping the Band-Aid on her cheek.

"Luck of the draw. Or maybe fate knows exactly what you need. Besides, I was the one who got the thing about fake tripping."

Pru narrowly resisted telling Hope what she thought of *that*. She would not end up with another one of these stupid slips this week. She was vowing it here and now. Whatever impulses she had to lock down, she would.

"I'm headed to the store. I'm not waiting around for you slowpokes." She grabbed her keys and started for the door. "Some friends you are."

"The best!" Kit shouted after her.

Which meant that as much as Pru might want to hold on to her anger, she was grinning by the time she got to her truck.

This wasn't what she'd planned for herself when she'd been a kid having sleepovers with her three best friends. But it was almost as good—maybe even better—living under the same roof at the old Gable farmhouse which Pru had always thought was particularly pretty and magical looking—not that she'd ever admit that either.

She took a moment to look at it. The white against the gold-tinted mountains in the background, the cozy porch that was perfect for morning cups of coffee and late-night stargazing. The redbud tree waving gently in the yard just inside the little gate.

There was a warmth to it. A sense of home, even though it was temporary.

She knew she was very lucky, even if she preferred grumbling over gratitude.

Maybe staying here wasn't permanent, but considering the four of them hadn't been in the same state for years now, living together was amazing.

Pru had always avoided roommates. In college, she'd worked an extra job just to afford a dorm room all to herself after her disastrous freshman year sharing with a *philosophy* major who'd always asked about Pru's feelings.

Pru shuddered. Who wanted to talk to people about that? Let alone strangers.

But she wasn't living with strangers now. She was living with her best friends, which was also way better than being under the same roof with her parents and brothers. She loved her family but she also wanted to strangle them. Then there was the whole ranch thing, which she preferred not to think about.

She got in her truck and began the drive to the quaint town of Jasper Creek and her store. She enjoyed the drive, taking in the beauty of the little Oregon town she'd always loved. Historical brick buildings lined Main Street—many were on the national register. A lot of them were shops, some were restaurants. But being a tourist town meant the ebb and flow of disrepair and revitalization. While it was doing well these days, there were still some pockets of town that had empty buildings as the owners had lost their businesses over the years.

The four buildings she and her friends were revitalizing sat on the corner of Main and Maple. The big brick building had long ago been split into four separate stores that shared a common basement.

Her building stood on the corner, taller than the rest. The end side was exposed brick with old advertisements faded but visible. She parked her truck and got out.

The sun shone on the brick, the sky above a bright summer blue. The mountains in the distance made a pretty horizon. She'd worked here in high school before Mr. Simmons had closed up shop.

Now it was hers.

They'd done it. She was going to open a feed store. It wasn't ranching, as had been her dream as a girl, but it was supporting ranchers and that mattered to her.

She'd spent years in agricultural sales, and while it wasn't the same as owning a business, she knew her product. Being a hometown girl who'd grown up on a ranch, she understood her customer, and together with her friends they were learning the ins and outs of business ownership.

Their grand openings would be in August in time for the centennial of when Horace Jasper found gold in the creek and seceded from Gold Valley to become Jasper Creek.

The previous leaser of her building had used it mostly as a catchall for stuff since it was open with high ceilings. Having to deal with all the junk that had come with the building had been more of a chore than she'd anticipated. Two weeks in, and it felt like she hadn't made much progress at all. Especially with the Fourth of July looming next weekend.

But the worst part was actually getting rid of some of it. Pru loved old things. Especially old ranch things. The more pointless the better. She was happy to toss rusty nails and faded feed sacks, but it had been tough to part with little pieces of history.

She'd kept the antique cash register that needed a good cleaning and probably would never be in working order, but looked *right* sitting on the checkout counter. There was the creepy goat statue she hadn't been able to part with next to the front door. It was too weird and made her laugh every time she looked at its eyes which were painted the oddest shade of pink.

She figured she'd dress it up for the seasons like old Mrs. Mooney had done with her goose lawn ornaments back when they were kids.

She gave the goat a pat as she stepped inside. She blew out a breath and refused to be overwhelmed. There were piles and piles of junk, and every morning it felt a bit like she *hadn't* spent the last two weeks trying to clear it out.

She would get it done. Just put one rusty rat trap in the Dumpster after another. She turned some music on loud and an hour later she was sweaty and her muscles ached, but she would power through till lunch or die trying.

When her music abruptly shut off she looked up to see her brother standing in her doorway. "You opened this dump yet?"

"Yes, that's why there's a Closed sign in the window and I'm drowning in baling twine." She opened her mouth to tell her brother to buzz off, but stopped herself when Grant Mathewson stepped in behind him.

Grant and Beau had been good friends since diapers. The Mathewson ranch and the Riley ranch bordered each other by way of a creek that the kids of both families played in.

Pru, the only girl on either side, had often been barred from such manly activities, which was why she'd had Hope, Kit, and Charity. Her parents had always felt very traditional about gender roles, down to her brothers getting shares in the ranch. And her getting jack diddly.

Which probably wasn't fair to say. They'd paid for college. They'd wanted her to have "better" than ranching and Jasper Creek.

And she'd given them everything they'd wanted, half believing they really did know best. She rubbed at the uncomfortable ache in her chest and scowled harder at her brother.

"Mom said you could use some help," Beau said, surveying her store.

Pru had regretted telling her mom she wasn't getting anywhere the minute the words were out of her mouth. Mary Riley didn't let problems go unsolved. Whether you wanted help solving them or not.

Grant still hadn't said anything. Pru probably hadn't seen him in the flesh in two or three years. He looked *about* the same. He'd always been the serious sort, but this quiet stoicism had only become a part of him after his father had died about six years ago. She'd been in California, but she knew the tragic story because her mother liked to tell it to make them all feel bad and want to do something for Grant. Luckily, that usually fell to her brothers who dragged him along like overzealous toddlers with a leash on a reluctant old dog. They meant well, but the Riley boys were not known for their finesse.

Maybe that was why Pru had taken such pride in becoming a good saleswoman. She could finesse, she could be slick, assertive, and even charming—*not* what Rileys were known for.

Of course, she wasn't much of any of those things when she was at home, even less so when she was in the company of her brothers.

"Prudence, I don't know what you were thinking," Beau said, sighing sadly as if she was dim.

"Well, you don't have to know. Long as I do. So Mom sent you both to help?"

"No, I've got ranch work, but she thought Grant could be of some help hauling."

She turned to the man in question, eyeing him suspiciously. He said nothing, just stood there tall and imposing. He was a little on the lankier side than he should be, but it gave his face a rough-hewn look that was a little too appealing. Then there was the dark hair, usually kept short but today a shade too close to being considered shaggy—at least by her mother. And then there were his eyes.

Which she didn't let herself think about too often, except that they were the exact shade of blue as that summer sky outside.

"I'm only in town because I've got some errands to run," Beau was saying. "But Grant said he could spend a few hours here playing grunt."

Pru frowned. "Maybe Grant could talk for himself."

"Why would I do that when I've got your brother to do it for me?" Grant returned.

Pru knew what her mother was up to. Not just solving Pru's problem, but solving Grant's as well. Her mom thought Grant needed fresh air and hard work outside his family ranch so he was being foisted on her.

"Look, I don't need—"

"Was that a mouse?" Beau asked, taking her elbow and dragging her deep into the store. She struggled to rid her arm from his grasp, but he held firm. When she thought about junk-punching him, he angled his body to make sure *that* didn't happen. Call it a brother's intuition.

"You need help. Grant needs to get out," Beau said, keeping an eye on Grant so that he was out of earshot. Beau pretended to point to a corner where there was *definitely* not a mouse. "He barely even comes into town anymore."

"I don't need your dour best friend helping me."

"Why not? All you need is someone lugging stuff around. Besides, the way Grant is these days, he won't even argue with you. Free, silent labor." Beau grinned at her. "Unless you'd rather have JT and me in here, arguing with you, telling you every move is wrong."

She scowled at him. He might be joking, but she knew that was exactly what her brothers would do if her mother sicced them on her.

"It was Mom's idea," he added. The Riley kids did not disobey Mary Riley. *Ever.*

"All right. Fine. I'll put him to work. But just so you know, if he's annoying or worthless, I'm telling him he's the current Riley pity project and he should get over himself."

"You're all heart, Pru. It's a wonder you haven't settled into married bliss yet."

"Yeah, yeah, yeah. Where's your ring?"

"A soul like mine is impossible to tame."

Pru rolled her eyes hard enough to hurt and made a shooing motion at her brother. "All right. You can go now."

Beau sauntered off, saying a few last words to Grant before sliding out the door.

Leaving her alone in her store with Grant Mathewson. *Joy.*

GRANT WASN'T A dumb man, so he knew exactly what his friend was up to. He also knew why. Mary Riley had been best friends with his late mother, which was why Beau had been *his* best friend since long before Grant could remember.

After his mother had died, Jasper Creek had stepped up in a lot of ways, but for Grant in particular it was the Rileys who'd made the biggest difference. Being thirty-seven years old didn't matter to the exuberant Riley clan when it came to trying to take care of him. Grant couldn't fathom why he put up with them.

But put up with them he did. Down to helping little Prudence Riley.

She wasn't little anymore. She had the height of her father and brothers, but the lighter features of her mother. She had the sharp Riley chin and a generous mouth. He wasn't sure where it had come from and knew better than to think about it.

"Don't talk so much, Grant," she said. "It's downright annoying."

He grunted. He wouldn't be goaded into talking. Typically, the only ones who could make that happen were his brothers, and only because they'd had a lifetime of knowing what buttons to push.

"Well, I've been working on clearing the place out."

He looked around. "Work's not done yet, is it?"

"Thank you for your astute observation." She gestured for him to follow her, and he did, sidestepping piles of rusty watering cans, canned beans with age-faded labels, and a towering mountain of baling twine. She led him all the way through the store and out the back door to the lot where there was a Dumpster, entirely filled with junk. It was impressive, considering how much junk was still inside. "Well."

"Well, indeed." She studied it herself, with a stubborn jut to her chin he remembered from when she'd fought with her brothers. Today, she had a Band-Aid on her cheek and a glossy ponytail instead of dirt streaks and braids.

"What happened to your face?"

"Huh?"

"Your face? The flower Band-Aid." It looked like something one of his nieces would wear. Considering they were ten and seven, it seemed a bit out of place.

Pru blinked, turned a strange shade of red, and...spluttered. "*You're* not supposed to ask me that!"

Puzzled by her insane reaction, he could only shrug. "Okay. Maybe don't put a bright one on your face then."

She shook her head then and began marching back inside. "I...scratched it on some of this junk. That's all."

"So why are you acting so squirrelly about it?"

"Why are you asking me about it?"

"I don't know. Just seemed weird. Forget I asked." *Jeez.* Who knew Pru Riley had gotten so, well, squirrelly?

"Let's work on moving this quadrant to the back room so when the Dumpsters get switched out I can just start tossing." She pointed to a corner of the store that was filled with mostly broken pieces of what had maybe once been furniture. Splintered wood, twisted metal frames.

"I had no idea this had become a dump."

"Yeah, me neither. When Mr. Simmons said he had a *few* things I'd have to take care of on my own, I clearly misunderstood." She blew out a breath, her hands fisted on her hips as she surveyed the store.

Then she shrugged as if it didn't matter at all. "Oh, well, best get back to work. No breaks till lunch."

That was fine with Grant. Carrying junk wasn't all that much different from what he'd be doing back on the Mathewson ranch. But here he could do it without constantly being poked at by his brothers, or their significant others.

They worked in silence—something his middle brothers were physically incapable of doing—and got a good chunk moved to the little room in the back. It was an oddly satisfying feeling to clear off some space on the wood-planked floor.

"Floor's nice. Once you get this junk out and do some deep cleaning, I guess you'll be ready to open."

"Yeah, that's the plan."

He glanced over at her. She was bent over, denim stretched over the round curve of her butt. And for a second, he must have forgotten who she was because he found the sight more intriguing than he should allow himself to. The low pull in his gut was so foreign to him these days that he didn't understand it at first, and didn't hear what she said about the floors as he studied her. Thought about putting his hands on—

"I should really get back to the ranch," he said abruptly, jerking himself out of a very, very, *very* disturbing daydream.

"Why?" she asked, wiping her forehead with her forearm. "Don't you have, like, a million brothers who help you?"

"Well, yeah, but…" He didn't have a good answer for that, and as she bent over again he had to turn away. "Cade's married with two kids and another on the way. And Mac has a girlfriend and…" She probably knew all that. It was a small town. She might have lived in California, but Mary would have kept Pru in the loop about all things Jasper Creek. So why was he babbling about his family and staring at a goat statue by the door?

"Sounds like you've got even more help than usual."

There was a painful pressure in his chest. That was what everyone was telling him. Plenty of help. Take a day off, Grant. *Relax.* Dole out the responsibilities a little more.

But Dad had wanted *him* to take care of the ranch. As he lay dying, *that* was the thing he'd said to Grant. "Take care of this place. Take care of the kids."

Grant hadn't been able to save his dad, there in the barn, waiting for the ambulance to arrive, but he would make sure the ranch ran without a hitch and that his brothers were taken care of. No matter how much help he had or how old his brothers got.

He looked at the goat's pink demon eyes instead and found a comeback that didn't give any of his feelings away. "Don't you have friends to help you?"

"Yeah, if I can't get this done fast enough. But they've all got their own stores and troubles to work on. Look, I can wrangle my brothers if you're busy, but you're much quieter to work with."

He looked at her, but she was still bent over. He needed to bow out. He needed to escape a world where he was looking at Pru Riley's ass. But Mary would only send him again, and how could he explain to them why he didn't want to be trapped in a store with Pru?

He stared at the goat some more. Maybe the goat was the answer. He'd just avoid looking at Pru. Or thinking about her. He could haul junk and keep his eyes to himself. How hard was that for a man who spent most of his life trying to keep everything to himself? "I'll come by tomorrow if you've got a need."

"Yeah. That'd be great." She stood up, a beheaded doll in one hand and a peeling lawn jockey in the other. Her hair was falling out of its band. She was dusty and sweaty and the Band-Aid she had on her cheek was falling off, revealing absolutely no injury behind it.

It should have been off-putting. A little grotesque. It should have loosened some of this weird tightness in his body.

It didn't. So he turned on a heel and left as fast as his legs would carry him.

CHAPTER TWO

PRU WATCHED GRANT MATHEWSON GO, thinking things she should never have allowed herself to think. He was *Grant*.

He'd asked her about her Band-Aid. Not that she'd expect some handsome cowboy to swoop in and magically be caught by some stupid magazine tip. But Grant was...

He was *Grant*.

So, watching him was stupid. Even if there was that... cloud around him that she didn't remember from before. Maybe it had always been there and she'd just never paid attention, but he hadn't smiled. Not once.

She rubbed at her chest, still watching even though his truck had disappeared. Something ached inside of her. She wanted to...do something. Like her mother always did. Which might have made her feel good or terrified— depending on how she felt about her mother at the given moment—but what truly bothered her was that she only ever felt that way with her friends.

She whirled away and the goat statue made her jump a little. She pointed her finger at it. "I'm *not* drooling over Grant," she said to the goat. "And you need a name. Beelzebub? Maynard? Maybe I'll put it to a vote."

She stalked back to her work and did everything she could to keep her mind off Grant Mathewson's unsmiling mouth.

The pounding knock from the wall her store shared with

Kit's had Pru looking at her watch. Lunchtime. Pru went to her truck and grabbed her lunch cooler and then entered Kit's future bookstore.

Kit and Charity were already seated at the table where they usually ate lunch. Pru felt grumpy and itchy and *tense*, but she forced a smile. "How's it going?" she asked, stealing one of Charity's chips before Charity could guard them.

"Well enough," Kit said. "What's up with you?"

"Got another few pounds of garbage moved."

"That's not what I meant," Kit said, tapping her cheek. "Your Band-Aid is gone."

"I didn't violate any rules. A man asked me about it. Then I got too sweaty and it fell off." Pru slumped into her chair and tried not to scowl as she unpacked her lunch.

Kit rubbed her hands together. "*Ooh.* A man? Where the hell is Hope?"

"Definitely not an *ooh*," Pru muttered, shoving a bite of sandwich into her mouth. "It was one of those Mathewsons." Pru waved that off, as if they were all the same. As if she didn't care.

"Which one?" Charity asked, plucking a grape from her pretty, neat bento box lunch. The chips on the side were what made her more human than robot in Pru's estimation.

"Who knows? They're all the same to me." That was a flat-out lie. Grant had always been a part of her brother's life, which in extension meant hers.

"And what did he say about it? What did you say?"

"He asked what happened to my face. I said I scratched it on some junk and no great love match was made." Pru frowned. "Then he called me squirrelly."

Charity waggled her eyebrows. "That's hot."

Pru narrowed her gaze. "It was *weird*."

"Why?" Kit demanded, as if zeroing in on a point she was going to argue.

"Because Grant and Beau are like best friends and he's *old* and…"

"Uh-oh," Charity said in a fake whisper.

"Uh-oh, what?" Pru demanded.

"Well, first, you lied," Charity said, keeping her expression completely placid though Pru saw the humor in her eyes. "So you have to take another slip."

A screeching sound erupted, unbidden, from her mouth. "I didn't—"

"You said you didn't know which Mathewson," Kit pointed out, studying her apple smugly, "when clearly, you did."

Luckily Pru found herself speechless with anger, so she couldn't get herself into any more trouble by arguing.

"Second, you've got the hots for him."

"Who does Pru have the hots for?" Hope asked, hurrying into the store, her lunch clutched to her chest.

"Where have you been?" Pru asked. Hope was suspiciously out of breath and…rumpled. She was also the perfect person to take the spotlight off her.

"Brooks came by." Hope sat, attempting to look very regal.

"Mm. We'll circle back to that," Kit replied, making a circling motion with her finger before pointing it at Pru. "But first. Pru. Grant Mathewson."

"I do not have the hots for him. He's almost *forty*."

"That doesn't stop you loving Harrison Ford."

"The man who played Indiana Jones and Han Solo is an exception to all rules."

"You have to give her that one," Charity agreed.

"So, Grant—an attractive man, by all accounts—asked

you about your Band-Aid and this made you uncomfortable." Kit grinned. "Why?"

Pru knew she should take it in good fun, and she wanted to. She just couldn't get there. She felt…well, the exact word Grant had used for her. *Squirrelly.* "It's like thinking my brother is hot."

Hope rolled her eyes. "But your brothers *are* hot."

"First of all," Pru said, shuddering, "you are disgusting. Second of all, you know what I mean."

"I guess I do, but I don't really understand why you're all shoulder tense about it."

Pru immediately dropped her shoulders from her ears and straightened her spine. "I don't like this line of conversation."

Her three best friends exchanged looks. Looks Pru understood all too well. They'd drop it because she was being too weird about it. But it wasn't *over* over. There was a pin in it until they were sure she wouldn't Pru-ricane.

"Well, whatever slip you pull out next you should definitely use on him," Kit said.

"I'm not using *anything* on him."

"Don't get all bent out of shape, Pru," Charity said with some concern. "It's all in good fun."

"I am not bent out of shape." And it wasn't fun. She was churned up and…and… "I have things to do."

"Oh, come on," Kit said. Charity started apologizing, and Hope said nothing. Pru walked out of Kit's shop, lunch remains left behind, mostly uneaten.

It was childish. She knew that, but she'd rather everyone think her childish and short-tempered than understand she was…confused. Weirded out. Uncomfortable and wholly out of her depth.

Like she'd ever do anything on the Grant score. Coming

home and hooking up with her older brother's best friend? She snorted as she walked back into her store. The sheer complication, the embarrassment of dealing with her family, and...and... Grant?

She shuddered. It was quite literally all a nightmare thought, and it bothered her beyond measure that her brain had even led her here to this horror-show hypothetical.

So, she firmly put it out of her mind and got to work.

GRANT STEPPED OUT of his house in a bad mood. Mary Riley had called him up this morning, flat-out told him she expected him to help Prudence with her junk removal until the job was done, and then invited him for dinner next week.

A man didn't turn down an invite to dinner from Mary Riley, no matter how much he tried. And boy had he *tried*.

What was it about women and dinners? And togetherness? Why couldn't they just let him alone? He'd spent his entire life surrounded by his brothers. And when he hadn't been, there'd always been Beau and JT. He was hardly *alone*.

Especially now that Cade had married JJ, bringing a new glow of happiness to the Mathewson Ranch. Mac was making noise about getting married to his girlfriend, and Violet had already moved into the main house, filling it up with frilly female things, including once-a-week mandatory *family dinners*.

Grant stalked out to the large gardens in the back. Even though he'd turned over his mother's flowers to JJ last year, he hadn't quite broken the habit of checking in. And since JJ often put him to work, he'd kept it up. JJ wasn't a chatter, so they could work quietly together.

He found her kneeling in the beds, weeding.

"Should you, ah, be doing that? You know…in your… condition?"

JJ looked at him, raising an eyebrow. "It's not a terminal illness, Grant. It's pregnancy." His sister-in-law stood from where she'd been weeding between the flowers she grew to supply her sister's florist shop.

"Sure, but it's terrifying."

JJ eyed him. "You've helped birth cows."

"Cows are not *humans*."

"Thank God for that. You want me to put you to work weeding instead?"

He rocked back on his heels and shoved his hands in his pockets. "I have to go to town."

"Twice? In one week? You okay?" She didn't say it mockingly like his brothers would have, but that didn't make the question any less grating.

"Beau's got me helping his little sister clear out some junk. She's one of the ones that rented those storefronts on Main. Well, you know that. They're renting your grandma's place too." He hoped the shrug was careless, but it hardly felt it. He hated being torn over his responsibility to the ranch and what he owed Mary for all her care of him over the years.

"Little sister?" JJ seemed to think that over. "How little?"

"Huh?"

JJ grinned. "And what does she look like?"

Grant blinked. He couldn't think of one thing to say. "What?"

JJ placed a hand over her stomach, though there was barely anything there to give away that she was busy growing human life. The grin on her face turned into something far too…seeing. It reminded him of Cade and he scowled.

His sister-in-law was not supposed to get all...*insightful* on him.

"You aren't getting any younger," she said gently.

His scowl deepened. "What's that got to do with anything?"

"Don't you want a life of your own? I'm not saying you have to have companionship to be happy, but you don't seem happy."

"Judas."

She smiled a little at that. "I know. I'm not supposed to talk to you about your feelings. Pregnancy is making me sappy." She moved to grab the watering can, but Grant was faster.

"I'll get it."

She sighed. "I'm not an invalid, Grant."

"Sure, sure. I'll get it all the same." He went and filled it and began to water the plants that needed watering while JJ watched him, traitor that she was. Because this was not their relationship. They talked about flowers. About Lora and Ellie—his nieces and her stepdaughters. Sometimes they discussed the ranch, or what was for family dinner.

They did not go any deeper than those things, because he got enough of that from his brothers and from the Rileys. It was a betrayal, plain and simple.

"You know, Grant, take it from the pregnant, married lady who always figured she'd be neither. Happiness isn't the enemy. It's scary, and it can be hard. It's not a state you can hold on to all the time. But it's not the enemy."

Of course it wasn't. He didn't deny anyone their happiness. He rolled his shoulders to rid himself of the tension that had centered there. He just had responsibilities. When a dying man told you to take care of the ranch and your brothers, you didn't have much of a choice in the matter. Which meant happiness was way down on the to-do list.

"I can pick you up something in town if you need it," he said, ignoring all talk of happiness and focusing instead on what his role in life was. Responsibility.

JJ was silent for a moment, then seemed to accept that was as far as she was going to get. "Thanks. I'll text you a list."

He nodded, put the watering can away, then left her to the rest of the weeding. He didn't head into town right away. First he had to find his brothers and check on what they had planned for the day.

He found Tate and Cade in the stables. Cade had Lora up on their old mare. He'd admit it to no one, but it was a strangely…enjoyable experience watching his youngest brother be a father, doing with his girls what their parents had once done with them.

"Morning," Grant greeted his brother who was closest in age with him. "You already been out?"

"Pepper and I needed a bit of a ride."

"Shouldn't you be in the north pasture checking on the calves?"

Tate kept brushing his horse, not even bothering to shoot Grant a look. "Unclench, big bro," Tate said. As he often did.

Grant felt unaccountably irritated by it. Some days he could shrug it off, and some days the weight of the responsibility he carried made the tension so tight in him he simply had to break. "Maybe you should clench a bit more."

"So you always say," Tate replied, setting the brush aside. He stepped out of the stall and eyed Grant. Tate liked to start fights. Usually Grant sidestepped them, especially with the girls around. So, he focused on what was important. "I hope the rest of the boys are out in the north pasture with the—"

"Dude. Let it go," Tate said on a groan.

"Let *what* go? Responsibility? Making sure we're all taking care of our livelihood instead of screwing it up?"

"That isn't fair," Cade said, coming to stand in between them.

"He's getting worse," Tate muttered to Cade. "Someone's got to do something."

"Worse at *what*?" Grant demanded, lost.

But Tate waved him off. "Let us do our job, Grant."

"Last time I checked, this entire ranch is my job, my responsibility, and you with it."

"I don't need micromanaging." Tate started moving forward, his fingers curling into fists. "I'm tired of saying it."

Grant matched his stance. "Then go somewhere else where you don't have to say it." It was too harsh. The last thing he wanted to do was run his brothers off—that was the opposite of what his dad had tasked him with. Grant didn't know why he said it except that he was in charge here, and they all acted like he'd wrestled that out of someone else's hands. Instead of having had that heavy mantle laid over him when he hadn't been able to save their dad.

But Tate kept talking. "I'm sure you'd like that. Drive us all away so you can sulk alone for the rest of your life. Sorry, big brother. Ain't happening. So you might as well get out of my face before we bloody each other a little."

Cade stepped in, giving Grant a push. Not a shove that would start a fight, just a push toward the stable doors. He kept nudging until Grant was outside.

"Lay off him," Cade said firmly, in the same way he talked to his elementary-school-aged daughters.

Grant wanted to bristle at that, but Cade didn't give him a chance.

"You want to check everyone's work, you go ahead and wear yourself out. Just do it where we don't have to see how little you trust us. It'll save everyone a lot of grief. And you can keep all those alone hours you like so much."

It wasn't about trust, but Grant didn't know how to say that. He didn't know how to...

"Go. Give Tate some space." Cade sighed heavily as his girls started shrieking and running toward him, clearly angry with each other. "We're not your responsibility, Grant," Cade said sadly. "Not the way you do it."

"What's that supposed to mean?" Grant demanded. But Cade was dealing with two wailing girls.

What Grant wanted was some good, hard physical labor far away from any human being. Instead, he had to drive into town and help Prudence. He scowled as he stalked to his truck. If he didn't show up, Mary would likely come over. He didn't need that. What he needed was more alone time. There was too little of it lately. That was why he was in a piss-poor mood and taking it out on people more than usual.

If he could just be alone for a bit, he'd find his equilibrium again. Figure out how to balance the responsibilities with that tightness in his chest that only seemed to get worse.

He's getting worse, Tate had said. Like he could see through him to the parts of himself he'd buried deep under all that responsibility.

We're not your responsibility. Not the way you do it. What? Making sure things were done the right way? Making sure the legacy their father left them didn't fall apart because Grant hadn't been diligent enough, careful enough, prepared enough.

Like he hadn't been when he'd found his dad gasping for air in the barn.

Grant allowed himself enough temper to jerk his truck into Park in front of Pru's store. It was such a pointless store. Jasper Creek ranchers had gotten used to going elsewhere for feed and the like. What did she think she was doing?

He stalked up to the door, ignoring the little voice that told him he was taking his bad mood out on the wrong people. He stopped short there as he caught sight of her through the big storefront window.

She was standing in the middle of the store, hands fisted on her hips, her profile to him. He didn't see anyone in there with her, but she appeared to be talking. She gave the creepy goat statue a head pat and he had to wonder if she'd been talking to *it*.

JJ's words flitted through his head. *What does this little sister look like?*

Quite unfortunately, she looked like something that was going to make his life far more complicated than he wanted it to be.

Join the club, Pru.

CHAPTER THREE

THE BELL ON the door tinkled and Pru looked over her shoulder as Grant stepped in. It was like a dark cloud entering the building, an impending storm, but currently contained.

Too bad that black cloud made her heart trip over itself.

There was just *something* about a man in boots and a cowboy hat that sent her heart to fluttering no matter how she tried...which was why she stayed the hell away from them.

Too bad she couldn't stay away from Grant Mathewson.

"Morning," she greeted. "You didn't have to come," she said, trying to sound casual instead of accusatory.

He made that grunting sound he seemed to think constituted communication.

"I'll assume, since you're here, you wanted to."

He shoved his hat back on his head, then looked around and settled it on an old hat rack in the shape of a turkey. His expression told Pru all she needed to know.

"My mother called you."

"I can neither confirm nor deny."

Pru snorted. "Don't be funny, Grant. It doesn't suit your dour expression."

He grunted again.

Pru rolled her eyes. Well, she wouldn't look a gift workhorse in the mouth. She turned to survey the store, then remembered the slip in her hand. Since she'd been alone, she'd been able to complain freely about the injustice of it, so that was just what she'd done, laying all her problems on… Stuart? Goaty Goatface?

She still needed to have that vote on his name.

The man-catching tip was particularly ludicrous today, and all because she'd left her umbrella in the entryway and it had created a puddle Charity had stepped in, soaking her socks.

Charity had been in such a foul mood, and the prospect of making Pru take a slip had cheered her so much, Pru hadn't had a choice. She'd taken a slip, complaining with enough zeal to make Charity laugh.

Carry a camera and ask strange, handsome men if they would mind snapping your picture.

With their phones locked safely away, Pru had thought she might sneak out of doing this one. But no, Kit had found a small digital camera in the attic of wonders at the Gable house.

Pru had then figured she wouldn't be in the vicinity of any strange men, but Grant was here and he certainly ticked both boxes. Handsome. *Strange.* And why not fling all this stupidity at him? It would keep her from embarrassing herself in front of anyone else, *and* hopefully embarrass her enough in front of Grant that she'd stop feeling all softhearted over him.

"Do me a favor?" She held out the camera. "Take a picture of me in the store."

He looked at the camera, then at the store. "Don't you want to wait until the place looks nice?"

"No, I want to document the whole process." She shook the camera at him, but he still didn't take it.

"Don't you have a self-timer deal? I don't know how to work one of those things."

"Good Lord, Grant. Would it kill you to punch a damn button?" She shoved the camera into his hand. "You look through here. You push this. The end."

He grimaced, holding the camera like it might bite. But he eventually held it up to his eye. "Okay. Smile, I guess."

"Okay." She shook back her hair, angled her chin, and fixed on her best smile. She felt a little rusty. Back when she'd been in sales, appearances had been everything. She'd been selling tractors, so the appearance had been that of sturdy, clean, wholesome ranch stock, but that still required a certain approach.

Grant frowned at her, looking a bit like he'd tasted something sour. "What is that?"

"I know you don't really recognize these, Grant, but when you turn the corners of your mouth up it's called a smile."

"You look like you're selling something."

"Funny, that *is* my specialty. Now take the picture."

He shook his head, grumbled, then hit the button on the camera a few times before handing it over to her.

She swiped through the pictures. "These are all blurry. You are a *terrible* photographer."

"I'll add that to the list of complaints about me today," he muttered. "I am surrounded by impossible people."

"If you're surrounded, you might consider the possibility *you* might be the impossible one."

He looked stricken by that. Like he was shocked he might be the impossible person in his life. Her heart did the fluttery thing. She almost wished she had something else stupid and slightly embarrassing to ask him to do.

Instead, she crumpled up the slip of paper and tossed it in the trash, racking her brain for a job to give him that would keep him as far out of her orbit as possible.

"What's that you just threw away?" he asked.

"My penance," she muttered darkly.

"Huh?"

"Don't worry about it."

"I don't remember you being this weird. Should I tell your mom she should be worried about you?"

"I'm not weird. And there's no reason for anyone to be worried." It wasn't all that embarrassing to tell him. Probably less embarrassing than continuing to act weird around him *without* explanation. "The girls and I have an agreement. We have house rules. When someone breaks one, they have to pick a penance from a jar. Every piece of paper has a terrible piece of 'catch a man' advice from this old magazine we found."

"You want to catch a man?"

"No. God no. We just had this thought and…it's…it's a girl thing." She decided the man with five brothers wouldn't touch that with a ten-foot pole. "But I swore I'd do it for the three months we're living together, so I have to no matter what. Since I don't have any designs on a man, you can be the way I keep my promise to do the penance."

"How is someone taking your picture going to catch a man?"

"Hell if I know. Why would a man asking why you've got a Band-Aid on your face catch a man? I guess it's just… attention. Ways to get attention. And the basic male urge is supposed to take over."

"Good thing I'm immune to basic male urges."

"I'd beg to differ."

"Huh?"

"Wasn't it you who got Mackenzie Bishop into the back seat of your car in high school that won you a bet with my brothers and a few of yours?"

"I'd forgotten about that." His mouth actually curved.

"Oh my God, Grant. Don't smile. I might faint." She patted her heart.

He grunted again, and though he scowled there was something very close to humor in his eyes.

"You used to do that," she remembered. He hadn't *always* been this way. She'd forgotten that sense of humor of his, that he used to be more…cheerful wasn't the right word. Lighter? Happier? She'd forgotten that phase of Grant Mathewson, and it wasn't a comfortable memory.

Neither was Mackenzie Bishop, which she most certainly hadn't forgotten about. She remembered how angry she'd been about their bet. How she'd lectured her brothers on feminism and respect, but had mostly stewed over Grant *winning it*.

"Used to do what?" he asked, shoving his hands in his pockets.

"Smile. Make bets with my brothers. Be a general goof."

He pulled back and straightened his shoulders as if she'd accused him of being a murderer. "I was *never* a goof."

"Okay, maybe not. But you weren't so…" She waved a hand. "This. Dour and dark and walking around with the weight of the world on your shoulders."

If there'd been any humor left, it was long gone now. "Dad died. The ranch and my brothers became my responsibility. That's a lot for one man."

"But you're not one man. Isn't that the good thing about having five brothers? A ranch is a lot of responsibility, but there are a lot of hands to help."

"I'm the oldest."

She studied him. "Oldest, sure, but you're all adults. I remember when he died, which means Cade was in his twenties too. Wasn't he already married to his first wife?

It's not like you had little kids to take care of. You had five adult brothers to share the burden."

"It's my name on the deed. It's my responsibility. Obviously my brothers carry their weight in terms of chores and stuff, but it's *mine*."

"But they're all ranchers, right? They know what they're doing. You all grew up there. A few extra years doesn't make you the expert or the only one who knows how to do stuff."

"But…"

She shrugged when he didn't seem to have anything else to say. "Take it from a youngest sibling: we actually can take care of ourselves. Not saying you can't offer advice, or be annoyingly superior on purpose, but if you're sincerely worried about their *capability*, you're off the mark."

"I'm…not."

"Sounds like you are. Or that they feel like you are if you're calling them impossible. Hey, it's your life. Your family. I'm just saying. It sounds like you're making problems for yourself."

"What would you know about it?" he demanded angrily.

She sobered. She'd hit a nerve. The truth was, Grant had lost both his parents and she didn't know how he bore it. "Nothing, I guess." How embarrassing. Why hadn't she shut her mouth? She *always* shut her mouth when things were complicated.

"You're damn right nothing." He stalked to the door, flung it open, then walked right out without another word.

The bell tinkled as the door fell closed and Pru winced. Well, she'd screwed that six ways from Sunday.

She sighed and turned around, but caught sight of his forgotten hat on the turkey rack.

She should stay put, let him storm off, maybe even tell
her mother and brothers to lay off...

Instead, she rushed forward and jogged after him with
the hat in her hand.

"Grant."

He stopped next to his truck, though he didn't turn
around. So she walked up to him and held out the hat.

He blew out a breath and after a moment's hesitation
took it. He still didn't say anything, but he didn't make a
move to get into his truck.

And she...she just couldn't let him go. Not like this. God
knew why when there was all this *emotion* in the air. "You
want to go get a beer?"

He blinked. "A beer."

"Yeah."

"It's lunchtime."

"So, we'll stick to one and get a burger to go with it.
Come on." She reached out and grabbed his arm, ignoring
the tense muscle. She tugged. She had a feeling he only allowed himself to be tugged because he was too surprised
to argue.

She used it to her advantage and dragged him down the
street to the Jasper Creek diner. When she walked in, a
few familiar heads turned their way and Pru realized this
looked...not at all like it was.

No, that wasn't going to work. "You go on and take a
seat. I've got to call the girls real quick and tell them I won't
be there for lunch."

GRANT SAT IN a booth at the town diner he hadn't been to in...
years, and wondered what the hell he was doing. He could
have escaped when she'd gone up to one of the waitresses

and asked to use the phone. Before that, he could have told her firmly no and walked in the opposite direction.

Instead, he waited for her to slide into the seat across from him. When she smiled with that same saleswoman smile from before, he knew he should tell her that, based on the looks of the people in the diner, a rumor about them would be making the rounds before they even ordered.

But the thought of explaining that to her made him so uncomfortable he just kept his mouth shut as Pru perused the menu. When the waitress came over, she ordered…a rather heavy lunch. But when the waitress turned to Grant, he didn't know what to get so he simply said he'd have the same.

She kept up with that saleswoman smile, one that made it absolutely impossible for him to remember she was far too young for him, but pretty easy to remember she had left Jasper Creek, and seen and existed in a world he'd never had any interest in.

"Since you probably don't want to have lunch with me," she said cheerfully, "I called in reinforcements." She slid out of the booth and he stared at her, completely lost. Beau came up to her and she smiled up at him. "I'll see you around, guys."

Grant watched her leave, some odd feeling mixing in with the irritation that she'd outmaneuvered him.

"So, how'd Pru manage this?" Beau asked.

"Manage what?" Grant growled.

"Getting you into a restaurant. I've been trying to get you out for a beer or a burger for years, but you always have *too much to do*," Beau said using air quotes around the words.

"She pissed me off."

"I piss you off."

"She did a better job, I guess." Grant should have got up and left. He wasn't sure what Pru's whole deal was, but he didn't want to be here. If he'd wanted to be here, he would have come of his own volition.

But if he got up now, it'd be like he'd come only because of Pru and that couldn't possibly be the case. Besides, he'd ordered. He was hungry. And Beau...

Beau would understand. Beau had always been there. He knew what responsibilities Grant shouldered. His best friend would agree with him, and then Grant could put all Pru's obnoxious points away. Firmly proved wrong.

"Do you think I take on too much responsibility?"

Beau laughed. And *laughed*. "I'm sorry I don't have a more emphatic, intelligent way of saying *duh*."

"But—"

"There ain't no buts, friend. You treat your brothers like dim-witted ranch hands at best. I've been telling you that for years."

Grant could only stare at his friend. When he managed words, they were weak at best. "No, you haven't."

"Yes, I have. You always tell me I'm wrong and list a litany of reasons why you have to double-check their work, or go over the books again even though Tate's perfectly capable. Maybe even more capable than you. But the years go on and you only hold on harder, and don't even listen when I point out that your brothers are grown men and good ranchers." Beau sobered. "Maybe I never said it in as many words, because I get it, Grant. Everything changed when your dad died."

"Everything." Grant thought about it. Sometimes he could barely remember the time before he found his father gasping for air in the barn six years ago. His mother's death had been a blow, but he'd been young enough, surrounded by family and friends enough. It had been a gradual thing he'd gotten used to as cancer had won, so it hadn't sat inside him with the same heaviness that losing his dad had.

Yeah, everything had changed when his dad died. "Including me."

"Especially you."

The waitress put their food in front of them as Grant let that sink in. It was true, but it felt like an accusation. Of course he had changed. His father had died in his arms, begging for promises before he'd gone unresponsive. The ambulance had been too late, and there'd been nothing Grant could do. What kind of person *wasn't* changed by that?

"Look, we don't have to have this conversation," Beau said, shifting uncomfortably. "We can eat our burgers, drink our beers, go back to…the way things always are."

The way things always are.

"Unless…"

Grant stared at his friend, who was watching him with careful eyes. It was the same kind of expression his brothers were always watching him with.

"There's no unless," Grant said firmly. "Everything's fine." He picked up his burger and forced himself to take a bite. It was good. Surprisingly good. Certainly better than the burgers he grilled and usually burnt at home. Tate was better at grilling. Grant usually handled it though, because…

Because.

He put the burger back down on his plate and stared hard at it. "What if everything's not so fine?" he mumbled, and then took a long pull of his beer.

Beau hunched his shoulders. "I guess you start figuring how it could be." He downed the rest of the beer Pru had ordered, possibly even more uncomfortable than Grant himself. "But you've got to decide what *fine* means to you first."

The question seemed impossible to answer but so much more impossible to ignore.

CHAPTER FOUR

PRU WAS IN a foul mood for the weekly meeting, though she couldn't understand why. Everything was great. She was making progress on the junk removal. She'd foisted off Grant on Beau for lunch, then her brother had stopped by to say thank-you.

A thank-you. From her *brother*. It was downright apocalyptic. The Rileys didn't *thank* each other. They did the good deed and then moved on.

She couldn't say why that made her mad when it should have made her feel good. She'd done something *kind*. Clearly it had helped Grant or her brother wouldn't have thanked her. She was a saint.

"Uh-oh. There's a Pru-ricane brewing," Hope said with a grin.

Pru pointed a finger at Hope. "I hate that term. I'm putting that on the house rules. No one can say Pru-ricane." She was not out of control. Her emotions did not rule her. And these three women were the only dang people on Earth who ever saw those very, very, *very* rare moments when her emotions won. They should know this wasn't one.

And even if it was, that didn't mean they could *call* her on it.

"You can't house-rule our free speech," Kit replied, affronted. "Besides, if the shoe fits. Strong winds. Dark clouds." Her eyes twinkled with mischief. "The threat of death and destruction."

"I'm fine."

"You're really not," Charity said. "I saw smoke coming out of your ears during dinner."

"You suggested making a salmon mousse. It wasn't smoke, it was my taste buds evaporating and running far, far away."

"The Pru-ricane has just been upgraded to a category four," Charity said in a fake newscaster voice.

"I hate all of you."

"Of course," Kit said, unbothered. She turned off the Victrola, though Pru wasn't sure who'd turned on the old Andrews Sisters record. "Meeting begins. Blah, blah. We're all still working on things. Meeting adjourned."

"You can't just—"

"I have a better idea of how to spend our Friday night." Kit clapped her hands in front of her. "Let's go out."

"Go out? In Jasper Creek?" Charity wrinkled her nose. "Where?"

"What's the one scandalous thing we never got to do as teenagers in this town?" Kit asked.

"Well, for Hope it was sex," Pru offered.

"Uh, for you too!" Hope shot back.

"Focus, ladies," Kit said. "The Rusty Nail."

"Ohh." Charity's eyes widened. "Well. Can't we just stay here and knit and listen to records?" she asked with a pout, though so far all she'd done was jab some needles at a ball of yarn.

"No. And we'll take some of our man-catching slips." Though there was grousing, Kit had already gotten the jar of slips. She picked one out herself first. "'Laugh wildly at anything a man says in your presence. Men like girls who do not challenge them, but find them funny!'" she read aloud. "Well, regrets, I have a few."

Charity took her slip. "'Walk up to him and tell him you need some advice,'" she read. "Who is getting advice at a bar?"

"Everyone," Kit supplied. "Hope. Your turn." She shook the jar at Hope.

Hope sighed and took one. "'Dropping the handkerchief still works.' I don't have a handkerchief."

"I think I saw one in my room," Kit offered.

"This house always has what we need," Hope said, a faint wrinkle across her forehead.

Kit turned to Pru, a teasing glint to her eye that Pru knew meant she was expecting an argument. A Pru-ricane.

Pru refused to give her the satisfaction. She smiled and took a slip. "'Be forward! Ask him to dance.'" She forced herself to smile. "Yay." She said it sarcastically, but as the little farmhouse became a flurry of getting ready to go out, Pru began to feel it.

Really feel it. Kit told her she couldn't wear *those* jeans, Hope loaned Charity a lipstick color that wasn't *nude*, and they all chimed in on convincing Hope to wear something more low-cut.

By the time they were in Kit's car, driving toward the Rusty Nail, Pru was laughing. Excited. *This* was why it was good to have her friends together. She didn't get so trapped in all those feelings she hated to dissect. They pushed each other, understood each other, all without having to *express* it all.

The Rusty Nail looked a bit like a barn, and inside it was decorated to the hilt with every Western thing imaginable: elk heads and rifles mounted on the walls; old Wanted posters and barbed wire; wagon wheels and six-shooters.

Pru rubbed her hands together. "Okay, who's going to do a shot with me?" Pru had her sights set on Hope, but Charity surprised them all.

"I will."

"*You* will?"

"I've never done a shot before. It's time I learned how."

Pru linked arms with her. "Atta girl." The four of them walked over to the bar. Pru ordered the shots while Kit and Hope got tamer drinks. Pru laughed through instructing Charity on how to do a shot, and the way she coughed and her eyes watered afterward.

"That's terrible," she croaked.

"I know," Pru agreed.

"Hey, Pru," Hope said over the din of an old eighties country song. "Isn't that your brother?"

Pru craned her neck to see where Hope was pointing. Her brothers with Tate and Ford Mathewson.

And Grant.

Grant was in a bar. He didn't look happy about it, but he was there, amidst his brothers and hers. He held a bottle of beer.

"And some Mathewsons," Kit added, as they all stared at the group of men. "Can you tell those apart now?"

Pru scowled at Kit. "Yes."

"And is one of them your little helper? No, don't answer. I can tell by the look on your face he is. The one talking to Beau. Wasn't he at our graduation party?"

"I don't remember," Pru lied.

"Oh!" Charity pushed her shoulder. "You should ask *him* to dance."

"I'm not going to..." The denial was reflex, but Pru considered it. Hadn't she decided she was going to use Grant as a kind of placeholder? He'd probably say no, and then she wouldn't have to dance. "Good idea."

She pushed away from the bar, and went straight for him. "Hey," she greeted over the din.

Shock fluttered over his face. "I didn't know you'd be here."

"Me? When was the last time *you* were here?"

He considered. "A while ago."

"So, really, *I* should be saying I didn't know you'd be here."

He said nothing else, and Pru knew she should blurt out her thing, but she could feel her friends' *and* brothers' eyes on her and—

"Look," he said. "I owe you one."

She blinked up at him. The alcohol was doing its work, making her body feel warm and loose. Still, she didn't think she was drunk enough for Grant to be speaking gibberish. "For what?"

"Lunch."

"You had lunch with Beau."

"Yeah, but I wouldn't have if you hadn't dragged me there."

"Well, consider it a thank-you for your help at the store." Her lungs felt tight, but she ignored it and powered through. "You still want to help?" She found herself holding her breath waiting for his answer. She didn't care. God, she didn't want to care.

"Yeah, I told my family I was taking the day off the ranch tomorrow, so I can be around all day. If you want."

"That'd be great. More hands make less work and all that." She glanced down at his hand which was wrapped around a beer bottle. Big, work-rough, a little scarred. She really shouldn't have done that second shot. "You're going to have to dance with me."

His eyebrows went so far up on his forehead they nearly disappeared. "Huh?"

"I need you to dance with me. One song. No big deal."

"Yeah, I don't dance." He lifted the beer bottle to his lips and took a long swig.

She could leave it at that. After all, her slip didn't say she *had* to dance. It just said she had to ask. But somehow words kept coming out of her mouth. "Look, I have to do it," she said, pointing to her friends.

"Why are you agreeing to stuff you don't want to do?"

"They're my friends. It's for Hope. I…just dance with me." She grabbed his arm and pulled him, just like she had that afternoon.

"The whole dragging me around is getting to be a habit. Can't say I like it."

"You're in my orbit, you get dragged. Riley Rule of Life. You should be used to it."

"True enough," he muttered as they stopped in the small throng of people on the dance floor. "I really can't dance."

But a crooning Patsy Cline song came on. Couples sidled closer together. "I can't either. That's why you just sway." Which meant she had to touch him. Why had she insisted?

But she wasn't a quitter. She wasn't *afraid*. Pru Riley had balls. She grabbed his hand and threaded her fingers with his. Then she struggled to breathe, which was so utterly unacceptable.

Where she might have awkwardly grabbed his other hand too, he put it on her hip. He looked about as comfortable as she felt, grimacing as they awkwardly began to sway in time with the music.

Pru wasn't sure she breathed. All she could do was stare

at his chest. His hand held hers, and his other hand was on her *hip*. Her body all but vibrated with it. What was *wrong* with her?

She glanced up to catch him studying her, a line dug into his forehead. But his eyes were that vivid blue and…

She thought he was hot. She had all these jangled, tangled feelings about him and the worst part was they weren't new. They'd always been there. She'd just been out of his orbit for so long she could always convince herself after a trip home that she'd imagined it. Romanticized a childish crush.

The song ended and she stepped back, bumping into someone behind her. She didn't even turn to apologize. Her eyes were on his and she couldn't break away. "Well, thanks," she managed.

He shrugged. "Yeah, sure. No big deal."

She turned abruptly and moved through the crowd, way too fast to look like anything other than running away. She found Kit and Charity at a table in the corner. She plopped next to Charity.

Her friends didn't say anything. They stared at her, but they didn't say anything.

Pru dropped her head into her hands. "So, whatever, I'm attracted to him. Big deal."

"If it's not a big deal you wouldn't be so…what was that word he used?" Charity said, looking at Kit.

"Squirrelly," Kit supplied.

"It's just weird," Pru said. Weird. *Terrifying.* "That's all. I'll get over it."

"Or you could jump him."

"Charity!" the two of them echoed in scandalized shock.

"Well. Isn't that what we're doing?"

"Jumping things?" Pru sputtered.

"No, putting ourselves out there. Shaking up those old lives we got caught up in and letting the universe take over."

"I'm not jumping Grant." She sucked in a breath. She didn't know what she was going to do about this attraction thing. She'd agreed to changing her old life because of Hope—at least that was what she'd told her friends.

But truth be told, she hadn't been all that in love with her old life. Shaking it up had sounded…good. Letting the universe take charge hadn't seemed so bad.

But changing anything with Grant would require dissecting feelings and… No, that wasn't an option.

She grabbed Charity's arm. "Come on. We need another shot."

GRANT PARKED IN front of Pru's store with severe trepidation. For more than one reason.

After his lunch with Beau yesterday, he'd gone home and told his entire family he wouldn't be around the ranch today. He'd made a big pronouncement because he'd known if he didn't act on that feeling of change right away, he would let it slide like he had so many times before.

It wasn't like he never looked around and realized he'd let himself fall into a not-so-great place. It was just that there was always something to worry about, some work to throw himself into. Why try to shift the weight of responsibility on his shoulders when he could stay firmly and comfortably in that place of overworking himself?

But something about Pru not just telling him his family was capable at the ranch—but that he was causing himself his own problems—without any of the judgment or hurt feelings his brothers came to him with, actually punctured something.

So, he'd stepped back—it was the only way he knew how

to *unclench*, as Tate so often told him to do—and gone to the bar with Beau last night. He hadn't gotten drunk like JT and Tate had, but he'd done it. He'd gone out. He'd had a good time, more or less.

He'd danced with Pru.

If he'd known what else to do with himself today away from the ranch, he wouldn't have come. There was too much Pru in his life suddenly.

He got out of his truck into the warm morning. Clouds were hanging around, and the red brick of her store shone with the rain from last night. Grant hadn't spent much time in town for the past few years, so maybe that was why it struck him that it was downright pretty.

He'd never questioned why tourists came to Jasper Creek. Never wondered overmuch how their little town survived and thrived. But he looked down Main Street now, with the flowerpots hanging from second-story porches or arranged next to storefront doors. Wild, colorful blooms spilled over. American and Oregon-state flags waved in the light breeze and some people had decorated with red, white, and blue in preparation for the Fourth. There were only a few empty storefronts left now that Pru and her friends had taken on this stretch.

A big burly man drove a motorcycle down the street, and Grant had to laugh when he saw that there was a tiny, fluffy dog in the sidecar who was clearly enjoying his ride.

The man waved, so Grant lifted his hand. Not a local. Someone taking a morning drive and enjoying the scenery.

He looked back at the store. If Pru was smart, she'd try to reach some of that tourism traffic.

It was absolutely none of his business what Pru did with her business. He shook his head and pulled open the door, stepping inside. He heard the bell on the door tinkle, and saw Pru wince from where she stood over by that monstrosity of a cash register she'd told him was an impressive antique. He considered it a waste of space.

"Shh," she said, pushing fingers to her temples.

Grant raised an eyebrow. She looked pale and miserable. He didn't know why that amused him. "A bit hungover?"

"A bit." She swallowed as if her stomach was unsteady. "Charity had never done shots before. I felt honor bound to teach her how."

"So why aren't you at home nursing it with a little hair of the dog?"

Pru pressed a hand to her stomach. "God, my entire stomach just turned over." She grabbed a water bottle and sipped from it. "You don't nurse a hangover. You take your punishment as penance and then muddle through whatever you've got to do."

"You're pretty big on penance."

"Have you met my mother?"

His mouth curved. "Fair enough." He moved to the spot they'd designated as trash. It had grown exponentially since he'd been here yesterday morning. She must have done a lot of work after lunch. "All right. This still the trash heap?"

"Yeah. Got the Dumpsters switched out this morning so it can all go. As soon as my head stops spinning I'll haul too. I just need a few more minutes of sitting."

Grant shrugged, grabbing the first box of spare, rusty parts. "Don't worry about it."

He hauled. She went through stacks of papers, books, and magazines, tossing some of it in a box on the floor, but setting most of it to her side. He shook his head. She was never going to get rid of all this junk if she wasn't better about throwing things away.

"Why'd you take the whole day?" she asked after a

while. "I'm not complaining, especially in my state, but it's a big turnaround from yesterday."

Grant blew out a breath and thought through his words carefully. How much should he tell Pru? "My brothers are a little tired of me breathing down their necks. I'm kind of tired of it too. But I can't be there and not...micromanage, Tate would say. So, I have to remove myself if I want anything to change."

She was quiet for a moment. When she spoke, she kept flipping through the old magazines, but she did look at him out of the corner of her eye. "You want things to change?"

"Not *things* so much as *me*, I guess. Plenty of things have changed. Cade got remarried. He's got another kid on the way. Mac's probably going to propose. There are all these changes around me. But... I'm stuck." He didn't know why they were having this conversation, but it weirdly felt okay to talk about it.

"Well, happy to help by giving you trashman duties."

He wasn't sure how long they worked after that. She got through a hefty amount of smaller stuff sitting there. He got almost the entire pile moved to the Dumpster.

It felt good. Like he'd accomplished something. It was a strange realization to find the ranch hadn't given him that feeling in quite some time. Guilt still crept in at the thought—after all, his dad had expected him to love the ranch as he had—but at least here there was no brother to bicker with until the guilt went away.

"Wanna break for lunch?" she asked.

He opened his mouth to argue, but she was already digging through a small cooler and tossing baggies onto the counter.

"I think I can only stomach crackers, so the sausage and cheese is yours if you want it."

"Sure." What was the harm? He found a stool to match hers and pulled it over to the counter. Then they sat there and ate the lunch Pru had packed.

"It's starting to look like a store," he offered.

"It is, isn't it?" She looked around, still a little bleary-eyed, but clearly pleased with her progress. "I can't say I'm looking forward to figuring out where to put things, but I *am* excited about ordering things and selling things."

Grant opened his mouth to tell her that the feed should stay where it had always been. Old-timers didn't like change. He had a whole list of ideas in his head. He could practically see it.

But it wasn't his store. So, he shoved a bite of summer sausage into his mouth.

"I know you're trying not to micromanage your brothers, but this can't be what you'd rather be doing."

"This isn't so bad."

"Really? I feel like my brothers would disagree with you."

"Your brothers love what they do."

Her eyebrows drew together. "You don't?"

"I used to love it." Grant frowned. When he was a kid, he'd never considered anything else. The ranch was it for him. But even before his father had died, the ranch had begun to feel more albatross than calling. "I'm not sure when I stopped. But I just…did."

She studied the cracker in her hand. "Yeah, me too."

"What happened?" he asked, wondering if she would say something that would make it make sense for himself.

She shrugged. "I didn't get a piece of it."

Since he knew the story well enough from her brothers, he didn't ask for details. Or whether she'd ever *asked* for a piece of it. "That killed your love of ranching?"

"Soured it some. I guess I didn't love ranching so much as the Riley ranch. College was fun enough, and then sales. I'm good at sales." She looked around the store. "I'm damn good at it. And the ranchers around here are going to come here and buy."

"I don't know, Pru." He knew he was being a downer, but he felt like she didn't have a full enough grasp on the challenge ahead of her. Forewarned is forearmed and all that. "We haven't had a feed store in Jasper Creek in years, and there's a reason the last one went under."

"Because Mr. Simmons was old and bored and didn't want to change with the times. I'm none of those things. The key to selling anything is to know thy customer." She studied him. "Let me guess. Mathewson Ranch. You've got a thousand acres or so." She rattled off a brand of feed, an amount per month, and some other monthly items that were eerily accurate.

Then she grinned at him. "You don't have to tell me I'm right."

Her pleasure was contagious and he found himself smiling right back. "Then I won't."

They were smiling at each other, when he couldn't remember the last time he'd sustained a smile like that except when he was alone with his nieces. They never made him feel grumpy or overbearing.

Pru brought out the same kind of ease in him. He wasn't sure what to do with it. So, he talked about the store. "You should do gardening stuff too. Supplies for kitchen gardens and the like. That way it's not just ranchers and you widen your client base. You could have a whole section."

"That's a really good idea. Put it up front so people can see it through the storefront window. Eventually, I want to partner with some ranchers and farmers and either have orders for beef here, or even a little local grocery section."

"That's a hell of an idea. We've got the farmers market of course, but you're open more often."

"Exactly," Pru said, excitement lighting her eyes. He felt a twin pang of excitement inside him.

They argued about what feed brands she should carry, and it was weirdly fun. He suggested a few more things, and Pru wrote them down in her notebook like she was seriously considering them.

In the afternoon, they went back to junk removal. There was something satisfying about the way the store opened up more and more. He was starting to think if he could give her a full week of days, they'd have most of it taken care of…minus all the junk she insisted on keeping.

"I think I'm ready to take off. I gave Hope a ride this morning, and she'll be ready to head home any minute."

"I can give you another full day tomorrow if you could use the help. I'm bringing my own lunch though."

"Really?" she asked, walking toward the door with him.

"Sausage and cheese and a Coke is not my idea of a lunch."

"No, I mean the full day thing." She grabbed his hat off the weird hat rack and handed it to him.

"Sure. Long as you need it."

She chewed on her bottom lip, which was when he realized they were standing a shade too close. And he was staring at her mouth.

He remembered exactly how it felt to have his hand on her hip, no matter how lightly. To have those hazel eyes fixed on him like she wasn't so sure of herself. He could forget who she was—a Riley, his friend's baby sister, his surrogate mother's daughter—and just see and feel Pru. He could forget who he was *supposed* to be, and just be him.

The bell tinkled and Pru jerked so hard she nearly tripped over her own feet. Her cheeks turned a bright red. As if she'd been thinking the same kind of thoughts he had.

Without jerking or blushing, he turned to face the intruder. It was one of her friends. Hope. The one with the failed wedding and the candy store.

"Sorry to interrupt," she said.

"Not at all," Grant replied. He slid his hat on his head. He didn't look back at Pru, but he offered a wave. "See you tomorrow."

Tomorrow. Tomorrow he'd remember to keep his distance.

CHAPTER FIVE

PRU BLEW OUT a slow, steady breath. Boy, had her imagination gone off in a very bad direction. Because there could not have been a moment where Grant's gaze had dipped to her mouth.

Ha! Ha. Ha. Ha. Not in a million years.

But Hope's eyebrows were raised. "What did I walk into?"

"Nothing," Pru said, and knew she sounded desperate to believe it.

"Didn't look like nothing. Especially considering how red your face is. I thought you didn't want a man."

Pru wanted to blame the churning of her stomach on the hangover, but she knew that wasn't it. "I don't. I really don't."

"Okay, so—"

She couldn't let Hope talk. Or joke. Or anything. She had to make this go away. "I'm just hungover." She waved her hands, knew the gesture was a little too wild, but couldn't seem to help it. It was silly to get this worked up over a look. To let that flutter in her chest lie to her. "He just puts me off balance."

"That's not such a bad thing. James never put me off balance. I always thought I had everything under control. Then…" Hope made exploding noises and mimed things blowing up.

Pru laughed, some of the panic leveling out at Hope's joke. "I'm glad you can do that."

"Do what?"

"Make a joke about it and mean it."

Hope shrugged. "I wasted a lot of time on him. On that life."

"Not anymore." No more wasted time. She swallowed because that caused a strange bubble of panic to center itself in her chest. But panic could be dealt with. You stepped back. You took everything one day, one hour, one minute at a time. She'd maneuver Hope away from this conversation, and everything would be fine.

"So…" Hope slid onto the stool Grant had sat at for lunch. He'd sat there and eaten lunch with her and batted ideas back and forth and it had been…

Best not to think on that.

"Let's talk about Grant."

"Nothing to talk about. He's been helping me out." That was all. With time, she could convince herself of it.

"You danced with him."

"Well, yeah, that was my slip. Ask someone to dance."

"But you chose him."

"Because I knew he wouldn't think anything of it. Just because I think he's hot, doesn't mean I'm *interested*." Pru forced herself to relax. To be flippant. Bored. Not all *churned* up. "Grant's a whole thing, Hope. Think of the mess I am and multiply it by like a hundred. Man's a wreck."

Hope tilted her head, studying Pru in a way that told Pru she'd said something wrong, but Pru couldn't think what.

"Why would I think you're a mess, Pru?"

Because I am such a damn mess. Pru breathed in deep then forced a smile. "I just mean in general, you know. We agreed to come here because we weren't happy, right? That was the pact." Her heart was thundering in her chest, but she had to pretend it wasn't. Had to pretend...

"But you acted like...like you were doing it for me. For the pact. Not because you weren't happy enough in California."

"*Enough* being the operative word." This was leading somewhere she hadn't anticipated. She had to nip it in the bud. "Look, I don't want to talk about— "

"Pru." Hope's hand curled around her arm. There was a look of confusion and hurt on her face and Pru didn't know what to do but stare at it. "What haven't you been telling us?"

"I tell you guys everything." As close to everything as anyone in her life.

"Clearly not. If you think you were a mess. If you're saying you weren't happy. That's not what you told us when you agreed to this. You mentioned being a little dissatisfied in your job. Not being unhappy."

"All I had was my job."

"That's *not* what you told us. You had friends. Dates. You were playing beach volleyball of all damn things."

"I did. I was. For a while. The last year or so... I didn't. I just sort of pulled myself in. Gradually. Without noticing it. I just stopped wanting to do any of it or be involved in that sort of thing."

"You were *depressed*?"

"No. Not like that." She pulled away from Hope. This was getting out of hand, but Pru was failing at being clear. "Not clinically. I didn't want to hurt myself. I was just sad." Had she realized that? Had she admitted it to herself?

God, she didn't want to. She needed to power through and change the subject. "I don't know why. So, congratulations, your wedding imploding fixed my problem. I haven't felt sad here. This store…" She looked around, but the emotions swamping her weren't going away. And, as only ever happened with her friends, words she wanted to keep inside tumbled out. "It wasn't what I wanted, or thought I wanted, but it feels exactly like what I've needed."

"You should have told us."

Pru thought about that. She had never felt like she was lying or keeping something from her friends. She wasn't sure she understood what she'd been doing or feeling until she'd left it behind. "I didn't know how."

"'I'm sad.' That's all you needed to say."

That sounded horrible. *Terrifying.* Why would anyone tell people they were sad? Then you had to deal with it, when life would probably come along and fix it well enough on its own. She'd come home because of her friends and happenstance, not because she was sad. "Did you ever tell us you were unhappy with James?"

Hope wrinkled her nose. "Point taken."

"Sometimes you just don't…know." That wasn't exactly right. She'd known…something. She just hadn't had the words for those feelings. And talking about them would have made it worse, she was sure. This here wasn't helping anything. She felt like her heart was going to beat out of her chest. Or worse, that she might start *crying.*

"But now you do. We do," Hope said. "So, if it happens again, you *tell* us."

Pru nodded. She didn't agree, not fully, but this wasn't just about Pru. It was about Hope. Hope hadn't been happy and she hadn't said it or acknowledged it… She needed to believe that was the answer, and for Hope it might very well be.

It definitely wasn't for Pru.

"And in the here and now you tell me what's going on with Grant."

"I think I like him," Pru said, even though she didn't want to admit it. But the words just fell out. "A little too much. For a little too long."

"Why's that so bad?"

She had a litany of reasons, but they would all get more commentary from Hope than Pru wanted, so she used the easiest one that couldn't be refuted. "He doesn't look at me like that."

"I wouldn't be so sure. He was looking at you when I walked in."

Pru chewed on her lip. She didn't *hope* for that or anything. Or if she did it was only because it was embarrassing to be the only one feeling something. Which was the only reason she wanted confirmation. "Really?"

"Big time. I mean, he might not have looked altogether sure of what to do about it, but he was looking."

Pru laughed and shook her head. It had loosened something inside her, but it was still ridiculous. Even if he *looked*, Grant wasn't going to *touch*. Not Beau's little sister. And anyway, she didn't want him to, right? She wanted to make this store work. That was all she could think about.

"Come on, let's go home," Hope said, nodding for the door. "Charity has us going to some church potluck thing."

"No. No. I can't stomach salmon. I can't *bear* it."

"That's what the potluck is for. Other people have to eat the salmon."

JUNE ROLLED INTO JULY, the Fourth seeing Grant actually attending the big Jasper Creek Fourth of July celebration with Cade and his family. Grant had caught a glimpse of Pru with her friends and done his level best to avoid her.

He spent more and more of every day helping her at the store, and was careful to keep his distance from her everywhere else.

By mid-July, they'd finally gotten most of the clear-out taken care of, and were now working on putting shelves and bins together. Pru was ordering things and figuring out when to have her soft open.

He didn't question whether she still actually needed his help. It worked—weekdays at the store, weekends at the ranch. Why it worked and when it would end wasn't worth thinking about.

But every weekend at the ranch, he found himself worrying about the time coming when he'd have to be back to it full-time. When he'd have to face the weight of what his father had asked of him that he'd been shirking for *weeks*.

But a strange side effect to spending more time off the ranch was that he enjoyed the time he *did* spend there with his family. It was why, no matter how many Sunday nights the guilt started to creep in like his father's ghost was hanging out in the corner, Monday morning he got up and went to Pru's.

To avoid the guilty feelings *this* Sunday, he offered to handle the dishes while everyone else scattered to various chores. As he was finishing up, all five of his brothers entered the kitchen.

Grant looked at them. When they didn't say anything, just stood there with their arms crossed as they blocked the exit, Grant dried his hands on a towel. "What's this?"

"An intervention," Tate said.

"What do I need an intervention for?"

"The past few weeks you've been scarce. Off our backs. Doing exactly what we've been asking you to do for like five years."

Grant looked at each of them like they were crazy, since they clearly were. "So, I give you guys what you want for a few weeks and suddenly I need an intervention?"

"I saw you *smiling*," Adam said with a shudder.

"I caught you whistling," Mac said, as if it were on par with running through the house naked and on fire.

"The girls said you made cookies with them yesterday." Cade threw his hands in the air. "Cookies."

"Aren't those all good things?" Grant asked.

"Are you dying?" Ford demanded. "Because that isn't cool if you're keeping it from us."

"I'm good. I'm fine."

"You started with *good*. You."

"He's got to have a woman," Mac insisted. "You don't magically start acting nicer and looking healthier without a woman's influence."

"Where would his sour face come up with a woman?" Adam retorted.

"Well, if you guys are going to talk about me like I'm not here, you really don't need me for this conversation." He tried to move, but his brothers only tightened the circle around him.

"He's been spending a lot of time at Pru's store," Cade said softly, studying Grant with a careful eye.

"He danced with her at the Rusty Nail a few weeks ago," Tate added, nodding thoughtfully. "Awkward as hell. But they danced."

"Little Prudence Riley?" Adam scoffed.

"Little? She's my age," Cade retorted.

"Yeah, *your* age. In other words, too young."

"I've had two wives and I'm about to have a third kid. I wouldn't call it too young."

"The point isn't you. It's Grant," Tate said firmly. "What fixed you?"

"Was I broken?"

"Yes," they all said in unison.

"For years," Cade said, and he didn't sound…mad about it. This wasn't an accusation, even if that was how it seemed. This was concern. Maybe even hope.

A hope Grant had forgotten how to recognize. How to feel. He wasn't sure why it was coming at him now or what had changed exactly. It had been so gradual he hadn't fully noticed it himself until his brothers seemed surprised to find him smiling, whistling, or enjoying time with his nieces.

"I'm not fixed. I just…" Grant rubbed at his chest. He didn't think people just got fixed, but while he'd been busy getting off the ranch and not thinking about their dad and his responsibilities, something that had been tied tight around his lungs for years had eased. "I just…"

"Got out for a while?" Mac supplied. "Stepped away from Dad's ghost? And look. It didn't kill you. It made you happy."

Happy. After their dad had died, happy hadn't mattered, only making sure everyone was okay. But his brothers *were* okay, and the ranch was good. Even with him spending time away. Grant shook his head. "Look, I don't know why you're all surrounding me. Things have been good. Why question it?"

"Because the good is directly stemming from you not being here," Tate pointed out.

Grant felt a stab of guilt, then that familiar pressure in his chest, around his lungs. He was going to have to give it up, start pulling his weight here again. It was the right thing to do. The thing *Dad* had asked him to do. "I'm sorry. I'll start putting more hours in. The ranch needs—"

"You misunderstand us, Grant," Mac said with a certain gentleness his brothers rarely trotted out. "Did it occur to you that *not* working the ranch might be what you need?"

"How could I not work the ranch? Dad—"

"Isn't here," Tate said firmly. "He's gone. I know you blame yourself. But we don't."

"And he had six sons," Ford added. "I'm pretty sure five of us can handle it. This store stuff seems to interest you more. Maybe try that."

"Running a store?"

"Or working at Pru's," Cade said. "Even just part-time. You're not expendable here, but we can certainly step up and fill your shoes if they're shoes you don't want."

Grant had never thought of the ranch as being a choice. That wasn't how he'd been brought up.

"So?" Ford prodded.

"So what?"

"What do you want?" Adam asked, and all his brothers looked at him expectantly. Grant hadn't allowed himself to answer that question in years. Not once since his father had died. Even before then. Ed Mathewson had been devoted to his family. Everything was about the good of the family—not the individual.

Grant wasn't sure he'd ever seen himself as one of those. Wasn't sure the word *individual* even made sense. How could he know what he wanted if he didn't think about the ranch and his brothers?

But maybe that was it. The thing that had unlocked that suffocating cloud of grief weighing on his shoulders. He'd wanted to solve an unsolvable problem. Not for himself. But for his brothers. For his family.

A family that was more than fine, even with his absence. If he thought about himself and himself alone, he wanted something very different. Away from the responsibility his father had left him. While *dying*. Not while alive and having a normal conversation.

"I don't...know."

Cade slapped him on the shoulder. "You've got time to figure it out. We just wanted to make sure it was happiness. Not like..."

"Terminal illness," Ford finished.

"No. No illness."

"Good, then. We've got it covered here while you figure it out," Tate said.

"Because we want you to be happy, Grant. Not a martyr to this place," Cade added.

Eventually his brothers scattered, but everything they'd said stuck with Grant as he tried to sleep, as he got ready for the following day.

He *had* been a martyr to the ranch. In a way, that had been his grieving. There was part of him afraid to leave it behind.

But there was another part of him that couldn't stop turning over and over what Cade had said. *We can certainly step up and fill your shoes if they're shoes you don't want.*

They'd asked him flat out, what *did* he want? At first it had simply been to change, to stop feeling the way he had been. But something had opened up.

He pulled up in front of the feed store. There were pots overflowing with blooms on either side of the door, and he could see the goat's creepy head staring at him just by glancing at the window.

In the privacy of his own mind, Grant had taken to calling him Victor.

He got out of his truck and simply watched. Pru was moving around inside. It looked like she was trying to set up the front where they'd both agreed the gardening section should go.

He'd been helping her out for weeks, but he'd been careful ever since that moment when they'd stared at each other a little too long. There had been other moments like it, but he'd been careful. Stepped back. Made space. Had *not* made eye contact.

If he thought back over the past few weeks, he realized they'd *both* been being particularly careful about their individual physical spaces. But they'd also worked together to get this store to where it was. Grant felt invested.

But being part of it came with her.

She opened the door and popped her head out. "What are you doing just standing there?"

"Thinking."

"Well, you look like a creeper staring at me."

Yeah, she was probably right. It shouldn't amuse him. But it did, and instead of ignoring what he felt, what he *wanted*, Grant went ahead and said something completely and utterly out of character. "You're not so bad to stare at."

She looked at him like he'd lost his mind and he found he kind of liked it.

"What is with you?" she asked, as he followed her into the store. She stalked straight for a pile of stuff that had been delivered yesterday.

"My brothers asked me the same thing last night," he said, considering the gardening supplies. And then her.

"Oh yeah? You have an answer for them?" She didn't look at him.

"Not really. Not fully. I'm getting there though." Yeah, he was getting there. It wasn't just getting away from the ranch—though that was some of it. There'd been a noose around his neck, one he'd placed there himself, and stepping away from it had given him the slow realization of how little he needed it.

Part of it was the store stuff. He liked the planning and figuring out where things would go and what customers would like.

And then there was her. She'd dragged him to lunch with her brother. Forced him to dance with her at the bar. She was confident and straightforward—things he'd been missing himself for a while. But when it came to *him*, there was a very careful part of her. One that looked at him with enough trepidation to give his ego a boost.

Beyond that, she made him laugh, and it didn't come with the strings his brothers did. Or even her brothers. Because he'd always been very aware that Beau and JT were conduits for their mother. Not that they didn't care about him, but Mary Riley was part of it.

Pru never treated him like a project though. She'd put him to work because her mother wanted it, but she'd used him for her own sake. She'd treated him like she wasn't afraid to break him, or ask too much of him, or like she needed to fix him.

She treated him like he was a man. One who hadn't changed after his father had died. It reminded him of who he'd been. And in the reminding, he found himself stepping back into those old pieces of himself.

What do you want? All the people in his life he loved the most had asked him that lately.

But standing here in Pru's store, with Pru staring at him like he'd grown two heads, he didn't know what he wanted.

But he knew he wanted to stop being careful. Stop keeping his damn distance. So, he walked right up to her.

"What...are you doing?" she asked, backing away from

him. For every step she took backward, he took another one forward, until she found herself backed into a corner.

"I'm going to kiss you."

"What?" She slapped a hand to his chest, her eyes wide and panicked. "Oh my God. No, you're not."

He kept her cornered there, and though she had her hand plastered against his chest, she certainly wasn't running away.

He angled his head just so. His hat was still on, so it created a little shadow around them. A tremor went through her and his mouth curved.

"Don't you want me to?" he asked, softly, his mouth just a whisper away from hers.

She sucked in a breath, still wide-eyed. But she looked right at him. And said nothing.

Which made him grin. "Let's give it a shot."

CHAPTER SIX

PRU DIDN'T HAVE a chance to suck in another breath before Grant's mouth was on hers.

His *mouth*. And it was an actual fantasy come to life.

Not that she'd ever imagined that he'd just walk up to her, slide his big, rough hand around the back of her neck, and *kiss* her. Like he was in charge. Like he knew what he was doing.

God, he knew what he was doing. Every last thought, rejection, and tension in her mind was simply melting away until she felt like little more than a puddle in his arms. Strong arms, strong body. He smelled like soap and sky.

His hands were on her face, his body was as hard and uncompromising as the wall behind her, and the *taste* of him was a dream. The rolling sensation of need and heat *had* to be a dream. This couldn't be a real thing. A kiss had never made her feel like she was underwater, like nothing else existed.

A kiss had never shaken her down into her bones. Never made her hold on and let the road take her wherever. *Anywhere.* As long as his mouth was on hers.

When he eased away, she nearly went with him, before remembering herself. Before remembering *him*.

She was clinging to his shirt. His hat was still on, but had been precariously tipped back. And those blue eyes stared right at her. It felt like they stared *into* her.

She didn't want *that*. She uncurled her fingers from his shirt, slowly rocked back on her heels, and leaned away from him. "I am very confused."

He fixed his hat, and his expression was contemplative. "I'm not sure I can clarify it."

"You *kissed* me. Like, in every definition of that word possible."

"Yeah." His mouth curved.

Who *was* this guy? He looked so damn pleased with himself. He'd had all these walls up when he'd first walked into her store in June, and slowly he'd begun to tear them down. Himself. He'd worked on himself.

It was terrifying to watch someone do that. To strip away their protections, to find a certainty inside themselves.

"*Why* did you kiss me?"

"Because I wanted to."

"That's not an answer."

He shrugged. "Best answer I can think of."

Under normal circumstances, Pru did not consider herself a coward. Even if she didn't know how to fight something, she still powered through. More or less.

She had no idea how to power through this emotional tide inside of her.

"It was a good kiss," he said. No question. No grin. No smirk. Just the look of a man who was quite satisfied with himself.

What on earth had happened? "Yeah, okay. But where did it *come* from?"

"I've been wanting to do it for a while."

Her mouth hung open. *For a while.* What? *What?* "Why now?"

"My brothers surrounded me last night and demanded to know why I was so happy. I still don't have all the answers to that. Part of it was letting go of the ranch, and the guilt that kept me so tied to it in the first place. Part of it was the store stuff, but part of it was you. I like you, Prudence."

Pru didn't think she breathed for a full minute. What even *was* breathing? He liked her. He'd kissed her. It did not compute.

"I thought I didn't want any complications in my life, but the truth is, I was more comfortable wrapping the grief and overwhelming responsibility around me. But I've realized that I've avoided everything difficult or complicated in the name of a misplaced responsibility. I'm not interested in that anymore."

"Well, *I* am." She hadn't meant to say it out loud exactly. But she wanted no misunderstanding. She'd upended her life, and she didn't want to think of upending it any more. She wanted to get her store ready in time for the centennial, and then...

What was she supposed to do with some...guy? Some fantasy brought to life? Relationships required work. Give and take. She'd watched her friends struggle with anger and broken hearts and the sort of soaring joy that could only end by crashing to the ground in a million fiery pieces.

When you were alone, you could control all that. Avoid all that. *That* was what she wanted. The space to keep everything on an even keel and not feel like a kiss could break her to pieces.

He stepped forward and cupped her cheek with his hand. It was a sweet, gentle gesture that made her want to cry, of all damn things. "What complications have you had, Pru?" His words were as gentle as the hand on her face, because he was genuinely asking her. Not telling her she had it easy. Not surprised she didn't have her act together.

She didn't know how to answer that question. She didn't

want to answer it, and even thinking about it had tears stinging her eyes. Which was absolutely unacceptable. "What would my family think?" she said, instead of anything that answered his question.

"Does it matter?" His thumb brushed back and forth on her cheek as though that was normal and her heart fluttered like she wanted it to be.

Matter? She'd built her *life* around what they thought. She'd left Jasper Creek to make her parents proud. She'd been successful to prove to them they were right.

And then you came home when all of that turned out to be an empty shell.

But she'd done that for Hope. Not for herself. Doing it for herself would have meant there was too much at stake.

Just like there was way too much at stake in the here and now. Grant kissing her and acting like there was something to pursue here? No. It just wasn't going to happen. She didn't want it. Good kiss or not. Liking him or not. She didn't *want* it. "I'm not interested in anything like this."

"Okay."

She blinked at his easy agreement. "Okay? Just okay?"

He dropped his hand from her face, finally giving her some space. "I like you, and I'm attracted to you. I'm definitely interested in seeing where that kiss leads, but if you're not…" He shrugged. "You're hardly the only attractive woman in Jasper Creek."

The sound that came out of her mouth was an outraged squeak.

He seemed wholly unbothered. "So, are we setting up the gardening section today?" He gestured at her piles of stuff. Casually.

As if it didn't matter. As if kissing her was the norm.

As if being rejected was the norm and she was as easily replaced with Alice at the diner or Kit next door.

Which was good. *Great.*

I like you, Prudence.

Had anyone ever said something so simple and had it upend...everything?

But she didn't want to be upended. He could totally go off into town and find someone else. She didn't care.

Not one bit.

They worked together to set up the gardening supply area and when JT came to help out that afternoon, she was the only one who felt tense and awkward. JT and Grant joked around like old times and she...brooded.

When she finally got back to the farmhouse that night, all Pru wanted to do was hide. Maybe punch her pillow a few hundred times.

But her friends were gathered around the kitchen table, perusing those damn salmon recipes. Something held her in place, as though hands held her right there until she felt compelled to say something.

"I need an emergency meeting."

Kit didn't even look up. "Please see the rules about excessive and unnecessary meetings."

"Grant kissed me."

Chairs scraped against the floor and her three friends immediately got to their feet. It felt like the thing holding her in place gently let go because she was suddenly surrounded by her friends.

"Okay, no violation whatsoever," Kit said, heading for the wine rack. "This is a very important meeting."

Charity wound her arm around Pru's waist and began to lead her to the living room. Hope grabbed her fudge and Kit pressed a large glass of wine into Pru's hands.

Pru took a very long sip.

"So, what kind of kiss?" Charity asked.

"What do you mean what kind? The kind where his mouth was on my mouth."

"Tongue?" Kit asked, which earned a shoulder slap from Hope.

Pru nodded. "Tongue. Touching." She took another gulp of wine. "He said he liked me."

"Why wouldn't he like you?"

She didn't know how to answer that question, so she ignored it. "I don't know how to play dating games."

"It doesn't sound like he was playing games," Hope replied. "I'd have thought you'd appreciate that."

"Well, I don't. At all."

"Was he pushy?" Charity asked with some concern.

"No! I told him I wasn't interested and he had the *gall* to say there were plenty of other women out there. The asshole."

Kit snorted out a laugh, and Charity looked shocked to her core. Pru much preferred Charity's reaction.

"You told him you weren't interested," Hope pointed out.

"I know."

"What was he supposed to do? Cry?" Kit asked.

"I don't know! He wasn't supposed to kiss me or like me in the first place."

"But you told me a few weeks ago that you liked him," Hope said. "Too much. I don't understand the problem."

"I didn't mean the kind of like I wanted reciprocated."

"There's a kind of like people don't want reciprocated?" Charity asked, clearly confused.

But Kit was looking right at her, not confused at all. And it was that calm, insightful study that made Pru realize she'd made a giant tactical mistake. She should have never confided in her friends. *This* was why she hadn't told them she'd been sad in California.

Because one of them would have been able to tell her why.

"There is if you're Pru," Kit said, never breaking eye contact with Pru.

The panic fluttered, so Pru tamped it down with anger and offense. "What does that mean?"

"It means nothing scares you more than something you want a little too much."

"That isn't true."

Her friends exchanged uncomfortable glances, and Pru couldn't believe this had somehow turned into some... confrontation of her own flaws.

"The ranch is the prime example."

"The ranch? My parents wouldn't give me a piece of it. How is that—"

"No, your parents told you they were splitting off portions for JT and Beau, but you'd get the same monetary value to spend on college. You never told them you didn't want that. That you would rather have had a piece."

"That wasn't about wanting. It was about..." But Pru didn't have the words to explain what she felt. She never did.

"Okay, maybe not. Parents are complicated," Charity said kindly. "But then there was that co-op farm thing you wanted to be a part of during college, but you backed out."

Pru gaped at Charity's betrayal. "It was too risky! They needed a big investment, and I would have had to quit school."

"Then there was Owen Landry," Hope added, because of course they would all gang up on her.

"I did *not* want Owen Landry."

"Exactly. Which is why you dated him for two years even though you never had any intention of marrying him."

She had a million comebacks for that, but Pru had the terrible feeling they'd just keep finding more examples, and she didn't want her smart, careful, and definitely not *fear-based* choices thrown at her. "This isn't what I needed."

"We're sorry," Charity said.

"Are we?" Hope asked. "I'm not. It's time for some tough love, baby."

"Well, you can all shove your tough love." Pru got up, thought about leaving the wineglass behind, then snatched it up instead. "Right along with the salmon."

"The truth only makes you run if you're afraid of it," Kit called after her.

Afraid? No, she wasn't afraid.

And she'd prove it.

GRANT WAS PULLING UP to his ranch after a night watching the baseball game at the Riley ranch with JT and Beau when his phone rang. He took it out and didn't recognize the number. But it was local. "Hello?"

"Hi."

"Pru?" He didn't get out of his truck like he'd planned. He sat there, engine still running, but he flicked the headlights off. "Couldn't you text like a normal person?"

"You know I can't use my cell phone," she said, sounding irritable. "This is the landline here at the farmhouse."

"Okay. What's up?" There was a long pause that made him grin. "You want to talk about today?"

"No," she said emphatically. "But can you meet me at the store?"

He could question that. He probably *should* question

it. Make it harder on her, and on himself, before this went somewhere irrevocable.

But he didn't. "All right. I'll meet you there. Right now?"

"Yeah. Good. Great. Bye."

He chuckled and ended the call. This was an interesting development. Deep down, he knew he should be more careful. There were the Rileys to think about, but wasn't this whole…change about doing something for himself without worrying about everyone else?

He drove to town and didn't let himself think too far ahead. They were just going to have a conversation. Maybe she was going to ask him not to help out at the store anymore.

For the first time since this morning, a real bolt of unease went through him. He really couldn't imagine the Rileys turning their backs on him just because he got involved with Pru. They were too much like family. But he could see Pru barring him from the store and that was a surprisingly awful thought.

He'd grown to love the store.

He drove down a dark and empty Main Street and saw her truck parked in front. He pulled up his truck next to hers. There was one lone light on so he could see her pacing in and out of the shadows. Talking to herself. Hand gesturing.

She'd changed her clothes. Instead of jeans, a T-shirt, and boots that had been her uniform all these weeks, she was wearing denim shorts that showed off her long legs. Her tank top was the color of grapes and gave a glimpse of just how toned her arms were.

She was pretty as a picture, and his hands itched to touch her.

Any thoughts of being careful or discussing things faded

as he stepped inside. She stood in the middle of her store, staring at him like he was some kind of bogeyman. But that changed, gradually, into a kind of grim determination. "We can't tell anyone," she said by way of greeting.

He could have pretended he didn't know what she was talking about, but he didn't. He raised an eyebrow as he walked toward her. "We can't?"

"Okay, 'anyone' is relative because I will tell Hope, Charity, and Kit. But I mean, my brothers." She didn't back away like she had this morning.

Her eyes were wide, but there was a determined light in them. She looked up at him, licked her lips, and stood her ground.

"What exactly are you afraid of there? That they're going to try to beat me up? I've got five brothers to back me up. I'll be fine."

She shook her head. "I'm not afraid. It's not about fear," she said. "Do you remember Marianne Fleming?"

Confused, Grant struggled to follow what she was saying because her tank top dipped low enough to give him a tantalizing glimpse of the soft swell of her breasts. "Marianne? JT's ex?"

"Yes. And I got to be really good friends with her. She even came and visited me in California a few times. Kit and Charity and Hope were so far away and I thought I was finally finding a local friend again. Then she broke up with JT and it changed everything. I couldn't forgive her for that."

"Pru—"

"Your friendship with JT and Beau is deeper and longer and far more important than that friendship I had with Marianne," she said earnestly. "I wouldn't want it to be ruined because something happened here. And it could be. My brothers love me and are overprotective of me. They're protective of you too. It's too much when this is just about sex."

Just about sex. No. There was more between them than just that kiss this morning.

"It's more than sex, Pru."

She looked like he'd slapped her. "No. I invited you here for *sex*."

"And I'm telling you there's more between us than sex, whether you like it or not."

She shook her head. "Just kiss me again," she demanded.

She seemed to think sidestepping the conversation changed it, but it didn't. Not for him. "Why?"

"Because I am *not* afraid." She proved it by grabbing his shirtfront and pressing her mouth to his without waiting for him to make the move.

It wasn't quiet. It wasn't testing or teasing. This morning had been born out of a feeling of…a new lease on life or something. Bright. Confident. Grabbing the good.

This was an explosion. Heat and need, like she'd poured every last careful look over the past few weeks into this moment. Into lips and tongue and teeth.

She wrapped her arms around his neck and pressed her long, lean body to his. She was close, but he pulled her closer. She kissed him deep, but he kissed her deeper. He wasn't sure how they ended up pressed up against the back wall, but they were.

She raked her fingers through his hair. He slid his hands over every curve of her. He scraped his teeth over her bottom lip and she made a noise in the back of her throat that had his vision going hazy.

She was panting, and he wasn't all that sure his heart hadn't beaten straight out of his chest. He slid his hands under her shirt and groaned against her mouth. She was perfect. Soft and strong.

In some deep, very annoying part of his brain, alarm bells were clamoring. He didn't particularly want to listen to them, but they were rather insistent. "Pru—"

She shook her head. "I want you, Grant."

Alarm bells sufficiently quashed. "Here?" he asked her, aware that there was nowhere soft to lay her down.

But she was tugging at his T-shirt. "Yeah, here's good. Here's great."

"I don't have any—"

"I'm good. We're good. Promise." She pulled his shirt up and over his head and then undid the button of his pants and whatever else he'd been about to say was lost to the mist of *need*.

He pulled her shirt up and didn't bother with the task of unclasping her bra, simply yanking it down.

"God, Pru." She was like a delicacy he'd denied himself too long. So he tasted her. Everywhere he could reach standing here in the back of her store. Then they were pulling off each other's clothes as best they could, like groping teenagers.

When he kicked his jeans off, her faint *oh* was a nice little boon to his ego. He wanted more, but… "How are we going to do this?"

"I brought a blanket," she muttered, grasping blindly behind her at the counter. She grabbed the folded bit of fabric and held it out to him. He spread it out on the floor. The floor. *Of her store.* Granted, they were far enough in the back that the windows were blocked, but…

Any doubts he had about the venue were gone when she rid herself of her underwear and unclasped her bra and tossed it aside.

"Beautiful."

She made an odd noise, and she blushed. Then she gestured at him. So, he took the rest of his clothes off then pulled her to him. He laid her down on the blanket. It hardly hid the fact that they were on the hard ground, but she didn't seem to care. She kissed him and held on to him, until he forgot anything else. Just Pru, and how right this felt. How right it *was*.

"There's no going back from this," he said against her neck. Because it needed to be said. Because it needed to be understood.

This changed everything, and he found that was perfectly okay with him.

CHAPTER SEVEN

PANIC SPURTED THROUGH HER, but it was wrapped up in all the other sensations. The way her skin throbbed everywhere he'd kissed or touched. The pull in her stomach, the dull ache that could only be solved by one thing.

No going back? There was always a way to go back. She opened her mouth to tell him but he slid inside of her. So *big*. So encompassing. She could scarcely breathe and when she did it was only to whisper his name as he held still, deep inside her.

He sighed against her neck, his hands sliding down her sides. Then his mouth covered hers as he began to move. It was a slow, maddening rhythm that stoked a fire too big and too bright to be recognizable.

Sex had never been like this. Had she ever let it be? But she didn't have a choice with Grant. There was the physical sensation taking her out of that mental space, but it was deeper. Because it was Grant. He pulled some *feeling* out of her that made everything that much bigger and brighter. And it altered her.

She didn't want to be altered but she had no choice. The orgasm shuddered through her like a storm, and whatever thoughts she'd had were washed away into sensation and pleasure. Into his mouth, his hands.

Somehow it didn't end there. He kept touching her and kissing her, moving with her. Like it could go on forever.

She found herself whispering his name, holding on to him as something too complicated to mention worked through her, heightening the pleasure in a way she didn't understand.

Until it all broke, and him with it into a perfect moment of pure sensation.

He rolled off her, but kept an arm around her, drawing her close.

She was lying on a blanket in her store, having just had sex with Grant Mathewson. She was breathing like she'd run a marathon and every last inch of her was perfectly, wonderfully relaxed. She should probably freak out right now, but she couldn't muster it up just yet. For now she'd enjoy the aftershocks of really, really, *really* amazing sex. The kind she had fully believed did not exist.

"This wasn't some slip thing, was it?" he asked, his voice sounding a little sleepy. "Seduce a guy on the floor of your store."

"I didn't *seduce* you."

"Hm." He kissed her shoulder absently, then her neck more purposefully. Then her mouth again.

"No slip," she murmured against his lips. Just a purposeful decision because she wasn't afraid of anything. Least of all any strange feelings about Grant. It was just attraction mixed with an old crush she'd never fully admitted to herself she'd had. Those were both things she could handle. And would.

"Okay." He rubbed his mouth against the underside of her jaw. "I guess I'm just rusty enough to think it was that."

"Rusty?" She pushed at him so he had to pull back. "How rusty?"

He blew out a breath and looked at the ceiling. "Well... not really worth talking about, is it?"

She poked his chest. "How long?"

"I don't see how that's pertinent information."

"It is to me. You've allegedly been this sad sack, mopey, tragic figure and—"

"All right," he muttered, scowling at her.

"How long?" She drilled him in the chest again, just to see what he would do. Grant. Naked. After having had really amazing sex with her. On a blanket in her store. That was going to take some time to fully compute.

He grabbed her hand so she couldn't poke him again. "Three years," he muttered.

"Years?" She nearly shrieked. "*Years? Three years.*"

He looked at her dolefully.

"Years," she whispered. She didn't want to laugh *at* him. It wasn't that. It was just that she could hardly imagine him being this beautiful and not having at least random hook-ups, no matter how much of a tragic figure he'd been.

"What about you?" he asked, shaking the hand he held.

"Oh, a lady never tells." She fluttered her eyelashes at him, trying to pull her hand away, but he held firm, keeping those blue eyes pinned to hers.

"Tit for tat, Prudence."

She lay back and sighed. It was really strange not to be self-conscious around Grant, but he'd touched her, kissed her, been inside her. Clearly he saw something he liked. She wasn't exactly racking up the notches on her bedpost, but it had hardly been three years. "Less than three years." She smiled slyly at him.

He was propped up on one elbow, which showed off the intriguing curve of his bicep muscle. "At least tell me it's been more than three weeks. I can deal with something under three years and over three weeks."

"Yes."

"Okay, good."

"By about eleven months."

He pointed his free hand at her. "Ha!"

"One year is hardly the same as *three*. When you look like you do."

"And how do I look?"

She waved a hand at him. "Look at you. I bet you can do a lot of pull-ups."

"What does that have to do with anything?"

"Naked pull-ups could have a lot to do with a lot of things. The point is, sad sack or not, you could have had a slew of one-night stands if you'd wanted to."

"Maybe. I guess I didn't want to." He studied her until she *did* start to feel self-conscious about being naked in front of him.

Her heart bumped against her chest. It was the sign. The one she always listened to. When that heart bump happened, it was time to ease up. To ground herself to earth. Listening to the heart bump only ever ended in heart*ache*.

But his mouth was on hers again and she couldn't quite follow a thought to completion. To action. His fingers trailed through her hair and she melted into him. Again.

"We could go to the farmhouse," he said, his mouth traveling down her neck. "You said you were going to tell them anyway."

She shook her head even as she tilted it to give him more access. "House rules. No hookups."

"You guys have a lot of really annoying rules." Then he started to laugh. He rolled onto his back and laughed like he'd heard the funniest joke ever.

"What?" she demanded.

"All those man-catching tips," he said, then chuckled again. "They worked."

She gently smacked his bare chest. "They did not!"

"You used them on me to do your duty or whatever, but here I am." He spread his arms wide. "Sufficiently caught."

She wrinkled her nose. "I wasn't trying to catch you or anyone else."

He rolled on top of her. "Too late." The kiss was sudden, sweet, and gentle. It had a warmth seeping through her that felt like kryptonite. The panic or fear was ready to rear its ugly head, but he kept talking as he kissed her.

"A bed, Pru. I want you in a bed. My house or yours, but one of them."

She couldn't go to his house. Not when he shared it with four of his brothers. It was breaking the rules to take him back to the farmhouse, but she was too…overwhelmed to argue with him. "All right. Follow me home, Grant."

GRANT WOKE UP in a strange bed in a strange house, but the woman wrapped around him wasn't strange at all.

Grant allowed himself to lie still and absorb the moment. He'd set out to change his life when he'd realized he was happy away from the ranch, working at Pru's store. He hadn't planned on changing it quite *this* much. But it *fit*.

What that meant long-term…well, that was still a mystery. But there was time to figure that out. He glanced at the alarm clock on the dainty nightstand. Late for him, all in all, considering he was used to ranch hours.

No doubt one of his brothers would notice his absence— or his arrival—if he didn't get home soon. That didn't bother him so much, but Pru wanted to be careful and, given the choice, Grant would rather avoid his brothers' notice than be forced to lie to them.

He rolled out of bed and gathered his clothes. Pru began to stir, and he allowed himself the pleasure of watching her wake up. There were none of her usual quick, precise movements or bullet-like focus. It was slow. She tossed and turned a little bit, seemed like she was going to settle back into sleep, then made grumbling complaints.

But once her eyes opened fully, they were sharp and alert and landed on him. "Oh my God. You have to get out of here before everyone wakes up."

"Good morning to you too."

She yawned, and looked damn appealing lying there in the rumpled bed. But he knew sex wasn't on the table again this morning. Not when there had to be some subterfuge. But that didn't mean he'd hurry away. "What are you guys going to do when you're done renting this place?"

"Huh?"

He gestured at the walls around him. "You can't rent a vacation house forever."

"I don't... I haven't really thought about it."

He stopped pulling on his clothes for a second and looked at her. She was sitting up in the bed, sheet pulled up to her chin, looking perplexed.

"You haven't thought about where you're going to live come September?"

"No. I have a store to focus on. If we're not all ready by the centennial, the rent goes up astronomically and I'll have to quit."

It seemed odd to him that it was all or nothing, but maybe...

He shook the thought away.

She hopped out of bed, gathering clothes and muttering to herself about the time. Her hair was wild and her cheeks were flushed. She pulled a T-shirt on, but realized it was his and had to strip it off again and toss it at him.

He caught it, and her when she tried to scurry by him.

"Hi."

"Grant, I—"

He didn't let her finish. He put his mouth on hers in a lazy, affectionate good-morning.

She sank into the kiss for approximately three seconds before she shoved him away. "Get dressed," she ordered, but there was humor in her tone as she pulled the right shirt on this time.

He did the same, fastened his belt, and shoved his feet into his boots. Pru was dressed now, but her hair was still wild. "You're going to need to do something about that. That is sex hair."

She patted her head. "It isn't... Oh, hell. My brush is in the bathroom. Listen, I'll go out, make sure the coast is clear, then give you the sign to sneak away."

"Yes, sir."

She rolled her eyes at his mocking salute, but eased the door open. "You have to stop being funny. Now be good and get gone. If you get caught, *I* get in trouble."

"All you have to do is one of your silly man-catching things. I give you permission to use whatever it is on me." He grinned at her. She didn't grin back. He leaned down and gave her a quick kiss. "I'll see you at the store in a bit."

She nodded, chewing that bottom lip fretfully. The hall was clear so she eased into it, then motioned him to go downstairs. He followed her instructions, though one stair creaked ominously as he put his weight on it, but he sped through. Surely it was early enough they were all still—

He heard the quiet murmur of female voices when he reached the bottom of the stairs. The hallway went directly through the kitchen, which was where he assumed the women were gathered. But if they were eating, they'd be focused on the table. Not this side of the room. All he had to do was be very quiet, and very quick.

That proved impossible when he tripped—over what he'd never know. He wasn't a clumsy man, but it was almost like the floor had jumped up to conspire against him. He glanced at the kitchen.

Three pairs of female eyes blinked at him, in varying states of pajama wear.

He did the only thing he could think to do. Tipped his hat and said, "Morning, ladies." When they all continued to gape at him, he managed a smile. "Have a nice day."

And he got the hell out of Dodge, as strains of old-timey big band music followed him out.

Though the Mathewson ranch wasn't far off, there was no direct route so he had to take the main road around which added time. He took the side entrance, which meant a drive by Cade's cabin. If he could get past the cabin without Cade or JJ spotting him, he could figure out a way to get back into the house without anyone catching him.

Of course, it wasn't that easy. As Grant drove toward Cade's cabin, Cade was getting out of his truck, a box in his hands.

Grant slowed to a stop, working through the various excuses he could use for coming into the ranch this way. He rolled down his window, mind blank. "You're out early."

Cade held up the box. "JJ's having a hard time keeping stuff down. I went and grabbed some bagels from the bakery." Cade studied Grant and then where he'd come from. "Pru, huh?"

It was a relief not to have to come up with a lie, and that it was Cade who'd caught him. Cade might be the youngest, but he was the more mature of the other brothers. "Can you keep that on the down low for the time being?"

"Sure. Why?"

"She's not ready to spread it around yet."

"Why not?"

Grant shrugged, not sure why Cade's questions bothered him. "It's the Rileys, and Mary's been so good to me, I guess."

"You don't sound sure."

"It's no big deal, Cade."

"Okay." Cade looked like he was about to step back, but then he shook his head. "Listen, you don't need advice from me, but speaking as someone who had their wife walk out on them, you want to make sure you're on the same page. If it's more than sex, that is."

"The same page?"

"Yeah, I mean you don't have to have the same opinions, or even want the same things, you just have to be clear about that. It's…keeping it to yourself that sours things. Trust me." Cade patted the truck door and stepped back.

Grant nodded and drove the rest of the way to the barn.

Pru was definitely keeping some things to herself. But it was early yet. Cade was talking about a failed marriage, not the beginnings of something that might not even be feasible.

But it worried Grant how much he wanted to make it feasible.

CHAPTER EIGHT

PRU WAS WHISTLING when she walked down to breakfast. It was much later than she usually appeared, but she could use a million different excuses for that. Her hair no longer looked sex tangled, and she felt...

Good. Really good. Relaxed and happy and...*mmm*. When she reached the kitchen, everyone was there, still in their pajamas, speaking in earnest, excitable tones.

"You guys are slowpokes this morning," Pru greeted. "I'm ready to head for the store."

"You hooked up in the house!" Charity pointed an accusing finger at her. "You hardcore broke the rule."

Pru should have known it wouldn't be that easy. And yet, she couldn't work up any outrage or irritation. As her friends stared at her accusingly, she couldn't even work up guilt.

They wouldn't tell anyone and there was no use lying about it. Besides, it proved how not scared she was.

Even if she felt the flutter of fear every time Grant looked at her with those serious, studying eyes. But that was a problem for another day.

"Yeah, I did. And you know what? It was totally, one hundred percent worth it. I'll take all the slips in all the land. *That's* how good breaking the hooking-up rule was."

"Well, that's a far cry from Prudence Riley's usual 'sex is fine' stance," Kit said blandly.

"It was not fine. It was *fantastic*." She walked over to the coffeemaker and poured herself some. Why not gloat?

"The right guy makes all the difference, huh?" Hope said.

"Yes, I… I mean, not that Grant's the *right* guy." There was no room in her head to think about that. About what came next. There was too much that could still go wrong for her to leap ahead like that. She had to focus on the moment. On the now.

And she felt *great* about the now.

"It doesn't prove anything," Kit said loftily.

"Excuse me?"

"You wanted to prove you're not afraid. But sex doesn't prove anything. It's all the stuff that comes with it that's the scary part."

With that, Kit sailed out of the kitchen, one of her scarves trailing behind her, and Pru could only stand there, all that *great* leaking slowly out of her.

She drove to the store alone, because she was ready and they weren't. Because she didn't know how to share air with her friends when they'd ruined her lovely post-sex buzz.

They hadn't even remembered to make her take a man-catching slip. For the first time, she stepped out of her truck, looked at her store, and didn't feel calmed.

It was a dream come true to make these stores theirs, and for Pru, specifically, to be in Jasper Creek. Everyone else had wanted to leave, to build their lives somewhere else. She was the only one who'd wanted to be here.

She might not have the ranch like she'd always wanted, but she had just about everything else.

Her breathing came in shallow gasps. What was she going to do when it all fell apart the way things inevitably did? *She* would fall apart. She couldn't bear it. She couldn't...

She pulled herself back. She was thinking too far ahead. One step at a time. They had to survive the centennial first.

She wouldn't cross *any* bridge until they'd proved themselves a success at the centennial.

She went inside and put herself immediately to work. The harder she threw herself into it, the less she had to think. When the bell tinkled, she looked up, and Grant entered her store.

She had a vivid memory of what they'd done in her store last night. And then in her bed. When he smiled, like he was remembering too, everything inside of her jittered with something she recognized. And it terrified her.

She used to feel that way about her plans. Excited and scared, but sure. Sure she'd have a piece of the Riley ranch, sure she'd build a life she loved.

When that had been such a bust, she'd taught herself to avoid that feeling. Any time it threatened, she bolted. Just like her friends had accused her of—the ranch, the farm in California.

She didn't know how to bolt from Grant. Send him away? Tell him the sex sucked?

"Morning. What's on the list today?" he asked cheerfully. Grant Mathewson was being cheerful, and she'd had something to do with it.

Which gave her such joy and that would lead to what? Complicated feelings and emotional needs and no. *No, thank you.* "I have a couple online orders I want to get filled and ready for pickup."

He nodded and they got to work in easy, silent teamwork.

"You're going to need help," he said as they stepped back and surveyed their work. "A cashier. Or a stock boy.

Someone who understands the merchandise and the customer, just as you do."

She considered the store. It wasn't open yet. They weren't at the centennial yet. How could she think about after when the here and now was scary enough? She waved a hand. "I'll think about that after."

He took the waving hand in his, surprising her enough to look up. Why did that dark blue make her heart kick so hard?

"Think about it now," he said, giving her hand a squeeze before he released it. "Easy choice. Me."

Her eyebrows drew together. "You want a job here?"

"Yeah. I'm enjoying myself. I know hiring me is probably more paperwork, but I'll help you figure it out. You can pay me minimum wage. I don't need health insurance or anything like that. We've got all that covered through the ranch."

"You can't...be my stock boy." He'd be here. Always here. Entwined with the one thing she'd believed she could have. *That was your first mistake.*

"Why not? I like the work, and it'd just be part-time. I still have some responsibilities at the ranch I'd keep."

She blinked and she shook her head. It was too much to consider. She didn't want to picture it. "We'll talk about it after the centennial."

"That seems to be your answer for everything."

"Because if that's not a success then we don't *have* stores." And if it *was* a success, if everything they'd been building came to fruition, how would she deal with it when things went wrong?

Suddenly, not having a store felt like the better option. "And if I don't have a store, I have to go back to California." She'd been safe in California. Sad maybe. But safe.

"Why?"

"What do you mean why?"

"Why couldn't you stay here? Why does that have to mean you run off to California?"

She didn't know how to answer that. Things were spiraling too far out of control. If she succeeded, things would be hard. If she failed, she'd have to live with the knowledge she'd failed her friends and with the loss of this thing she genuinely loved. It was all rock and hard place. How had she let herself end up here? "I...couldn't live in this town a failure."

"You'd hardly be a failure, Pru."

She could only stare at him. Of course she'd be a failure. Her old life had been safe and she'd been good at it, but she'd given it up to go after what she'd wanted.

And what she wanted was right here. But she was never any good at the things she loved. And she loved this store so much. She...

He was looking at her funny, worry starting to creep into his expression. She was freaking out and she couldn't possibly talk to *Grant* about the freak-out. About her feelings.

She sucked in a breath. She wouldn't let herself think beyond the next step. If she survived the centennial, she would think about the next step.

But only then.

"We have work to do," she said firmly, closing the conversation.

And when he didn't push, she told herself she felt relieved and vindicated.

IT WAS A strange thing getting more and more involved with someone you'd known most of your life, and was the sister of your closest friend. There were the impressions Grant had of Pru as a kid, or even as an adult. Impressions formed by his own experiences, but also formed by the Riley family's interpretation of Pru.

But the more Grant got to know her, got to be around her, the more he saw there was a thread of disconnect somewhere. She wasn't exactly what her family thought she was, any more than she was exactly what Grant had thought she was.

She was so much more than the Pru-ricane everyone joked about. She had a vulnerability about her that she shored up so hard, he only saw little glimpses of it at odd moments.

She worked herself to the bone on the store, but she flitted around like she was building on sand. Like it could all shift and sink away through no fault of her own. But also like she'd have to flee the wreckage.

And any time he made a suggestion that might firm up that foundation, she closed him off and out. Never fully. Never for long. There'd been approximately one night in three weeks when they hadn't been together, though she rarely let him talk her into either bed.

But something wasn't right. It was good. *They* were good, but something was off-kilter and it took him a while to figure out what it was.

No matter the weeks that passed, she wouldn't talk about what might happen after the centennial. Not when it came to where she was going to live, whether she'd hire him to work at the store, or what they meant to each other.

It was like a talisman. *After the centennial.*

And he couldn't for the life of him figure out why. The more he poked and prodded, the less she opened up to him.

The worst part was, that conversation with Cade haunted him. He'd always thought Cade's first wife had been halfway out the door long before their second daughter had come around. She'd been searching for a reason—or for the courage—to leave, and there was something similar in Pru's eyes.

It wasn't the same, but it wasn't fully different either.

He should be fine with keeping it strictly casual. He kept telling himself so, but it stuck in his craw and made each passing day a little more dissatisfying. He drove into town, just a few days away from this magical centennial and tried to convince himself Prudence was right.

They'd figure everything out after the centennial.

The town was starting to prepare. Mrs. Kim and the decorating committee were standing in the middle of the square as he drove past, likely planning everything they'd do on Friday night and Saturday morning with the gravity of a military campaign.

He parked his truck around back now that the Dumpster was gone, and entered through the back door. The stockroom was full and organized, and it gave him a quick zing of satisfaction.

It was Pru's store, no doubt about it, but he'd played a part in building it.

When he entered the main section, she was standing behind the counter, organizing the impulse-buy stock. He walked up to the counter and leaned across to give her a quick kiss, but she ducked away. "Windows."

He glanced at them. They were big and the sun shone through, but he doubted anyone would see a quick kiss. "Right." It hurt. He kept telling himself it shouldn't. That her reasons were valid, even if *he* was past them. But it hurt nonetheless, and it was reminding him a little too much of what he'd done after his dad had died.

He'd sacrificed himself for everyone else. Put responsibility above everything else. Never let anyone see how hard it was to do it on his own.

"It looks good, doesn't it?" she said, surveying the store.

It looked good *and* it looked ready for the big reveal on Saturday. "It looks great. We make a good team."

Something flickered in her expression and her shoulders tensed, but she smiled at him, no matter how forced it was.

She said nothing.

And that did it. Because he couldn't see past this wall, and he wasn't going to fling himself at it. Not if she didn't want him to be on the other side. There was no point.

"I need you to give me some answers, Pru."

"About what?" she asked, studying Victor the goat with her head cocked, clearly only half paying attention to him.

"About everything you've been avoiding."

She froze, then very carefully turned her eyes away. "Grant. I've got two more days. Can't the answers wait two more days?"

"I'm not sure they can." It wasn't fair, but being fair hadn't gotten him anywhere. "Pick one question to answer. I don't care which one. Where are you going to live when your rental is up? Are you going to hire me after the centennial? Are we going to tell your family about us after the centennial? If you struggle here, are you going to give up and go back to California because that's where you really want to be?"

"I don't really want to be in California," she said softly, almost as if it was some grave admission.

"Then where do you want to be?"

CHAPTER NINE

How could Grant not understand here was exactly where Pru wanted to be? How could she possibly tell him that she wanted this store and him and this life she'd been building more than she'd ever wanted anything?

More than the ranch. More than that farm back in college. And the bigger it became, the more real it felt in her hands, the more it was like sand dripping through her fingers.

Because this was her. *She* was building her store. *She* was sleeping with Grant. These weren't things happening to her, things held back from her. The universe wasn't pulling the strings. It was the life she'd always wanted and she'd built it with her own two hands.

Her own two hands—and a heart that didn't know how to handle how much she wanted this.

She'd tried to talk to her friends, but they were wrapped up in their own stores, their own romances. Besides, Kit would only call her a coward and Charity would only tell her what she wanted to hear, and Hope would ply her with fudge and that didn't fix…

This. Her. Only *she* could handle that task and she… couldn't. Clearly. It wasn't fear, it was…what?

"Maybe you don't know," Grant said gently, but it felt like razors against her heart. She was hurting him and she didn't fully understand how. "I don't think there's anything so wrong with that, except it means you're keeping one foot out the door."

One foot out the door? When she'd flung herself at him and this store? "I am not. How can you say that? I left my life. All the time we've spent together—"

"Secretly. Secretly together. But I don't just mean me. I mean the whole thing. No house. No planning beyond the centennial. Talking about going back to California. Why are you halfway out the door?"

He sounded so hurt, and he was so wrong. He just didn't understand, and it was hardly her fault she didn't have the words to get through to him.

"There is no door," she said, trying not to cry. What an utter embarrassment to cry in front of him.

"You said you'd have to go back to California. That's a door." He shook his head and looked away. Then he squinted and pointed. "There's your dad in the square. Call him over. We'll break it to him. Together. Prove there's no door."

"Are you insane?" Tell her father she was sleeping with Grant Mathewson?

"What are you afraid of? We build something and then break up and your family has to have a complicated emotion about their family friend? I promise, we'd all survive, Pru."

"Have you *met* my family?"

He shook his head. "The thing is, no matter what you say, your actions aren't backing it up. So I have to form my own conclusions. And they don't work for me, Pru."

He was breaking things off. And that was fine. Just fine. She'd do better without him muddying up the waters anyway. "I'm sorry this isn't working the way you want," she said, wondering why her voice sounded so strangled when she was trying to be firm.

"No. No, you won't put it on me, Pru. I've played martyr

too long to let you do that. Maybe you are afraid of your family's reaction to us—it doesn't explain the other stuff, but we'll go with it for a second. It messes up your life, or so you think. Okay? So that's more important than anything we've got going? You're afraid of—"

"I'm not afraid."

"Okay, you're not afraid. Then the other option is you want an escape hatch. You play tough, but the truth is, Pru, you like an easy way out when stuff gets hard. And you know it will, because life is hard."

Utterly horrified, she reared back because it felt like he'd slapped her. An escape hatch? "That isn't true."

"Then what *is*, Pru?"

She knew there had to be something to say. Something true and firm and putting him in his place.

No words came out.

"This is what's true for me. I'm in love with you. I want to work at this store with you. I want to build a life with you. I want to tell your parents, your brothers. Mine. I want to *build* something. But you can't build when someone won't build with you."

Love. In love with her. Love. *Love.* She wasn't sure she breathed. Her vision went a little gray. *Love.* She wanted to throw herself at him and sob and the urge was so overwhelmingly embarrassing she was sure she turned bright red.

And managed *no* words, because what could she *say*? While Grant stood there staring at her like she'd shoved something sharp right through him.

The bell tinkled and her father walked in, grinning in greeting. "Well, look at this place!" he said, missing the tension in the room.

But Grant didn't pretend like it wasn't there. "Jack," Grant said curtly. "I've got somewhere to be."

Dad watched Grant stride out, then looked at Pru with some confusion. "Well, don't go running off your help, honey."

She wanted to burst into tears. Nothing would horrify or terrify her father more. An emotional outburst? He'd never survive.

"Now look at this place. Isn't it something? Your mother and I knew you'd make it work. Nothing you can't do that you put your mind to." He nodded, as if that was that, because in Jack Riley's world, such was the case. He said it, and that was that.

And she had nothing. No defenses. No strength. Just everything stripped away because Grant was in *love* with her, and somehow those words had crumbled every wall she'd ever built.

The wall between her and her father and the way he'd hurt her. "If that's so true, why didn't you give me a piece of the ranch?"

Her dad seemed surprised by the question, but not taken totally off guard. He hunched a little, defensively. "It didn't suit you. Now, this store—"

But she wouldn't let him change the subject or avoid it, not when for the first time in twelve years she had the courage to broach it. "I love the ranch." She fought back the tears, because they'd only send her father running. "Is it because I'm a girl?"

Her dad laughed. Actually laughed. "What's that got to do with anything?"

"It's the only difference between me and Beau and JT."

"Now that isn't so. You never could stand to be alone or work alone. Why do you think we had those girls over all the time? You didn't even like to do chores on your own. You like people. You like interaction. A ranch ain't the place for that. School was though, so that's what we gave you. And look how well it's all worked out." He gestured around to the store.

"I wanted the ranch," she managed to whisper.

"Well, I know." Her father blushed, itching his head—which she knew was his nervous tic. He usually lasted about one more minute before foisting the topic off on her mother, but her mom wasn't here. He raised his hands. "I didn't want to embarrass us both with some kind of fight over it. Better to press you to do the right thing."

Embarrass us both. With emotions. A Riley could be angry, but they couldn't be mushy. They couldn't be sad. Not around anyone else.

The terrible thing was, she couldn't find her anger in the moment. Because he was right, in a way she'd never allowed herself to admit. She *loved* the ranch, but the process of running one would have been isolating. Lonely.

If he'd told her his reasons back then, she would have made it her life's work to run a ranch, no matter how miserable it would have made her.

Grant had called himself a martyr. She wasn't sure what she was. So determined to prove she was right? And for what? To end up like she had in California, pulling herself away from anything that brought her enjoyment because she'd been sucked soul dry by trying to prove she could be good at this life her parents had chosen for her?

Afraid to say I love you to the man who'd raised her, ecause it would embarrass him. Afraid to say she'd been urt when they didn't offer her a piece of the ranch. Beause you didn't show that kind of emotion in the Riley ouse. It just wasn't done.

Somehow, she'd taken the Riley way to heart without ever seeing it for what it was. Cowardice.

No. She simply couldn't accept that she was afraid. Even knowing it was true. So, she did something utterly insane. She told her father what she was feeling. "Daddy, I'm in love with Grant."

If it was possible, her father blushed an even deeper shade of red. "Well, I don't know that it's any of my business what—"

"And he's in love with me. He told me so, and I didn't handle it very well."

"This seems like a conversation better suited to you and your friends, Prudence."

She laughed, despite it not being funny. Because he was right. It was a conversation much better suited for her friends. She couldn't change her father, the way he'd been raised or how he dealt with his own emotions. She didn't fully want to. He was a good man who did his best.

But she could change herself. And Grant had just given her the key to where that change started. "Daddy, I love you."

"Well, I love you too, Pruey," he muttered, deeply uncomfortable but saying it anyway. He might not be comfortable with it, he might run from it, but when push came to shove, love helped him stand there and do all those uncomfortable things. Love allowed him to survive it.

How had she missed that for so long? The love of her friends had *always* been her safe place to land, even when she hadn't known how to say it. They were her sisters. The place she could go for what her family couldn't give her— through no fault of their own.

And that was…okay. For the best, even. To have both. A

family she loved, and who'd always be a safe place to land. Her friends, who weren't afraid to call her out on her fears.

And now Grant loved her, and it *was* scary, and hard, and she didn't know how to fix what she'd messed up. But it was love, and that was worth...*this*. The churning stomach. The red face. The fear and discomfort.

Because love might be hard, but it was also *good*.

"If it needs saying, you can always come home if you need to," he muttered, deeply embarrassed to his soul.

She couldn't stop herself. She crossed the store and gave him a hug.

"I know, Dad." She'd always known she could go home, and maybe that was the escape hatch Grant had been talking about. A place to go. To hide. Because her parents would never cause her to have any emotional breakdowns.

Her father awkwardly patted her back then stepped away. "Well, I'll just be headed home now. You...you take care, Pruey. We'll be by for the centennial of course." He was backing out of the store and shoving his hat back on his head before practically sprinting outside.

That was essentially what she'd done to Grant. She'd run away, even while standing right there. And he'd seen through her.

And loved her anyway.

She didn't know what to do with that. Not his love, or her own. But she knew the first step to figuring it out.

GRANT EYED BEAU'S truck coming up the lane to the Mathewson ranch. Grant had thrown himself into some basic ranch chores after leaving Pru and the store. Mucking and hauling and anything physical, dirty, and sweaty to deal with his temper.

"Didn't expect to see you here," Beau said with a frown.

"Haven't been able to pry you out of Pru's store these past few weeks."

"Been busy. What are you doing here?"

"I was just coming by to get Tate for..." Beau trailed off as his phone rang. "It's Mom. Hold on." He turned away, said a few words into the phone, and eyed Grant with some confusion. After a few more minutes of what sounded like uncomfortable *uh-huhs*, Beau hung up and shoved his phone in his pocket.

He glared at Grant. "What's this about Pru being in love with you?" Beau demanded.

Well. *That* was a surprise. Surely Pru hadn't gone to talk to her mother? Not about him. Unless she'd actually gotten some sense knocked into her by her father and was going around telling her family. Proving something?

But then why wasn't she here? Telling him herself?

He supposed those questions were moot until he dealt with Beau. "Actually, you've got that mixed up."

Relief washed over Beau's face. "Thank God," he said with feeling. "Let's forget Mom ever—"

"No, I mean, *I'm* in love with *her*, not the other way around."

Beau's mouth hung open, then he shook his head.

"I told her this morning. And she looked about as stupefied as you do, and handled it worse."

Beau pulled a face. "Don't tell me this. I don't want to know this. Let's just forget we ever said anything."

"Why would we do that?" Grant asked, truly baffled.

Beau looked at him like he'd grown three heads. "It's just not... It's none of my business. You'll keep it to yourself is what you'll do."

But Grant didn't want to keep it to himself. He didn't want to wait for the damn centennial. He wanted *someone* to deal with what he felt. Even if it was Beau clocking him one. "I slept with her."

Beau's mouth dropped, then he slapped his hands over his ears. "Stop."

"Multiple times."

"Damn it, Grant. I'm warning you. You're my best friend. I don't want to have to punch you. Whatever is between you and Pru is between you and Pru and I want nothing to do with it."

"Multiple places."

Beau swore a blue streak, and then did exactly what Grant had been aiming for. He cocked his fist and plowed it into Grant's jaw.

It hurt like hell, but Grant took it. He moved his jaw back and forth to make sure it wasn't broken and touched his lip gingerly when he tasted blood. "Well, now that you've got that out of your system, why don't we actually talk about it?"

"We'll forget this," Beau said darkly. "Put it behind us and never mention it again." Then Beau stalked away and into his truck, slammed the door, and peeled out without ever getting Tate for whatever he'd come here for.

And Grant saw, so clearly, and in a way he hadn't before, what all this was. What he'd known but never fully taken on board in a way that made sense.

Put it behind us and never mention it again.

Grant had been wrong back in the store today. Pru wasn't looking for an escape—that was why she'd looked so shocked when he'd suggested it. She just plain old didn't know what to do with a complicated emotion. Or maybe just a soft emotion.

She was *afraid* of love, or at least she didn't know how to talk about it. The same as Beau couldn't. Beau could shout and use his fists, but when it came down to it, he'd bolted rather than have a conversation about his best friend being in love with his sister.

The Rileys never dealt with feelings. Beau and JT hadn't stuck with a girl, because a woman always "wanted too much." Like an "I love you" or a promise. Mary Riley never could say, "I'm worried about you, Grant." She had to finagle him to dinners or get him into town with excuses and work-arounds.

They were a family who straight up didn't know how to express emotions or process them. It worked for Jack and Mary because they loved each other. Maybe somewhere in their inner lives away from their children, they knew how to deal with it.

His family, on the other hand... The Mathewsons certainly weren't perfect. In fact, their parents' deaths had done a number on all of them. But they'd never been afraid to have a knock-down-drag-out. Never been afraid to express an emotion, a fear.

But avoiding, well, that was the Riley way.

The realization soothed the irritation that had been simmering inside of him. It softened some of the hurt and heartbreak at the thought that Pru might not have the same feelings for him.

She did. Of course she did.

Now he just had to figure out how to get around her fear of that. And that was going to take some doing.

CHAPTER TEN

PRU HAD GONE through her to-do list at the store after her father had run out. She hadn't eaten lunch with her friends or with Grant. She'd taken some time to be alone. To think. To work out, in the inner quiet of her own head and heart, what she really felt and wanted.

When she started to get mad about this or that, she did what she'd never really done before: asked herself what she was really mad at. Was it the people in her life? Or the way she reacted to them?

For the first time since she'd set foot back in Jasper Creek, she allowed herself to think about what she wanted her life to look like *after* the centennial.

She pretended the store would succeed, and she could have anything she wanted—if she was willing to work for it. She wouldn't run away or *escape* when things got a little too complicated. She would embrace the good, and let that good help her through the bad.

It felt a bit like a panic attack that didn't fully form—the lack of air, the dull beating throughout her body—and yet it never went to that space of full-on inability to breathe.

Because in a way, Grant had made her feel like her friends did. He'd said he loved her and wanted to tell everyone. Wanted to *build* things.

It still scared her.

It was *terrifying*, and she wasn't ready to face it yet. First, she needed to talk to her friends.

She locked up then went to Kit's store and looked through the windows. The bookshelves Browning West had built were full of colorful paperbacks—books about hope and love and redemption. But no one was there. She found them in the next building, surrounded by candy in the bright Willy Wonka daydream that was Hope's store.

She stepped inside. Through mouthfuls of candy, they called her over to where they were taste testing Hope's offerings. Pru didn't take a piece. She didn't think her stomach could handle it.

"I need to ask a serious question."

Her three friends looked at her, and they didn't shift or look uncomfortable. They didn't bolt like her brothers would have done, or change the subject like her parents would have done. Her friends watched and waited.

It was what Grant would have done too.

"What if we fail?"

"Well, the statistical chances of all four stores failing aren't as high as you might think," Charity said. "I did a lot of research before the move. About the businesses here, the tourism. It's certainly feasible that for whatever reason one or two of the stores just don't resonate with the client base, but we won't know that until we give it a good shot. Still, if one store fails, we'll concentrate on the three that are left. And so on and so forth. Surely, between the four of us, we can make at least one of the stores a long-term success."

It sounded so reasonable. So simple. And because Charity had done the research, Pru knew it was correct. Still, it wasn't exactly what she meant.

"Don't worry so much, Pru. We came home for this.

We'll find a way to make it work." Charity smiled reassuringly.

"But not just for this," Hope said. "You guys came home in part for me. We all agreed not just for ourselves, but for each other. I love my store. I really love it, and I'll be bummed if it doesn't work out. But it's you guys, it's love and *home* that makes it different from where I was before."

Love and home. What she'd always wanted. Jasper Creek and her friends. She had it now. She *had* it. But she didn't know what to do with the mix of joy and fear and love and hope.

So Pru did what she never did. Not in front of anyone, and certainly not when she was alone with only herself to handle the mess.

She began to cry.

Her friends immediately circled around her. Soothing pats and back rubbing and words, but it didn't help. It only made it worse. She just cried and cried.

And the world didn't end. She wasn't going to *die* just because she was crying in front of her friends.

"Are you pregnant?" Charity whispered.

"What?" Pru croaked, as she began to pull herself together. "No. Jeez. I am very religiously on the pill. I'm just… I told my dad I loved him today."

"Oh my God. Is he sick?" Hope asked.

"Are *you* sick?" Charity asked.

It made Pru laugh. "Which I did after Grant told me he loved me."

"Woah, woah, woah. Back it up. Start from the beginning," Kit demanded.

So, Pru did. She told her friends everything.

"So, to be clear. You figured out you were in love with him back, and instead of running over to tell him, you finished your tasks at the store and then came here to talk to us."

"It's just…" Pru held up her hands. "I don't know how to do this. I don't know how to be in love with someone. I don't know how to… He just said it to me. Out loud."

"Oh, Pru." Kit came over and squeezed her shoulders. "You've always known how to complicate things."

"Haven't we all?" Charity replied. "It's part of growing up, I think. And coming into our own."

"Let's break it down in a way you'll understand," Hope said. "Grant loves you. You love him. He told you. Now the next step is…"

"Move to Antarctica?" Pru said, offering a weak smile. "You guys know I suck at this expressing emotional stuff."

"Yeah. We do," Kit agreed. "And you'll notice that we're still here. And when we need more from you, we ask for it. And you do your best. When you need to let something out, we needle it out of you. It's called a relationship. Even if you're bad at the words, you've never been bad at backing it up with actions."

Actions. She tried to be good at those, and she had to admit that even if her family wasn't good at the words… they were always there. Saying I love you had never been par for the course, but she *knew* her parents loved each other, because of how they talked to each other and looked at each other. She knew her brothers loved her because as much as they teased her and shied away from any deep conversations, they'd showed up to help at the store. They *did* things.

That was the Riley way.

And it was a good way, but somewhere in the past few years, she'd found she needed the words too.

"I love you guys." It still made her uncomfortable, even more so when they squeezed tight around her.

"Group hug!" Kit said, laughing and wrapping her arms around all of them and squishing them together.

"I did not consent to that," Pru managed, though her voice was muffled by the three bodies practically suffocating her. She laughed in spite of herself.

Because *this* was what she'd come home for.

WHEN GRANT WOKE up the next morning, he felt a bit like a soldier getting ready for battle. Tomorrow was the centennial, and he was hardly going to stay away from the store just because he'd stormed out yesterday.

No, he wouldn't play her game. If she didn't love him, or didn't want him around, she was going to have to come out and say it. Maybe the Rileys were bad at that kind of thing, but Grant didn't have to put up with it.

Still, there was a certain finesse to browbeating someone into admitting they were in love with you.

He slid his hat on his head and stepped out of the house, stomach already in knots. But he wasn't afraid. Not of words or feelings. And he was going to prove to her that she didn't have to be either.

Then there she was. Leaning against his truck hood. Talking to JJ and Cade. The morning sunlight made her hair look like a golden halo, giving her the look of an angel. A very Western angel, but an angel nonetheless.

He stopped in his tracks and watched as she laughed at something Cade said, her eyes darting over to the house as if she kept checking. Waiting.

Their gazes met. Held. He couldn't read her expression, but she was here. Which had to mean…something.

He walked over to the trio. "Morning," he offered.

JJ was all smiles, her hand resting on her slightly rounded stomach. "Good morning. Pru, it was so good to officially meet you, but I've got some things I need Cade to take care of ASAP." She was already pulling Cade away. "We'll see you later, Grant."

Then it was just Grant and Pru.

She frowned at him. "What happened to your lip?"

"Oh, right. A gift from your brother. I didn't expect you to spill the beans. Especially to your mother."

"I didn't." She frowned. "I guess my father told her. He's who I told. I can't believe he'd spread it around." She shook her head and studied the fat lip. "Why would Beau hit you over that?"

"Beau said you were in love with me. I corrected him that it was the other way around. He said he wanted to forget it, and I kept telling him things he didn't want to hear."

Some of that cool bravado failed her and she wrinkled her nose. "You know it's not just the other way around."

Some of the tension in him unwound, but it couldn't be *that* easy. "Do I?"

She blinked and opened her mouth to speak, but no sound came out.

"Beau hitting me, then running away like he'd just seen a bull coming straight for him, crystallized something for me. About you. About the whole damn lot of you Rileys."

"Does it have anything to do with how badly we suck at this whole love thing?"

"You don't suck at love. Not a one of you." He touched her face. "You're maybe bad at expressing it, but not at being it."

She inhaled deeply. "But...some people need the expressing. I mean..." She swallowed. "It can be important."

"It can be learned."

She looked up into his face. And he waited, but when she finally spoke it didn't make any sense. "I think I'm going to need your help to move Maynard onto the sidewalk," she blurted.

"Who's Maynard?"

"The goat statue," she said, as if that was common knowledge. Or obvious. Or *sane*.

"Huh. I've been calling him Victor in my head."

Pru blinked up at him and swallowed, tears filling her eyes. "Really?"

He had no idea why that would make her cry, so he only nodded.

She flung her arms around his neck and almost knocked him clear over. "God, I love you," she said. It was a bit like a deathbed confession, but she was saying it nonetheless. "It's not that I'm afraid of that, exactly. I don't know how to...just say it. To not feel... It's just, you named the goat."

"Well, *you* named the goat. Maynard is a much better goat statue name than Victor."

She laughed into his shoulder. "I want you to keep working with me. After the centennial."

More of the tightness unwound. Because he wanted her, but he wanted to be a part of that store too. "I was planning on it."

"I want all that stuff you said in the store. I'm in such a habit of shying away from anything that seems too good to be true."

"I'll screw up if it'll help."

She managed a laugh and he could see how hard she was fighting with the tears.

"Pru, you don't have to do that. You don't have to be afraid with me. Tears don't bother me, except of course I don't want to see you cry. Fears don't scare me. I've been afraid so often since my father died, I'm old hat. I'm not going to run away."

"I love you so much that I don't know what to do with it all," she said in a rush of breath. Like it was terrible.

But it wasn't. At all. "Good."

Before he could finally kiss her again, she pushed him back a little. "I need you to tell me when you need the words and when I'm not doing a good enough job. I need you to promise me that," she said earnestly.

"Okay, as long as same goes."

She wrinkled her nose. "I don't need words."

"I think you do. And I'll give them to you. I'll give whatever I've got to you."

She rubbed at her chest. "Okay, maybe words work." She pressed her body to his. "But other things work too." And she kissed him. With a gentleness she hadn't shown before, a sweetness he knew terrified her. And she'd given it to him anyway.

"Yeah, that works," he said, leaning his forehead to hers.

She sighed dreamily, if he did say so himself. "Come to the store, Grant. Let's get ready for the centennial."

"And after the centennial?"

"Well, you're going to have to help me figure out the paperwork for hiring you."

"Done. What else?"

"I'm going to move home for a little while. Until I find a place in town to rent."

"Close enough to the store you could walk to work?"

"Exactly."

"Big enough for two?"

She arched a brow. "That depends on how much I want to horrify my mother and live in sin."

"And if you don't?"

"I guess at that point you'll just have to make an honest woman out of me." She grinned up at him. "That's what I'm looking to build, Grant. What my parents have. What yours did. Nothing half-assed. Partners. In everything. No matter how hard or scary it is."

He pulled her closer. "I'm counting on it." He lowered his mouth to hers, but paused before he kissed her. "All right, Riley. How about those words."

She held his gaze and smiled. "I love you, Grant."

"See, you didn't even sound like you had a gun to your head this time."

"Oh, shut up," she said on a laugh, and pressed her mouth to his.

It was a kiss, but it was also a promise. To build the future they both wanted.

EPILOGUE

THERE WAS RED, white, and blue bunting everywhere. It was a miserably hot day, and still people had packed the parade route.

Riley Feed & Gardening Supply celebrated the day with a tuxedo-clad goat statue moved onto the sidewalk. Happy Ever After Books had a sidewalk sale of used romance novels that attracted young and old. The Sugar Shack needed only to have the doors opened to waft the smells of maple fudge outside. And A Simple Thread had decorated its big store window with knitted flowers and free patterns for knitters who wanted to replicate them.

Each store had been filled with interested Jasper Creekians, eager tourists, and then finally the *test*. The mayor had come through each of their stores. Inspecting buildings. Inspecting traffic flow. Then with a nod, she gave each of them the seal of approval. Their affordable rent would stay intact.

None of them had stopped for lunch. Pru didn't know what she would have done without Grant there to help. It was a never-ending parade of customers. Not everyone bought, but getting even a few knickknacks sold and gardening supplies ordered made her feel good about the future. Even better, quite a few ranchers had wandered in to discuss her feed selection.

Many of them mentioned that her dad had sent them.

When it was time to close up for the day, Pru, Hope, Kit, and Charity all did it simultaneously, and breathlessly… then immediately met in the basement.

Pru worked to finagle the safe. It took just as long, and just as much muscle to pry it open as it originally had. And here they were, just a few months later, their cell phones in hand.

"I'm not sure I want it," Hope said.

"I want it," Pru said, snatching hers out immediately. "I can *text* instead of calling again. Like God intended." But none of them spent any time *looking* at their phones. They slid them in their pockets.

They were a nice slice of convenience, but they weren't necessary. Not when they had each other.

"Well, we did it," Hope said. "We really, *really* did it."

They all grinned at each other, exhausted and pleased to the bone. They had *done* it. They had created the happiness they'd dreamed of and made a pact about as kids.

"Well, what the hell do we do now?" Pru asked.

"We go watch the fireworks," Kit said. "Make out with our very fine significant others. Get a little drunk on Jill Vargas's summer punch and enjoy ourselves."

"Hear, hear!"

The fireworks would start in about ten minutes, so the women went out to their storefronts. Basking in the glow of their success, they turned to the town. People were scattered all over the square's lawn—blankets filled with families, couples, and screeching teenagers.

There was one big quilt being guarded by four men holding plastic cups of the infamous punch. Four true-blue cowboys, four really good men.

They were good enough men to stand there and wait while the girls closed up their shops and had their moment.

"What are you looking at?" Charity asked, when Pru came to a stop on the boardwalk.

Pru gestured to the guys. "Not a bad-looking group of gentlemen."

Kit sighed appreciatively. "We did good, girls. Real damn good."

"You all owe me a thank-you. My wedding implosion is what started all of this," Hope said.

"Actually I think we should thank James Field Warner IV," Kit replied with a grin.

"Nah," Pru said. "Let's thank ourselves. Just a couple of badasses who know how to run a business and hook a man."

"With the help of a few magazines," Hope offered with a laugh.

"And that house, complete with hatbox, lasso, camera, and so on."

"And each other," Charity said in her solemn way. She reached across to find Kit's hand with hers, then Kit gripped Hope's, and Hope Pru's until they were a connected chain.

In tandem, they looked up at the stars, finding Aquila. Their constellation. The arrow that had led them here. Right where they each belonged.

When the fireworks began to sparkle through the night sky, reflecting on the compass necklaces they had always kept their promise to wear, they each walked to the man waiting for them.

They knew exactly what their pact had given them. Not just a store. Not just a man.

Home.

* * * * *

"Come away with me this weekend."

The invitation tumbled from his lips before the idea had fully formed. A warning alarm blared in his head, loud and screaming. But he didn't rescind the offer. Though she stiffened against him, he didn't release her, just shifted his hand from her face to her hip, steadying her.

"I have a cabin in Colorado. You, Ben, me—we can fly there tonight after you're finished at the restaurant, spend tomorrow there, and I'll have you back Monday in time for work. We can talk over the details of the move and how we're going to proceed with our families. I want to spend time getting to know my son with his mother. Take a risk and a day off work, Charlotte."

"I don't have to take a day off," she murmured, almost absently. "One of my conditions when I accepted the job at Sheen was that I have Sundays off to be with Ben."

Whether she realized it or not, she was halfway to agreeing to go with him. He pushed his advantage, because the invite might've been spontaneous, but he wanted this. Wanted her and Ben alone.

"Say yes, Charlotte," he said, finally stepping back even though his body screamed in rebellion and promised swift retribution. Even though his palms tingled with the need to cup that rounded, firm hip again. To squeeze it. Mark it. "This is about Ben. What happens afterward—if something happens—is up to you."

Her eyes darkened, and the thick fringe of her lashes lowered. But not before he caught the gleam of arousal in her eyes. The uncertainty, too. Yes, she'd understood his meaning. He hadn't been referring to their coparenting plan or how they intended to break the news to her parents that he was Ben's father.

He'd meant that kiss.

When he'd proposed their…cohabitation, he'd stipulated it would be platonic. And that had been his plan. Up until she'd moaned into his mouth.

"Come away with me." The offer, roughened by the lust tearing at him, still hung between them.

Her lips parted, moved, but nothing emerged. She bowed her head, pinching the bridge of her nose. Anticipation and the need to press for an answer whipped inside him like a gathering summer storm, but he held back. Granting her space and time to come to her decision. Because it had to be hers, freely given.

Finally, she lifted her head, met his gaze. Desire still simmered in her eyes as did the doubt. But so did resolve. He had his answer even before she murmured, "Yes."

He exhaled. "Good," he said. "Call me when you're about to leave work. I'll come by to pick up you and Ben tonight."

"Okay." She sighed. Then whispered, "I hope we're not making a mistake, Ross."

The assurance that they were doing the right thing hovered on his tongue, but he couldn't utter it. Because it would be a lie.

He didn't know.

And right now, he didn't care.

Don't miss what happens next in…
Back in the Texan's Bed *by Naima Simone,*
the first in the Texas Cattleman's Club: Heir Apparent series.

Available February 2021 wherever
Harlequin Desire books and ebooks are sold.

Harlequin.com